Theodor Fontane

EFFI BRIEST

TRANSLATED
WITH AN INTRODUCTION BY
DOUGLAS PARMÉE

PENGUIN BOOKS

Penguin Books Ltd, Harmondsworth, Middlesex, England
Penguin Books Inc., 3300 Clipper Mill Road, Baltimore, Md 21211, U.S.A.
Penguin Books Australia Ltd, Ringwood, Victoria, Australia

—

This translation first published 1967
Copyright © Douglas Parmée, 1967

—

Made and printed in Great Britain by
Hazell Watson & Viney Ltd
Aylesbury, Bucks
Set in Monotype Fournier

INTRODUCTION

No single factor has had more profound consequences on the fate of Europe within the last hundred years than the emergence of Prussia, from being a vigorous provincial kingdom, as the energetic, confident and dominating partner in the prosperous and powerful new nation of Germany. It is a measure of Theodor Fontane's greatness that it was in him that this golden age of Prussian civilization found its most adequate witness and chronicler – and formidable critic.

Born near Berlin in 1819, Fontane lived, until his death in 1898, largely in this city that became, during his lifetime, the capital of the new Reich. He was thus admirably placed to follow the social, political and cultural manifestations of the birth of this new world power, and it reveals Fontane's awareness of the nature of Prussia's achievement that his first novel, *Vor dem Sturm*, published in 1878, was a historical novel dealing with the critical period of Prussia's successful resurgence against Napoleonic domination; and years later, in *Effi Briest*, we still find him half admiringly, half exasperatedly exploring those militant virtues of his homeland, which was to bring two cataclysms on the world.

Fontane's early life had provided him with an excellent preparation to become the chronicler of his age. His early years were spent in his father's profession of apothecary, during which time he was already showing an amateur interest, and more than an average amateur competence, in literary matters, at this stage chiefly as a ballad-writer and critic. In 1849, having already developed considerable literary associations in Berlin, he decided to devote himself entirely to writing as a journalist. In the course of this career, which was not always uniformly successful, he spent some years as a foreign correspondent in London and wrote a number of works of travel, including one on Scotland, based on his own experiences. More exciting, although not necessarily more rewarding for the development of his talent (in which the novels of Sir Walter Scott and Charles Dickens played an important part), were his experiences as war correspondent in the three conflicts which provided Prussia

5

with the important stepping-stones towards her hegemony in Europe east of the North Sea: the wars against Denmark in 1864, Austria in 1866 and France in 1870. During this last war, Fontane was taken prisoner and detained for some months on suspicion of spying. This is perhaps less surprising than might appear at first sight, for Fontane was of French origin, albeit distantly, on both sides of his family. This fact may or may not explain why his attitude towards certain aspects of the rise of Prussian imperialism was markedly ambivalent – the squabble between geneticists and ecologists over the relative importance of heredity and environment is still unresolved; but it is undeniable that, despite his birth (and his taking a wife similarly of French origin), there was no writer steeped more profoundly in the history and legend of Brandenburg nor more appreciative of the natural beauties of its landscapes, as certain pages of *Effi Briest* bear witness. It would be idle – albeit fascinating – to speculate on the extent to which Fontane's novels gain their rich complexity from the paradox that they were written by a novelist of southern French extraction who felt himself very much at home in the north of Europe.

By 1878, the date of publication of *Vor dem Sturm*, Fontane had achieved financial security as a dramatic critic and had leisure to devote himself increasingly to his novels. In 1880 appeared the first of his modern studies of relationships between the sexes, *L'Adultera*, but it was not until 1887, when he was already sixty-six, that he published what is generally recognized as one of his masterpieces: *Irrungen, Wirrungen*. In this, a study of love between an officer of aristocratic connexions and a Berlin girl of humbler origins, Fontane has found his permanent theme and field: the study of individuals in their social milieu. In 1891 appeared another masterpiece, *Unwiederbringlich* ('Beyond Recall'), also a study of adultery, although in this case the clash of temperaments takes priority over the social study; in 1892, on the other hand, *Frau Jenny Treibel* gives increasing attention to the close depiction of milieu; in 1894 there appeared *Effi Briest*, the novel in which Fontane achieved perhaps his most perfect balance between individual conflict and a careful and accurate study of social milieux. His last novel, *Der Stechlin*, was published in the year of his death, 1898, at the age of seventy-eight. Life in Prussia in the latter years of the nineteenth century had been triumphantly chronicled.

6

The medium of this chronicling was the novel, as it had been perfected in the course of the nineteenth century, notably by such writers as Stendhal, Balzac and Flaubert in France and Turgenev and Dostoyevsky in Russia, until it had become an instrument of extreme flexibility, equally well adapted to probing the recesses of an individual's mind and feelings as to brushing in the detailed background of social life; and it was Fontane's role to raise the novel in German to a rank where it could become part not of a purely national but of a European tradition. This tradition in the novel – we have already mentioned Walter Scott and Dickens – may be broadly described as realism, which we may roughly define as the depiction of mankind – often the ordinary run of mankind, the middle classes or lower middle classes – in its habitat at a particular time in a particular place, with considerable emphasis on physical and social detail. Thus defined, realism may sound rather dull; but it was Fontane's originality and greatness to bring to the writing of realistic novels his own personal emphasis and method, both of content and technique. He specifically states, first of all, that 'it is not the purpose of the novel to describe things which happen or ... can happen every day'. It is true that the novelist must create an *image* of life and society and that it must not be a distorted one; but this image is no mere photographic reproduction, it is the product of the author's imagination, and he must ensure, Fontane says, that it has 'the intensity, clarity, lucid composition, roundness and consequent heightened intensity of feeling achieved by the transfiguration which is the task of art'.

Thus we find in *Effi Briest*, for example, that, although we are throughout convinced of the verisimilitude of Fontane's portrayal of life in the little Baltic sea-port and resort of Kessin, we are never in doubt either that, by his use of certain ironic or humorous details, we are being invited by the author to pass some kind of judgement, albeit a good-humoured one, on the quality of life led there; nor, indeed, as far as the *dramatis personae* are concerned, would we be tempted to see in the slightly hunch-backed, kind-hearted, cultivated, comic and rather sad little apothecary Alonzo Gieshübler an average inhabitant of such small Baltic ports, even though he may possess no qualities that are inherently improbable. Fontane's realism, in fact, depends as much on his profound knowledge of the type of people and the milieu involved in his novels as

7

on his imaginative, often ironic approach to them, although this irony or humour is administered with a subtlety and unobtrusiveness which warn us that the author himself is not forcibly imposing his views on us nor, indeed, trying to pass definitive judgements on his characters. In *Effi Briest* it would be difficult to point to any single character as being entirely blameworthy; even the hardened seducer Major Crampas, through whose agency the tragic adultery occurs, is far from appearing a wholly unsympathetic person.

Fontane's greatness as a novelist springs from two strong concerns, of which we are constantly aware in reading *Effi Briest*: first, his concern for the individual and, as a corollary, for the actions and reactions produced when these individuals meet and, especially, when they clash; secondly, his concern for the society from which his individual characters spring, in which they have their being, and with which they are in harmony or, more commonly, in conflict. It will readily be seen that from these two major concerns we are led directly to ask ourselves, when reading Fontane's novels, those questions which form the basis of civilized man's existence: how free is the individual? to what extent are his actions dominated by environment? what right has society to justify its domination? what are the relative roles of reason and instinct in the individual? And having made us ask these questions and propounded various solutions, Fontane leads us on to consider even wider issues that, for most people, are the most important questions of all: what is happiness? is it attainable and, if so, how? what becomes of individual happiness when faced by social pressures? Nor must we forget, where *Effi Briest* is concerned, the question that is the whole crux of the novel – a question which conceals beneath an apparent triviality a host of moral and even philosophical implications, as well as being a question of practical relevance to more people than one might at first suspect – how long ago must an act of adultery have been committed in order to have become, if not innocuous, at least forgivable?

In other words, Fontane's characters can frequently be looked upon as being more than just individuals, because although they never cease to be individuals, they bear considerable traces of their social origins and their environment or of their heredity, although Fontane never indulges in Zola's pseudo-scientific claptrap on the subject. Some of the characters have, indeed, as their principal function to bear witness to their origins, while others in their breadth of conception seem intended to transcend their social origins, even though firmly rooted in them, and to become exemplars of types of humanity. Of such characters, Effi Briést herself may be considered the epitome: despite her marked individuality, it is tempting to see her as a representative of certain broader characteristics of her sex, as well as offering all the subsidiary characteristics belonging to her provincial family upbringing. In fact, such a generalizing approach must be made only with great caution, for the truth of the matter is that her generally human and feminine characteristics are flawlessly and indissolubly combined in the circumstances of her birth and upbringing to form one whole, rounded, complex individual human being.

Effi is shown as a very natural and instinctive creature, very close to the roots of life, impetuous, frank, open; there can hardly be a more charming apparition in modern literature than that of Effi at the beginning of the novel indulging in her Swedish exercises – lithe, pure, simple – or playing, like the young girl she still is, with her childhood companions. And yet – there is always an 'and yet' with Fontane – we are plainly warned that being natural is not enough, at least unless you are prepared for complete self-sufficiency: for Effi not only has the faults of her virtues – rashness, thoughtlessness, even a certain callousness in her attitude towards others – she also has faults springing no doubt in part – to what extent, we ask ourselves – from her social origins and upbringing: the most serious of these is her pride – pride of birth as well as personal pride which takes the form of conceit and even arrogance.

Her husband von Innstetten also has great family pride; but his faults flow from a different source: while she is too natural and unconventional, Innstetten relies too much on reason and will-power: Effi is too impulsive, her husband too scheming, while yet being, in many ways, affectionate and, of course, within his conventional lights, the soul of honour. Paradoxically, it is this excessive dependence on the social code of his caste that brings about the downfall of his own marriage; if only Innstetten could have shown a little more moral courage, in braving public opinion – his physical courage is never in doubt – his marriage could have been saved; and it is once more a typically ironic touch that it is through the temporary failure of nerve of this iron-willed man that his wife's adultery is placed in danger of becoming public property. We may feel sorry for Innstetten; but it is Effi whom we love, perhaps because, although she can hardly be said to love her husband, we feel that in happier circumstances she would have been capable of love, whereas we doubt whether Innstetten is so capable.

It is an excellent and typical example of Fontane's novelistic skill that the basic differences between husband and wife which are to lead on to the tragic outcome first appear during their honeymoon in humorous, almost comic form. In her first letter to her parents, Effi describes, rather amusingly, how Innstetten, guide-book in hand, insists on dragging her round all the cultural monuments of the towns at which they stay in the course of their wedding trip to Italy; only later, when there are other suspicions aroused in the reader of sexual inadequacy on Innstetten's part, do we begin to suspect a deeper significance in the fact that, in this honeymoon letter, Effi's exhaustion is chiefly associated with . . . sore feet! The letter takes on a further significance later: during the honeymoon, it is Innstetten, the 'culture vulture', who is determined to open Effi's eyes to the beauties of art; but later, in her hour of lonely need, Effi is the one to seek and find consolation in art, not by looking at the work of others but by devoting herself to learning to paint in order to create, rather than merely passively absorb, a work of art. This letter is, in fact, but one example amongst many of the skilful way in which Fontane uses apparently trivial detail to form an illuminating pattern; the whole structure of the novel is taut, yet not so taut as to become artificial.

This avoidance of excessive rigidity of structure can be exemplified from the role played by the character who is the catalyst in Effi's relationship with her husband, the middle-aged, ginger-moustachioed militia major, Crampas. Married to an embittered and, at this stage in their marriage, justifiably suspicious wife somewhat older than himself, but whom he nonetheless refuses to leave in the lurch, Crampas is the professional amorist, gambler and society-man, a most important character in his own right; yet he has more than a personal role, for what could be more appropriate than that it is this gambler, always taking risks, who represents the element of chance in the novel?

However tightly Fontane draws the noose of fate around his heroine's neck, however much his characters may seem to be the tools of their temperaments or their origins or circumstances, he insists that there is always in life an element of chance; nothing is really inevitable until it has happened: Crampas, on one certain October morning, might not have been passing by while Effi was sitting on her veranda having breakfast and, further, he might not have approached to speak to her – invited to do so, ironically enough, by the husband himself; Gieshübler's servant Mirambo might not have received the kick from the horse that causes Innstetten to leave his wife alone in the sleigh with Crampas on the return from the ill-fated excursion to the head forester's house. In fact, Fontane is as attentive to the *occasion* of a particular happening as he is to its *cause*, and while chance is allowed its due role, coincidence, that *deus ex machina* of even some of the greatest novelists, is just as carefully excluded. His characters are given room to breathe and act freely; as in life, it is only after the event that we can see what was coming and can assess the deeper inevitability of what actually took place.

Around the protagonists are ranged a variety of minor, yet fully realized, characters: Effi's parents in Hohen-Cremmen; in Kessin, apart from Gieshübler, there are a number of less important, although essential, characters; the tough, uncharitable, pious Sidonie; the emancipated and gifted Trippelli (alias Fräulein Trippel!); all the bigoted, jingoistic country gentry, the backbone of Prussia; the sinister *starost* Golchowski and the even more sinister Frau Kruse, steadfastly refusing to be parted from her black hen; in contrast, the kindly, rather stupid and completely loyal Roswitha, whose most poignant experience of life has been (as she continually reminds anyone whom she can persuade to listen to her) the occasion when her father, a village blacksmith, came after her with a red-hot iron bar on learning that she was in the family way; and yet, be it remarked in passing, this stupid country girl convinces us without a shadow of doubt when, with earthy common-sense, she condemns her master for duelling with Crampas because of her mistress's adultery; whereas the much smarter, prettier, and livelier maid Joanna, who trots out, second-hand, all the clichés of aristocratic society with regard to 'honour', appears as a calculating sham.

Fontane's range of characters is thus extremely wide, and each is skilfully incorporated into the general structure of the novel; but Fontane's genius shines with particular brilliance in his methods of characterization. Its essence can be best expressed in the novelist's own words: 'the author's intrusion', he writes 'is almost always wrong and, to say the least, superfluous'; and as a corollary, he resolutely turns his face against the convention of the omniscient author, the writer who can pry into all the secrets of his characters to interpret all their thoughts and, above all, to distinguish all their motives. Almost all our knowledge of the characters in *Effi Briest* comes from what they themselves do and from what they say, from their conversations with each other as well as from their letters, which are always most revealing and self-revealing – if not self-condemnatory – and often full of unconscious irony; the dialogues between Effi's parents, for example, have a subtlety and a richness of suggestion that can match the best of Jane Austen. Another method occasionally used by Fontane is to give glimpses of unsuspected sides of certain characters by showing them through the opinions of others.

A striking example of this can be found in the important revelations made by Crampas regarding Innstetten's early life as an ambitious young officer – although it is to be noted that here, as often, Fontane deliberately introduces a note of doubt. How reliable is Crampas's testimony? Not only has he a personal axe to grind, he also has a specific aim to achieve – Effi's disillusionment concerning her husband; and so the reader finds himself asking questions: to what extent can Crampas be believed, and is Innstetten really such an artful schemer and hypocrite? Sometimes such questions receive their answer in the novel; more frequently, as in real life, no definite answer is forthcoming and so we are left, exactly as when we are face to face with living people, with large areas of ignorance about the characters' feelings and motives, their intentions and their sufferings. How deeply, for example, does Geert love Effi? We never learn, and no doubt Fontane is suggesting that no one can ever know, not even Innstetten himself; and doubtless, too, as in life, the amount of affection that Innstetten feels towards his wife ebbs and flows constantly. Fontane is, in fact, telling us that states of mind can never be simple, and it is this rich ambiguity that gives his characters their constant depth and vividness. Very rarely does he have recourse to more explicit means of revealing character; occasionally, for Effi herself, he resorts to the less realistic device of soliloquy, but even here, apart from suspecting that this soliloquy may be misguided, we feel that this device serves the structural purpose of underlining Effi's desperate loneliness, her feeling – and ours – that all the world and fate are leagued against her. Such use of soliloquy is rare, and on the whole, by constructing character through external action and dialogue, Fontane unerringly avoids, as he pointedly expresses it, the temptation of 'judging, preaching, being clever and wise'.

Having said this, we must at once add that such complete lack of involvement in one's characters is a pious hope, a tendency rather than a permanent fact. Fontane himself admits that it is difficult to discover where such lack of intrusion begins or ends: 'the author must, as such, do and say a great deal'. After all, he was seventy-four years old when *Effi Briest* was published and no one attains that age without having reached some sort of personal philosophy of life that is bound to seep through his works. In fact, certain passages of heightened intensity in *Effi Briest* do suggest personal involvement on the author's part and when, from passages involving two such different people as Effi and Innstetten, it seems possible to draw similar moral conclusions, we may feel justified in seeing in these passages an expression of Fontane's own ripe wisdom. The message is a simple one: Be content in the enjoyment of peace and quiet. It is expressed in strictly practical terms by Innstetten: live where you feel at home and be satisfied with small pleasures – he instances the enjoyment of a good night's rest and wearing good, comfortable boots! Effi's solution to the difficulties of life, which she is able to put into practice in her last few months, is similar, albeit more emotional: she finds her happiness in return to Hohen-Cremmen, where she feels at home, not only because she is surrounded by parental love but also – natural, instinctive creature that she is – because she discovers the deep satisfaction of communion with nature and the elements; and it is ironically appropriate, too, that it is through exposure to the elements that she contracts her final illness. All the same, it is in the acceptance of modest pleasures that she enjoys the happiest months of her life.

Such a modest philosophy, however serene, may appear rather selfish and narrow, the philosophy of a resigned old man; it is counterbalanced by another, vividly embodied in what is perhaps the most heavily charged passage of the whole work. After the divorce, custody of the child has been given to the husband, but having glimpsed her daughter by chance one day in the tram, Effi is seized by a yearning to speak with her again. Through the good offices of the wife of the Minister who is Innstetten's chief, this meeting takes place, but to Effi's fury and despair she discovers that Annie has been indoctrinated, parrot fashion, to be on guard against her own mother. It is this realization, more than anything that has previously happened, which at last breaks Effi's spirit, and we are made to feel very strongly that Innstetten's inhibiting, for his own selfish social and personal purposes, of the child's natural feelings towards her mother is a graver sin even than his killing of his wife's former lover in a duel. Treason against the individual is surely the blackest of all crimes in Fontane's scale of values.

It has been said that the 'meaning' of a poem is what is left over when all the poetry has been removed; and the same may be said, *mutatis mutandis*, of the 'message' of a novel. It would, indeed, be gravely unjust to Fontane to end on any purely moralizing conclusion: and the only proper way to end any study of *Effi Briest* must be simply to invite the reader to plunge, with delight, and full awareness, into Fontane's rich and skilfully constructed world; to follow Effi and Crampas over the snow into the gloomy pine forest which provides the mysterious background for so many of the central happenings of the novel; to let our flesh creep as we piece together the uncanny story of the little Chinaman who lies buried in that very forest; to suffer with Innstetten as he meditates on the enigma of Crampas's dying expression of pain and sympathy; and to grieve with Effi, surely one of the most appealing heroines of modern literature, in her agonizing and unavailing struggle against the massive forces of Prussian moral rectitude.

D.P.

I

In front of the von Briests' house in Hohen-Cremmen – their family house since the reign of the Elector George William – the village street lay bathed in the glare of the midday sun, whilst towards the park and gardens, a side-wing, built on at right angles, cast a broad shadow, first on a white and green flagged path and, beyond, on a large round flower-bed with a sundial in the middle and cannas and rhubarb growing round its edge. A dozen yards further on, exactly symmetrical with the wing, ran a churchyard wall with small-leafed ivy growing along its whole length except where it was pierced by a small, white-painted iron gate; beyond the wall rose the tall tower of Hohen-Cremmen, with its shingle roof and its glittering, recently regilded weather-cock.

The house, the wing and the churchyard wall formed a horseshoe enclosing a small ornamental garden, open on one side to reveal a little lake and a jetty to which a boat was moored and, close by, a swing with its wooden seat suspended from two ropes at each end; the posts supporting the wooden crossbar were already somewhat askew. Between the lake and the circular bed, however, half hiding the swing, stood a few immense old plane trees.

Even the front of the house, consisting of a terrace on which stood aloes in tubs and a few garden chairs, offered a pleasant and entertaining place for relaxation and recreation on a cloudy day; but on scorching sunny days, the garden side was definitely favoured, particularly by the lady and the daughter of the house, who today were once again sitting in the full shade of the paved pathway, with their backs to some open windows framed by masses of creeper; beside them, a small projecting flight of stone steps led from the garden up to the flower-beds adjoining the wing. The two of them, mother and daughter, were busily at work embroidering a square, patchwork altar-cloth; countless skeins of gaudy wool and silk lay strewn in disorder on a large round table, together with a few dessert-plates left over from lunch and a majolica dish filled with magnificent large gooseberries. The needles, threaded with wool, moved skilfully and quickly to and fro, but while the mother kept her gaze fixed on her work, now and again the daughter, whom her friends called Effi, would put her needle down and stand up to do the appropriate bending and stretching exercises that formed part of her course of gymnastics.

It was obvious that she was greatly enjoying the exercises, which she deliberately turned into something slightly comical, and when she stood there, slowly raising her arms and bringing the palms of her hands together above her head, her mother, too, would look up from her work, if only for a quick furtive glance because she did not want to show how entrancing she found her own child. It was a gesture of maternal pride which was fully justified. Effi was wearing a sort of linen smock with blue and white stripes, tightly held in at the waist by a bronze-red leather belt; a wide low-cut sailor's collar covered her shoulders, leaving the front and side of her neck exposed. Her every movement showed a combination of pertness and grace, while her laughing brown eyes gave evidence of considerable native wit, high spirits and kindness of heart. People called her 'Tiny', a title which she had to accept only because her lovely, slender mother was a good four or five inches taller.

Effi had just got up to do some more gymnastics – alternate body swinging to left and right – when her mother, who had just looked up from her sewing once again, called out to her: 'Effi, you ought really to have been a circus rider, always flying through the air on a trapeze. I half believe you'd like to be something like that.'

'Perhaps I should, Mama. But if so, whose fault would it be? Where do I get it from? Not from anyone but yourself. Or do you imagine I get it from papa? That makes even you laugh. And then why do you put me into this sort of boy's smock? Sometimes I imagine I'm going back into short skirts. And if I have *those* again, I'll be making curtseys like a young thing all over again, and when the Rathenowers come over I'll sit on Colonel Goetze's lap and ride galloppy-galloppy. And why not? He's three parts uncle and only one part flirt. It's your fault. Why don't you get me any grand clothes? Why don't you make me into a lady?'

'Would you like that?'

'No.' She ran up to her mother and eagerly flung her arms round her to kiss her. 'Don't be so wild, Effi, and so impulsive. It always worries me when I see you like this . . .!' And her mother seemed anxious to proceed with her recital of cares and fears, but she was unable to go on, because at this very second, three girls appeared in the garden through the iron gate in the churchyard wall and came along a gravel path leading to the sundial and its round flower-bed. All three waved their sunshades at Effi and went over at once to pay their respects to Frau von Briest, who, after asking a few questions, invited them to stay and keep them both, or at least Effi, company for half an hour. 'I've all sorts of things to do, anyway, and young people like to be by themselves. Be good!' With this, she went up the stone steps leading from the garden to the side-wing of the house. And so the girls were left all to themselves.

Two of the new arrivals – chubby young girls whose freckles and good humour made an excellent match with their curly auburn hair – were the twin daughters of the schoolmaster Jahnke, who, as a sworn devotee of the Hanseatic league, Scandinavia and Fritz Reuter and under the influence of this Mecklenburg compatriot, also his favourite poet, in imitation of Mining and Lining, had given his own twins the names Herta and Berta. The third young lady was Hulda Niemeyer, Pastor Niemeyer's only child. More ladylike than the other two, she was also boring and conceited, a lymphatic blonde with rather protruding, stupid eyes, which none the less seemed always on the look-out for something, for which reason even Klitzing, from the Hussars, had once said: 'Doesn't she seem as if she's expecting the angel Gabriel to appear at any minute?' Effi's view was that the slightly hypercritical Klitzing was only too right, but nevertheless she refrained from making any distinction between her three friends. At this moment, such a thought was certainly far from her mind, and resting her arms on the table, she said:

'This embroidery's boring! Thank goodness you've come!'

'But we've scared your mama away,' said Hulda.

'Not really. As she told you, she would have had to go anyway. She's expecting a visitor, an old friend from her younger days, whom I must tell you a story about some time – a love story with a hero and heroine who gave each other up. It will make your eyes pop out of your head. Incidentally, I've already seen mama's old friend over in Schwantikow. He's a provincial governor, with a good figure and very manly-looking.'

'That's the main thing,' said Herta.

'Indeed it is. "Men should be men and women women" – as you

know, that's one of papa's favourite sayings. And now, first of all, help me tidy up this table here or else there'll be another sermon.'

In less than no time the skeins were packed away into the basket, and when they had all sat down again Hulda said: 'Well Effi, now for your love-story with the unhappy ending. Or wasn't it as bad as all that?'

'A story that ends in self-sacrifice is never *bad*. But I can't begin until Herta has taken a few of those gooseberries, because she can't take her eyes off them. Incidentally, do take as many as you like, because we can pick some more later on, only do throw the skins right away – or better still put them on the newspaper supplement here and then we'll make a paper bag out of it and get rid of the whole lot. Mama can't bear skins lying about all over the place, she always says someone might slip up on one and break their leg.'

'I don't believe it,' said Herta, busily addressing herself to the gooseberries.

'I don't either,' agreed Effi. 'Just think, I fall down two or three times a day and still haven't broken anything. A decent leg doesn't break as easily as all that, at least mine doesn't, nor yours either, Herta. What do you think, Hulda?'

'You shouldn't tempt Providence. Pride comes before a fall.'

'There speaks the governess, as always. You really are a born old maid.'

'Who still has hopes of getting married. And perhaps before you.'

'That's all right as far as I'm concerned. Do you think I'm waiting to get married? That would be the end. Incidentally, I shall get my man and perhaps quite soon. So I'm not worrying. Only quite recently young Ventivegni from over the way said to me: "Miss Effi, what's the betting that we have a wedding breakfast and a marriage before the year's over?" '

'What did you say to that?'

'Quite likely, I said, quite likely; Hulda's the eldest and might well get married any day. But he would have none of it and said: "No, I mean another young lady who's just as dark as Miss Hulda is fair," looking at me very soulfully as he spoke. . . . But I'm talking nineteen to the dozen and forgetting my story.'

'Yes, you keep changing the subject. You don't really want to tell us.'

'Yes, I do, but I keep on changing the subject because it's all a bit strange, almost romantic.'

'But you said that he was a provincial governor.'

'Yes, that's right, provincial governor. And his name is Geert von Innstetten, Baron von Innstetten.'

They all laughed.

'What are you laughing at?' asked Effi, rather indignantly.

'Oh Effi dear, we didn't mean to offend you or the baron. Innstetten, you said? And Geert? Nobody round here has a name like that. The aristocracy do really often have rather funny names.'

'Yes, my little one, so they do. That's why they're the aristocracy. They can allow themselves this privilege and the further back they go, I mean in time, the more they can allow themselves. But if such things are beyond you, you mustn't blame me for that. We can still remain friends. So he is Geert von Innstetten and a baron. He's exactly mama's age, to the day.'

'How old is your mother exactly?'

'Thirty-eight.'

'A nice age.'

'Yes, indeed it is, if you still look like my mama. She really is beautiful, don't you think? And she knows her way about, she's always so confident and elegant and never improper like papa. If I were a young lieutenant, I'd fall in love with mama.'

'How can you say a thing like that!' said Hulda. 'It's against the fourth commandment.'

'Nonsense. How can it be against the fourth commandment? I think mama would be delighted to know that I'd said something like that about her.'

'Maybe,' interrupted Herta. 'But what about that story?'

'All right, don't be impatient, here it is. Well, when Baron Innstetten was still under twenty, he was garrisoned with the Rathenowers and used to know lots of the landowners around here and best of all he liked my grandfather Belling's house, in Schwantikow. Of course, it wasn't for the sake of my grandfather that he used to visit him such a lot, and when mama talks about it, it's easy for anyone to see whom it really was for. And I think it was mutual.'

'And what happened then?'

'Well, what was bound to happen, just as always happens. He was still far too young and when my father turned up he was already a district governor and owned Hohen-Cremmen, there was nothing further to think about and so she accepted him and became

Frau von Briest! . . . And what followed, well, you know all about that . . . . What followed was me!'

'Yes, it was you, Effi,' said Berta. 'Thank goodness, we shouldn't have had you if things had gone otherwise. But tell me, what did Innstetten do, what became of him? He didn't kill himself, otherwise you wouldn't be expecting him here today.'

'No, he didn't kill himself. But something rather like it.'

'Did he make an attempt?'

'No, not even that. But he didn't feel like staying in the neighbourhood any longer and he must have been generally tired of his whole life as a soldier. It was peace-time, too. To cut a long story short, he resigned his commission and began to study law "like mad" as papa says. But when the war came in '70, he joined up again, but with the Perlebergers instead of his old regiment, and he won the Cross. Naturally enough, because he's very dashing. And immediately after the war he went back to his documents and it's said that Bismarck thinks very highly of him and the Kaiser too, and so he became a provincial governor in the district of Kessin.'

'What's Kessin? I haven't heard of any Kessin hereabouts.'

'No, it's not near here, it's quite a good distance away, in Pomerania, on the other side of Pomerania as a matter of fact, although that doesn't mean anything, because it's a seaside resort like all the towns round there, and Baron Innstetten is now on a holiday trip which is really a visit to some cousins or something like that. He wants to see old friends and relations.'

'Has he got relatives here then?'

'Yes and no, it depends what you mean. There aren't any Innstettens here, in fact I don't think there are any left anywhere. But he has got some distant cousins on his mother's side here and above all he wanted to see Schwantikow and the Bellings' house, which still have so many memories for him. He was over there the day before yesterday and today he intends to be in Hohen-Cremmen.'

'And what does your father say about all this?'

'Nothing at all. He's not like that. And anyway he knows mama. He just teases her.'

At this moment it struck twelve, and before it had finished striking, Wilke, the Briests' old family retainer and general factotum, appeared to request Miss Effi, from her mother, to make sure she was dressed in good time, since the Baron was expected to be arriving just after one o'clock. And while Wilke was making this announcement, he started at once to clear away the ladies' work-table and began by reaching out for the newspaper on which the gooseberry skins were lying.

'No, Wilke, not that. Those skins are for us to deal with ... Herta, you must make a paper bag and put a stone in it, so that the whole thing sinks properly. And then we'll form a long funeral procession and commit the packet to the deep.'

Wilke gave a chuckle. 'Miss Effi's a card, she is,' must have been roughly what he was thinking. However, as Effi placed the bag down on the table-cloth which had been hastily gathered up, she said: 'Now we must all catch hold, one at each corner and sing something sad.'

'That's all very well, Effi, but what are we going to sing?'

'Anything. It doesn't matter at all as long as it has lots of *ain* in it, *ain* always has a nice mourning sound. So here we go: *Oh main, oh main, receive our sad remains.*'

And as Effi solemnly intoned this dirge, all four girls set off slowly towards the jetty, clambered on to the boat that was moored alongside and slowly let the bag, weighted down with a stone, slide into the pond.

'Herta, your guilt is now washed clean,' said Effi, 'and incident-ally I've just remembered that in days gone by, poor unfortunate women are supposed to have been drowned in the same way, as faithless wives of course.'

'But not here.'

'No, not here' laughed Effi, 'we don't do that sort of thing here. But they did in Constantinople, and that reminds me, you must know all about that too, because you were there when the pupil teacher Holzapfel told us about it in the geography lesson.'

'Yes,' said Hulda, 'he was always telling us things like that. But one forgets that sort of thing.'

'I don't, I remember things like that.'

2

THEY chatted on for a while in this way, recalling with mixed indignation and satisfaction various common experiences in class and a whole string of Holzapfel's indiscretions. Indeed, they were going happily on and on, when all at once Hulda said: 'Now it's really time for you to go, Effi. You look – well, what shall I say – you look as if you'd just been picking cherries, all crumpled and untidy. Linen always creases and there's that broad white sailor's collar . . . yes, that's right, now I realize what it is, you look like a cabin-boy.'

'A midshipman, if you don't mind. I must get some advantage from my noble birth! Anyway, midshipman or cabin-boy, my father has just recently promised to get me a mast again, right beside the swing, with yard-arms and a rope ladder. I really would enjoy that and I wouldn't let anyone fasten the pennant to the top but myself. And Hulda, you would climb up from the other side and we'd give three cheers up aloft and give each other a kiss. Shiver me timbers, that'd be something!'

'Shiver me timbers! What an expression . . . you really are talking like a midshipman. But I'll be careful not to climb up after you, I'm not so keen on risking my neck. Jahnke is quite right when he keeps saying there's too much of the Bellings in you, from your mother. I'm just a parson's daughter.'

'Get along with you! Still waters run deep. Do you still remember that time when Cousin Briest was here, when he was still a cadet, but quite grown-up, and you crept along the barn roof? And why did you? Well, I won't give you away. But come along, let's have a swing, two on each side; I don't think we'll break it, but if you're not keen, because I see you're pulling a long face, then let's play tig. I've still got a quarter of an hour. I don't want to go in yet, especially just to meet a provincial governor, and one from the depths of Pomerania at that. He's getting on, too, he's almost old enough to be my father, and if he really does come from a seaside town, which Kessin is supposed to be, more or less, then he'll like me best in this sailor's dress, won't he, and he ought to look on it as a great compliment. When the aristocracy receive anyone, from what my father tells me, they always put on the uniform of the other person's district. So don't get alarmed. Quick, I'm off, and home is beside this bench here.'

Hulda tried to raise further objections but Effi was already running up the nearest gravel path, first left, then right, until suddenly she was nowhere to be seen. 'Effi, that doesn't count.

Where are you? We're playing tig, not hide and seek.' And with these and similar protests, the three friends pursued her, well beyond the round flower-bed and the two plane trees growing beside it, until all at once Effi reappeared from her hiding place and without any trouble, because she was behind her pursuers, with a 'one and two and three', she was home beside the bench.

'Where were you?'

'Behind the rhubarb. They've got such big leaves, even bigger than fig-leaves.'

'Ugh . . . .'

'Well ugh to you, because you weren't any good. Hulda with her great big eyes still didn't see anything, she's always hopeless.' And so saying, she took off again through the flower-bed towards the lake, perhaps because she intended first to hide behind the thick hazel-nut hedge that was growing there and then to make a long detour round the churchyard and the front of the house to reach the side-wing and so back again to home. Everything was all worked out but, in fact, before she was half-way round the lake, she heard her name being called from the house, and turning around she saw her mother waving her handkerchief from the stone steps. She quickly dashed back.

'Now you've still got your smock on and our visitor has arrived. You're never on time.'

'But I am on time, it's the visitor who isn't. It's not one o'clock yet, nowhere near,' and turning round to the twins – Hulda had still not caught up – she called to them: 'Keep on playing, I'll be back in a second.'

A second later, Effi went with her mother into the big conservatory which occupied almost the whole of the side-wing.

'Mama, you mustn't be cross with me. It's really only half past. Why has he arrived so early? Young men mustn't arrive late but it's even worse to come too soon.'

Frau von Briest was obviously embarrassed, but Effi snuggled up to her and said: 'Sorry, I really will hurry up now; you know that I can be fast as well and in five minutes Cinderella will be transformed into the princess. He can wait that long or have a chat with papa!'

And with a nod of her head, she set off up the small iron staircase that led upstairs from the room. But Frau von Briest, who, in certain circumstances, was capable of being unconventional, suddenly stopped Effi as she was already rushing away, and looking at the ravishing young creature who was standing there, a picture of health and gaiety, still flushed from the excitement of her game, she said, almost confidentially: 'I think it's better for you to stay as you are after all. Yes, do that. In fact, you look very nice indeed. And even if you didn't, you look so unready, so completely untidy, and that is how you want to be at this moment. Because I've something to tell you, my darling Effi . . . .' and she took hold of both her daughter's hands . . . . 'I've got to tell you . . .'

'But Mama, what's the matter? You're making me all scared and frightened.'

'I've got to tell you, Effi, that Baron Innstetten has just asked to marry you!'

'To marry me? Seriously?'

'It's not something that one would joke about. You saw him the day before yesterday and I think you liked him, too. It's true that he's older than you, which, all things considered, is an advantage, and he's a man of character and he's well-bred and he has a good situation, and if you don't say no, which I can hardly imagine my clever Effi doing, then by the age of twenty you'll have gone as far as others have at forty. You'll go much further than your mother.'

Effi said nothing and tried to find words to reply. But before she could do so, she could hear her father's voice coming from the next room, the drawing-room at the front of the house, and immediately afterwards Ritterschaftsrat von Briest, a well-preserved and inordinately genial man of fifty, came through into the conservatory, accompanying Baron Innstetten, slim, brown-haired, and military in bearing.

When she saw him, Effi felt a sudden nervous tremor, but not for long, for almost at the very same moment that Innstetten approached her with a friendly bow, the auburn heads of the twins appeared in the middle of the two wide-open windows half-overgrown with creeper, and Herta, the most exuberant of them, shouted into the room: 'Come on, Effi!'

Then she ducked away and the pair of them jumped down again into the garden from the back of the seat that they had been standing on and all you could hear was their subdued tittering and laughter.

3

BARON INNSTETTEN became engaged to Effi that very day. Although not yet quite at home in his solemn role, the father of the bride drank to the young couple in the course of the subsequent celebration, a toast which did not fail to stir his wife's emotions, for she liked to recall what had happened barely eighteen years before. But not for long: *she* hadn't been able to marry Innstetten, but now it was her daughter's turn instead and that was, on the whole, just as good or perhaps even better. It was possible to get along with Briest, even if he was a trifle prosy and, now and again, rather silly.

Towards the end of the meal, when the ice-cream had already been served, the old councillor made a further speech, to propose that they should all use '*du*' in future, as a family. So saying, he clasped Innstetten to his bosom and gave him a kiss on the left cheek. However, this still didn't suffice; on the contrary, he proceeded to suggest even more intimate names and titles for use at home, in addition to the 'thou', a sort of order of precedence in familiarity, while naturally respecting any justifiable peculiarities – justifiable because well earned. For his wife, therefore, he proposed that the best thing would surely be to continue using the term 'Mama' – there were, after all, young mamas; as for himself, he would renounce the honorary title of 'Father' in definite preference for the simple appellation 'Briest', if only because it was nice and short. And as for the children – and looking across at Innstetten, only about a dozen years younger than himself, he had to nudge himself as he used the expression – well, Effi was just Effi, and Geert, Geert. If he were not mistaken, the name Geert meant a tall, slim tree trunk and so Effi would be the luxuriant ivy clambering round it. At this the young couple looked at each other with a somewhat embarrassed expression which in Effi's case also betrayed childlike amusement. But Frau von Briest said, 'Briest you can say what you like and give the toasts as you please, but, if I may say so, please leave poetic images alone – that's outside your competence!' This correction met with more acceptance than disagreement from Briest. 'You may possibly be right, Luise.'

As soon as they left the table, Effi excused herself in order to go over to the pastor's. On the way, she said to herself: 'I think Hulda is going to be annoyed. I've got in before her after all – she always was stuck-up and pleased with herself.' But Effi was not quite right in her assessment; Hulda restrained herself and behaved well, leaving it to her mother to show anger and bad-temper and also to make some most peculiar comments. 'Oh yes, that's how things are. As it couldn't be the mother, it has to be the daughter. We know what it's like. Old families always hang together, and to those who have shall be given.' Old Niemeyer, sorely embarrassed at this flow of acid remarks, as ill-bred as they were improper, complained once more at having married a housekeeper.

From the pastor's, Effi naturally went on to the schoolmaster Jahnke; the twins were already on the look-out and met her in the front garden.

'Well, Effi,' said Herta, as they all three walked up and down between the blossoming rows of the pupils' flowers, 'how do you feel?'

'How do I feel? Oh, quite all right. We've already started using Christian names. He's called Geert, incidentally, as I seem to remember having told you before.'

'Yes, you did. But I feel rather scared about it all. Is he really Mr Right?'

'Of course he is. You don't understand, Herta. Anyone is Mr Right. Of course, he's got to have a title and a situation in society and look presentable.'

'My goodness, Effi, the things you say. You used to talk quite differently.'

'Yes, I used to.'

'And so you're really happy already?'

'When someone's been engaged for two hours, they're always really happy. Anyway, it seems so to me.'

'And don't you feel, I don't quite know how to express it, don't you feel a bit awkward?'

'Yes, I do, a bit, but not very much. And I think I'll get over it.'

After these two visits to the parson and the schoolmaster, which had lasted less than half-an-hour, Effi had returned home across the way, where coffee was being taken outside, on the garden veranda. Father-in-law and son-in-law were strolling up and down the gravel path between the two plane trees. Briest was talking about the difficulties of being a provincial governor; he had been offered the post on a number of occasions but he had always turned it down. 'I've always preferred to be able to do exactly what I like; in any case I like it better – forgive me, Innstetten – than always having to look upwards for approval. Then you only have thought or care for your immediate superiors, or those at the very top. Here, I can live in complete freedom and enjoy every green leaf and the creeper that's growing over the window there.' He went on in this strain, attacking officialdom, apologizing now and again with an abrupt 'Forgive me, Innstetten'. The latter kept nodding his agreement but was, in fact, paying very little attention, for he kept on looking, as if fascinated, over towards the masses of creeper growing over the window which Briest had just mentioned, and as his thoughts followed his eye, he seemed to see the auburn heads of hair of the girls through the tendrils and hear the saucy voice calling 'Come on, Effi!' He had no belief in signs and portents; on the contrary, he rejected any sort of superstition completely. But all the same, he could not stop himself hearing those three words, and while Briest continued with his peroration, he had the constant feeling that that tiny incident had been more than a mere chance.

Innstetten had only taken a short leave and on the following day he went away again, having promised that he would try to write every day. 'Yes, you must do that,' Effi had said, earnestly, for she had not had any greater treat for years than receiving large numbers of letters on her birthday. On that day, everyone had to write to her. Effi heaped scorn on any expressions such as 'Gertrude and Clara join with me in sending you their very best wishes'; if Gertrude and Clara wanted to remain friends with her, they had to see to it to provide a letter with its own stamp – if possible, because her birthday fell in the holidays, a foreign stamp from Switzerland or Carlsbad.

Innstetten, as promised, really did write every day, but what made it particularly nice to receive his letters was that he only expected to have one short letter each week in reply. This he also received, full of charming little trifles that never failed to delight him. When there was anything more serious to discuss – matters concerning the wedding, questions of trousseau and household arrangements – it was Frau von Briest who dealt with it with her son-in-law. Innstetten, who was approaching the end of his three years in office, was, if not magnificently, at least very adequately set up, and it was desirable to obtain some idea, by correspondence, of what things he had, so as not to acquire anything unnecessary. When finally Frau von Briest had obtained sufficient information about all this, mother and daughter decided on a trip to Berlin in order, as Briest put it, to purchase Princess Effi's trousseau.

Effi looked forward intensely to their stay in Berlin, the more so as her father had agreed to allow them to stay in the Hôtel du Nord. 'We can deduct the expense from the dowry; Innstetten is going to get it all anyway.' In complete contrast to her mother, who refused once for all to descend to such 'pettiness', Effi joyfully accepted her father's offer in complete indifference as to whether he had spoken in jest or in earnest, and was much, much more concerned with the impression that the two of them, mother and daughter, would make when they appeared at dinner than with Spinn and Mencke, Goschenhofer, and similar firms which had been provisionally selected. And her behaviour when the great week in Berlin finally came was in accordance with her cheerful expectations. Cousin Briest, who was in the Alexander Regiment, and an uncommonly spirited young lieutenant who took the *Fliegende Blätter* and collected all the wittiest jokes, placed his services, whenever he was off-duty, at the ladies' disposal, and so they found themselves sitting with him in a corner-window at Kranzler's or even at the appropriate time in the Café Bauer, while in the afternoon they drove to the Zoological Gardens to look at the giraffes, which inspired Cousin Briest, who incidentally was called Dagobert, to remark that they looked like old maids.

Every day went according to plan and on the third or fourth day they went, as arranged, to the National Gallery, because Cousin Dagobert wanted to show his cousin the *Island of the Dead**. Cousin Effi was on the point of getting married, true enough, but perhaps it was still a good thing to have made the acquaintance of the *Island of the Dead* beforehand. His aunt gave him a tap, but with such an indulgent look that he felt no reason to change his tone. They were blissful days for all three of them, not least for the cousin, who was wonderful as a chaperone and skilfully and speedily ironed out any little differences of opinion. As might be

* A famous painting by Böcklin, gloomily mysterious.

expected, there was never any lack of such differences between mother and daughter, but fortunately they never arose when they went to make their purchases. Effi was completely indifferent to whether they should acquire six dozen or three dozen of something, and if, as they were on their way back to the hotel, any mention was made of the price of the objects they had just bought, she regularly confused the various amounts. Frau von Briest, very critical in other ways, even where her darling daughter was concerned, not only took this apparent lack of interest lightly, she even recognized its advantages. 'All these things,' she said to herself, 'don't mean a great deal to Effi. She's not pretentious. She is living in her dreams and her imagination, and if Princess Friedrich Karl nods a friendly greeting to her as she passes in her carriage, that means more to her than a whole chest of linen.'

All that was true enough, but only half the truth. Effi did not care a great deal whether she possessed a larger or smaller quantity of everyday things, but when she was going along the Unter den Linden with her mother and, after sizing up the best displays, went into Demuth's store to make all sorts of purchases for her projected honeymoon in Italy, then her real character showed itself. Only those things that were supremely elegant found favour in her eyes and if she couldn't have the best, she would give up the idea of having the second-best, because this second-best had no further interest for her. She did indeed, as her mother said, know how to do without certain things and there was something unpretentious in this quality; but if, by way of exception, she had really set her heart on something, this thing had always to be quite outstanding. And in this she *was* pretentious.

4

COUSIN DAGOBERT was at the station to see the ladies off on their return to Hohen-Cremmen. They had been happy days, particularly in that they had not been afflicted with any awkward or indeed unsuitable relatives. 'We must remain incognito for Aunt Theresa this time,' Effi had declared immediately on their arrival. 'She can't possibly come to our hotel. Either it's the Hôtel du Nord or Aunt Theresa, the two don't go together.' Eventually, her mother had fallen in with this and even given her darling daughter a kiss on her forehead to seal the agreement.

As far as Cousin Dagobert was concerned, it was, of course, quite a different matter, for not only was he every inch the guards-officer, he also possessed in full measure that special kind of good humour which has almost become traditional with officers from the Alexander regiment, by means of which he was successful, from the beginning, in stimulating and amusing both mother and daughter, and this cheerful mood lasted till the end. 'So, Dagobert,' were Effi's last words, 'you'll be coming to my eve-of-wedding celebration – not by yourself of course, because after the performances are over, there will be a ball – but don't bring any pressed men or mouse-trap dealers. And remember that my first big dance is perhaps going to be my last one. I shan't accept less than six brother-officers and best-quality dancers, naturally. And you can go back on the early train!' Dagobert promised faithfully and so they parted.

Towards noon, the ladies arrived at their station in the Havelland, in the middle of the Luch, and drove for half an hour to reach Hohen-Cremmen. Briest was very pleased to see his wife and daughter back and asked innumerable questions, most of which he did not wait for an answer to. Instead, he launched into an account of all that had happened to him meanwhile. 'You spoke to me earlier about the National Gallery and the *Island of the Dead* – well, while you were away, we've had something of that sort here, too: our overseer Pink and the gardener's wife. Of course, I've had to dismiss Pink, unwillingly, incidentally. It's absolutely inevitable that this sort of thing almost always takes place at harvest time. And apart from this, Pink was an uncommonly useful man. Unfortunately he was in the wrong place here. But let's not talk about that; Wilke's already getting restless.'

At table, Briest listened more attentively; the excellent understanding with the cousin, of whom much had been spoken, received his complete approval, the treatment of Aunt Theresa rather less. You could see, however, that his disapproval was not unmixed with pleasure, for a little trick of this sort was just the kind of thing he liked and Aunt Theresa really was a figure of fun. He clinked glasses with his wife and daughter. He even showed interest when, after lunch, they unpacked some of their purchases for him to examine; an interest which still remained, or at least did not vanish completely, when he had a quick look at the bill. 'Somewhat expensive, or rather, let's admit it, very expensive. But it doesn't matter. Everything is so chic – I might almost say so exciting – that I can see quite plainly that if you give me a trunk and travelling rugs like those as Christmas presents, then we'll be spending Easter in Rome, too, and taking our own honeymoon eighteen years after the event. What do you think, Luise? Shall we do some extra drill? Better late than never!'

Frau von Briest made a gesture as if to say 'Incorrigible' and left him to his own shame, which was not, however, excessive.

August had drawn to a close, 3rd October – the wedding-day – was approaching and the preparations for the festivities were proceeding uninterruptedly in the vicarage and the school, as well as at the Briest's house. Faithful to his passion for Fritz Reuter, Jahnke had hit on the idea that it would be particularly appropriate to let Berta and Herta play the parts of Lining and Mining, in dialect of course, while Hulda should play Käthchen von Heilbronn in the dream scene, with Lieutenant Engelbrecht of the Hussars as Wetter vom Strahl. Niemeyer, who could have claimed the credit for the idea himself, was not slow to point out the moral application to Innstetten and Effi. He was himself very pleased with his work and immediately after the rehearsal (with books) he received many complimentary remarks from all concerned, with the exception, indeed, of his old friend and patron Briest, who, having listened to the mixture of von Kleist and Niemeyer, protested in a lively fashion, albeit not on literary grounds. 'Lord and master, lord and master all the time. What's it all about? It's misleading and distorts everything. Agreed, Innstetten is a splendid fellow, a man of character, a man of spirit, but the Briests – forgive the expression, Luise – the Briests are after all not exactly upstarts, either. We are, in fact, a family with a history, thank God, if I may say so, and the Innstettens are merely old, very old if you like, but what does very old mean? I don't want a female Briest, or at any rate a character in a performance at these celebrations whom everyone will *take* as a counterpart of Effi – I don't want any female member of my family, direct or indirect, to be continually talking about her "lord and master". In that case, Innstetten would have to be a secret Hohenzollern. Such people do exist, but he isn't one, so I can only repeat that it gives a false picture.'

And Briest did in fact maintain this opinion most stubbornly for a considerable while. Only after the second rehearsal, partly a dress rehearsal, when Käthchen wore a very tight-fitting velvet bodice, did he find himself impelled to utter the remark – and he was normally not slow to compliment Hulda either – that 'Käthchen looked very nice lying there', an observation which amounted to something like a surrender or, at any rate, led up to one. That all these preparations were kept secret from Effi need hardly be pointed out. Had the latter shown more curiosity, such a thing would, of course, have been quite out of the question, but Effi had so little desire to be involved in these preparations and surprise plans that she had told her mother quite bluntly that she was prepared to wait for them; and when her mother still expressed doubts, Effi cut them short by reiterating that she really meant what she said and her mother could believe her. And why shouldn't she? After all it was only just a play and it couldn't be more poetic and more lovely than the *Cinderella* which they had seen on their last evening in Berlin. She would really have liked to have acted in that herself, if only to have been able to make a chalk mark on the back of the stupid schoolmaster. And how charming it had been in the last act when Cinderella woke up to find herself a princess or at least a countess; it really was just like a fairy-tale.

She talked a great deal in this sort of way and was generally jollier than before; if anything did annoy her, it was her friends' constant whispering and secrecy. 'I wish they made less of a fuss about it for themselves and thought more about me. When it comes to the point, they're only going round in circles and it's I who have to worry about them and be ashamed that they are like that.' Such were Effi's malicious remarks and it was quite obvious that she was not greatly concerned about the wedding and all its festivities. Frau von Briest had her own views on the matter, but she did not worry unduly, because Effi was taking her future quite seriously, which was a good sign, and with her usual imagination would launch into descriptions of her life in Kessin that went on for a good quarter of an hour, descriptions which, much to her mother's amusement, revealed a remarkable notion of life in deepest Pomerania – or perhaps were skilfully supposed to reveal such notions. Effi in fact enjoyed making Kessin out to be well on the way to Siberia, where it hardly ever stopped freezing or snowing.

'Goschenhofer has just sent the last lot today,' said Frau von Briest, as she was sitting with Effi as usual, in front of the side-wing of the house, at the work-table, which was piling up higher and higher with every sort of linen. 'I hope that you've now got everything, Effi. If there are still some things that you'd like, you must say so now, at once if possible. Your father has just got a very good price for his rape-seed and is in an unusually good humour.'

'Unusually? He's always in a good humour.'

'In an unusually good humour,' repeated her mother, 'and we must take advantage of it, so you must speak up. Several times when we were in Berlin, I had the impression that you wanted something or other rather specially.'

'Well, Mama, what do you expect me to say? In a way, I've got everything one needs, at any rate everything one needs here. But as it seems to be my fate to go so far north – please note that I've nothing against that, on the contrary, I'm looking forward to it, the northern lights and the stars shining more brightly – but since it's been decided that I shall, I should quite have liked a fur coat.'

'But my dear girl, that's just a lot of nonsense. You're not going to Petersburg or Archangel.'

'No, but I shall be on the way there. . . .'

'Of course, my dear, you're on the way there. But what does that matter? When you go from here to Namen, you're on your way to Russia too. Incidentally, if you feel like one, you shall have your fur coat. But let me say first that I advise you not to. A fur coat is for older people – even your old mama is too young for one – and when you make your appearance at seventeen dressed in mink or ermine, the people of Kessin will think you're in fancy dress.'

It was 2nd September when this conversation took place, and it would probably have been continued, had it not been Sedan Day. So they were interrupted by the sound of drum and fife, and Effi, who had heard previously about the proposed procession but had then forgotten, sprang up at once from their work-table and ran past the round flower-bed and pond to a small balcony on the churchyard wall approached by six steps that were hardly wider than the rungs of a ladder. She was up there in a second and, yes, there was the whole school approaching in procession, with Jahnke gravely marching on the right wing whilst a tiny drum major, far in front, led the way, with an expression on his face as if his task were to fight the battle of Sedan all over again. Effi waved her handkerchief to him, to which he immediately responded by saluting with the knob of his staff.

A week later, mother and daughter were sitting in the same place once again and once more busy at their sewing. It was a magnificent day; the heliotropes in the decorative flower-bed round the sundial were still in flower and a gentle breeze wafted their fragrance towards them.

'Oh, how nice I feel,' said Effi. 'Nice and so happy. I don't think heaven could be nicer. And after all, who knows whether they've got such wonderful heliotropes in heaven?'

'Effi, you mustn't talk like that. You've got that from your father – nothing is sacred for him. He even said recently that Niemeyer looked like Lot. Incredible. What can he mean by it? Firstly he doesn't know what Lot looked like and secondly it shows extraordinary lack of consideration for Hulda. It's a good thing that Niemeyer only has the one daughter, so that the comparison really falls to the ground. It's true that in one respect he was only too right – what he said about Lot's wife, our dear Frau Niemeyer, who once again completely spoiled Sedan Day with her stupidity and pretentiousness. Which reminds me incidentally that when Jahnke came by with the school he interrupted us in our conversation – at least, I can't imagine that a fur coat is the only thing you want. So tell me, darling, what else have you set your heart on?'

'Nothing, Mother.'

'Nothing at all?'

'No, really nothing; I'm quite serious. But if there *had* to be something after all . . .'

'Yes?'

'It would be a Japanese bedroom screen, black with gold birds on it, all with long beaks like cranes. And a bulb for our bedroom lamp to give a red light.'

Frau von Briest said nothing.

'Now you see, Mama, you're refusing to speak and you look as if I'd said something quite improper.'

'No, Effi, not improper. And in front of your mother, quite definitely not. Because I know you very well. You're a strange little girl and you like dreaming about the future and the more colourful your dreams are the lovelier and more desirable they seem. I realized that when we were buying your luggage. And now you think it would be wonderful to have a bedroom screen with all sorts of fantastic beasts on it and lit by a dim red light. You think of it as a fairy-story and you'd like to be a princess.'

Effi took her mother's hand and kissed it. 'Yes, Mama, I am.'

'Yes, so you are. I know that. But Effi dear, we must be careful how we live, above all because we're women. And when you arrive in Kessin, a little place where you'll hardly see a street lamp at night, people will laugh at that sort of thing. And they won't just laugh! The people who aren't very fond of you – and there always are such people – will say that it's bad upbringing and a lot of them will say worse things than that.'

'All right then, nothing Japanese and no red light! But I confess that I had imagined it all lovely and poetic to see everything bathed in a red glow.'

Frau von Briest was touched. She stood up and kissed Effi. 'You're just a child. Lovely and poetic indeed, that's just imaginings. Reality is different and it's often a good thing, instead of a red glow, to have it quite dark.'

Effi seemed on the point of making some reply but at that moment Wilke came in bringing the letters. One was from Innstetten in Kessin. 'Oh, one from Geert,' said Effi and putting it on one side she continued quietly: 'But all the same you must let me put the grand-piano diagonally across the room. I'm more interested in that than in the fireplace that Geert promised me. And that picture of you I shall put on an easel; I can't do without you completely. Oh, how I'm going to long to be able to see you, perhaps even during my honeymoon and quite definitely in Kessin! People tell me it hasn't any garrison and not even a chief medical officer but thank Heavens at least that it's a seaside resort. Cousin Dagobert – and I rely on him – his mother and sister always go to Warnemünde. Well, I don't see why he can't direct his dear relatives to Kessin for once. Direct – that sounds just like the General Staff, which, if I'm not mistaken, he has designs on. And then of course he'll come with them and stay with us. Incidentally, someone told me only recently that Kessin has quite a big steamer that goes twice a week to

Sweden. And there'll be dancing on board – there must be music there, of course – and he's a very good dancer.'

'Who is?'

'Why, Dagobert.'

'I thought you meant Innstetten. But anyway, it really is time for you to see what he's written. . . . You've still got his letter in your pocket.'

'So I have. I'd almost forgotten it.' And she opened the letter and perused it quickly.

'Well, Effi, why don't you say something? You don't seem overjoyed and you haven't even laughed once. And yet he always writes such cheerful and entertaining letters, and not at all like a heavy father.'

'No, and I wouldn't put up with such a thing either. He's older and I'm younger. I'd just wag my finger at him and say: "Geert, just you think it over and you'll see what's best." '

'And he would reply: "What you say is best, Effi," because he's not only an extremely polished and cultivated man but also fair and understanding and he knows very well what it's like to be young. He's always reminding himself of this and adapting himself to the young, and if he remains the same after he's married, yours will be a model marriage.'

'Yes, I think so too, Mama. But do you know, I'm almost asham-ed to tell you, I'm not so very keen on what people call a model marriage.'

'That's just like you. Tell me what you are in favour of, then.'

'I'm in favour of . . . well, I'm in favour of equality and, of course, of love and tenderness, and if there can't be love and tenderness, because love, as papa says, is just a lot of claptrap – which I don't believe – well, then I'm in favour of wealth and a lovely big house, a real stately home, one where Prince Frederick Karl would come shooting for elks or capercailzie, or where the old Kaiser would drive up and have a gracious word for all the ladies, even the young ones. And when we're in Berlin, then I want court balls and gala performances at the opera, always sitting close to the Imperial box.'

'Are you saying all this for fun, just out of high spirits?'

'No, Mama, I'm saying it in all seriousness. Love comes first but immediately after that comes honour and glory and then comes amusement – yes, amusement, always something new, always something to make one laugh or cry. What I can't stand is boredom.'

'How have you managed to put up with us?'

'Oh, Mama, how can you say such a thing! It's true that when all our dear relatives call on us in the winter and stay six hours or more and Aunt Gundel and Aunt Olga look me up and down and find me cheeky – and Aunt Gundel once told me so – well, I must agree that that doesn't make it very nice for us sometimes. But apart from that, I've always been happy here, so happy . . .'

And as she was speaking, she burst out crying and flinging herself on her knees in front of her mother, she kissed her hands.

'Do get up, Effi. Those are just the sort of moods that come over someone when they're young like you and faced by the uncertainty of marriage. Now, you read out the letter to me, unless it contains something very special or perhaps secrets.'

'Secrets,' laughed Effi, jumping to her feet with a sudden change of mood. 'Secrets! Well, he always starts off with a dash but most of it I could have pinned up in the local bailiff's office, where all the governor's ordinances are displayed. And of course, Geert *is* a provincial governor.'

'Go on, do read it.'

' "Dear Effi". . . . he always starts like that and often he calls me his "little Eve" too.'

'Keep reading . . . you're to read it to me!'

'All right, then: "Dear Effi, The nearer we come to our wedding day, the less you write to me. When the post comes, the first thing I always do is to look for your handwriting but, as you know (and I admit that I agreed to it), usually there's nothing. The labourers are now in the house preparing the rooms – not many, it's true – for your arrival. I suppose that the most important things will be done while we are on our travels. The decorator Madelung, who is supplying everything, is a real character whom I must tell you about in my next letter, but above all I must tell you how happy I am about my dear little Effi. My urge to see you is unbearable, and at the same time good old Kessin is becoming quieter and quieter, and more and more lonely. The last bather left yesterday and the last bathes he took were at a temperature of 48°; the attendants were always pleased to see him come out safe and sound. They were afraid that he might have a stroke which would bring the bathing into disrepute, as if the waves were worse here than anywhere else. I'm rejoicing at the thought that, in four weeks from now, I shall be leaving the Piazzetta to go over to the Lido or Murano, where they make glass beads and beautiful jewelry. And the most beautiful will be for you. My regards to your parents and a very tender kiss, from Your Geert." '

Effi folded the letter up again to put it back into the envelope.

'That's a very nice letter,' said Frau von Briest, 'and the fact that he's moderate in everything he does is an additional advantage.'

'Yes, he's certainly moderate enough in everything he does.'

'Effi dear, let me ask you a question. Would you like him not to be so moderate in his letter, would you like him to be more tender, perhaps even over-tender?'

'No, Mama, not at all. Really and truly not, I don't want that. That's why it's better like it is.'

' "That's why it's better like it is." How peculiar that sounds. What a strange girl you are. And earlier on you were crying! Is there something that's worrying you? There's still time. Don't you love Geert?'

'Why shouldn't I love him? I love Hulda and I love Berta and I love Herta. And I love old Niemeyer too. And I don't bother to mention that I love you and father. I love everybody who's well disposed towards me and treats me kindly and spoils me. And I expect Geert will spoil me too. In his own way, of course. He's already thinking of giving me jewelry. He hasn't the slightest idea that I'm not interested in jewelry. I'd sooner climb trees and have a go on the swing, and most of all I always like being scared that something will give way or break and fall down. After all, it's not bound to kill me.'

'And do you perhaps love Cousin Briest as well?'

'Yes, a lot. He always keeps me amused.'

'And would you have liked to marry him?'

'Marry? Goodness me no! He's still half a boy! Geert is a man, a handsome man, someone I can cut a dash with, someone who is going to be somebody in life. What were you thinking about, Mama!'

'Yes, that's quite right, Effi, I'm pleased to hear it. But I think you've still got something on your mind.'

'Perhaps.'

'Tell me what it is, then!'

'You see, Mama, it doesn't matter about his being older than me, perhaps it's really a good thing, because he's not actually old and he's fit and well and very military and dashing. And I could say that I'd have absolutely nothing against him if only . . . well, if only he were just a teeny weeny bit different.'

'How ought he to be then, Effi?'

'How? Well, you mustn't laugh at me. It's something that I've only just heard about recently, over at the vicarage. We were talking about Innstetten over there and all at once old Niemeyer gave a frown, but in an admiring and reverent sort of way, and said: "Oh yes, the baron! He's a man of character, a man of principles!" '

'So he is, Effi.'

'Certainly. And I think Niemeyer even said later on that he was a man of fundamental principles, too. And that seems to me something rather more. And I'm afraid that I . . . that I haven't got any. So you see, Mama, that's something that worries and frightens me. He's so kind and good to me and so considerate but . . . I'm scared of him.'

5

THE festivities were over. Everyone had left, including the young couple, on the evening of the wedding-day.

The celebrations on the eve of the wedding had given pleasure to everyone, especially to those who were taking part, and Hulda was the toast of all the young officers, from the Rathenower Hussars to the somewhat more critical brother-officers of the Alexander Regiment. In fact, everything had gone off smoothly and well, almost better than expected. Only Berta and Herta had been sobbing so violently that Jahnke's dialect poetry had been more or less inaudible. But even that had not caused much harm. A few connoisseurs had even expressed the view that this was the right way to do it; forgetting your lines and sobbing and mumbling incomprehensibly – by such means, above all when the speakers were such pretty auburn curly-heads, victory was always most decisive. Cousin Briest could boast of having achieved outstanding success in a part that he had invented for himself: he had pretended to be a salesman from Demut's who, acting on the information that the bride intended to leave for Italy immediately after the wedding, wished to deliver a suitcase. This suitcase was then revealed as an immense comfit box from Hövel's. Dancing had gone on until three o'clock, and old Briest, under the growing influence of the champagne, was led to make all sorts of comments on the fact that at many courts a torch dance was still commonly performed and to draw attention to the remarkable custom of the garter-dance. He went on making these remarks so frequently and indeed so blatantly that a stop had had to be put to them.

'Pull yourself together, Briest,' his wife had whispered to him, with some urgency; 'you're not here to indulge in *doubles-entendres* but to act as host. This is *not* a shooting party.' To which Briest's reply was that he didn't see much difference and that in any case he was a happy man.

The wedding had also gone off very well. Niemeyer had made an excellent speech, and one of the old gentlemen from Berlin, who moved partly in court circles, during the journey back from the church to the bride's house had remarked, in this connexion, how extraordinary it was 'to see how richly endowed with talent our State is. I attribute it to the excellence of our schools and, perhaps even more, to our philosophy. When I think of that Niemeyer, an old village parson who at first glance looked like a simple almoner . . . well now, my friend, wouldn't you say that he preached just like a court chaplain? His tact and his skill in antithesis, just like Kögel, and even superior to him in feeling. Kögel's too cold. It's true that a man in his position has to be cold. What really prevents anyone from succeeding in life? Always too much emotion.' The distinguished person to whom these words were addressed, still a bachelor, and doubtless for that reason at the moment involved in his fourth liaison, naturally agreed.

'Too true, *cher ami*,' he said. 'Too much emotion . . . quite superb . . . and incidentally I must tell you a story later on.'

The day following the wedding was a bright October day. The morning sun was sparkling, although it was already cool and autumnal, and Briest, who had just had breakfast with his wife, got up from his chair and stood, with both hands behind his back, beside the slowly dying fire in the grate.

Frau von Briest, who was doing some sewing, also moved nearer to the fire and told Wilke, who came in at that moment, to clear away the breakfast.

'And then Wilke, when you've cleared up everything in the drawing-room – that must be done first – will you see to it that the cakes are taken over the way, the tart with the nuts to the pastor and the dish of small cakes to Jahnke's. And be careful with the glasses. I mean the thin cut-glass ones.'

Briest, already on his third cigarette, was looking in very good shape and volunteered the statement that 'there was nothing as good for anyone as a wedding, excluding one's own, of course.'

'I don't know what makes you produce remarks like that, Briest. It's news to me that you consider yourself to have been the loser by it. Nor can I imagine why you should have.'

'Luise, you're a spoilsport. But I never complain, even about that sort of thing. By the way, who are we to say anything about it when we ourselves didn't even have a honeymoon? Your father was against it. But Effi is having hers now. Lucky girl. Left on the ten o'clock train. They must already be somewhere near Regensburg by now and I assume that he's telling her all about the main art treasure of the Valhalla there – without getting off the train, of course. Innstetten is an excellent fellow but he's got a thing about art, and our dear Effi, well, she's a child of nature. I'm afraid that he may be getting on her nerves a bit, with all his keenness on art!'

'All men get on their wives' nerves. And there are worse things than being keen on art.'

'Yes, of course, there are. In any case, we don't want to quarrel over that; it's a big subject. And then people vary so much, too. Now *you* would have been able to cope. You would have been altogether more suited to Innstetten than Effi. Pity it's too late.'

'How flattering you are, apart from the fact that it's irrelevant. Anyway, however that may be, bygones are bygones. He's my son-in-law now and it's pointless to keep going back over what took place when I was young.'

'I only wanted to buck you up a little.'

'Very kind, I'm sure. But as a matter of fact, it's quite unnecessary. I'm already in quite a lively mood.'

'And a good one?'

'I think so, almost. But you're not going to spoil it. Well, what's the matter now? I can see that you've got something on your mind.'

'What did you think of Effi? Did you like the whole thing? She was so peculiar, half childish and then on the other hand very self-possessed and not at all overawed as she ought to be by such a man. It can only be explained by the fact that she doesn't yet quite realize what sort of a husband she has. Or is it simply that she doesn't really love him? That would be a bad thing. Because, with all his good qualities, he's not the sort of man who'd find it easy to make her love him.'

Frau von Briest said nothing and counted up the stitches on her canvas. After a while she said:

'What you've just said, Briest, is the most intelligent thing I've heard from you so far in the last three days, including what you were saying at table. I've had misgivings of my own, too. But I think we can rest assured.'

'Did she pour her heart out to you?'

'I shouldn't like to call it that. She certainly feels the need to talk now and again but she doesn't feel the need to empty her heart out, and she keeps a lot to herself; she's informative and discreet at the same time, almost secretive, a very strange mixture altogether.'

'I quite agree. But if she didn't tell you anything, how did you come to know?'

'I only said that she didn't pour her heart out to me. That sort of general confession, baring her soul, is not her style. It all came out in fits and starts and all of a sudden and then it was over. But because it came out of her so involuntarily and almost by accident I thought it was terribly important.'

'When was it, then? What happened exactly?'

'It'll be just three weeks ago when we were sitting in the garden, seeing to all sorts of things, big and small, connected with the trousseau. Wilke brought in a letter from Innstetten. She put it away and I had to remind her a quarter of an hour later that she had a letter. Then she did read it but it seemed to make hardly any impression on her. I must confess that my heart sank when I saw that, so much so that I wanted to be certain about it all – as far as one can be in these matters . . .'

'Very true, very true.'

'What does that mean?'

'Well, I just meant . . . But it doesn't matter. Go on, I'm all ears!'

42

'So I asked her bluntly how things were, and since, because of her character, I wanted to avoid being solemn and take everything as lightly as possible and even almost as a joke, I suddenly asked her whether she would perhaps have preferred to marry her cousin who had been extremely attentive towards her in Berlin. . . .'

'And?'

'You ought to have seen her. Her first reaction was a saucy little laugh. Her cousin was really only a big cadet dressed up as a lieutenant, she said. And she couldn't even love a cadet, let alone marry one. And then she talked about Innstetten, who seemed suddenly to be a model of all the manly virtues.'

'And how do you explain that?'

'Quite simply. Although she's so lively and high-spirited and almost passionate, or perhaps because she is all these things, she's not the sort of girl who is really set on love, at least not on what is properly called love. She talks about it, of course, as if she believes in it and she even harps on it, but only because she has read somewhere or other that love is the noblest, the finest, the most splendid thing there is. It may be that she has only heard that sentimental girl Hulda talking about it and is just imitating her. But she doesn't have strong feelings about it. It's possible, of course, that she may have one day, God forbid, but she doesn't at the moment.'

'And what is there at the moment? What does she feel?'

'To my mind and according to what she herself says, too, there are two things: love of pleasure and ambition.'

'Well, she may get over that. I feel reassured.'

'I don't. Innstetten is ambitious – I won't say a careerist because it's not true of him, he's too much of a gentleman – just ambitious, and that will satisfy Effi's vanity.'

'Well, that's all right.'

'Yes, that's all right. But that's only half the story. Her vanity will be satisfied but will her love of fun, her love of adventure? I doubt it. Where day-to-day entertainment and excitement are concerned, all those little things that keep away boredom, that deadly enemy of clever young women, Innstetten will be a very poor help. He won't leave her in a spiritual desert because he's too intelligent and too much a man of the world for that, but he won't particularly amuse her either. And the worst thing is that he won't even try properly to tackle the question of how he should set about it.

They'll jog along like that for a while without much harm being done, but finally she'll notice it and then she'll feel hurt. And then I don't know what will happen. Because although she's so gentle and easy-going, there's also a touch of the devil in her and she can take lots of risks.'

At this moment, Wilke came in from the drawing-room to report that he had counted everything up and it was all complete, but one of the best wine-glasses had been broken – it had been done yesterday, when they were drinking the health of the bride and groom – Fräulein Hulda had clinked her glass too hard against Lieutenant Nienkerken's.

'Of course, she's always been only half awake and, naturally, the dream scene didn't help matters. A silly girl, and I can't understand Nienkerken.'

'I can understand him perfectly.'

'But he can't marry her.'

'No.'

'What's the point, then?'

'A big subject, Luise.'

This conversation took place the day after the wedding. Three days later there arrived a few words scribbled on a card from Munich. 'Dear Mama, This morning visited the Pinakothek. Geert wanted us to go on afterwards to the other one opposite, which I'm not going to mention because I'm not certain how to spell it and I don't want to ask him. In any case, he's terribly kind and explains everything to me. Everything absolutely wonderful but strenuous. I suppose it'll calm down a bit in Italy and be better. We're staying at the Four Seasons Hotel, which has inspired Geert to make the remark that it's autumn outside but that I'm his spring. I think it's very clever. He's extremely attentive towards me. It's true that I have to be, too, especially when he says something or explains something. Moreover, he knows everything so well that he doesn't ever need to look anything up. He was captivated by you both and particularly by mama. He thought Hulda a trifle affected, but old Niemeyer completely won his heart. All love from your wildly happy but rather tired Effi.'

From now on such letters arrived daily, from Innsbruck, Verona, Vicenza, Padua, and each one began: 'This morning visited the famous local art gallery' or if not the gallery, the arena, or some church called Santa Maria something or other. From Padua, together with the card, came a proper letter:

'We spent yesterday in Vicenza. Vicenza is a "must" because of Palladio; Geert told me that all that's modern originates from him. Of course, only modern as far as architecture is concerned. Here in Padua, where we arrived early this morning, while we were driving in the hotel carriage, he muttered several times to himself: "He's buried in Padua"* and was surprised to learn from me that I had never heard those words before. In the end, he said that it was really quite a good thing and an advantage that I didn't know anything about it. He's altogether a very fair man. And above all, he's terribly kind to me and not at all superior and not at all old, either. My feet are still troubling me and I find all the looking up and standing about in front of pictures rather strenuous. But it has to be done. I'm looking forward a great deal to Venice. We shall stay five days there, perhaps even a whole week. Geert has already been telling me great things about the pigeons on the square in front of St Mark's and how you can buy bags of peas and feed the pretty birds. Apparently there are photographs showing it all, with beautiful blonde girls, "à la Hulda", he says, which brings to mind the Jahnke girls. Oh, what I'd give to be sitting with them on the shaft of a cart in our yard and feeding our pigeons. You mustn't kill the fantail. I want to see it again. Oh, it's so lovely here. In fact, it's supposed to be the loveliest of all. Your happy but rather tired Effi.'

When she had read out the letter, Frau von Briest said: 'Poor child! She's homesick.'

'Yes,' said Briest, 'she's homesick. All this damned travelling.'

'Why are you saying that now? You could have stopped it. But that's just like you, to be wise after the event. It's only when the child has fallen into the stream that the council puts up a fence to stop it.'

'Now, Luise, don't try that sort of thing with me. Effi's our daughter, but ever since 3rd October she's been Baroness Innstetten. And if her husband, our son-in-law, wants to go on a honeymoon and seizes the opportunity to recatalogue all the art galleries, I can't do anything to stop it. That's what is meant by "getting married".'

*Said by Mephistopheles in Goethe's *Faust*, Part I.

'So now you admit it. With me you've always denied, *always denied*, that the wife loses her freedom.'

'Yes, Luise, I always have. But why talk about it now. That's really too big a subject.'

6

In the middle of November – they had reached as far as Capri and Sorrento – Innstetten's leave came to an end, and in keeping with his character and habits, he was punctilious concerning his time-table. And so on the morning of the 14th he arrived in Berlin on the express and was greeted, with Effi, by Cousin Briest, who suggested that they might spend the intervening couple of hours before the departure of the Stettin train in going to look at the view at St Privat and combine this visit with a light lunch. Both these suggestions were gratefully accepted. By noon, they were once more at the station and parted again with hearty handshakes, not before both Effi and Innstetten had issued the customary invitation, which is fortunately very rarely to be taken seriously, to 'come over one of these days'. As the train was already moving off, Effi waved from the compartment. Then she made herself comfortable and shut her eyes; only now and again she sat up and took hold of Innstetten's hand.

It was a pleasant journey and the train arrived on time at Klein-Tantow station, whence a causeway led to Kessin, two miles further on. During the summer, that is during the bathing season, instead of using the causeway, people would prefer to go by water and took an old paddle-steamer down the little river Kessine, to which the town itself owed its name. However, on 1st October every year, they suspended the service and people had long been wanting this boat, the *Phoenix*, to be true to her name and go up in flames one day when she wasn't carrying any passengers. So Innstetten had already sent his coachman Kruse a telegram from Stettin: 'Klein-Tantow station five o'clock. If fine, open carriage.'

And the weather was fine and Kruse drew up at the station in an open carriage, to greet the new arrivals with the decorum appropriate to a first-rate coachman.

'Well, Kruse, everything all right?'

'At your service, m'lud.'

'Then climb in, Effi, will you?' And Effi followed him, and while one of the porters stowed a small suitcase beside the driver, Innstetten gave instructions for the rest of the luggage to be sent on by the omnibus. Then he immediately took his seat as well, asked for a light from one of the by-standers, to show the common touch, and called to Kruse: 'Drive on, Kruse!'

And off they went over the many rails of the level-crossing, diagonally down the station approach and then straightaway past an inn, standing right on the road, which was called 'The Prince Bismarck'. At this spot, there was a fork branching off right to Kessin and left to Varzin. Standing in front of the inn was a broad-shouldered man of medium height dressed in a fur coat and cap. He removed the cap as the governor went by.

'Who was that?' asked Effi, greatly interested by everything they saw and, for that reason, in a good humour. 'He looked like a village elder, although I must confess that I've never seen a village elder.'

'And there's no harm in that, Effi. All the same, you guessed very well. He really does look like a village elder and is something of that sort. He is, in fact, half Polish and is called Golchowski, and when we have an election here or a shoot, he's always in the forefront. He's really rather a tricky customer whom I wouldn't trust out of my sight, and he must have quite a lot of things on his conscience. But he pretends to be loyal and when the gentry from Varzin come by, he'd be happy to throw himself under the wheels of their carriage. I know that Prince Bismarck finds him repulsive. But what can one do? We can't fall out with him because we need him. He's got the whole district feeding out of his hand and he knows more about manipulating votes than anyone, and he's also said to be well-off. And what's more, he lends money for interest, which Poles rarely do; on the whole they do the opposite.'

'But he was a good-looking man.'

'Yes, he has good looks all right. Most people have around here. A handsome lot of people. But that's the best that can be said for them. The people from your part of the world are not so prepossessing and look more morose, and they're less respectful in their attitude, but when they say yes or no, they mean yes or no and you can rely on them. Here, there's nothing certain.'

'Why are you telling me this? I've still got to live here with them.'

'You won't have to, because you won't be hearing or seeing much of them. There's a big difference here between the town and the country, and you'll only get to know our townsfolk, our nice, kind people of Kessin.'

'Our nice, kind people of Kessin. Are you making fun of them or are they really so nice and kind?'

'I wouldn't exactly say that they're really nice, but they are at least different from the others. Yes, there's no similarity at all to the country people.'

'And why is that?'

'It's because they're quite a different sort of people, by their origin and by their connexions. The people you find in the interior are the so-called Kaschubes, whom you may have heard of, Slavs who have been settled here for a thousand years and probably much longer. But the people who live in the little seaside resorts and trading towns all along the coast are immigrants of long standing who pay very little attention to the Kaschubes, because they have little to do with them and their interests lie in quite a different direction. Their interests, in fact, lie in the areas where they trade and as they trade with the whole world and have connexions with everybody, you'll find people from all four corners of the world amongst them. Even in our good old Kessin, although it's really only a God-forsaken hole.'

'But that's delightful, Geert. You're always talking about it's being a dreary hole and now I see that unless you've been exaggerating there's a whole new world to discover. All sorts of exotic people. That's right, isn't it? You meant something like that?'

He nodded.

'A whole new world, then, perhaps a Negro or a Turk or perhaps even a Chinaman.'

'Even a Chinaman. How clever you are at guessing. It's possible that we may still have one, but in any case we did have one. Now he's dead and buried on a little plot of earth enclosed by an iron fence, right beside the cemetery. If you're not scared, I'll show you the grave when we have the chance. It's among the sand-dunes, with nothing but wild oats all around and a few everlasting flowers here and there, and you can hear the sea all the time. It's very lovely and very awe-inspiring.'

'Yes, that's the word and I should quite like to know more about it. But perhaps I'd better not, because I'll immediately have dreams and visions, and as I hope to sleep well tonight I shouldn't like to see a Chinaman heading for my bed straightaway.'

'Nor will he.'

'Nor will he. D'you know that sounds strange, as if it were possible all the same. You want to make Kessin sound interesting for me, but there you're going a bit too far. And are there many such foreigners in Kessin?'

'Very many. The whole town consists of foreigners, of people whose parents or grandparents lived somewhere quite different.'

'How extraordinary. Please tell me about it. But not anything creepy again. I think there's always something a bit creepy about a Chinaman.'

'Yes, so there is,' laughed Geert, 'but the rest are quite different, thank God, nothing but pleasant people, perhaps rather commercially-minded, thinking rather too much about their own interests, and always ready with some rather dubious bills of exchange. Yes, you have to be careful with them. But, apart from that, nice. And in order to convince you that I haven't misled you, I'll give you a small sample, a sort of index or list of names.'

'Yes, do that, Geert.'

'Well then for example, less than fifty yards from us – our gardens back on to each other – we have Macpherson, the engineer in charge of the dredging, a real Highland Scot.'

'And does he behave like one?'

'No, thank God, because he's a wizened little man whom neither his own clan nor Walter Scott would be particularly proud of. And in the same house as Macpherson, there lives an old surgeon as well, by the name of Beza, nothing but a barber, really. He comes from Lisbon where the famous General de Meza comes from too – Meza, Beza, you can hear that the two names are related. And then higher up the river, on the mole – that is, in fact, the wharf where the ships tie up – we have a goldsmith by the name of Stedingk, who comes from an old Swedish family, in fact I think there are even counts of that name. And in addition – this is the last one for now – we have good old Dr Hannemann, who is, of course, a Dane and who spent a long time in Iceland and has even written a short book on the last eruption of the Hekla or Krabla.'

'But that's splendid, Geert, that's as good as six novels and you'd never get to the end of them. At first it sounds dreadfully bourgeois and then you can see that it's something quite special. And just because it's a town by the sea, you must also have people who aren't just surgeons or barbers or suchlike. You must have sea-captains, too, some flying Dutchman or . . .'

'You're quite right. We've even got a captain who was a pirate with the Black Flags.'

'Never heard of them. What are Black Flags?'

'They're people on the other side of the world, in Tonkin and in the South China Sea. . . . But since he's come back to civilization, he's become very respectable again and quite entertaining.'

'But I'd still be frightened of him.'

'Which you need never be, not even when I'm travelling or dining with the Prince, because in addition to everything else that we've got, thank goodness we've got Rollo as well. . . .'

'Rollo?'

'Yes, Rollo. It makes you think of the Duke of Normandy, as-suming that Niemeyer or Jahnke told you about such things, and our Rollo is something like that. But he's only a Newfoundland, a splendid animal, who is fond of me and is going to be fond of you, too. You see, Rollo is a connoisseur. And as long as he's about, you can feel quite safe and nobody will be able to come near you, alive or dead. But look at the moor over there. Isn't it lovely?'

Effi, absorbed in her own thoughts, had silently been taking in every word with a mixture of eagerness and anxiety; she now sat up and looked over towards her right where the moon had just risen behind white clouds which were rapidly vanishing. From behind an alder wood, the big copper-coloured disc was casting its light on to the Kessine, which formed a broad expanse of water at this spot. Or perhaps it was already a bay formed partly by the sea beyond.

Effi was enraptured.

'Yes, Geert, you're right, how lovely it is; but it's got something uncanny about it as well. I never had an impression of that sort in Italy, not even when we drove over from Mestre to Venice. There was water and marsh and moonlight then and I thought that the bridge was going to break; but it wasn't so spooky. Why's that? Is it because of the north?'

Innstetten laughed.

'We're fifteen miles further north here than in Hohen-Cremmen and you'll have to wait a long time to see your first polar bear. I think you're strung up because of the long journey and the view from St Privat and the story about the Chinaman.'

'But you haven't told me anything about him at all.'

'No, all I did was to mention him. But a Chinaman is a story in himself . . .'

'Yes,' she laughed.

'And in any case, you'll soon have got over it. Can you see that little house with the light in front of you? It's a smithy. The road turns off there. And when we've gone down the turn, you'll be able to see Kessin's steeple, or rather two steeples. . . .'

'Has it got two?'

'Yes, Kessin is progressing. It's got a Catholic church as well now.'

Half an hour later the carriage pulled up at the governor's residence at the far end of the town; it was a simple, somewhat old-fashioned frame-house facing on to the main street leading to the bathing-places but with a gable overlooking a copse, which people called 'the plantation', separating the town from the dunes. This old-fashioned frame-house was, incidentally, merely Innstetten's private house, not the official government house, which stood obliquely across on the other side of the street.

Kruse had no need to announce their arrival by three cracks of his whip: the occupants of the house had long been on the watch, from door and window, for the arrival of the master and his wife, and even before the carriage drew up, they had all gathered on the entrance steps which took up the whole width of the pavement, and Rollo, who was also there, began to run round the carriage as soon as it had stopped. After first helping his young wife to climb down from the carriage, Innstetten offered her his arm and with a friendly acknowledgement walked past the servants, who followed the young couple into the vestibule, with its superb old wall-cupboards.

The maid, a pretty woman, no longer very young, whose impressive embonpoint suited her almost as well as the neat little cap she wore on her blonde hair, helped her new mistress off with her muff and coat and was just about to bend down to take off her fur-lined rubber boots as well, when, before she could do so, Innstetten said:

'The best thing is for me to introduce our whole household to you straightaway, with the exception of Frau Kruse, who is rather chary of appearing – I presume that she's busy with her inevitable black hen once again.'

Everyone grinned.

'But let's forget Frau Kruse. . . . This is my trusty old Frederick who has been with me ever since I was up at the university . . . that's right, isn't it Frederick, in the good old days? . . . And this is Joanna, a compatriot of yours from Mark Brandenburg, assuming you are prepared to accept as such someone who comes from the region of Pasewalk; and this is Christel, whom we rely on to look after our needs at lunch and supper – and she knows all about cooking, I can promise you. And here is Rollo. Well, Rollo, how goes it?'

Rollo seemed to have been waiting only for this cue, because the moment he heard his name he gave a woof of pleasure, stood on his hind-legs and placed his paws on his master's shoulder.

'All right now, Rollo, all right then. But now look here, this is your mistress. I've told her all about you and said that you're a handsome animal and would look after her.' Hereupon Rollo desisted and sat down at Innstetten's feet, at the same time looking up with curiosity at his young mistress. And when she held out her hand to him, he nuzzled against it.

During these introductions, Effi had found time to look around her. She was enchanted by what she saw and at the same time dazzled by the amount of light. In the front part of the hall, there were four or five lighted candelabra on the walls, the sconces themselves being very primitive and made only of tin, a fact which, however, only helped to increase the brilliance and glare.

Two astral lamps covered with red shades, a wedding present from Niemeyer, were standing on a folding table placed between two oak cupboards, and in front of the table were the tea-things, with the little lamp already burning under the kettle. But there were many, many more things than these, some of them most peculiar. Right across the hall ran three beams dividing the ceiling into sections; on the first beam, there hung a fully rigged ship, with a high poop and port-holes for cannons, while further along an immense fish seemed to be swimming in the air. Effi raised her umbrella, which she was still carrying, and gingerly poked at the monster.

'What's that, Geert?' she asked.

'That's a shark.'

'And right at the back there, that thing that looks like a big cigar?'

'That's a young crocodile. But you can look at all that much better tomorrow, in detail. Come and let's have a cup of tea now. You must be frozen in spite of all those rugs and plaids. It was getting definitely chilly towards the end.'

He offered Effi his arm and while the two maids went away, leaving only Frederick and Rollo to follow, they all moved off to their left into the main living-room, which was also a study. Effi found herself as surprised here as she had been out in the hall; but before she could say anything, Innstetten flung back a curtain masking a doorway which led into a second, larger room overlooking the courtyard and garden.

'And this, Effi, is your room. Frederick and Joanna have done their best to arrange it according to my instructions. I think it's quite tolerable and I shall be happy if you like it.'

She slipped her arm out of his and reached up on tip-toe to give him an affectionate kiss.

'How you do spoil your poor little Effi! The grand piano and carpet, which I do believe is Turkish, and the aquarium with those dear little fishes and the flower-piece as well! I'm being spoilt in every direction!'

'Yes, Effi dear, I'm afraid you'll have to put up with it – it's the penalty of being young and pretty and lovable, which the inhabitants of Kessin seem already to have discovered. Heaven knows how. Because at least where the flowers are concerned, I'm not responsible. Frederick, where does the flower-piece come from?'

'The chemist Gieshübler. . . . There's a card there as well.'

'Ah, yes, Gieshübler, Alonzo Gieshübler,' said Innstetten and with a laugh that was almost gay he passed the card with its rather strange-sounding name to Effi. 'I'd forgotten to tell you about Gieshübler – incidentally, he's also got the title of doctor but he doesn't like it when people use it, because he thinks that it would merely annoy the proper doctors and I've no doubt that he's right there. Well, I imagine you'll be meeting him and quite soon at that;

he's our trump card here, cultivated, something of a character and, above all, a heart of gold, which is still the most important thing. But let's leave all that now and sit down and have some tea. Where shall we put it? In here with you or out there with me? There's no alternative. Poor and humble is my dwelling.'

Without further thought, she sat down on a small corner settee. 'We'll stay here for today, I invite you to be my guest. No, let's have this arrangement: tea with me and breakfast with you; then we shall each have our proper turn and I shall be curious to see which I like best.'

'It's a question of morning versus evening.'

'Certainly, but the point is just how it turns out or rather how we look on it ourselves.'

And she laughed and snuggled up to him and was going to kiss his hand.

'No, Effi, for goodness sake, don't do that. I don't want to be someone to be respected. That's what I am for the inhabitants of Kessin. For you I'm . . .'

'What are you?'

'Now, now Effi, I certainly won't tell you that.'

7

It was already broad daylight when Effi woke up the following morning. She found it difficult to realize where she was. Where was she? Of course, in Kessin in Baron Innstetten's, the provincial governor's house, and she was his wife, Baroness Innstetten. She sat up and looked around with curiosity; the previous night, she had been too tired to examine closely all the half strange, half old-fashioned things around her. The beam of the ceiling was supported by two pillars, and the sleeping space, a kind of alcove in which the beds were standing, was shut off from the rest of the room by green curtains; only in the middle there was no curtain, or else it had been drawn to one side, giving her a clear view from her bed. Between the two windows there stood the tall but narrow cheval glass, while beside it, to the right, against the wall next to the entrance hall, towered the big black Dutch-tiled stove which, as she had noticed last night, was stoked in the old-fashioned way from outside the room. She could feel the heat from it coming across the room towards her. How lovely it was to be in one's own home; never had she experienced so comfortable a feeling during the whole journey, not even in Sorrento.

But where was her husband? Silence reigned everywhere, there was no one to be seen. The only thing she could hear was the tick-tock of the small clock and now and again a dull thud in the stove, from which she deduced that a few fresh logs were being pushed in from the hall. Slowly she recalled, too, that last night Geert had mentioned an electric bell; it did not take her long to find it; right beside her pillow was a small ivory knob, which she gently pressed. Joanna appeared at once.

'You rang, m'lady?'

'Oh, Joanna, I think I must have overslept. It must be quite late.'

'Just nine o'clock.'

'And the master . . .' she couldn't bring herself to use the word 'husband' yet – 'the master must have been very quiet. I didn't hear anything.'

'Yes, he was indeed. And your ladyship will have been sound asleep. After the long journey . . .'

'Yes, I was. Does the master always get up so early?'

'Always, m'lady. He's strict about that; he can't bear sleeping too long and when he goes into his room over there, the stove has to be going well and he mustn't have to wait for his coffee.'

'Has he already had breakfast then?'

'Oh no, m'lady . . . the master . . .'

Effi had the feeling that she shouldn't have asked that question, nor voiced the suggestion that Geert might not have waited for her. So, as she was anxious to make good her mistake as best she could, when she had got out of bed and sat down in front of her dressing-mirror, she referred to the matter again.

'The master was quite right, of course. Always up with the lark was the rule in my home too. When people stay too long in bed everything stays disorganized for the rest of the day. But the master won't be too hard on me; I stayed awake last night for quite a while and I was even a little bit worried.'

'What's that, m'lady? What happened then?'

'There was quite an uncanny sort of sound above me, not a loud one but very penetrating. First it sounded like long dresses brushing over the floor and in my excitement once or twice I thought I saw some small white satin shoes. It was as if there were dancing overhead, but very gentle dancing.'

While Effi was saying all this, Joanna looked over her young mistress's shoulder into the long narrow mirror in order better to observe the expression on her face. Then she said: 'Yes, that's in the big room above. Before we used to hear it in the kitchen, too. But now we've got used to it.'

'Is there something special about it, then?'

'Oh no, Heaven forbid, not in the least. For some time we didn't really know where it was coming from and the pastor used to look rather embarrassed, in spite of the fact that Dr Gieshübler only laughed about it. Now we know that it's the curtains. The drawing-room is rather close and stuffy and so the windows are always kept open unless the weather's really unsettled. And so there's nearly always a strong draught up there which sweeps the old white curtains, which are very long ones, to and fro over the floor. So it sounds like silk dresses or else like satin shoes, as your ladyship just said.'

'Of course that's what it is. But in that case I don't understand why the curtains haven't been taken down. Or else they could be shortened. It's such a strange noise that it gets on your nerves. And now, Joanna, please will you give me that little towel again and dab my forehead. Or better still, fetch the spray from my toilette-case. . . . Ah, that's beautifully refreshing. Now I'll go along to the other room. Is he still there or has he gone out?'

'His lordship has already been out, I think, over to the office. But he came back a quarter of an hour ago. I'll tell Frederick to bring breakfast.'

Thereupon Joanna left the room while Effi, giving herself a final look in the mirror, went across the hall, which had lost much of its magic by day, into Geert's room.

He was sitting at a writing table, a somewhat massive roll-top desk, which he did not want to get rid of because it was inherited from his parents. Effi came up behind him and gave him a kiss and hug before he could get to his feet.

'So soon?'

'So soon, you say. You're poking fun at me, I know.'

Innstetten shook his head, 'How could I?' However, Effi was in a self-accusing state of mind and she refused to listen to her husband's protestations that he really had been sincere with his 'So soon?'

'You must have realized during our trip that I never keep anyone waiting in the morning. During the day perhaps, but that's something different. It's true that I'm not very punctual but I'm not a lie-abed. As far as that's concerned, I think my parents brought me up properly.'

'As far as that's concerned? As far as everything's concerned, Effi dear.'

'You're saying that because we're still on our honeymoon ... well, no, the honeymoon's over. .... For goodness sake, Geert, I hadn't realized that we've been married for more than six weeks, six weeks and one day. In that case, it's another matter, and I won't take it as a piece of flattery, I'll accept it as true.'

At this point Frederick brought in breakfast. The breakfast table was standing at an angle in front of a small, rectangular sofa that exactly filled one corner of the living-room. They both sat down.

'The coffee is really delicious,' said Effi, looking round at the room and its arrangement as she did so. 'I must write to mama about it – we haven't got coffee like this in Hohen-Cremmen. In fact, Geert, I've only now realized what a splendid match I've made. At home, everything was much more ordinary.'

'Ridiculous, Effi, I've never seen better housekeeping than in your home.'

'And then there's the way you live. When papa bought himself the new gun cupboard and had a buffalo-head fixed over his desk and old Wrangel immediately underneath – he'd once been adjutant in the old man's regiment – he thought he was doing something marvellous; but if I look round here, all our magnificence at Hohen-Cremmen looks very petty and ordinary. I really don't know what to compare it with; even yesterday evening, when I just had a fleeting glimpse of it, all sorts of ideas came into my mind.'

'And what were they, may I ask?'

'Yes, what were they? You mustn't laugh at them. I once had a picture book in which a Persian or Indian prince – I knew that because he was wearing a turban – was sitting on a red silk cushion with his legs tucked under him and at his back you could see a big roll of red silk billowing out on each side and the wall behind the

Indian prince was bristling with swords and daggers and leopard skins and shields and long Turkish muskets. And you know, it looks just like that in your house, and if you tuck your legs under you the likeness will be perfect.'

'Effi, you're a dear, delightful creature. You don't know how much I think so and how much I'd like to show you every moment that I do think so.'

'Well, you've got plenty of time to do so; I'm only seventeen years old and I don't intend to die yet.'

'At least not before me. To tell the truth, if I were to die, I'd prefer to take you with me. I don't want to leave you behind for anyone else. What do you think about it?'

'I must think it over. Or better still let's not talk about it at all. I don't like talking about death, I'm all for living. But now tell me, what sort of a life shall we be leading here? On the way you were telling me all sorts of strange things about the town and the country but not one word about the sort of life we shall be living. I can see that everything is different from what it is in Hohen-Cremmen and Schwantikow, but we must surely be able to find some sort of company to frequent in the "excellent town of Kessin" as you keep on calling it. Are there any good families in the town?'

'No, my dear Effi, you're in for grave disappointments on that score. In the neighbourhood there are a few gentry whom you'll be getting to know, but here in the town there's absolutely nobody.'

'Nobody at all? I can't believe that. There are nearly three thousand people and out of three thousand people, apart from the small fry such as Barber Beza (I think that was his name), there must surely be some kind of élite or something of the sort.'

Innstetten laughed. 'Oh yes, there is an élite all right – but they hardly stand up to close examination. Of course, we have a preacher and a judge and a headmaster and a harbour master, and taking all the officials of that sort I suppose you could collect together a dozen people, but most of them are just nice people with nothing to them at all. And apart from them you're merely left with consuls.'

'Merely consuls? But really, Geert, how can you say "merely consuls". That means something very high and mighty, I'm almost tempted to say frightening. Aren't consuls the ones with the bundle of rods, with an axe sticking out of it, I think!'

'Not exactly, Effi, those are lictors.'

'That's right, lictors. But consuls are also something very distinguished and magisterial. After all, Brutus was a consul.'

'Yes, Brutus was a consul. But ours aren't really very much like him and they are quite happy dealing in sugar and coffee or opening a crate of oranges and selling them off at a penny each.'

'It's not possible.'

'Indeed it is. They're just cunning little tradesmen, and if a foreign ship puts in here and isn't quite sure about something or other connected with its business, they'll offer their advice and when they have given it and done a service to some Dutch or Portuguese ship or other, eventually they become the accredited representatives of those foreign states. We have as many consuls in Kessin as there are ambassadors and ministers in Berlin and when there's a public holiday – and we have a good deal of those here – then all the pennants are hoisted and if we happen to have a bright sunny day that morning, you can see all the flags of Europe flying from our roof tops, and the star-spangled banner and the Chinese dragon in addition.'

'You're being facetious, Geert, and you may well be right. But as for my humble self, I must confess that I find it all entrancing and that the towns in our province are nothing in comparison. When they celebrate the Kaiser's birthday, they only put out black and white flags with occasionally a bit of red here and there, but that can't be compared with the whole panoply of flags you were talking about. In general, as I was telling you, I feel all the time that there's something foreign about everything here and everything I've seen and heard somehow makes me feel surprised. Even yesterday evening, there was that extraordinary ship out in the hall and the shark and then the crocodile beyond and your own room here! It's all so oriental, just like being with an Indian prince. . . .'

'Certainly! My congratulations, princess. . . .'

'And then the drawing-room upstairs with its long curtains which sweep the floor.'

'And what do you know about the drawing-room, Effi?'

'Nothing apart from what I've just said to you. When I woke up last night, for a good hour I seemed to be hearing the sound of shoes sliding over the floor and dancing and something like music as well. But it was all very soft. I told Joanna about it this morning, merely to make an excuse for having slept on so long afterwards.

59

And she told me that it was the curtains in the drawing-room upstairs. I think we'll show them short shrift and cut something off them or at least close the windows; in any case, we're going to have storms enough soon. The middle of November is the time for them, isn't it?'

Innstetten looked blank and somewhat embarrassed, seemingly hesitating whether to make any reply to these remarks. Finally he decided not to. 'You're quite right, we'll shorten those long curtains upstairs. But there's no hurry, particularly as it's not certain whether it will help. It may be something else, in the flue or worm in the wood or a pole-cat. We do have pole-cats here, in fact. But in any case, before we undertake any changes, you must first see how our household is organized; of course, I'll show you round – we can manage it in a quarter of an hour. And then you can get dressed – you needn't do very much, because you're most attractive like that – for our friend Gieshübler. It's after ten o'clock and I should be very mistaken in my judgement of him if he doesn't make his appearance here at eleven, or at least by noon at the latest, to pay you his humble respects. That's the kind of expression that he indulges in. And, as I've already told you, an excellent man withal, and one who will become a friend of yours, if my knowledge of both him and you is correct.'

8

IT was long past eleven, but Gieshübler had still not put in an appearance. 'I can't wait any longer,' Geert had said, since he had work to do. 'If Gieshübler does appear, be as affable as possible, and then everything will go smoothly; he mustn't be embarrassed; if he is, then he's either tongue-tied or else says the most extraordinary things; but if you can succeed in giving him assurance and putting him into a good humour, then he'll prattle away like a book. Anyway, you'll be able to do it. But don't expect me before three o'clock, I've got all sorts of things to do over the way. And we'll think over what we said about the drawing-room upstairs, but I expect that the best thing will be to leave things as they are.' With this Innstetten went off, leaving his young wife to herself.

She sat leaning slightly backwards in a corner of the window where she could look out without being seen, supporting her arm on a small side tray pulled out of the roll-top desk. The street was the main road leading to the beach, extremely busy during the summer months but now in the middle of November quite deserted and still; only a few poor children whose parents lived in some thatched cottages on the extreme edge of the plantation were clumping by in their wooden clogs. But Effi had no feeling of this loneliness, because her imagination was still full of all the fascinating things which she had just seen during her tour of inspection of the house.

It had started in the kitchen, which had a stove of modern construction and where, along the ceiling, leading into the maid's room, there ran an electric wire – both recently installed. Effi was very pleased when Innstetten had told her about this, and then they had left the kitchen and gone back into the hall and from there into the courtyard, the first half of which was not much more than a narrow passage between two wings of the house. In these wings there was accommodation for all the other services required for the running and upkeep of the house; on the right the maid's room, a servant's room and laundry, on the left the coachman's premises, situated between the horse-box and coach-house and occupied by the Kruse family. Above these the chickens were housed and a trapdoor in the roof over the horse-box provided access and egress for the pigeons. Effi looked at all this with great interest, but showed far greater interest when, after returning from the courtyard into the front part of the house, she had gone, under Innstetten's guidance, upstairs to the floor above.

The staircase was crooked, decrepit and gloomy, but the landing on which it ended seemed, in contrast, almost cheerful, because it was very light and had a good view of the surrounding country: on one side you looked out over the roofs at the edge of the town and over the plantation towards a Dutch windmill perched on a high sand-dune; on the other, towards the river which, being on the point of joining the sea, was quite wide and very grand. It was impossible not to be struck by this and Effi had immediately given enthusiastic expression to her pleasure. 'Yes, lovely, lovely, very picturesque,' Innstetten had replied and without further comment had pushed open a rather unevenly hung double-door leading off to the so-called drawing-room on the right. This room extended

61

over the entire upper floor. The windows were open at the front and the back, and the strong draught was blowing the famous long curtains to and fro. In the centre of one of the main walls, a chimney breast with a large stone hearth projected into the room whilst a few plain metal candelabra hung on the opposite wall, each with places for two candles, exactly like those in the downstairs hall; but everything was tarnished and neglected.

Effi was somewhat disappointed and said so, adding that instead of this dreary old drawing-room she would like to see the rooms on the opposite side of the landing. 'There really is absolutely nothing there at all,' Innstetten had replied, but opened up the doors none the less. There were four rooms here, each with one window and distempered in yellow, like the drawing-room, and all equally empty. In one of them only were three rush-seated chairs, whose seats had collapsed, and on the back of one of these there had been stuck a tiny picture, only half an inch or so high, depicting a China-man in a blue tunic and baggy yellow breeches with a broad flat hat on his head. Effi saw it and asked: 'What's the Chinaman doing there?' Innstetten seemed surprised himself by the little picture, and replied that he did not know what it was.

'Christel must have stuck it there, or Joanna, for fun. You can see that it's been cut out of a spelling-book.' Effi thought so too, and was only perplexed that Innstetten took it all so seriously, as if it did have some importance. Then she had taken just one more look into the drawing-room, saying as she did so that it really was rather a pity that it was all empty. 'After all, we've only got three rooms downstairs, and if someone comes to visit us, we don't really know what to do. Don't you think that we could turn the drawing-room into two nice guest-rooms? It would suit my mother; she could sleep at the back and look out on to the river and the two jetties, and in front she would have the town and the Dutch windmill. In Hohen-Cremmen we've only got a trestle windmill. What do you think about it? I imagine mama will be coming next May.'

Innstetten had agreed with everything and only at the end had added: 'That's splendid. But all the same it will be better, eventual-ly, to put your mother up over the way in the government building; the whole of the first floor is entirely free, like this one here, and she will be more to herself there.'

This, then, had been the outcome of her first inspection of the house. Effi had then gone to get dressed, not quite as quickly as Innstetten had assumed she would, and now she was sitting in her husband's room, her mind occupied alternately with thoughts of the little Chinaman and of Gieshübler, who still failed to put in an appearance. True enough, a quarter of an hour earlier, a small man with crooked shoulders, indeed almost a hunchback, and dressed in an elegant short fur-coat and a tall, very smooth and well-brushed top hat had passed by on the other side of the street and looked up at her window. But that surely couldn't have been Gieshübler! No, this gentleman with the crooked shoulders and at the same time such an air of distinction must have been the high court judge, and she recalled once having actually seen someone like that at a reception at her Aunt Theresa's, until she suddenly remembered that Kessin would only have an assize judge.

While she was still pursuing these thoughts, the object of them, who had obviously just been taking a morning stroll round the plantation, perhaps to pluck up courage, reappeared, and a minute later Frederick entered and announced the chemist Gieshübler.

'Excuse me, your ladyship.'

The poor young woman's heart was beating fast, for this was the first occasion on which she was having to make her appearance as the lady of the house and, in addition, as the first lady in the town.

Frederick helped Gieshübler off with his fur coat and opened the door again.

As the chemist came gingerly in, Effi offered him her hand, which he proceeded to kiss with some fervour. The young woman seemed to have made an immediate and considerable impression on him.

'My husband has already told me. . . . But I'm receiving you in his room . . . he's over at his office and may be back any minute. . . . Won't you please come into my room?'

Gieshübler followed Effi as she led the way into the next room, where she indicated one of the armchairs and herself sat down on the sofa. 'I wish I could tell you what pleasure you gave me yesterday with your beautiful flowers and your card. It made me feel at home straightaway, and when I mentioned this to my husband he told me that we should certainly be good friends.'

'Did he say that? The dear governor! And if I may venture to say so, your ladyship, the marriage of the governor and yourself has brought together two good, kind people. As for your dear husband, I know what he is like and for yourself, my dear lady, I can see it.'

'As long as you're not looking at me in too kindly a light! I'm so very young. And youth . . .'

'Ah, my dear lady, you must not say anything against youth. Youth, oh yes, even when youth makes mistakes they remain splendid and endearing ones, and as for age, even its virtues don't make it worth much. For my own part, I'm afraid that I cannot speak on this point – I don't mean about age of course, but about youth, because I was never really young. I may even say that that is the saddest thing about it all, one lacks the right courage and self-confidence, one barely ventures to ask a lady for a dance because one wants to avoid causing her embarrassment and so the years go by and one grows old and life has been dull and empty . . .'

Effi stretched out her hand to him. 'Oh, you mustn't say things like that! We women are not as bad as all that.'

'No, indeed, of course not . . .'

'And when I think back,' Effi went on, 'over all my experiences . . . not very many, because I never went out very much and lived almost all the time in the country, but when I think back, I still think that we do always love those who are worth loving. And I can also see at once that you're different from other people; we women have got a sharp eye for that sort of thing. Perhaps it's your name, too, that helps in your case. That was something our old Pastor Niemeyer always maintained; he liked to say that a name, particularly a Christian name, contained something fateful and mysterious and it seems to me that the name Alonzo Gieshübler opens up a whole new world for anyone; in fact, I'm almost tempted to say that Alonzo is a romantic name, a really precious name.'

Gieshübler gave a quite unusually delightful smile and was encouraged to put down his top hat – far too tall for his size – which he had hitherto been twirling in his hand. 'Yes, dear lady, that is true.'

'Oh, I can understand. I've heard about the consuls that Kessin is supposed to be so full of, and your father, I imagine, met the daughter of a sea-faring *capitano* in the house of the Spanish consul, I expect some beautiful girl from Andalusia. Girls from Andalusia are always beautiful.'

'Exactly as you have assumed, dear lady. And my mother really was a beautiful lady, although it is hardly fitting for me to undertake to prove it personally. But when your husband came here three years ago, she was still living and she still had fire in her eyes. He'll bear me out. For myself, I rather take after the Gieshübler side of the family, unpretentious in appearance but respectable in standing. There have already been four generations of us, a good hundred years, and if there were such a thing as an aristocracy of chemists . . .'

'You would have claims to belong to it. And as far as I'm concerned, I consider your case proven, without any reservation whatsoever. It's easiest for people like us, who belong to old families, because we are prepared to accept any sound opinion wherever it may come from, or so at least I was taught by my father, and my mother too. My maiden name is Briest and I'm descended from the Briest who, on the same day as the battle of Fehrbellin,* carried out the surprise attack on Rathenow of which you may have heard. . . .'

'Indeed, your ladyship, that's a special interest of mine.'

'A Briest, then. And my father has said to me hundreds of times: "Effi" – that's my name, Effi – "that's the long and short of it, there's nothing else and at the time Froben exchanged his horse, he was of noble birth and when Luther said: 'Here I stand',† he was really and truly of noble birth." And I think, Herr Gieshübler, my husband was quite right when he assured me that we should be good friends.'

At this moment, Gieshübler would have liked nothing better than to make a declaration of love and ask for permission to fight and die for her, like El Cid or some other *campeador*. But since all such things were impossible and his heart was strained to bursting point, he stood up, looked for his hat, which, fortunately, he was able to find at once and, kissing Effi's hand, once more beat a hasty retreat, without having added a single word.

9

So passed Effi's first day in Kessin. Innstetten gave her another three or four days' grace, so that she could settle in and write her letters – very different kinds of letters – to Hohen-Cremmen, to her mother, to Hulda and to the twins; then they began to make calls

* At the battle of Fehrbellin in 1675 against the Swedes, the head groom Froben is said to have exchanged horses with the Great Elector, whose own horse was too conspicuous.

† In 1521.

in the town, part of the time in a closed carriage, because it was raining so hard that they were able to allow themselves this breach of custom. When these were finished, it was the turn of the country gentry. This took longer, since, because the distances were usually considerable, only one visit could be made on each day. First they went to the Borckes in Rothenmoor, then they went to Morgnitz, Dabergotz and Kroschentin, where they made the appropriate calls on the Ahlemanns, the Jatzkows and the Grasenabbs. There followed a few more, amongst whom old Baron von Güldenklee at Papenhagen was also included.

Effi's impression was the same wherever they went: second-rate people mainly of dubious amiability who, while pretending to be talking about Bismarck and the Crown Princess, were in fact merely eyeing Effi's clothes, which were considered by some to be too pretentious for a young woman and by others as barely proper for a lady of her social position. The influence of Berlin was, indeed, obvious in everything, they seemed to be saying: a taste for externals and a remarkable awkwardness and uncertainty in handling important questions. The Borckes in Rothenmoor as well as the families in Morgnitz and Dabergotz declared that she was 'tainted with nationalism', while the Grasenabbs in Kroschentin stated bluntly that she was an 'atheist'. It is true that old Frau von Grasenabb, a south German, *née* Stiefel von Stiefelstein, had made a faint attempt to redeem Effi for the ranks of the 'deists', but Sidonie von Grasenabb, an old maid of forty-three, had abruptly cut her short: 'I'm telling you, Mother, she's just an atheist, neither more nor less, and that's the truth,' whereupon the old lady, who was scared of her daughter, had wisely held her peace.

The whole round of tours had lasted about two weeks and it was only late on 2nd December that they returned to Kessin from the last of their calls.

This last visit had been to the Güldenklees' at Papenhagen and on this occasion Innstetten had not escaped the fate of having to talk politics with old Güldenklee.

'Yes, my dear governor, when I think how times have changed. A generation ago, more or less, it was another 2nd December and good old Louis Napoleon, Napoleon's nephew – if he was his nephew and didn't have quite a different origin – was giving the Paris mob a whiff of grape shot. Well, he may be forgiven for that

– he was the right man for that sort of job and I maintain that everyone gets as good or bad as he deserves. But that he should lose all sense of proportion and in '70 without so much as a by-your-leave wanted to have a go at us, too, well, Baron, you know, that's – how can I express it? – a confounded impertinence. And he had to pay for it. The old man at the top won't stand for that sort of caper, he stands by us.'

'Yes,' said Innstetten, who was shrewd enough to pretend to take this sort of narrow-mindedness seriously, 'the hero and conqueror of Saarbrücken didn't realize what he was doing. But you ought not to hold it too much against him personally. Who is there who's able to rule his own house? No one. I'm already resigning myself to handing over the reins to other hands, and Louis Napoleon, well, he was completely wax in the hands of his Roman Catholic wife – or shall we rather say, his Jesuitical wife.'

'Wax in his wife's hands and she made a fool of him. Of course he was, Innstetten. But you're not trying to stand up for this puppet, are you? He was and is condemned. Of course, in itself, it's not at all proven' – and as he said this he tried, somewhat anxiously, to catch the eye of his better half – 'whether government by women may not be an advantage, provided, of course, it's the right kind of wife. But who was his wife? She wasn't a real wife at all, at best she was a "lady" – that's enough said. "Lady" is an expression that always leaves a nasty taste in the mouth. That Eugénie – and I'm prepared to pass over her affair with the Jewish banker, for I hate self-righteousness – had something of the *café chantant* about her, and if the town she lived in was Babel, then she was a woman of Babel. I don't want to express myself more plainly, because I know' – here he bowed to Effi – 'the respect due to German womanhood. Your forgiveness for having touched on such matters at all in your hearing, dear lady.'

Such was the conversation they had had after they had discussed the election, Nobiling* and the price of rape-seed, and now Innstetten and Effi were home again. The two maids had already gone to bed, for it was almost midnight.

Innstetten was walking up and down in a short house-coat and morocco-leather slippers; Effi was still in her dress; her fan and gloves were on the floor beside her.

'Yes,' said Innstetten, halting for a moment, 'we ought really to

*An anarchist who made an attempt on the Kaiser's life in 1878.

celebrate today but I don't know how. Shall I play you a victory march or set the shark swinging or bear you in triumph across the hall? Something ought to be done because, as you know, today's visit was the last.'

'Yes, it was, thank goodness,' said Effi, 'but I think that the feeling of peace and quiet that we shall now have is a good enough celebration. You might give me just one kiss. But you don't ever think about that. Throughout the whole long journey, you didn't touch me once, you're as chilly as a snowman. All you can do is smoke a cigar.'

'Don't, Effi, I'm going to reform, and for the moment I'd merely like to know how you feel about all these meetings and visits? Do you feel drawn to anyone particularly? Did the Borckes win the day against the Grasenabbs or vice-versa? Or do you support old Güldenklee? What he said about Eugénie made a great impression of nobleness and purity.'

'Fi, fi, Herr von Innstetten, so you can be sarcastic as well! I'm getting to know quite another side of you.'

'And if the gentry won't do, what's your view of the notables of Kessin itself? What do you think of the club? *That* really is a matter of life or death. I saw you talking recently with our magistrate who's a lieutenant in the reserve, an elegant little man who would be almost bearable if he could only rid himself of the opinion that he had been instrumental in recapturing Le Bourget by his appearance on the flank. And his wife. She's said to be the best whist-player in the club and also has the prettiest collection of stamps. But once again, Effi, what's it going to be like in Kessin? Will you get used to it? Will you become popular and help me to get my majority when I want to stand for the Reichstag? Or are you in favour of seclusion and shutting yourself off from the people of Kessin, town and country alike?'

'I suppose I'll opt for seclusion unless the blackamoor chemist doesn't drag me out of it. No doubt I shall thereby sink even further in Sidonie's estimation but I shall have to put up with that; that's a battle that has to be fought. I stand or fall with Gieshübler. It sounds rather funny but he really is the only person with whom one can talk, the only real human being here.'

'Yes, he is,' said Innstetten. 'How discriminating you are.'

'Would I have got *you* otherwise?' asked Effi, hanging on to his arm.

68

This was on 2nd December. A week later Bismarck was in Varzin and Innstetten realized that from now until Christmas, and even after, he could not expect to be left in peace. Bismarck had had a particular liking for him ever since Versailles and frequently invited him to dinner when there were guests, but also by himself, because the young governor, whose manners were as distinguished as his clothes, was also a favourite of Princess von Bismarck.

On the fourteenth, the first invitation arrived. Snow was lying and Innstetten intended to go to the station by sleigh, a journey of almost two hours, with a further hour's journey by train.

'Don't wait up for me, Effi. I can't be back before midnight; probably it will be two, or even later. But I won't disturb you. Look after yourself – I'll see you tomorrow morning!' So saying, he climbed in and the two fallow-dun Graditzer horses sped off through the town and then inland towards the station.

This was the first time they had been separated for any length of time – almost twelve hours. Poor Effi! How was she going to spend the evening? It would be a mistake to go early to bed, because then she'd wake up and not be able to go to sleep again and would lie awake listening to everything. No, the best thing would be to become really tired and then have a good sound sleep. She wrote a letter to her mother and then went to see Frau Kruse, for whose state of mind she felt a good deal of sympathy – the poor woman would often keep her black hen clutched on her lap until well into the night. Effi's kind gesture elicited, however, no spark of response from the woman as she sat brooding and completely silent in her overheated little room and so, when Effi realized that her visit was causing more disturbance than pleasure, she went away again, merely inquiring whether the sick woman wanted anything. The woman retorted that she didn't.

Meanwhile evening had come and the lamp was already lit. Effi installed herself by the window of her room and looked out on to the copse, whose branches were sparkling with snow. She was completely absorbed by the sight and paid no attention to what was going on in the room behind her. When she looked round again, she saw that Frederick had quietly and silently laid a place at table and put a tray on the sofa-table. 'Oh yes, supper. . . . I suppose I'll have to go and sit down.' But she had no appetite and so she stood up again and re-read the letter she had written to her mother. She had felt lonely before, but now she felt twice as lonely. What would she not have given to see Jahnke's two red-headed daughters come into the room, or even Hulda? It's true that she was always so sentimental and usually only concerned with her own conquests; but however much one might doubt or dispute them, Effi would, at this particular moment, have been glad to hear about them. In the end, she opened the grand-piano to play, but that was no good, either.

'If I do that, I'll become completely maudlin; I'd better read.' She started looking for a book. The first one that she discovered was a thick red travel guide, out-of-date, perhaps even dating from the time when Innstetten was a lieutenant. 'Yes, let me read some of this, there's nothing more tranquillizing than this sort of book; the only trouble is the maps; but I'll avoid that dreadfully small print.' And so she turned at random to page 153. Nearby she could hear the tick-tock of the clock and, outside, Rollo who, since the longer evenings, had given up his place in the coach-house and tonight, as on every night now, was lying on the big mat in front of the bedroom. His presence made her feel less lonely and she even began to feel more cheerful, so, without delay, she began to read. The page she had just turned up was concerned with the Hermitage, the well-known country seat of the Margraves, near Bayreuth. She was attracted by this – Bayreuth, Richard Wagner – and so she started reading: 'Amongst the pictures in the Hermitage, let us mention one more, interesting not only for its beauty, but for its age and for the person whom it represents. It is a portrait, greatly darkened by age, of a woman, with a small head, sharp and somewhat weird features and a ruff, which seems to be supporting the head. Some claim that it is an old Margravine of the end of the fifteenth century, others that it is the Countess von Orlamünde, but all are agreed that it is the portrait of a lady who has since achieved some notoriety in the history of the Hohenzollerns under the name of the "White Lady".'

'What a good choice!' said Effi, pushing the book away. 'I wanted to calm my nerves and the first thing I read is the story of the "White Lady" who's been frightening me for as long as I can think back. But now I've given myself the creeps, I might as well read on.'

So she opened the book again and read on: 'This old portrait itself, the original of which played such an important part in the family history of the Hohenzollerns, also played, as a picture, a role in the private history of the Hermitage, which is no doubt connected with the fact that it hangs on a concealed door, invisible to any stranger to the house, behind which is a staircase leading up from the basement. The story goes that when Napoleon was spending the night here, the "White Lady" came down from her frame and walked over to his bed. The emperor started up in horror and called for his aide-de-camp; and until the end of his life, he would talk indignantly about that *"maudit château"*.'

'I must stop trying to calm myself by reading,' Effi said. 'If I read any more I'll surely come across a vaulted cellar where the Devil rode away on a barrel of wine. I think that Germany is full of things like that and naturally everything has to be put into a guide book. So I think I'll shut my eyes and try and remember my wedding-eve as well as I can: the twins who couldn't go on because they were crying so much and Cousin Briest who, while everyone was looking at each other in embarrassment, produced the remark, with amazing solemnity, that tears like those were the key to paradise. He really was charming and always in such high spirits. . . . And how about me? And here I am. . . . Oh, I'm not really any good as a grand lady. Now mother would have fitted in here. She would have been able to set the trend as a governor's wife ought and Sidonie probably would have been properly respectful and wouldn't have worried so much about her beliefs or lack of belief. But I'm . . . a child . . . just a child, and I suppose I'll remain one. I once heard that that was a good thing. But I don't really know if it's true. Anyway, you've always got to adapt yourself to the circumstances you find yourself in.'

At this moment, Frederick came to clear the table.

'What's the time, Frederick?'

'Getting on for nine o'clock, your ladyship.'

'Well, that's something! Send Joanna in to see me.'

'Your ladyship asked for me?'

'Yes, Joanna. I'm going to bed. It's rather early, I know, but as I'm all alone. . . . But first, will you please post the letter and when you've done that, I expect it'll be time to go. And even if it isn't . . .'

Effi took the lamp and went into her bedroom. Rollo was lying on the rush mat in front of the door. When he saw Effi coming, he got up to let her pass and rubbed his ears against her hand. Then he lay down again.

Meanwhile, Joanna had gone over to the government building to post the letter. She was making no particular attempt to hurry herself; in fact, she preferred to have a word with Frau Paaschen, the wife of the caretaker of the building. As might be expected, it was about the young mistress.

'What's she like?' asked Frau Paaschen.

'She's very young.'

'Well, that's no misfortune, rather the opposite. The nice thing about young people is that they don't do much except stand in front of the mirror all the time and try on clothes and give a tug here and a tug there and don't see a lot or hear a lot and don't worry about counting all the candle-ends or not letting anyone get a kiss from someone just because they're not getting any kisses themselves any more.'

'Yes,' said Joanna, 'my last mistress was like that, and for no reason at all. But my ladyship's not like that.'

'Is he very fond of her?'

'Oh yes. You can imagine how he would be.'

'But he leaves her alone all the time . . .'

'Yes, but you mustn't forget, Paaschen dear . . . there's the prince. And then, after all, he *is* the provincial governor. And perhaps he wants to be something bigger.'

'Of course he does. And he will be, too. Paaschen's always saying so and he knows what people are like.'

In the course of this visit to post a letter a quarter of an hour must have gone by, and when Joanna returned Effi was already sitting in front of her mirror and waiting.

'You were a long time, Joanna.'

'Yes, m'lady. Please excuse me. . . . I met Frau Paaschen over there and I talked to her for a minute. It's so quiet here. One's always pleased to meet someone who one can talk to. Christel is a very nice girl but she never says a word and Frederick is so dull and so careful, too, that he'll never speak out. I know that one must be able to hold one's tongue, too, and that Paaschen is so inquisitive and common that she really isn't the sort of woman I like; but it's still rather nice to hear something and see something.'

Effi gave a sigh. 'Yes Joanna, that's the nicest thing there is. . . .'

'Your ladyship has such lovely hair, so long and silky.'

'Yes, it's very soft. But that's not a good thing, Joanna. Hair shows what your character is like.'

'Of course, m'lady. And a soft character is surely nicer than a hard one. My hair's soft, too.'

'Yes, Joanna. And blonde as well. Men like blonde hair best.'

'Oh, that depends a lot, m'lady. A lot of them like black hair as well.'

'Yes, indeed,' laughed Effi, 'I've already discovered that. It must depend on something quite different. But blondes have always got a pale complexion as well. You too, Joanna, and I wouldn't mind betting that you have a lot of followers. I'm still very young but I do know that. And I've got a friend, too, who was just as blonde, a real flaxen blonde, even fairer than you, and she was a parson's daughter.'

'Oh well . . .'

'Now, Joanna, what do you mean by "Oh well"? It sounds rather rude and strange. Surely you don't have anything against parsons' daughters? She was a very pretty girl, even our officers always thought so – we had officers, red Hussars at that – and she had very good taste in dress, with a black velvet bodice, and a flower, a rose or a heliotrope, and if she hadn't had such big protruding eyes . . . Oh, you should have seen them, Joanna, at least as big as this' – and Effi laughed as she pulled down her right eyelid – 'she would have been a real beauty. She was called Hulda. We weren't really such close friends as all that with Hulda Niemeyer; but if I had her sitting here now, over there in the corner on the sofa, I'd want to talk and talk with her till midnight or even later. I feel such a longing and . . .' as she said this she clutched Joanna's head and pulled it close against her . . . 'I'm so scared.'

'Oh, of course, m'lady, we all were.'

'You all were? What do you mean by that, Joanna?'

'And if your ladyship is really so scared, I can camp out here. I'll take the straw-mat and turn this chair round so that I have something to lean my head against and then I can sleep here till tomorrow morning or until the master comes back.'

'He doesn't want to disturb me. He promised me himself.'

'Or shall I just sit on the sofa in the corner?'

'Yes, that might do. But no, it won't do either. The master mustn't know that I'm frightened, he doesn't like that. He wants one always to be brave and determined like himself. But I can't be, I always was rather subject to nerves.... But of course, I realize that I must make an effort and do what he wants in things like that, in fact, in everything. And after all, I've got Rollo. He's lying in front of the door.'

Joanna nodded her head in agreement to all that her mistress was saying and lit the light standing on Effi's bedside table. Then she picked up the lamp.

'Does m'lady want anything more now?'

'No, Joanna. Are the shutters closed tightly?'

'Just pushed together, m'lady. Otherwise it's so dark and stuffy.'

'Very well, Joanna.'

Joanna now left, but Effi went over to her bed and wrapped herself up in her bed-clothes. She left the light on because she was determined not to go to sleep at once but rather, just as she had previously done with her wedding-eve party, to go over her honeymoon and review it all again. But it didn't work out as she had planned, and when she had reached as far as Verona and was looking for Juliet Capulet's house, her eyes were already closing. The candle-stump in the tiny silver candlestick burned gradually down and then flickered once more before going out.

For a while she slept quite soundly. But all at once, she started up from her sleep with a loud cry, a scream which she could even hear herself, and she also heard Rollo outside starting to bark: Wuf, wuf, he went, all through the hall, hollow and almost scared himself. Her heart seemed to stop beating; she was unable to call out and at that moment something brushed past her and the door leading to the hall flew open. But this instant of excruciating fear was also the moment of deliverance, because instead of something horrible, Rollo came towards her, nosing for her hand with his head, and when he had found it, he lay down on the rug beside her bed. However, Effi herself had already, with her other hand, pressed the bell-button three times, and in less than half a minute Joanna arrived barefoot, her dress over her arm and a large check shawl over her head and shoulders.

'Thank God you've come, Joanna.'

'What was the matter, m'lady? Did you have a dream?'

'Yes, I had a dream . . . I must have had a dream . . . but it wasn't only a dream.'

'What was it then, m'lady?'

'I was fast asleep when all of a sudden I started up and screamed . . . perhaps it was a nightmare . . . we have nightmares in our family, my father has them, too, and scares us with them, only mama always says he shouldn't give way to them so much but that's easily said . . . well, I started up from my sleep and screamed and when I looked round as well as I could in the dark, something brushed past my bed, just where you're standing at the moment, Joanna, and then it was gone. And if I ask myself what it really was . . .'

'Yes, m'lady?'

'If I ask myself what it really was . . . I don't like to say so, Joanna . . . but I think it was the Chinaman. . . .'

'The Chinaman from upstairs?' Joanna tried to laugh. 'Our little Chinaman whom Christel and I stuck on the back of the chair? Oh your ladyship must have been dreaming, and if you had already woken up, that must have all been part of the dream too.'

'I'd like to think so. But it was exactly at the same moment that Rollo barked outside, so he must have seen it too and then the door flew open and the faithful old dog gave one leap towards me as if he were saving me from something. Oh, my dear Joanna, it was dreadful. And I'm so young and all alone. Oh, if only there was someone whom I could cry to. . . . But I'm so far from my home. . . .'

'The master may be here at any time now.'

'No, he mustn't come, he mustn't see me like this. He would laugh at me perhaps and I could never forgive him for that. It was so terrible, Joanna. . . . You mustn't go away now. . . . But don't wake Christel or Frederick up. No one must know.'

'Or perhaps I can fetch Frau Kruse as well. She won't be asleep, she sits there all night.'

'No, no, there's something strange about her, too. That business with the black hen is peculiar as well. No, Joanna. You stay here alone with me. And what a good thing that you only pushed the shutters to. Push them open, hard, so that I can hear a sound, a human sound . . . I'll have to call it that, however strange it sounds ... and then open the window a bit, to let some air and light in!'

Joanna did as she was ordered and Effi, sinking back on to her pillow, soon afterwards fell into a heavy sleep.

10

INNSTETTEN had not come back from Varzin until six o'clock next morning and, warding off Rollo's affectionate approaches, had returned to his room as quietly as possible. Here he made himself comfortable, merely letting Frederick cover him up with the travelling-rug. 'Wake me up at nine.' And he had been woken up at that time. He got up at once and said: 'Bring in breakfast.'

'Her ladyship is still asleep.'

'But it's late. Has anything happened?'

'I don't know; I only know that Joanna has had to sleep the night in her ladyship's room.'

'Well, send Joanna to see me.'

She came. Her complexion was as pink and rosy as ever and she seemed not to have been particularly affected by the night's events.

'What's wrong with her ladyship? Frederick tells me that something happened and you slept the night with her.'

'Yes, m'lord. Her ladyship rang the bell three times quickly, one after the other, so I thought at once that something was wrong. And there was, too. I expect she'd been dreaming, or perhaps it was something else.'

'What else?'

'Well, your lordship must know.'

'I don't know anything. In any case, we must put a stop to it. What was my wife like?'

'She was dreadfully upset and holding on to Rollo's collar very tightly, and he was standing beside her bed. And the dog was disturbed, too.'

'And what had she dreamt about or, if you like, what was it that she'd heard or seen? What did she say?'

'That it had brushed by her, very close.'

'What had? Who had?'

'The man upstairs. The man from the drawing-room or the little room.'

'Nonsense, I say. Always the same stupid talk; I don't want to hear anything more about it. And then you stayed with my wife?'

'Yes, your lordship. I camped out on the floor beside her. And I had to hold her hand and then she went to sleep.'

'And is she still asleep?'

'Fast asleep.'

'That worries me, Joanna. People can get well through sleeping but they can also get ill. We must wake her up, carefully, of course, so that she's not scared again. And tell Frederick not to bring breakfast. I want to wait until her ladyship is here. And do it gently!'

Half an hour later, Effi appeared. She looked charming, as pale as a ghost and leaning on Joanna's arm. But when she saw Innstetten, she ran towards him and kissed and hugged him, with tears running down her face.

'Oh Geert, thank God you're back! Now everything will be all right. You mustn't go away again, you must never leave me alone another time!'

'Effi dear ... Frederick, put it down there, I'll see to everything ... Effi dear, I don't leave you alone because I'm inconsiderate or just because I feel like it, but because I have to. I have no choice, I'm an official, I can't just say to the Prince or Princess: "Your Excellency, I can't come, my wife feels lonely" or "my wife is scared." If I were to say that, we should appear in a very strange light, at least, I certainly should and you, too. But have a cup of coffee first!'

Effi took a drink of her coffee, which visibly refreshed her. Then she clutched her husband's hand again and said: 'Of course, you must be right. I realize that that wouldn't do. And we want to be promoted, too. I say "we" because I'm really more ambitious for that than you ....'

'*Così fan tutte*,' laughed Innstetten.

'Then we're agreed. You continue to accept all the invitations as you have been doing and I shall stay here awaiting my "lord and master", which reminds me of Hulda waiting under her elderberry tree in the dream scene. I wonder how she is?'

'Women like Hulda are always all right. But what was it you wanted to say?'

'I wanted to say that I'll stay here and alone, if I must. But not in this house. Let's move somewhere else. There are such nice houses on the riverside, one between Consul Martens' and Consul Grützmacher's and one in the market, just opposite Gieshübler's, why can't we live there? Why must we live here? When we had friends and relatives visiting us, I've often heard that in Berlin families move out because of piano-playing or because of cock-roaches or because the porter's wife is unpleasant. If that can be done for such petty reasons . . .'

'Petty reasons? The porter's wife? Don't say that.'

'If it can be done for things like that, it must surely be possible here where you're the governor and people do what you like and many of them have obligations towards you. Gieshübler will certainly be of assistance to us if only for my sake, because he'll sympathize with me. And now tell me, Geert, shall we give up this haunted house, with its . . .'

'Chinaman, you were going to say. You see, Effi, it's possible for you to utter the dreadful word without conjuring him up. What you saw or what you thought glided by your bed was the little Chinaman whom the maids had stuck on the back of the chair upstairs; I'll wager that he was wearing a blue tunic and a broad flat hat with a shining button on top.'

She nodded.

'Well, you see then, it was a dream, a hallucination. And I expect that Joanna told you a story yesterday evening, about the wedding upstairs . . . .'

'No.'

'That's a good thing.'

'She didn't say a word. But I can see from all this that there *is* something strange. And then there's the crocodile. Everything's so queer here.'

'When you saw the crocodile the first evening, you thought it was like a fairy tale. . . .'

'Yes, then I did.'

'And you see, Effi, I should find it difficult to move from here, even if it were possible to sell the house or exchange it. It would be exactly the same as declining the invitation to Varzin. I can't have the people here in the town saying: Governor Innstetten is selling his house because his wife saw beside her bed the ghost of a little Chinaman whose picture had been stuck up on a chair back. It would be fatal, Effi. I should never recover from the ridicule.'

'Well, are you really so convinced that such a thing doesn't exist?'

'I'm not saying that. It's something that one can believe or, better still, refuse to believe. But assuming that such a thing does exist, where's the harm? The fact that there are germs flying about in the air that you *have* heard of is much more serious and dangerous than all these spirits rushing about, assuming that they are rushing about, that such things do exist. And then, I'm amazed to find someone like yourself, a Briest, so upset and scared. It's as if you came from a family of petty bourgeois. A ghost is a privilege, like a family tree and things like that, and I know families that would as soon lose their family arms as their "white lady" – who may equally well be a black one, of course.'

Effi said nothing.

'Well, Effi, don't you have anything to say?'

'What am I to say? I've given in and accepted, but I do think that you might be a trifle more sympathetic towards me. If you knew how much I longed for it. I was very unhappy, really unhappy, and when I saw you, I thought to myself, now I shall be able to get rid of my fear. But all you can say to me is that you don't feel like making yourself ridiculous in the eyes of the Prince or the town. That's no consolation. I don't find it so, and even less of one because in fact it turns out that you're contradicting yourself and not only seem to believe in these things yourself but even expect me to show proper pride in this noble ghost. Well, I don't feel any. And when you talk about families who value their ghost as highly as their family arms, that's a matter of taste; I attach more importance to my family arms. We Briests don't have a ghost, thank God! The Briests were always decent people and that probably explains it.'

This squabbling would have continued and perhaps led to the first serious quarrel if Frederick had not come in with a letter for Effi.

'From Herr Gieshübler. The messenger is waiting for an answer.'

All trace of ill-humour vanished from Effi's face, for just to hear Gieshübler's name did her good and her feeling of well-being increased as she looked more closely at the letter. In the first place, it was not a letter, but a note with the address: Baroness von Innstetten, *née* von Briest, written in a lovely court-hand, and instead of a seal, a small picture had been stuck on, a lyre with a staff in it. The staff might have been an arrow. She passed the note for her husband to admire it, too.

'But now do read it.'

So Effi broke the seals and read: 'Your most gracious Ladyship, Please allow me to venture to add to my most respectful greetings this morning one humble request. A dear friend of mine, of long standing, Fräulein Marietta Trippelli, a daughter of our excellent town, will be arriving here on the midday train and staying with us until tomorrow evening. She has to be in Petersburg on the seventeenth, where she will be giving recitals until the middle of January. Prince Kotschukoff will be offering her the hospitality of his house, as he has done previously. With the unfailing kindness that she has always shown me, la Trippelli has promised to pass the evening under my roof and present a few songs, personally chosen by myself, since nothing is beyond the range of her accomplishments. Might your Ladyship find it possible to be present at this musical evening? Seven o'clock. Your dear husband, whom I am relying upon to come without fail, will support my humble request. There will be no one else present except the accompanist Pastor Lindequist, and, of course, the widowed mother, Frau Pastor Trippel. With my deepest respects, A. Gieshübler.'

'Well,' said Innstetten, 'shall we go or not?'

'Of course we shall go. It will take me out of myself. And I certainly can't snub my dear old Gieshübler the first time he invites us.'

'All right, then. So Frederick, will you tell Mirambo, since it must be he who's brought the message, that we shall be honoured?'

Frederick went away. When he had gone, Effi asked: 'Who's Mirambo?'

'The genuine Mirambo is a bandit chief in Africa ... Lake Tanganyika, if your geography can stretch that far ... but our Mirambo is only the man who dispenses Gieshübler's coal and acts as factotum and who very probably will be waiting on us this evening in evening dress and white gloves.'

It was very plain that this small incident had had a good effect on Effi and largely restored her to her cheerful, easy-going self; but Innstetten wanted to do something himself to hasten her convalescence.

'I'm delighted that you said yes so quickly, without hesitation, and now I'd like to make another suggestion, to set you completely on your feet. I can see that you're still worried by something from last night that doesn't really suit my Effi and that we must get rid of, and for that there's nothing better than fresh air. The weather's superb, fresh yet mild, and there's hardly a breath of wind. What would you say to an excursion, a long one, not just through the plantation, in the sleigh, of course, and with the bells on and the white snow-rugs and when we get back at four you can go and rest and at seven o'clock we'll go along to Gieshübler and listen to Trippelli.'

Effi took hold of his hand: 'How kind and considerate you are, Geert! Because I must have seemed very childish to you, or at least adolescent, first because I was scared and then afterwards because I was suggesting selling this house and also that business with the Prince. You were supposed to shut the door in his face — how ridiculous! After all, he is the man who holds our fate in his hands. My fate as well. You can't believe how ambitious I am. I really only married you out of ambition. But you mustn't pull such a solemn face about it. I do love you . . . what do they say, when you break off a branch and pull the leaves off — I love you, I love you a little, I love you a lot.' And she gave a loud laugh. 'And now tell me,' she went on, as Innstetten still said nothing, 'where shall we go?'

'I thought we might go to the railway station, but on a roundabout route and then back on the main road. And we can eat at the station or better still at Golchowski's in the Prince Bismarck, the inn we went past the day we arrived, as you perhaps still remember. It always makes a good impression to call on people and I can have a talk about the election with the *starost*,* as appointed by Effi, and even if he is personally not worth much, he looks after his hotel well and his cooking is even better. People are great eaters and drinkers round here.'

This conversation took place at about eleven o'clock. At twelve,

* Village elder.

Kruse brought the sleigh up to the door, and Effi climbed in. Joanna wanted to bring a foot-muff and furs, but with all that was still on her mind, Effi felt such a need for fresh air that she said no to them all and merely took a double rug. But Innstetten said to Kruse:

'Kruse, we want to go to the station, where we both went this morning. People will be surprised but that doesn't matter. I think we'll drive along by the plantation and then go left towards the Kroschentin church tower. Give the horses their head. We must be at the station by one o'clock.' So off they went. Smoke was hanging about above the roofs, because the air was practically still. Utpatel's mill was only turning slowly and they flew past it at speed, close by the churchyard, where the berberis was growing out over the railings and the tops of their branches brushed against Effi so that the snow fell on her travelling-rug. On the opposite side of the track there was an enclosed space, scarcely bigger than a flower-bed, and inside it there was nothing to be seen but a young fir-tree, rising straight out of the middle.

'Is there someone buried there, too?' asked Effi.

'Yes, the Chinaman.'

Effi gave a violent start, as if she had been stung. But she still had the strength to control herself and with apparent indifference asked: 'Ours?'

'Yes, ours. Naturally, he couldn't be buried in the municipal cemetery, and so Captain Thomsen, who was something of a friend of his, bought this plot and had him buried here. There's a stone there, too, with an inscription. Of course, this was all before my time. But people are still talking about it.'

'So there is something in it after all. Some story. You were saying something like that earlier today. So the best thing after all will be to let me know all about it. As long as I don't know, in spite of my good resolutions, I shall always be imagining something. Tell me the truth. The truth can never hurt me as much as my imaginings.'

'Well done, Effi. I didn't want to talk about it. But now it's all come out by itself and that's a good thing. Moreover, it's not really anything very much at all.'

'I don't mind whether it's nothing or a lot or a little. Just tell me!'

'That's easy to say. The beginning is always the most difficult, even in stories. Well then, I think I'll begin with Captain Thomsen.'

'Good.'

'Well, this man Thomsen, whom I've already mentioned to you, was for many years on what they call the China run, carrying rice between Shanghai and Singapore, and must have been about sixty when he came here. I don't know whether he had been born here or whether he had other connexions with the town. Anyway, here he was, and he sold his ship, which was an old crate that didn't fetch much, and he bought himself a house, the one that we're living in at the moment. Because he'd become a wealthy man in the course of his life. And that's where the crocodile and the shark come from and the ship, too, of course. So there Thomsen was, a very smart man (at least, people have told me he was) and well liked, even by Kirstein the mayor and above all by the then vicar of Kessin, a Berliner who had come here shortly before Thomsen and met with a lot of ill-will.'

'I can imagine. I've noticed that, too, that they're very strict and self-righteous here. I think that the Pomeranians are like that.'

'Yes and no, it depends, there are districts where they're not at all strict and where everything's at sixes and sevens. But look, Effi, there's the church tower of Kroschentin just in front of us. Shall we not give up the railway-station and drive on to old Frau von Grasenabb? If my information is correct, Sidonie is not at home. So we can risk it.'

'But please, Geert, what are you thinking of? It's heavenly speeding along like this and I'm really beginning to feel freer and freer and all my fears are flying away. And now I'm supposed to give all that up so we can make a surprise visit to those old people and very probably cause embarrassment. For goodness' sake, let's not. And I do want to hear the story more than anything else. Well then, we were talking about Captain Thomsen, whom I think of as a Dane or an Englishman, very spick and span with white stand-up collars and snow-white linen . . .'

'Quite right. He is supposed to have been like that. He had with him a young woman of about twenty, who some people said was his niece but most people said his granddaughter, which incidentally was hardly possible, taking into account his age. And in addition to the granddaughter or niece, there was also a Chinaman, the one who is buried there in the dunes and whose grave we've just passed.'

'Yes, all right . . .'

'Well, this Chinaman was Thomsen's servant and Thomsen thought so highly of him that he was really more of a friend than a servant. And so that was how things were. Then all of a sudden it was said that Thomsen's granddaughter, whose name was Nina, I think, was going to be married, according to the old man's wishes to another captain. And it turned out to be true. There was a big wedding in the house, the pastor from Berlin made them man and wife, and Miller Utpatel, a Dissenter, and Gieshübler, who was also not considered very reliable in church matters in the town, were both invited, and above all lots of sea-captains, with their wives and daughters. And as you can imagine, there were high jinks. In the evening, there was a ball and the bride danced with everyone and eventually with the Chinaman, too. Then all of a sudden it was said that she, that is the bride, had gone away, and she really had gone off somewhere and no one knew what had happened. And a fortnight later the Chinaman died; Thomsen bought the plot that I showed you and he was buried there. The pastor from Berlin, however, is said to have remarked that he could easily have been buried in the Christian cemetery, because the Chinaman had been a very good man and just as good as the others. Gieshübler told me that no one quite knew what he had meant by "the others".'

'But I'm strongly against the pastor on this matter; people ought not to say things like that because it's unwise and improper. Even Niemeyer wouldn't have said that.'

'And in fact the poor pastor, who incidentally was called Trippel, was much blamed for saying it, so that it was really a fortunate thing that he died meanwhile, since he would have lost his post otherwise, because the town, in spite of having chósen him, was against him, just like you, and of course the consistory court really was, too.'

'Did you say Trippel? So then he is connected with Frau Trippel, whom we're going to see this evening?'

'Of course he's connected with her. He was her husband and is Signorina Trippelli's father.'

Effi laughed: 'Trippelli! Now I can see the whole thing. Gieshübler had already told me in his letter that she had been born in Kessin but I thought that she was the daughter of an Italian consul. There are such a lot of foreign names here. So she's really a genuine

German and her real name's Trippel. Is she so wonderful, then, to dare to turn herself into an Italian like that?'

'Fortune favours the brave. Moreover, she's quite good. She was in Paris with the famous Mme Viardot for a number of years, where she made the acquaintance of the Russian prince, too. Russian princes are very enlightened and quite indifferent to petty social prejudice and Kotschukoff and Gieshübler, whom she incidentally calls "Uncle" – and you could almost say that he's a born uncle – the two of them are mainly responsible for making little Marie Trippelli what she now is. It was through Gieshübler that she got to Paris and Kotschukoff then turned her into la Trippelli.'

'Oh Geert, how charming that all is and what a dull sort of existence I've been living in Hohen-Cremmen! Never anything at all out of the ordinary!'

Innstetten took her hand and said: 'You mustn't talk like that, Effi. You can take what attitude you like about ghosts. But beware of anything odd or what people call odd! What seems so attractive to you – and I'm also including in that the sort of life that Trippelli leads – usually has to be paid for at the expense of your happiness. I'm well aware how much you like Hohen-Cremmen and how attached you are to it, but you often poke fun at it as well and you've no idea what the peace and quiet of Hohen-Cremmen can mean.'

'Oh yes, I have,' she replied. 'I know quite well. Only I do like hearing about other things once in a while and then the urge seizes me to take part in them. But you're quite right. And in fact, I do have a longing for peace and quiet.'

Innstetten wagged an admonishing finger. 'My dear and only Effi, there you are, imagining things again. You're always doing it, first in one way and then in the other.'

11

THE excursion went off as planned. At one o'clock the sleigh stopped at the foot of the railway embankment in front of the Prince Bismarck, and Golchowski, happy to see the governor at his inn, took pains to prepare an excellent lunch. When finally dessert was served with the Tokay, Innstetten called to the host, who had been making an occasional appearance and seeing that everything was in order, and asked him to come and sit down at table with them and tell them a story. And indeed Golchowski was the right man to do so; within a radius of two miles all around, not an egg was laid without his knowledge. He gave proof of this gift today. Sidonie Grasenabb, as Innstetten had correctly surmised, had gone away, as she had done last Christmas, on a month's visit to the 'Imperial chaplain'; Frau von Palleske had been obliged to dismiss her maid on the spot because of an unfortunate incident, and old Fraude was in a bad way – although it had been put about that he had merely slipped and fallen, he had in fact had a stroke, and his son, who was in the Hussars at Lissa, was expected at any time. After this gossip, they had turned to more serious matters, to Varzin: 'Well now,' said Golchowski, 'how can one imagine the Prince as a paper-maker! It's all most extraordinary; he can't bear writing and even less the printed page and now he's acquired a paper-mill.'

'Yes, indeed, my dear Golchowski,' said Innstetten, 'but life is full of contradictions of this sort and it doesn't matter whether you're the Prince or however great a man you may be.'

'No, it doesn't matter how great a man you are.'

This conversation would probably have been very greatly prolonged had not the railway signal-bell suddenly rung to announce that a train was shortly arriving. Innstetten looked at the time.

'What's that train, Golchowski?'

'It's the Danzig express. It doesn't stop here but I always go up and count the carriages and in addition there is occasionally someone at the window whom I know. Directly under my yard here, there's a staircase, leading up the embankment to signal-box 417 . . .'

'Oh let's take advantage of that,' said Effi. 'I love looking at trains.'

'Then it's time we went, m'lady.'

So they all three went off and when they reached the top they placed themselves beside the signal-box on a little strip of garden which was now, indeed, covered with snow but where a patch had been shovelled clear. The signalman was already standing here, flag in hand. And now the train came rushing along the track, through the station, and a second later sped past the little hut and garden. Effi was so excited that she saw nothing and, as if bewildered, was only able to follow with her eyes the last carriage, with the brakeman sitting on top. 'It will be in Berlin at six-fifty,' said Innstetten, 'and an hour later, if the wind's in the right direction, the inhabitants of Hohen-Cremmen can hear it rattling along in the distance. Would you like to be on it, Effi?'

She said nothing. But when he looked over towards her, he saw that she had tears in her eyes.

As the train thundered past, Effi had been seized by a deep longing. However pleasant things might be, she still felt that she was in a foreign world. Whenever she had enjoyed something or other, immediately afterwards she became aware of all that she lacked. Over there lay Varzin and in the other direction the Kroschentin church steeple was glittering, and further on the one at Morgenitz and there the Grasenabbs and the Borckes were living, not the Bellings and the Briests. 'Yes, them!' Innstetten had been quite right about her sudden changes of mood and now she saw everything that belonged to the past as if transfigured. But although she certainly looked longingly after the train, she was of too mercurial a temperament to persist in her mood, and on the return journey, as the red ball of the setting sun cast its glow over the snow, she was already feeling better again; everything seemed fresh and lovely and when, having got back to Kessin, she entered the hall of Gieshübler's house almost on the stroke of seven, she was not only pleased, she even felt almost aggressively cheerful, a cheerfulness increased by the scent of valerian and violet roots prevailing in the house.

Although Innstetten and his wife had arrived punctually, they had nevertheless been preceded by the other guests; Pastor Lindequist, old Frau Trippel and Signorina Trippelli herself were already there. Gieshübler, in a blue tail-coat with dull golden buttons, with a pince-nez attached to a wide black ribbon which rested on his gleaming white piqué waistcoat like the ribbon of some decoration – Gieshübler could scarcely contain his excitement: 'May I introduce: Baron and Baroness Innstetten, Frau Pastor Trippel, Fräulein Marietta Trippelli.' Pastor Lindequist, who was known to everyone, stood close by, smiling.

Trippelli, in her early thirties, very masculine and an obviously humorous character, had, up to the moment when the introductions had been made, been occupying the place of favour. After these were completed, however, she went over to a high-backed chair standing nearby, saying: 'Please, your Ladyship, will you take over the burdens and perils of your high office. In this case perils' – and she pointed to the sofa – 'is the right word. I've been drawing Gieshübler's attention to it for years, unfortunately without success; he's as obstinate as he is kind.'

'But Marietta . . .'

'This particular sofa, in fact, which saw the light of day some half a century ago at least, is constructed in accordance with an old-fashioned trap-door technique and anyone who entrusts himself to it without first having underpinned himself with a pile of cushions will sink into the abyss, in any case, certainly deep enough for the knees to rear upwards like a monument.' Fräulein Trippelli pronounced these words with a perfect blend of good-humour and assurance, in a tone which made her position quite clear: 'You're Baroness Innstetten and I'm Trippelli.'

Gieshübler was very fond indeed of his gifted friend and valued her talents highly; but all his enthusiasm could not blind him to the fact that she had only been granted a modest share of social finesse. And it was on this sort of finesse that he prided himself personally. 'My dear Marietta,' he interjected, 'you have such a charmingly light-hearted way of treating these matters, but as far as my sofa is concerned, you are quite mistaken and I leave it to any expert to judge between us. Even a man like Prince Kotschukoff.'

'Oh, for goodness sake, Gieshübler, leave him out of it! Kotschukoff, Kotschukoff all the time! You'll make the baroness suspect that I'm proud to be his thousand and first soul – and incidentally, the prince is only one of the small fry and only has a thousand souls, or rather had, in the days when you still counted by the number of souls. No, the situation is quite different; my motto is "Always straight from the shoulder", as you know, Gieshübler. Kotschukoff is a friend of mine, a good friend, but he doesn't understand a thing about art and matters of that sort and certainly nothing about music, however many requiems and oratorios he may compose – most Russian princes, when they're artistically minded, tend to become rather spiritual or orthodox – and amongst the many things that he doesn't know anything about, one of them certainly is questions of interior decoration and furnishing. He is, in fact, sufficiently aristocratic to let himself be talked into buying anything that's flashy and costs a lot of money.'

Innstetten was amused and Pastor Lindequist made no attempt to hide his delight. Dear old Frau Trippel, however, was on tenterhooks at her daughter's embarrassing frankness of tone, while Gieshübler deemed it advisable to cut short a discussion that was becoming so awkward. For that purpose the best thing was to have a few songs. Marietta would not be likely to choose songs of a dubious nature, and even if she did, her talent was so considerable that the songs would be raised to a higher level.

'My dear Marietta,' he interposed, 'I have ordered our modest supper for eight o'clock. That means that we might have three quarters of an hour, unless you perhaps prefer to sing one of your cheerful songs during the meal, or perhaps not until we have left the table . . .'

'Please, Gieshübler, please! You, the aesthete! There's nothing more unaesthetic than a song recital on a full stomach. What's more – and I know that you're a man interested in *recherché* cooking, a *gourmand* even – what's more, it tastes better when the rest is over and done with. Art first and then *glace noisettes*, that's the proper order.'

'So may I bring you the music, Marietta?'

'Bring me the music? What do you mean, Gieshübler? If I know you correctly, you've got whole cupboards full of music, and I really can't possibly sing the whole lot. Music – but the important thing is, *what* music. And then it must be in the right range. Alto . . .'

'All right, I'll fetch it.'

And he busied himself at a cupboard, pulling out one drawer after another, while Trippelli moved her chair further along the table so that she was sitting close to Effi.

'I'm curious to see what he brings,' she said.

Effi was slightly embarrassed at this. 'I imagine,' she replied, rather awkwardly, 'something by Gluck, something really dramatic. . . . In any case, Fräulein Trippelli, if I may make the observation, I'm surprised to hear that you're only a concert singer. I should have thought that you would have been suited to the stage more than most. Your appearance, your energy, your voice. . . . I haven't yet had the opportunity to hear much of that sort of thing, only a short visit to Berlin . . . and then I was still almost a child. But I should have thought possibly Orpheus, or Kriemhild or the Vestal Virgin.'

Trippelli shook her head to and fro and gazed into space but made no retort, because at this moment Gieshübler reappeared and handed his friend half a dozen books of music which she quickly went through one by one: ' "Erlkönig", oh dear, "Bächlein, lass dein Rauschen sein" . . . but Gieshübler you're a Rip Van Winkle, you've been asleep too long. . . . And four ballads by Loewe, that's not very modern either. . . . "The Bells of Speyer", oh dear, that everlasting ding-dong, it's almost like ranting on the stage, it's so tasteless and stale . . . but here we are, "Ritter Olaf" . . . that'll do.'

And she stood up and while the pastor accompanied her, sang 'Olaf' with great assurance and *bravura*, to everyone's applause.

Then something similarly romantic was found, pieces from *The Flying Dutchman* and from *Zampa*, then the *Heideknabe*, all of which she sang with a virtuosity only equalled by her lack of emotion, whereas Effi was gripped by the words and by the music.

When Trippelli had finished the *Heideknabe* she said: 'That's the lot!' with such emphasis that neither Gieshübler nor anyone else had the courage to press her further. Least of all Effi.

But when Gieshübler's friend was sitting beside her once again, she said to her:

'I wish I could tell you, dear Fräulein Trippelli, how grateful I am to you! It was all so lovely, so sure, so skilful. But there's one thing, if you'll forgive me, that I admire more than that, and that is the calm way in which you've been able to sing these things. I'm so impressionable and if I hear the least talk of ghosts, it sends a shiver down my spine and I have a job to regain my composure. And you can sing these songs so powerfully and so movingly, and yet remain so happy and cheerful yourself.'

'Yes, Baroness, art is like that. And particularly in the theatre, which, incidentally, I've luckily been spared so far. Because however certain I may feel personally proof against its temptations, it ruins one's reputation, that is, it ruins the most important thing that one has. Moreover, as colleagues of mine have assured me hundreds of times, it blunts your talents. You're poisoned and stabbed and when Juliet's dead, Romeo whispers a so-called joke into her ear or a malicious remark or slips her a billet-doux.'

'I can't understand it. And to return to what I was saying about how grateful I am to you for this evening, for example, talking of the ghostly element in "Olaf", I assure you that if I have a nightmare or think I can hear some music or soft dancing above me, when there's nobody really there, or someone brushes past my bed, I completely lose my head and can't forget it, at least not for days.'

'Yes, but what you're describing now is something different – something real or at least someone that could be real. A ghost in a ballad doesn't make me shudder at all, but a ghost in my room is as unpleasant to me as it is to anyone else. So where that's concerned our feelings are the same.'

'Have you ever had that sort of experience then?'

'Certainly. And it was at Kotschukoff's too. And I've made the condition that this time I shall sleep somewhere else, perhaps with the English governess. She's a Quaker, so one can feel quite safe there.'

'And do you think such things are possible?'

'My dear Baroness, when someone is as old as I am and has been around a great deal and has been to Russia and even for six months in Rumania, you think anything is possible. There are so many wicked people and so the other things exist as well, the two belong together, so to speak.'

Effi pricked up her ears.

'I come from a very enlightened family,' continued Trippelli, '– only my mother was not quite like that – but when the question of spirit-writing came up, my father said to me: "Listen to me, Maria, there's something in that". And he was right, there is something in it. There are things lurking everywhere, all around us. You'll come to realize that.'

At that moment, Gieshübler approached and offered his arm to Effi while Innstetten accompanied Marietta, followed by Pastor Lindequist and the widowed Frau Trippel. They went in to dinner.

12

It was late when they broke up. When Effi had said to Gieshübler shortly after ten o'clock: 'It's time to go now, Fräulein Trippelli has to leave Kessin at six o'clock tomorrow if she's not to miss the train,' Trippelli, who was standing beside her, heard what she had said and, with her usual bluntness and fluency, had protested against receiving such delicate consideration.

'Ah, dear Baroness, you're thinking that people like me need regular sleep, but that's not the case; what we regularly need is applause and high fees. Yes, you may laugh. Anyway, as you may discover, one can sleep in the train, in any situation, and even on one's left side and even without undoing one's dress. It's true that I never wear anything tight; your chest and lungs, and above all your heart, always need to be free. Yes, Baroness, that's the main thing. And then with regard to sleep in general, it's not a matter of quantity, the deciding factor is quality; a good five-minute nap is better than twisting and turning restlessly for five hours. What's more, people sleep wonderfully well in Russia, in spite of the tea. It must be the air or the late dinner-hour or because one's so spoiled. There are no worries in Russia and in this respect Russia is even better than America – they both pay the same.'

After this explanation of Trippelli's, Effi had dissociated herself from all attempts to bring the evening to a close and it had gone on until midnight. They all parted in good humour and with a certain familiarity.

It was a fair distance from the 'alchemist's' to the governor's residence, although it was made shorter by Pastor Lindequist's asking to accompany Innstetten and his wife for a short distance; a night drive under the stars was the best way to remove the effects of Gieshübler's hock. On the way, the most varied Trippelliana were, of course, an unfailing topic; Effi began with all that she could remember, followed in turn by the pastor. The latter, something of an ironist, after asking her a great deal about mundane matters, had finally inquired as to her religious affinities and had been told that she recognized only orthodox religion. Her father had certainly been a rationalist, if not an agnostic, and this was why he would have liked to have seen the Chinaman buried in the communal cemetery, but for her part she was completely of the opposite view, in spite of the fact that she personally had the great advantage of not believing in anything at all. But in her definite absence of belief, she remained conscious all the time that it was a special luxury that one could only afford as an individual. Where the state was concerned, this was no joking matter and if she were in charge of the ministry of public worship or even an ecclesiastical court, she would act with ruthless severity. 'I feel that I'm something of a Torquemada.'

Innstetten was greatly amused and said that, for his part, he had sedulously avoided anything as delicate as questions of dogma but had concentrated all the more on moral questions. The main topic had been the fatal attraction, the perpetual feeling of danger inherent in any public appearance, whereupon Trippelli had lightly replied, referring particularly to the second half of the sentence: 'Yes, perpetually in danger, particularly with regard to one's voice.'

Chatting thus, before they parted they had reviewed the happenings of the evening spent with Trippelli and it was not until three days later that they were reminded of Gieshübler's friend when she sent a telegram to Effi from Petersburg. It ran: 'Madame la Baronne d'Innstetten *née* de Briest. Bien arrivée. Prince K à la gare. Plus épris de moi que jamais. Mille fois merci de votre bon accueil. Compliments empressés à Monsieur le Baron. Marietta Trippelli.'

Innstetten was delighted and expressed his delight more vigorously than Effi could grasp.

'I don't understand you, Geert.'

'That's because you don't understand Trippelli. I'm delighted to see how true to type she is; it's all there, down to the last dot on the *i*.'

'So you think it's all just play-acting?'

'But what else can it be? Everything calculated to appeal to everybody, to Kotschukoff and to Gieshübler. Gieshübler will set up a trust, I suppose, or perhaps only make a legacy to Trippelli.'

The musical evening at Gieshübler's took place in the middle of December; preparations for Christmas followed immediately afterwards and Effi, who would have found time heavy on her hands, blessed the fact that she herself had a domestic establishment whose claims had to be satisfied. She had to consider, inquire, procure, and all that left no room for gloomy thoughts. The day before Christmas Eve, presents arrived from her parents in Hohen-Cremmen and all sorts of little things from the schoolmaster's house had also been packed into the crate: lovely russet apples from a tree that Effi and Jahnke had budded together some years before and also some brown wrist and knee protectors from Berta and Herta. Hulda wrote only a few lines because, as she said to excuse herself, she still had to knit a travelling rug for Mr X. 'Which is simply a lie,' said Effi, 'I bet that X doesn't exist. Why can't she stop surrounding herself with admirers who aren't there.'

And so Christmas Eve arrived.

Innstetten himself put up the tree for his young wife and it was then lit and a tiny angel hovered in the air. There was even a crib with pretty coloured transparencies and inscriptions, one of which hinted delicately at a happy event that was going to take place in the Innstetten household in the coming year. Effi read it and blushed. Then she went up to her husband to thank him, but before she could do so, in accordance with the old Pomeranian custom, a Christmas box came shooting into the hall: a large case containing a whole host of things. Finally, the main gift emerged, a pretty little sweet-meat box covered with all sorts of tiny Japanese pictures and containing, in addition to its real contents, a little note, on which was written:

> Three kings did come to the blessed Christ,
> A blackamoor was among these kings;
> And now you can see a blackamoor chemist
> Coming to bring some dainty things,
> Not incense or myrrh, they wouldn't do,
> But pistachio and almonds, meant for you.

Effi read it two or three times and was delighted. 'When a nice man sends you his regards it really does you good, don't you think, Geert?'

'I do indeed. In a way it's the only thing that does give pleasure or at least ought to give pleasure. Because everyone is somehow or other involved in some sort of nonsense or other. I am too. But after all, we are what we are.'

The first day of Christmas was a church festival; on the second day they went over to the Borckes, and everyone was there except the Grasenabbs, who refused 'because Sidonie was away', which was considered on all sides to be a rather strange excuse. There were even a few who whispered: 'On the contrary, that's the very reason why they should have come.' On New Year's Eve there was the Club Ball, that Effi would have to attend and indeed wanted to attend, because it at last gave her the opportunity of seeing all the flora and fauna of the town gathered together. Joanna had her hands full preparing her ladyship for the pomp and ceremony;

Gieshübler, who had everything, including a hot-house, sent some camellias, and Innstetten, pressed though he was for time, had to go off that very afternoon across country to Papenhagen, where three barns had been burnt down.

All was quiet in the house. Christel, having nothing to do, had sleepily dragged a foot-stool up to the fireplace while Effi retired to her room and sat down at a small desk which had been specially made to fit in between the mirror and the sofa, as she wanted to write to her mother, whom she had thanked by card for her letter and Christmas presents, but to whom she had not sent any proper news for weeks.

Kessin, 31st December

Dear Mama, I imagine this will be a long letter because apart from the card, which doesn't count, I haven't written to you for a long time. Last time I wrote, I was still in the middle of preparing for Christmas and now all the Christmas festivities are over. Innstetten and my good friend Gieshübler did their utmost to make me as happy as possible on Christmas Eve but I still felt a little lonely and longed to see you both. In fact, in spite of all my reasons for being grateful and glad and happy, I still can't quite get rid of a feeling of loneliness, and if on previous occasions (perhaps more often than necessary) I've laughed at Hulda's everlasting crocodile's tears, I'm being punished now, because I find I have to fight against crying like that now. Because Innstetten mustn't see it.

But I'm sure that everything will turn out better when our household becomes a little livelier, and that is going to happen, Mama dear. What I hinted at earlier is now a certainty and Innstetten never stops proving to me all the time how pleased he is about it. I don't need to tell you how happy I am myself, if only because it will bring some life and something to distract me or, as Geert puts it, a 'precious toy'. I suppose he's right to use that word, but I'd rather he didn't, because it always gives me a slight jolt and reminds me how young I am and still not quite out of the nursery. I can't get rid of this idea (Geert says it's unhealthy) and so something that ought to make me as happy as possible seems almost a constant source of embarrassment to me. Yes, dear Mama, when the dear Flemming ladies were asking me all sorts of things, I really felt as if I were undergoing an examination that I hadn't properly prepared for and I think I answered very stupidly, too. I was annoyed, too. Because a good deal of what looks like sympathy is only curiosity and it's all the more out of place since I've still a long time to wait for the happy event, till the summer. Early July, in fact. Then you must come here, or better still, as soon as I'm more or less fit again I'll come, I'll take a holiday and head for Hohen-Cremmen.

Oh, how I'm looking forward to it and the air there – it's almost always raw and cold here – and then a trip to the Luch every day, with everything red and yellow and I can see the baby holding out its hands, because it'll surely feel that its real home is there. But I'm only writing this for *your* eyes. Innstetten mustn't know about it and you must forgive me too, Mama, for wanting to bring the baby to Hohen-Cremmen and telling you at once that I'm coming, instead of sending you an urgent and hearty invitation to come to Kessin, which after all receives 1,500 visitors for the bathing every year and ships of every possible flag and even has a hotel in the dunes. But the fact that I'm not offering much hospitality doesn't mean that I'm not hospitable, I haven't degenerated that much, it's just the governor's house, which, however pretty and quaint it may seem, is not really a proper house at all but only an apartment for two people and even hardly that, because we haven't even got a dining-room, which makes it awkward if a few people come to visit us. It's true we've got accommodation on the first floor, a big reception room and four small rooms, but they're all rather uninviting and I should call them lumber rooms, if there was any lumber in them; but they're quite empty, apart from a few rush chairs, and they make a very peculiar impression, to say the least.

Well, I expect you're thinking that would all be easy to change; but the house we're living in is a haunted house. Now I've said it. Incidentally, please, please don't mention this piece of information when you reply, because I always show Innstetten your letters and he would be dreadfully cross if he heard that I had told you that. I shouldn't have done it, either, particularly because I've been left in peace for several weeks now and I've stopped being scared; but Joanna tells me it always comes back, especially when someone new appears. And I can't expose you to such a risk or if that sounds too strong, to such a strange and unpleasant happening! I don't want to tell you about it today, at least not in detail. It's the story of an old captain, a so-called 'China run' sailor, and his grand-daughter, who was engaged for a short time to a young local captain and then suddenly disappeared on her wedding-day. That's not so bad. But what is more important is that a young Chinaman who had been brought back by her father from China, and who was first of all the old man's servant and then his friend, died shortly afterwards and is buried in a lonely spot next to the cemetery. I drove by there recently but quickly turned my head and looked in the other direction, because I think that I might otherwise have seen him sitting on the grave. Because, oh you see, Mama, I really did see him once or at least so it seemed to me, when I was fast asleep and Innstetten was on a visit to Prince Bismarck. It was dreadful, I shouldn't like to experience anything like that again.

So I can't very well invite you to a house like this, however pretty it is otherwise – strangely enough it's pleasant and uncanny at the same time. And Innstetten, although I really agree with him in many ways, didn't really, I think I may say this, behave very well over this. He told me to consider it as an old wives' tale and laugh about it, but all of a sudden he seemed as if he was believing in it himself and put forward the strange suggestion that it was distinguished and aristocratic to have a ghost in the house. But I can't and won't believe it. And however kind he is normally, he's not been kind and considerate enough towards me on this point. I know from Joanna that there's some truth in it and I also know it from Frau Kruse. She's the wife of our coachman and she spends all her time in an overheated room with a black hen. That's creepy enough in any case.

And now you know why I want to come as soon as I can travel. Oh how I wish I could come now! There are so many reasons I want to. This evening there's a New Year's Eve Ball and Gieshübler – the only nice person here, in spite of the fact that he has one shoulder higher than the other, in fact, it's a bit worse than that – has sent me some camellias. I may perhaps dance in spite of my condition. Our doctor says it won't do me any harm, on the contrary. And Innstetten has agreed, too, which rather surprises me, and now let me send my love and kisses to papa and all the other dear ones at home. A Happy New Year!

Your loving daughter,
Effi

13

THE New Year's Eve Ball went on till dawn and Effi had been abundantly admired, though less unreservedly than her bunch of camellias, which were known to have come from Gieshübler's hothouse. For the rest, everything remained much as before the New Year's Ball, with scarcely any attempt to develop further social contacts. And so the winter dragged slowly on and on.

Visits from the neighbouring gentry were rare and the obligatory return visits were always prefaced by the half-mournful remark: 'All right, Geert, if it has to be, but it's deadly boring.' A remark with which Innstetten never failed to agree. The talk of family, children, and even agriculture which took place during these afternoon visits was just about tolerable; but when ecclesiastical questions arose and the clergy present were treated like minor Popes or, indeed, even considered themselves as such, Effi's patience was tried beyond endurance and she used to think sadly of Niemeyer, always reserved and modest, although on every important occasion it was said that he might easily find himself called to the diocesan chapter. However well disposed the Borckes, the Flemmings and (with the exception of Sidonie) the Grasenabbs might be, not everyone was so amiable and it might often have gone very hard with Effi in the way of pleasure, distraction or even ordinary well-being, but for the presence of Gieshübler.

He looked after Effi like a minor Providence and she was grateful for it. In addition to everything else, he was naturally a keen and attentive newspaper reader, apart from the fact that he was a leading spirit in the reading club, and thus barely a day passed without Mirambo's bringing over a big white envelope full of all sorts of papers and periodicals, in which the appropriate passages were marked, usually with small, light strokes of a pencil, but occasionally, too, with a thick blue pencil accompanied by an exclamation or question mark. Nor did he leave it at that: he would also send over figs and dates, blocks of chocolate in glazed paper tied round with a red ribbon, and if he had some particularly lovely flower blooming in his greenhouse, he would bring it over himself and spend a happy hour chatting with the young woman whom he found so congenial and for whom he found himself feeling each and every sort of love mingled together, as if she were his daughter, niece, pupil and idol all in one.

Effi was touched by all this and frequently wrote about it to Hohen-Cremmen, so much so that her mother began to tease her about her 'love for the alchemist'; but this well-meant teasing missed its mark and indeed almost caused her pain because it made her realize, if but dimly, what her marriage really lacked: she needed someone to adore her, stimulate her, show her small attentions. Innstetten was good and kind, but he was not a lover. He felt that he loved Effi, and his good conscience in this respect led him to neglect making any special effort to show it. It had almost become a regular practice when Frederick brought the lamp for him to leave his wife's room and go back to his own. 'I've still got an awkward matter to look at.' And then he would leave. True, the door-curtain was left open, so that Effi could hear the rustle of the documents or the scratching of his pen, but that was all. Then Rollo would come and lie down on the hearth-rug, as if to say: 'I must look after you again, since there's no one else doing it.' And she would bend down over him and whisper: 'Yes, Rollo, we're alone.' At nine o'clock Innstetten reappeared for supper, usually holding a newspaper, and would talk about the Prince, who was once again very annoyed, especially over this Eugene Richter,* whose attitude and language were unspeakable, and then would go over the appointments and awards of decorations, most of which he objected to. Finally, he would talk about the elections and say how lucky he was to be head of a province which still showed respect. When he'd had his say on this, he would ask Effi to play something from *Lohengrin* or the *Valkyries*, because he was an enthusiastic Wagnerian. It was not quite clear what had made him like this. Some people said it was his nerves, because, although he seemed such a sobersides, in reality he was a nervous person; others attributed it to Wagner's anti-Semitism. Both parties were probably right. At ten o'clock Innstetten was sufficiently relaxed to indulge in a few well-meant, if somewhat tired, caresses, which Effi accepted without much response.

So winter passed and April came and the plants in the garden

* A liberal politician.

99

beyond the courtyard began to show green, which made Effi feel happy. She could hardly wait for summer to come, with its walks on the beach and its bathers.

When she looked back, she felt that while the evening with Trippelli at Gieshübler's and the New Year's Eve Ball had been all right, in fact rather nice, the following months had left much to be desired and above all they'd been so monotonous that she'd once written to her mother: 'Can you imagine, Mama, that I've almost become reconciled to our ghost. Of course, I certainly shouldn't like to experience another dreadful night like the one when Geert was away at the Prince's, naturally, but always being alone and nothing happening at all is very trying, too, and when I wake up in the night I occasionally listen to see if I can't hear the shoes sliding on the floor, and if everything is still quiet, I'm almost disappointed and say to myself, "If only it would come back again, only not too much and not too close." '

It was in February when Effi wrote this and now it was almost May. Over in the plantation, things were coming to life and you could hear the finches singing. It was in that same week, too, that the storks arrived and one hovered slowly over the house and then settled down on a barn standing beside Utpatel's mill. It had nested there before. Effi even reported this event; in any case, she was now writing more and more frequently to Hohen-Cremmen, and at the end of that same letter she wrote:

'I'd almost forgotten something, Mama: the new commandant of the district militia who has been with us now for almost four weeks. Well, is he really with us? That is the question and an important question at that, however much you may and will laugh about it, because you don't know the parlous social state we're still in here. Or at least, which I'm in, as I don't really manage to get on well with the local gentry. Perhaps it's my fault. But the result's the same and the fact remains: a parlous state, and for that reason I've been looking forward all winter to the new C.O. for comfort and salvation. His predecessor was a dreadful man, with bad manners and worse morals, and, if that weren't enough, hard-up. We've been suffering from him all this time, Innstetten even more than I have, and when we heard at the beginning of April that Major von Crampas (that's the new man's name) had arrived, we hugged each other as if no further harm could befal us in good old Kessin. But as I hinted above, it seems as if nothing much is going to come of it after all. Crampas is married, with two children of ten and eight years old, his wife one year older than he is, let's say forty-five. Well, there wouldn't be any great harm in that, why shouldn't I manage to have wonderful conversations with a motherly woman friend? Trippelli was close on thirty, too, and that went off quite well. But it's not much good with Frau von Crampas, who incidentally is certainly not of gentle birth herself. She's always bad-tempered and almost melancholy (like our Frau Kruse, whom she very much reminds me of) and all through jealousy. He, Crampas, is said in fact to have lots of affairs, rather a ladies' man, which I always find silly and which I should consider silly in this case, too, if he hadn't had a duel with a brother officer over some affair of that sort. His left arm was shattered just below the shoulder and you can see this straightaway, in spite of the fact that, as Innstetten told me, the operation (I think it's called a resection and it was done by Wilms) was said to be a masterpiece of surgery. The two of them, the two Crampases, called to pay their respects on us here a fortnight ago; it was a very awkward situation, because Frau von Crampas kept looking at her husband in a way that made him rather embarrassed and me completely so. I realized that he can be quite different, cheerful and gay, when he was alone with Innstetten three days ago and I could follow the conversation from my room. Afterwards I talked to him as well. Extremely gallant and extraordinarily quick-witted. Innstetten was in the same brigade with him during the war and they used to meet frequently at Count Gröben's, north of Paris. Well, my dear Mama, that would have been something that could have brought new life to Kessin; he, the Major, doesn't share the prejudices of the Pomeranians, although he's said to come from Swedish Pomerania. But the wife! Without her it's no good, and with her it'd be even worse!'

Effi was quite right: no closer relationship did, in fact, develop with the Crampases. They saw each other occasionally over at the Borcke's and on another occasion, just in passing, on the railway-station, and a few days later on a boat-trip excursion to the big beech and oak woods called Schnatermann, on the Breitling; but these meetings did not go beyond exchanging brief greetings and Effi was glad when, at the beginning of June, the start of the season approached. It was true that there were as yet hardly any visitors and, in any case, they used to appear only singly before midsummer's day, but the preparations for them were something of a distraction. In the plantation, a merry-go-round and shooting-booths were set up, the boatmen caulked and painted their craft, each little house got new curtains and the rooms that were damp and had dry rot in their floors were fumigated with sulphur and then ventilated.

In Effi's own house everything was in somewhat of a turmoil, not indeed because of any visitors but because of another new arrival; even Frau Kruse wanted to lend a hand, to the best of her ability. But Effi was horrified at the thought and said so: 'Geert, Frau Kruse really mustn't touch anything; that will bring bad luck and I'm already scared enough as it is.' Innstetten promised to see to it; after all, Christel and Joanna were not short of time, and in order to lead his young wife's thoughts into another direction he dropped the subject of preparations and, instead, asked whether she had yet noticed that a visitor had already moved in over the way, not perhaps the very first but one of the first of them.

'A man?'

'No, a lady. She has been here before, always in the same lodging. And she always arrives so early because she can't bear it when everything is so full up.'

'I don't blame her for that. Who is it?'

'The widow of a registrar, Frau Rode.'

'Strange. I've always thought that widows of registrars were poor.'

'Yes,' laughed Innstetten, 'as a rule they are. But this one's an exception. In any case, she has more than a widow's pension. She always brings a lot of luggage, infinitely more than she needs, and seems in general a quite peculiar woman: moody and delicate and, in particular, rather unsteady on her feet. For this reason, she's always on her guard and has an old servant with her all the time who's strong enough to protect her or lift her up if anything happens to her. She's got a new one this time, but the same sort of very thick-set woman, rather like Trippelli, but even stronger.'

'Oh, I've seen her already. Nice brown eyes that look you frankly and honestly in the face. But a bit stupid.'

'You're right, so she is.'

This conversation between Innstetten and Effi took place in the middle of June. Henceforth, every day brought more and more visitors, and a stroll down to the harbour to wait for the arrival of the steamer now became, as always at this time of the year, a sort of daily occupation for the inhabitants of Kessin. It is true that Effi had to forgo this occupation because Innstetten could not accompany her, but at least she had the pleasure of seeing the street leading down to the beach and the beach hotel come to life, whereas it was normally quite empty, and in order to watch this scene she spent much more time than usual in her bedroom, the windows of which offered the best vantage point. Joanna would stand at her side and manage to answer most of the things that Effi wanted to know, for as most of the visitors came back year after year, the maid was not only able to give the names but to tell some story or other about them as well.

All this was very entertaining for Effi and cheered her up. However, on Midsummer Day itself, shortly before 11 a.m., when normally the traffic coming from the steamer was at its liveliest, instead of the cabs filled with married couples and their children and baggage, a black-draped hearse accompanied by two mourning carriages was to be seen coming from the centre of the town down the street leading to the plantation and stopping in front of the house opposite the governor's residence. The widow of the registrar, Frau Rode, had died three days ago and when the relatives, hastily summoned from Berlin, had arrived they decided not to take the body back to Berlin but to have it buried in the Kessin churchyard among the dunes.

Effi stood at the window curiously watching the strangely solemn scene which was taking place across the way. The four people who had come from Berlin to attend the funeral were two nephews and their wives, all roughly about forty years old and with an enviably healthy look. The nephews, in well-fitting morning clothes, were reasonably acceptable, and the sober, businesslike nature of all their gestures was basically more becoming than upsetting. But their wives! These two ladies were obviously intent on showing the inhabitants of Kessin what mourning really meant; they were wearing long black crêpe veils which spread from the tops of their heads down to the ground.

And now the coffin, on which were lying a few wreaths and even a bunch of palms, was lifted into the hearse and the couples climbed into the carriages. Lindequist got into the first carriage together with one of the two pairs of mourners, whilst behind the last carriage walked the landlady and, behind her, the portly woman who had accompanied the deceased to Kessin as her servant. The latter was deeply moved and this feeling seemed genuine, even if the emotion was not, perhaps, exactly sorrow; but on the other hand it could be seen almost too clearly that the extremely violent sobbing of the landlady, a widow, was continually inspired by the possibility of an extra gift, in spite of the fact that she was in the privileged position, much envied by other landladies, of being able to re-let accommodation which had already been rented for the whole summer.

When the procession had set off, Effi went into the garden beyond the courtyard to try to rid herself, amongst the groups of box trees, of the lifeless and loveless impression left by this whole scene. But as this did not seem to be succeeding, she suddenly felt the desire to go for a longer walk than her monotonous stroll round the garden, the more so as her doctor had told her that a lot of exercise in the fresh air was the best thing she could have in her condition. Joanna, who had come into the garden with her, fetched her shawl, hat and sun-shade and with a friendly 'Good-bye' Effi left the house and walked over towards the spinney, where, beside the wide centre causeway, a narrower footpath led over the dunes to the hotel down by the beach.

There were benches along the path and she sat down on each of them because she found walking strenuous, the more so as it was now high noon and hot. But as she was sitting down and saw, from her comfortable seat, the carriages and smartly dressed ladies driving along, her energy revived, for seeing cheerful activity was like the breath of life to her. After the copse, there was a difficult stretch of path, with sand and yet more sand and no trace of shade; but fortunately there were wooden planks to walk on and when she arrived at the beach-hotel she was in good spirits, albeit tired and hot. People were already eating in the restaurant inside, but outside everything was quiet and empty all around, which was what she most needed at this particular moment. She ordered a glass of sherry and a bottle of mineral water and looked out over the sea shimmering in the bright sunlight with small waves lapping at its edge.

'Bornholm's over there and then Wisby beyond, which Jahnke

in the old days always used to say was so marvellous. He almost preferred Wisby to Lübeck and Wullenweber. And then beyond Wisby there's Stockholm, the scene of the blood-bath*, and then there are the big rivers and then the North Cape and then the midnight sun.' And as she said this she was seized with a yearning to see it all. But then she bethought herself of the event that was going to take place so shortly and was almost shocked. 'It's really sinful of me to be so frivolous and be thinking things like that and dreaming about far-away things when I really ought to be thinking about what's going to happen now. Perhaps I'll be punished for it and we'll both die, the child and I, and then the hearse and two carriages won't stop opposite, they'll stop at our house.... No. I don't want to die here, I won't be buried here. I want to go to Hohen-Cremmen. And however nice Lindequist is, I like Niemeyer better. He baptized me and confirmed me and married me and he must bury me too!' And as she said this to herself, a tear fell on her hand. But then she laughed again. 'After all, I'm still alive and only seventeen years old and Niemeyer's fifty-seven.'

In the restaurant she could hear the clink of cutlery, but suddenly she had the impression that chairs were being moved – perhaps they were already leaving the table – and she wanted to avoid meeting anyone. So she quickly stood up too, and set off again towards the town by a roundabout route, which led her close by the churchyard set amid the dunes. As the gateway leading through the churchyard was open, she went through. Inside everything was in bloom, the butterflies were flying around the graves and a few gulls were flying high in the heavens. It was so quiet and so lovely that she would have liked to have stopped straightaway by the first graves that she came to; but as the sun was becoming hotter and hotter every second, she went further up towards a shady path formed by weeping willows and some weeping ashes growing beside the graves. When she reached the end of this path, she saw, on the right, a fresh mound of sand with four or five wreaths on it and close by, set back from the row of trees, a bench on which was sitting the sturdy, kindly figure who had walked with the landlady following the registrar's widow's coffin, as the last mourners. Effi recognized her again at once and was deeply touched to see this loyal, affection-

* Massacre carried out by the Danish King Christian II on a large section of the inhabitants of Stockholm in 1520.

ate woman, for this she must surely be, sitting here in the blazing heat of the sun. A good two hours must have passed since the burial. 'That's a very hot place you've chosen,' said Effi, 'much too hot. And unless you're careful, you'll get sunstroke.'

'That would be the best thing for me.'

'Why is that?'

'Because then I'd be out of this world.'

'I don't feel that anyone ought to say that, even if someone is unhappy or when someone has died that you were fond of. You *were* very fond of her, weren't you?'

'Me? Her? God forbid!'

'But you're so sad. There must be some reason for it.'

'Yes, there is, your ladyship.'

'So you know who I am?'

'Yes, you're the governor's wife from over the way. And I was always talking to the old lady about you. Towards the end, she wasn't able to talk any more, because she couldn't breathe properly, she had something here, I suppose it must have been water. But as long as she was able to talk, she kept on all the time. She was from Berlin and a real ...'

'Good old woman?'

'No, if I was to say that, it'd not be true. There she lies and we oughtn't to speak ill of the dead, especially when they're barely laid to rest. Well, I expect she'll find rest! But she was no good, always quarrelling, an old skinflint, and she didn't look after me at all, either. And all the relatives who came from Berlin yesterday ... they kept squabbling long into the night ... no, they're no good either, they really aren't. ... Real nasty lot, greedy and grasping and hard-hearted and they paid me off with all sorts of nasty, horrid words, and only because they had to and because there are only six days to go to the end of the quarter. But for that I wouldn't have got anything or else only a half or a quarter. Not willingly at all. And they gave me a torn five mark note so that I can get back to Berlin, just about enough for a fourth-class ticket and I suppose I'll have to sit on my luggage. But I won't go. I want to stay here and wait to die. ... My God, I thought that I'd found a place and quiet at last and I'd've stuck it out with the old woman. And now that's all no good and I'll have to let myself be kicked around again. And me a Roman, too. ... Oh, I'm fed up and wish I was lying where the old woman is, and as far as I'm concerned she could go on living ... She would've liked to go on living. Cunning old trouts like that, even if they haven't got any breath left, they're the ones who hang on most to life ... .'

Meanwhile Rollo, who had gone with Effi, sat down in front of the old woman with his tongue hanging out, watching her. When she stopped talking at last, he stood up, walked forward a step and laid his head on her lap.

All at once the woman was as if transformed. 'Gracious me, that's something. There's a creature who can put up with me, who can look me in the face and put its head on my lap. My goodness, it's a long time since something like that happened to me. Well, you little old dog, what's your name? You're a fine fellow.'

'Rollo,' said Effi.

'Rollo. That's strange. But the name doesn't matter. I've got a strange name, too, my Christian name, that is. And that's the only name people like us ever have.'

'What is your name?'

'Roswitha.'

'That's an uncommon name, that must be ...'

'Yes, you're quite right m'lady, it's a Catholic name. And I'm Catholic too, that's why. From Eichsfeld. And being Catholic makes it even harder and more horrible. A lot of people won't take a Catholic because they're always off to church – always confessing – and they still don't confess the main thing. My goodness, how often I've had to listen to that, first of all when I was in service in Giebichenstein and then in Berlin. But I'm a bad Catholic and I've given it up altogether and perhaps that's why things are so bad, one ought not to drop one's faith and one should never stop going to church!'

'Roswitha.' Effi repeated the name and sat down beside her on the bench. 'What are you going to do now?'

'Ah, your ladyship, what can I do? I've got nothing to do. As sure as I'm sitting here, I'd like to stay here and wait till I drop dead. That's what I'd like best. And then people would think that I'd been as fond of the old woman as a faithful dog and hadn't wanted to leave her grave and had died there. But it's not true, you don't die for old women like that. I just want to die because I can't go on living.'

'I want to ask you something, Roswitha. Are you what they call "fond of children"? Have you ever been in a place where there were small children?'

'Yes, indeed I have. I think they're the sweetest and nicest things. A woman like that old woman from Berlin – God forgive me, because she's dead now and standing in front of God's throne and she can accuse me there – an old woman like that, it's dreadful, all the things that you have to do and it makes you sick, but those tiny dear little things, like dolls, that stare at you with their little eyes, well, it goes straight to your heart. When I was in Halle, I was nurse to the wife of a director of the salt-mines there and in Giebichenstein, where I went next, I brought up twins on the bottle. Yes, your ladyship, I know all about that. I'm quite at home with that sort of thing.'

'Well, do you know, Roswitha, I can see you're a loyal, kind person, a bit blunt but there's no harm in that – they're sometimes the nicest people – and I felt at once that I could trust you. Would you like to come to my house? I almost feel as if Providence had sent you. I'm expecting a baby soon, God willing, and when the child's born, it will have to be looked after and watched over and perhaps even breast-fed. No one can be certain about that, however much one might like to be. What do you think, will you come and join us? I can't imagine that I've been mistaken about you.'

Roswitha had jumped up and caught hold of the young woman's hand and kissed it fervently. 'Oh, God is in his heaven, and when the need is greatest help is round the corner. You'll see, m'lady, it will be all right; I'm a decent woman and I've got good testimonials. You can see that when I bring you my book. The very first day I saw your ladyship, I thought to myself: "Oh, if only you were in service with her." And now I shall be. O dear God, and Holy Mother of Jesus, who would have said that when we had the old woman under the ground and the relations had taken themselves off and left me alone.'

'Yes, Roswitha, every cloud has a silver lining and often a real one. And now let's go. Rollo is getting restless and keeps on running towards the gate.'

Roswitha was ready in a second, but went over to the grave once more, muttered something to herself and made the sign of the cross. And then they set off down the shady path towards the cemetery gate.

Over the way was the enclosure where the white stone glittered and shone in the afternoon sun. Effi felt able to look at it more calmly now. The path led through the sand-dunes for a short way until, just before Utpatel's mill, she reached the edge of the wood. At this point, she turned left into the wood and following an oblique avenue, called the Reeperbahn, she went towards the governor's house with Roswitha.

14

In less than a quarter of an hour, they were at the house. When the two of them went into the chilly hall, Roswitha was somewhat bewildered at the sight of all the strange things hanging up; but Effi did not let her make any further comment and said: 'Now, Roswitha, you go in there. That is the room where we sleep. I want to go first to see my husband in the government offices over the way – the big house next to the small one where you lived – and tell him that I would like to have you to look after the child. I'm sure he'll agree to everything but I still must have his consent first. And when I have, we must move his quarters and you will sleep with me in the alcove. I think we'll get along well.'

When Innstetten heard what had happened, he quickly and cheerfully said: 'You're right, Effi, and if your wage book can stand it more or less, we'll take her, on the strength of her kind face. Thank God, that rarely lets one down.'

Effi was very happy to meet so little difficulty and said: 'Everything is going to be all right now. I'm not scared any more.'

'What about, Effi?'

'You know what ... But it's one's imaginings that are the worst, sometimes worse than anything else.'

Within the hour, Roswitha had moved into the governor's house with her few belongings and settled into the little alcove. When the day was over, she went early to bed and, tired out as she was, went to sleep at once.

Next morning, Effi, who, now that it was a full moon, had been feeling anxious again for some time, asked Roswitha how she had slept and whether she had heard anything.

'Heard what?' Roswitha asked.

'Oh, nothing, I was only thinking, something like a broom sweeping or as if somebody was sliding over the floor.'

Roswitha laughed and this impressed her young mistress very favourably. Effi had been brought up as a firm Protestant and would have been very shocked if anyone had discovered any trace of Roman Catholicism in her or about her; all the same, she thought that Catholicism protects us better against things 'like those up-stairs'; and in fact, this consideration had been an important factor in her plan to have Roswitha come to live with them.

They quickly became used to each other, for Effi had the engaging trait of most country girls from Brandenburg of enjoying listening to all kinds of tales, and the deceased registrar's widow and her meanness and her nephews and their wives were an inexhaustable store of these. Even Joanna liked listening to her. True, when Effi often laughed out loud at the critical moment, Joanna smiled and wondered to herself how her ladyship seemed to take such pleasure in such stupid nonsense. But this astonishment, which went hand in hand with a strong feeling of superiority, was a good thing none the less because it ensured that there should be no quarrels about status. Roswitha was just a figure of fun and for Joanna to have been envious of her would have been rather like envying Rollo because Effi felt affection for him.

In this way, a week passed gossiping, almost cosily, because Effi was now facing the coming event with less anxiety than before. She also did not think that it was so near. On the ninth day, all the gossip and cosiness was over and done with; everybody was scurrying and running about, even Innstetten departed from his customary sang-froid, and on the morning of 3rd July a cradle was standing beside Effi's bed. Dr Hannemann patted the young mother's hand and said: 'It's the anniversary of the battle of Königgrätz today. A pity it's a girl. But the next one may be different, and the Prussians have lots of victories to celebrate.'

No doubt Roswitha thought the same, but meanwhile she was unreservedly overjoyed at what had in fact arrived and without hesitation christened the child 'Wee Annie', which the mother took as a sign. 'It must really have been an inspiration that made Roswitha hit on that name.' Even Innstetten could find nothing to say against it and the baby was referred to as Little Annie long before the actual christening. Effi, who wanted to be with her parents in Hohen-Cremmen by the middle of August, would have liked to put the christening off until then. But this could not be done; Innstetten was unable to obtain leave and so the christening was fixed, in church of course, for 15th August, in spite of the fact that it was Napoleon's birthday, which also caused objections from some families. As the governor's house had no reception room, the accompanying banquet took place in the large Club Hotel down by the harbour and all the local gentry were invited and, indeed, came.

Pastor Lindequist gave the toast of mother and child in a friendly speech which aroused great admiration from everyone, although Sidonie von Grasenabb took the opportunity of remarking to her neighbour, an assessor of noble birth and strict religious convictions: 'Yes, his informal speeches are all right. But he can't defend his sermons before God or man. He's half-hearted, one of those who are damned because they're lukewarm. I don't want to quote the exact words of the Bible here.'

Shortly afterwards, old Herr von Borcke rose to toast Innstetten: 'Ladies and Gentlemen, we live in difficult times, rebellion, impudence, lack of discipline wherever we look. But as long as we still have men and may I add wives and mothers' . . . here he bowed and made an elegant gesture towards Effi . . . 'as long as we still have men like Baron Innstetten, whom I'm proud to call my friend, then all is still well with us, this old Prussia of ours can still hold its own. Yes, Pomerania and Brandenburg will hold the fort and we shall stamp on the poisonous dragon's head of revolution. Our firmness and loyalty will prevail. The Catholics, our brothers, whom we must respect while opposing them, have the rock of St Peter, but we have the *rocher de bronze*.* All health to Baron Innstetten.'

Innstetten made a short speech in reply. Effi said to Major von Crampas, who was sitting beside her: 'That reference to the rock of St Peter must have been a homage to Roswitha; afterwards, she'll be going up to old Judge Gadebusch and asking him if he's not of the same opinion.' Inexplicably, Crampas took this remark seriously and said that Roswitha would be well advised not to approach the judge, a remark which Effi found uncommonly amusing: 'I really thought you were a better psychologist than that.'

* A phrase of Frederick William I's; the reference is to Bismarck.

'Ah, dear lady, with young and pretty women of under eighteen, no psychology is any good.'

'You're going from bad to worse, Major. You may call me a grandmother if you like but I can never forgive you any references to the fact that I'm not yet eighteen.'

Just as everyone had risen from the table, the late-afternoon steamer came down the Kessine and moored at the jetty opposite the hotel. Effi was sitting drinking coffee with Crampas and Gieshübler by the open windows, and looking out over the scene below.

'Tomorrow morning at nine o'clock the same ship will be taking me up the river and by midday I shall be in Berlin and by evening in Hohen-Cremmen, and Roswitha is going with me and carrying the baby. I hope it doesn't scream. Oh, how I'm looking forward to it! Gieshübler my dear, did you ever have such a happy feeling at going back to see your parents at home?'

'Yes, I've also felt like that, your ladyship. Only I didn't take any little Annie with me, because I hadn't one.'

'Something to look forward to,' said Crampas. 'Let's have a drink together, Gieshübler. You're the only sensible man here.'

'But there's only brandy left, Major.'

'So much the better.'

15

EFFI had left in the middle of August and by the end of September she was back in Kessin. In the intervening six weeks she had many a time longed to be back, but when she arrived and went into the gloomy hall, which was lit only by the rather dim light from the stairway, she suddenly felt alarmed again and she said quickly to herself: 'You won't find a dim yellow light like that in Hohen-Cremmen.'

But although she had once or twice felt a longing for the 'haunted house' while in Hohen-Cremmen, all things considered her life at home had been full of happiness and contentment. It is true that she had not been able to get on very well with Hulda, who could never forget the fact that *she* was still having to wait for her husband or fiancé; but she got on all the better with the twins, and more than once, while she was playing ball or croquet with them, she had completely forgotten that she was married. Those were happy times. But best of all she had enjoyed standing on the swing and flying through the air and experiencing a strange tingling sensation, a shiver of pleasant apprehension at the thought: 'Now, I'm going to drop.' When she finally jumped off the swing, she would go with the two girls down to the bench in front of the school house and when they had sat down there she would tell old Jahnke, who quickly appeared on the scene, all about her life in Kessin, half Hanseatic and half Scandinavian, and in any case, very different from the life in Schwantikow and Hohen-Cremmen.

These were the small day-to-day distractions, to which were added summer excursions to the Luch, usually in the shooting-brake; but nicest of all for Effi were the chats she had almost every morning with her mother. They sat upstairs in the big airy room while Roswitha nursed the baby and sang all sorts of cradle-songs in a Thuringian dialect which no one properly understood, perhaps not even herself; but Effi and Frau von Briest moved their chairs to the open window and while they talked they looked down on to the park, on to the sundial or the dragon-flies hovering almost motionless over the pond or the flagged path where Herr von Briest would be sitting reading the papers beside the projecting steps. Each time he turned over a page, he first took off his pince-nez and waved up to his wife and daughter. When he had worked his way through to the last paper, generally the *Havelland Observer*, Effi would go down and either sit down with him or go for a stroll through the park and gardens. On one such occasion, they left the gravel path and walked over to a small monument, standing on one side, that Briest's grandfather had had erected to commemorate the battle of Waterloo, a rusty pyramid with a cast-iron figure of Blücher in front and a ditto of Wellington at the back.

'Do you go for strolls like this in Kessin,' Briest asked, 'and does Innstetten go with you and talk to you about things in general?'

'No, Father, I don't go for walks like these. It's not possible, because we only have a small back garden, which is really hardly a garden at all, just a few borders of box and vegetable beds with three or four fruit trees. Innstetten has no interest in such things and he doesn't expect to stay in Kessin very much longer.'

'But you must have exercise and fresh air, child, you're used to it, after all.'

'But I do. Our house stands close to a little wood which they call the plantation. And I go walking a lot there with Rollo.'

'You're always mentioning Rollo,' laughed Briest. 'If we didn't know better, we might almost think that you're fonder of Rollo than you are of your husband and child.'

'Oh, Papa, that would be dreadful, although I must confess that there was a time when I couldn't have done without Rollo. It was that time . . . well, you know all about it. . . . He as good as saved me, more or less, or at least I imagined that he had and since then he's been a good friend of mine and my real mainstay. But he's still only a dog. And people come first, of course.'

'Yes, people are always saying that but I have my doubts about it, really. The question of animals is a rather special one and I don't think we've really got to the bottom of it yet. Believe me, Effi, that's a big subject, too. When I think that if you have an accident in the water or perhaps on tricky ice and a dog like that, a dog like Rollo, is there when it happens, well, he won't give up until he's brought you back to land. And if you're already dead, then he'll lie down beside your dead body and bark and whine until someone comes along, and if no one comes then he'll remain there beside the dead body until he dies himself. A good dog would always do that. And now compare that with people! God forgive me for thinking so, but I sometimes feel that animals are better than people.'

'But Father, if I tell Innstetten what you say . . .'

'No, you'd better not do that, Effi.'

'Of course, Rollo would save me but Innstetten would save me, too. He's a man of honour, after all, and he loves me.'

'Naturally, of course, and where there's love, there's mutual love. That's how things are. I'm only surprised that he hasn't taken some leave for a quick visit to see you. When someone has got such a young wife . . .'

Effi blushed because she was thinking exactly the same thing. But she didn't want to admit it. 'Innstetten's so conscientious and he wants to create a good impression and has got plans for the future; Kessin is just one rung on the ladder. And after all, I'm not going to run away from him. I'm his. If someone is too affectionate . . . and then there's the difference in age . . . people just smile. . . .'

'Yes, Effi, so they do. But one must put up with that. By the way, not a word about this, not even to your mother. It's so difficult to know what and what not to do. It's a big subject.'

Conversations such as these took place more than once in the course of Effi's stay with her parents, fortunately without leaving any lasting impression, and similarly the somewhat melancholy impression aroused in Effi when she first saw her house in Kessin again also vanished quickly. Innstetten was attentive and considerate and when they had had supper and gaily discussed all the various gossip and scandal, Effi affectionately took his arm when they went to their room to continue chatting, and she heard a few more anecdotes about Trippelli, who had recently had another lively correspondence with Gieshübler, which always amounted to a renewed charge on her account, never properly balanced. Effi was in excellent spirits during the conversation and felt very much the young wife and was glad to be rid of Roswitha, who had been relegated to the servants' quarters for an indeterminate period.

Next morning she said: 'The weather's nice and mild, and I hope the veranda facing the plantation is still in order so that we can sit out in the open and take breakfast there. We're shut up in our rooms soon enough and the winter in Kessin really is a month too long.'

Innstetten was quite agreeable. The veranda that Effi had mentioned, and which would perhaps have been better called a marquee, had been put up in the summer, three or four weeks before Effi's departure for Hohen-Cremmen. It consisted of a broad wooden platform, open in front, with an enormous canopy over it and canvas hangings attached to rings running on iron rods on each side so that they could be opened and shut. It was a delightful spot which was admired all through the summer by every passing visitor.

Effi leaned back in her rocking-chair and pushing the breakfast tray sideways towards her husband, said: 'Geert, could you be the obliging host today? I'm so comfortable in this rocking-chair that I don't want to get up. So make an effort and if you're really glad to have me back, I'll be able to do something for you in exchange.' As she spoke, she pulled the damask table-cloth straight and rested her hand on it. Innstetten took hold of her hand and kissed it. 'Well, how did you get on without me?'

'Pretty badly, Effi.'

'You sit there and pull a long face as you say that, but it's not true at all, really.'

'But Effi . . .'

'I'll prove it to you. If you'd had the slightest longing to see your child – I won't talk about myself, after all, what am I for such a great man, who was a bachelor for so long and wasn't in any hurry . . .'

'Well?'

'Well, Geert, if you'd had just a slight longing, then you wouldn't have left me all alone in Hohen-Cremmen for six whole weeks, like a widow, with nobody but Niemeyer and Jahnke and once or twice the people from Schwantikow. And none of the Rathenowers came over at all, as if they were scared of me or as if I was too old now.'

'Oh, Effi, what a way to talk. Do you know that you're a little flirt?'

'Thank Heaven you say that. It's the best thing we can be for you men. And you're the same as all of them, although you pretend to be so solemn and dignified. I know very well, Geert. . . . You're really a . . .'

'Well, what?'

'No, I'd better not say. But I know you very well; you're really what my uncle from Schwantikow once called you – an amorous man, born under Venus, and Uncle Belling was quite right when he said that. Only you won't show it and you think it won't do and will spoil your career. Am I right?'

Innstetten laughed. 'Well, there's something in what you say. Do you know Effi, you seem to have changed. Till little Annie was born, you were still a child. But all of a sudden . . .'

'Well?'

'All of a sudden you seem transformed. But it suits you, I like you very much, Effi. Do you know something?'

'Well?'

'There's something seductive about you.'

'Oh, my one and only Geert, what you've just said is splendid – it really gives me a lovely warm feeling in my heart. . . . Did you know that that's what I've always wanted to be? We have to be seductive or else we're nothing at all.'

'Did *you* think of that?'

'I might easily have thought of it. But I got it from Niemeyer. . . .'

'From Niemeyer! Heavens above, there's a clergyman for you. No, really, we don't have anyone like that here. But what made him say it? It's the sort of thing that some Don Juan or Casanova would have said. . . .'

'Well, who knows,' laughed Effi . . . 'but isn't that Crampas coming over there? And coming up from the beach too. Surely he won't have been bathing, will he? It's the 27th of September. . . .'

'He often does things like that. Sheer swank.'

Meanwhile Crampas had come quite near and he waved his hand. 'Good morning,' Innstetten called out. 'Won't you come over?'

Crampas came up to them. He was in mufti and he kissed Effi's hand as she began rocking her chair to and fro again. 'Please forgive me, Major, for seeming so inhospitable; the veranda is not really the house and ten o'clock is not really a visiting hour. So we'll be informal or, if you like, familiar. And now sit down and give an account of your doings. To judge by your hair, which I suppose you wouldn't object to having a little more of, it's obvious that you've been bathing.'

He nodded. . . .

'No sense of responsibility,' said Innstetten, half serious and half joking. 'You saw yourself what happened four weeks ago with the banker Heinersdorf when he, too, imagined that the sea and those splendid waves would spare him for the sake of his million. But the gods are jealous of each other and Neptune had no hesitation in setting himself up against Pluto, or at least against Heinersdorf.'

Crampas gave a laugh. 'Yes, a million marks. My dear Innstetten, if I had that, then I wouldn't have ventured in either, because the water was only 48 degrees. But with people like us who are a million in the red, you must allow us to show off a little, because we can afford to do that sort of thing without fear of making the gods in any way envious. And then we have that saying to console us: If you're born for the gallows, you'll never be drowned.'

'But my dear Major, you surely don't intend, if I might use the expression, to hang something as unprosaic as that round your neck. . . . In any case, lots of people think . . . I mean concerning what you've just said . . . think that all of us deserve it, more or less. . . . All the same, Major, for a major . . .'

'It's not a traditional form of death. . . . I admit that, Baroness. Not traditional and in my case not even very probable, in fact, nothing but a quotation or, to put it better, a *façon de parler*. But all the same, there was something serious in what I just said about the sea not having any grudge against me. I am, in fact, convinced that I shall die like a soldier, and I hope it will be an honourable death. First the gypsies told me so and now it's my own conscience.'

Innstetten laughed: 'You're going to run into difficulties, Crampas, unless you intend to serve with the Grand Duke or under the Chinese. There's some fighting going on there. Here, all that sort of thing is over for another thirty years and anyone who wants to die a hero's death . . .'

'. . . will have to arrange with Bismarck to provide a war. I know all that, Innstetten. But for you that's a mere trifle. It's now the end of September; in ten weeks' time from now at the latest, the Prince will be in Varzin again and because he has a *faible* for you – I prefer to avoid the more ordinary expression, since I don't want to find myself looking down the barrel of your pistol – you'll be able to arrange a small war for an old brother officer. The Prince is only human, after all, and a little persuasion helps.'

During this conversation, Effi had squeezed a few lumps of bread together, played dice with them and arranged them into patterns in order to hint that a change of subject was indicated. In spite of this, Innstetten seemed tempted to reply to Crampas's jocular remark and this made Effi decide that direct intervention would be better: 'I don't see why we need concern ourselves with how you're going to die, Major. Life concerns us much more closely and is a more serious matter, after all.'

Crampas nodded.

'I'm glad you agree with me. How are we going to spend life here, that's the question at the moment and it's more important than anything else. Gieshübler has written to me about it and if it weren't indiscreet and vain, because there are all sorts of other things in it as well, I'd show you the letter. . . . Geert doesn't need to see it, he doesn't appreciate that sort of thing. . . . By the way, the handwriting looks as if it had been engraved, and the expressions he uses suggest that our friend had been brought up at the French court of the *ancien régime* rather than on Kessin's Old Market Place. And the fact that he's deformed and wears white frills on his shirts, which no one does any more – I wonder where he finds a woman to iron them – all seems terribly appropriate. Well, anyway, Gieshübler has written to me about plans for the club evenings and about an organizer by the name of Crampas. You see, Major, I like that better than a soldier's death or indeed the other sort.'

'And I'm the same. And we must make it a magnificent winter if we want to be sure that we can rely on your ladyship's support. Trippelli is coming. . . .'

'Trippelli? Then you've no need for me. . . .'

'Not at all, Baroness. Trippelli can't sing from one weekend to the next – it would be too much even for her, not to mention us. Variety is the spice of life, a truism to which every happy marriage seems to give the lie.'

'If there are any happy marriages, apart from mine . . .' She stretched out her hand towards her husband.

'Variety then,' continued Crampas, 'and we shall need help from every qualified person in order to achieve it for ourselves and for the club, whose vice-president I have the honour to be at the moment. If we all cooperate, then we can set the whole wretched town topsy-turvy. We've already chosen the plays: *Krieg im Frieden*, *Monsieur Hercule*, Wilbrandt's *Young Love*, and perhaps Gensichen's *Euphrosyne*. You'll be Euphrosyne and I'll be the old Goethe. You'll be amazed how well I play the tragic *poet-prince* . . . if play is the right word.'

'I've no doubt about it. I've been informed by the letter from my secret alchemist correspondent that, apart from many other things, you occasionally write verse as well. First of all I was surprised. . . .'

'Because you couldn't see me as a poet.'

'Yes, but since I've learnt that you go bathing when the temperature's 48 degrees, I've changed my mind. . . . 48 degrees in the Baltic is better than the Castalian spring. . . .'*

'The temperature of which is unknown.'

'Not to me; at least, no one will prove me wrong. But now I must get up. Here comes Roswitha with wee Annie.' She stood up and going to meet Roswitha, took the baby from her arms and proudly and happily held her high in the air.

* A spring at Delphi, supposed to inspire poets.

16

THE weather was fine and remained so right into October. One result of this was that the tent-veranda outside came into its own, so much so that the mornings at least were usually spent there. At about eleven, the major would arrive, first to inquire after Effi's health and exchange a little malicious gossip with her – something he was very good at – and then afterwards to arrange for a ride with Innstetten, often inland, up the Kessine as far as the Breitling, but more often down to the quayside. When the gentlemen had gone, Effi would play with the child or look through the papers and periodicals that Gieshübler continued to send her or would perhaps write a letter to her mother or would say: 'Roswitha, we'll take Annie for a walk,' and Roswitha would then take the wicker baby-carriage and, followed by Effi, go a few hundred yards into the little wood to a place where horse-chestnuts were lying on the ground to be picked up and given to the baby to play with. Effi rarely went into town; there was really no one there with whom she could have had a talk, since a fresh attempt to establish contact with Frau von Crampas had come to nothing.

This continued for some weeks until Effi suddenly expressed the desire to be allowed to go out riding with the men, seeing that she was passionately fond of it and that it was asking too much that she should be prevented from doing something that she felt so worth-while merely because it might cause gossip in Kessin. The major was all in favour of it and although Innstetten was obviously less pleased, so much so that he kept emphasizing that it would be hard to find a suitable horse for a lady, he was obliged to give in when Crampas promised that he would see to that. And, true enough, the appropriate horse was found and Effi was able to gallop blissfully along the beach, where the separate divisions of Ladies' Bathing and Gentlemen's Bathing no longer needed to deter her. Usually Rollo came along as well and because on one or two occasions they had wanted to take a rest on the beach or go part of the way on foot, they arranged to have servants accompanying them, for which purpose the major's orderly, Knut, a former Treptow

Uhlan, and Innstetten's coachman Kruse were pressed into service as grooms, albeit not completely successfully, since to Effi's regret they were made to wear rather comic makeshift livery which still revealed traces of their real status.

It was already the middle of October before the complete cavalcade, thus equipped, first set off, with Innstetten and Crampas in front and Effi in between, followed by Kruse and Knut. Rollo at first brought up the rear, but finding this position not to his liking he was soon ahead of everyone. When they had passed the now deserted beach-hotel and shortly afterwards, keeping to the right and following the path along the beach, in the spray from a moderate surf, had reached the quayside, they were tempted to dismount and walk out to the end of the jetty. Effi was first out of the saddle. The Kessine was flowing wide and calm, between the two stone jetties, towards the sea which lay before them in the sun, its surface broken by the occasional ripple of a wave.

Effi had never been out here because when she had arrived in Kessin, the previous November, the unsettled weather had already set in and when the summer had come she had been in no fit state to go for lengthy walks. Now, she found herself entranced and thought everything magnificent and grand, indulged in derogatory comparisons between the Luch and the sea, and whenever she had the chance picked up a piece of wood washed up on to the beach and flung it into the sea to her left. Rollo was always delighted to chase things thrown by his mistress, but all at once his attention was distracted in the other direction and creeping forward cautiously, indeed almost timidly, he suddenly hurled himself on to an object that appeared in front of him, albeit without any success, because at that same moment the seal, which had been lying in the sun on the rock covered in green seaweed, slipped smoothly and silently into the sea, which was only about five yards away. For a short while its head could still be seen and then that, too, dived under.

Everybody was excited and Crampas began to speculate on the possibility of a seal-hunt and suggested that next time they should bring a rifle. 'No good,' said Innstetten. 'The harbour police.'

'What an extraordinary thing to say,' laughed Crampas. 'The harbour police, indeed. The three officials that we have here will surely be able to turn a blind eye amongst themselves. Does everything have to be so legal? All legality is boring.'

Effi clapped her hands.

'Oh yes, Crampas, that sort of remark is all very well for you and as you can see, Effi's applauding you. Of course, women don't take long to start screaming for a policeman but they don't want to hear about the law.'

'That's an old established privilege of women, Innstetten, and we're not going to be able to change it.'

'No,' laughed the other, 'and I don't want to, either. I'm not interested in trying to justify myself. But someone like yourself, Crampas, who has grown up in the shadow of discipline and who knows very well that you have to have discipline and order, a man like you really ought not to talk like that. Of course, I know you have a sublime *je m'en fichisme* and think that the heavens aren't going to fall just yet. Well, they may not fall straightaway. But sooner or later they will.'

For a moment, Crampas was embarrassed, because he imagined that Innstetten had made this remark with a particular purpose in mind, although this was not the case: Innstetten was only delivering one of his homilies, to which he was in any case rather prone. 'That's why I admire Gieshübler,' he added, 'always gallant and yet a man with principles.'

Meanwhile the major had recovered his composure and said, in his old tone of voice: 'Oh yes, Gieshübler; the nicest chap in the world and his principles are even nicer, if that's possible. But at the end of the day, where does it get him, and why does he do it? Because he has a grudge against life. Normal people take things lightly. In fact, if you don't take things lightly, life's not worth a tinker's damn.'

'Now, be careful, Crampas, on occasion a tinker can produce something rather more powerful than a damn.' And as he spoke he looked at the major's shortened left arm.

Effi had not heard much of this conversation. She had walked up close to the spot where the seal had been basking and was waiting to see if the 'mermaid' would show itself again.

At the end of October, the election campaign began, which prevented Innstetten from taking any further part in the excursions, and Crampas and Effi would doubtless also have had to give up in deference to the respectable inhabitants of Kessin if Knut and

Kruse had not been there as a sort of guard of honour. In this way, the rides continued into November.

By now, the weather had changed and a steady north-wester brought driving masses of clouds, while the sea thundered and foamed, but as rain and cold still held off, the excursions were almost more lovely under these grey skies and with the thundering surf than previously when the sun had shone and the sea was calm. Rollo would run on ahead, sprayed now and again by the spume, and the veil of Effi's riding hat flapped in the wind. It was almost impossible to talk, but if one left the sea and branched off into the shelter of the dunes or, better still, into the even more secluded fir-wood, everything became quiet, Effi's veil stopped fluttering and the narrowness of the path forced both riders close together. The conversation, interrupted by the noise of the surf, could now be resumed, as the stumps and roots forced their horses to walk. Crampas, an excellent conversationalist, would then retail stories about the war or about his regiment, as well as anecdotes and stories about Innstetten's character, for, with his seriousness and his taciturnity, the latter had never really fitted into the high-spirited circle of his brother officers, so that he had been respected rather than liked.

'I can imagine that,' said Effi; 'fortunately, respect is the main thing.'

'Yes, at the right time and place. But it's not always the case. And in addition to all that, there was his mystical tendency, which sometimes gave offence, first because soldiers aren't generally very keen on that sort of thing, and secondly, because we formed the impression, perhaps unfairly, that his attitude towards things was not exactly what he would have had us believe.'

'Mystical tendency?' said Effi. 'But what do you mean by that, Major? Surely he didn't set up religious groups and make himself out to be a prophet? Not even the one from that opera . . . I've forgotten his name.'

'No, he didn't go as far as that. But perhaps it's better not to go on about this; I shouldn't like to say something behind his back that could be wrongly interpreted. Besides these are questions which could very well be talked about in his presence. Questions which, whether one intended it or not, can be blown up into something peculiar when he's not there and not able to intervene all the time to contradict us or even perhaps laugh at us.'

'That's sheer cruelty, Major. How can you torture me like this. First he is something and then he isn't. And mysticism, too. Is he a seer?'

'A seer. No, I wouldn't put it like that exactly. But he did have a weakness for telling us ghost stories. And when he had put us all on edge and probably made a lot of us scared, he would suddenly make it seem as if he had only been amusing himself at the expense of all those who had been so gullible. To cut a long story short, once I tackled him and said: "For goodness sake, Innstetten, that's just a lot of nonsense. You're not deceiving me. You don't really believe that any more than we do, but you want to appear interesting and you've got the idea that eccentricity is a good passport to success, that they don't want ordinary people in the upper hierarchy. And as you have something like that in mind, you've looked for something strange of that sort and hit on ghosts." '

Effi said not a word, and her silence finally became too much for the major.

'You haven't said anything, Baroness.'

'No.'

'May I ask why? Have I given offence? Or do you think it unfair to tease a – I must admit that in spite of any protests to the contrary – to tease a friend a little when he isn't there? But in that case, you really are doing me an injustice. I shouldn't be in the least embarrassed to continue this conversation in his presence and I'll repeat word for word what I've just said.'

'I believe you.' And having said this, Effi broke her silence and told him of all her experiences in her house and how strange Innstetten's attitude had been towards it on that occasion. 'He didn't say either yes or no and I didn't know what he thought.'

'So he hasn't changed,' laughed Crampas. 'He was just like that when we were quartered with him in Liancourt and later on in Beauvais. He was living in an old bishop's palace there – by the way, it'll perhaps interest you to know that it was a Bishop of Beauvais with the appropriate name of Cochon who condemned Joan of Arc to the stake – and not a day passed, that is, not a night passed but something extraordinary happened to him. Or not exactly *happened*. There might have been nothing in it. And I see that he's still working on the same principles.'

'Yes, I see. And now I want to ask you a serious question,

Crampas, to which I'd like a serious answer: how do you explain all this?'

'Well, Baroness . . .'

'No prevarication, Major! It's very important for me. He's your friend and I'm your friend. I want to know how all this fits in. What does my husband think himself about it?'

'Well, Baroness, God sees into people's hearts, but a major in the local militia doesn't see into anything. How can I solve that sort of psychological problem? I'm just a simple man.'

'Now, Crampas, don't talk such nonsense. I'm too young to know much about people, but I'd have had not to be confirmed or even hardly baptized to take you for a simple man. You're the opposite, you're a dangerous man.'

'That's the most flattering thing that could be said to someone well in his forties, and unfit for active service. Well now, what does Innstetten really think about it? . . .'

Effi nodded.

'Well, if I'm to speak frankly, he thinks that a man like the provincial governor Baron Innstetten, who may get a ministerial post or something similar at any moment now – because, believe me, he's high on the list – that a man like Baron Innstetten can't possibly live in an ordinary house, a farmer's cottage – forgive me, your ladyship – which is what the governor's house really is. So he helps things along. A haunted house is always something out of the ordinary. . . . That's one thing.'

'One thing? Goodness me, is there something else?'

'Yes.'

'Well then, I'm all ears. But if possible make it something nice.'

'I'm not quite sure about that. It's rather a delicate point, almost *risqué*, and especially for your ears, Baroness.'

'That makes me even more curious.'

'Very well then. In addition to his ardent desire to further his own career at all costs, even to the extent of dragging in a ghost if need be, Innstetten has a second passion: he always wants to be educational, he's a born pedagogue and he would really have been at home in Schnepfental or Bunzlau,* to the left of Basedow and to the right of Pestalozzi, but more religious than either.'

* Educational establishments with a sectarian bias.

'And so he wants to educate me, too? Education by the use of ghosts?'

'Educate is perhaps not the right word. But educate indirectly.'

'I don't understand you.'

'A young wife is a young wife and a governor is a governor. He often has to travel all over the district and then the house is deserted and empty. But a ghost like that is as good as a cherub with a sword. . . .'

'Ah, now we're out of the wood,' said Effi. 'And there's Utpatel's mill. We've only got to go past the cemetery now.'

A moment later they passed along the sunken path between the churchyard and the fenced-in enclosure and Effi looked towards the stone and the fir-tree where the Chinaman was buried.

17

It was striking two o'clock when they arrived back. Crampas took his leave and rode into town, as far as his house in the market-place. Effi changed her clothes and tried to sleep, but without success, because she was more upset than tired. That Innstetten was cultivating the ghost in order not to live in a completely commonplace house could be accepted; it fitted in with his fondness for distinguishing himself from the crowd; but the other thing, that he was using the ghost as a means of education, was horrible and almost insulting. And she realized quite clearly that the expression 'means of education' was not really the half of it; what Crampas had meant was much more than that, a sort of calculated means of inspiring fear. There was something heartless about it which almost bordered on cruelty. Her blood boiled as she clenched her little fists and began to think what she would do; but then suddenly she had to laugh. 'What a ninny I am. Who's to say that Crampas is right? He's amusing because he's a gossip but he's untrustworthy and just a buffoon. He can't hold a candle to my husband.'

At this moment, Innstetten drove up, having returned home earlier than usual. Effi jumped up and ran down to meet him in the hall and was all the more affectionate because she had the feeling that she owed him some reparation. But in spite of everything, she could not entirely forget what Crampas had said and in the midst of all her show of affection and while she seemed to be taking an interest in what he was saying, all the time she kept hearing the words: 'So it was a deliberately calculated ghost, to keep you in order.'

But in the end, all the same, she did forget and listened calmly to her husband's news.

Meanwhile, the middle of November had come and the north-westerly winds, building up to gale force, blew for a day and a half so strongly against the harbour that the Kessine was driven over the sea wall into the streets. But when it had died down, the weather settled again and this brought a few more sunny autumn days. 'Who knows how long they'll last,' Effi said to Crampas, and so they decided to go riding again the following morning; Inn-stetten had a day free and wanted to go, too. First of all, they wanted to go as far as the harbour, where they intended to dismount, go for a stroll along the beach and finally have a picnic in the dunes, out of the wind.

At the appointed time, Crampas rode up to the governor's house. Kruse was already holding Effi's horse and she quickly swung herself into the saddle, at the same time offering Innstetten's excuses because he had, after all, been prevented from coming; last night there had been another big fire in Morgenitz – the third within three weeks and obviously deliberately caused – and he had had to go over there, to his regret, because he had really been look-ing forward to the ride, which would probably be his last.

Crampas said he was sorry, perhaps merely in order to say some-thing but perhaps he was genuinely sorry, because however lacking in consideration in his affairs of the heart, in his relations with men he was a good friend, in a purely superficial way, of course. Helping a friend and deceiving him five minutes later were things that fitted very well into his conception of honour. He would do both these things with all the good will in the world.

As usual, the ride was through the plantation. Rollo was in the lead, then followed Crampas and Effi, and finally Kruse. Knut was absent.

'What have you done with Knut?'

'He's got the mumps.'

'How extraordinary,' laughed Effi. 'As a matter of fact, he always looks as if he had.'

'True enough. But you should see him now! Or better not, in fact. Mumps is catching, even by just looking.'

'I don't believe you.'

'Young women don't believe lots of things.'

'And they also believe lots of things that they'd better not believe.'

'Was that meant for me?'

'No.'

'A pity.'

'What a typical remark! Major, I really think that you would consider it quite in order for me to make you a declaration of love.'

'I wouldn't go as far as to say that. But I should like to meet the man who wouldn't like to hear something of the sort. Thoughts are free and so are our wishes.'

'That's questionable. And there is, after all, a difference between thoughts and wishes. Thoughts are normally something that we keep back. Wishes are usually on the tip of the tongue.'

'What an appropriate image. . . .'

'Oh Crampas, you're a . . . you're a . . .'

'Fool.'

'No. There you're exaggerating again. But you're something else. In Hohen-Cremmen we always used to say – and so did I – that the vainest person imaginable was an eighteen-year-old ensign in the Hussars.'

'And now?'

'And now I say that the vainest person there is, is a forty-two-year-old major in the militia.'

'And I forgive you all those hard words because you've granted me an extra two years of life. . . . I kiss your hand. . . .'

'Yes, "I kiss your hand" is the right expression for you! It's Viennese. I got to know what the Viennese are like four years ago in Carlsbad, when they flirted with me, although I was only a little titch of fourteen. The things they said to me!'

'Surely nothing more than you deserved.'

'If that's true, then the things that are supposed to flatter me are rather ill-bred. But look at the buoys floating and dancing about. The little red flags have been taken in. Wherever I saw those red flags this summer, the few times I ventured as far as the beach, I said to myself: there's Vineta, it must be there, there are the steeples. . . .'

'That must be because you've read Heine's poem.'

'Which one?'

'The one about Vineta.'

'No, I don't know it; I really don't know very much, unfortunately....'

'And yet you've got Gieshübler and all those newspapers that they circulate. As a matter of fact, Heine gave his poem another name, I think *Phantom of the Sea* or something like that. But he meant Vineta. And he himself – forgive me if I tell you the story of the poem like this – the poet is lying on the deck of the ship as he passes by the spot and looks down and sees narrow medieval streets and women in coifs tripping along and they're all carrying hymn books and going to church and all the bells are tolling. And when he hears that he's seized with the desire to go to church with them, if only because of the coifs, and so, filled with this longing, he is just about to dive down when at that very instant the captain catches his leg and shouts, "Doctor, you're lost." '

'But that's fantastic. I'd love to read it. Is it long?'

'No, it's short really, somewhat longer than *Du hast Diamanten und Perlen* or *Deine weichen Lilienfinger*.' He gently touched her hand. 'But whether it's long or short, what powers of description and how vivid he is! He's my favourite poet and I know him by heart, even although I don't go in much for poetry, in spite of certain weaknesses of my own in that direction. But Heine is very different. Heine is on the side of life and, above all, he understands love, which is the main thing, after all. And he's not just one-sided.'

'How do you mean?'

'I mean he's not only interested in love.'

'Well, even if he were one-sided about it, there could be worse things than that couldn't there? What else is he interested in?'

'Well, he's also very much interested in Romanticism, which in fact comes immediately after love, and in some people's opinion they both really belong together. But I don't think so, because in his later poems, which have also been called Romantic poems – in fact he called them that himself – in these Romantic poems executions take place all the time. It's true they were often caused by love, but all the same they usually had other more vulgar motives, in which I include first and foremost politics, which is almost always rather vulgar. For example, in one of his romances, Charles Stuart is carrying his head under his arm, and the tale of Vitzliputzli is even more dreadful. . . .'

'Who's that?'

'Vitzliputzli? Vitzliputzli is a Mexican god and when the Mexicans had taken twenty or thirty Spaniards as prisoners, these twetny or thirty were to be sacrificed to Vitzliputzli. That was quite normal there, the custom of the country, their religion, and it was all done in the flick of an eyelid – you slit them up and out came the heart.'

'No, you mustn't go on talking like that, Crampas. It's indecent and disgusting. And just when we're going to have our picnic, more or less.'

'Personally I feel completely uninfluenced by that and my appetite depends on the menu. . . .'

While talking, in accordance with their plan they had left the beach and reached a bench that had been set up, half in the shelter of the dunes, in front of an extremely primitive table. Kruse, who had ridden on ahead, had already prepared the meal: slices of cold meat with rolls and red wine, and beside the bottle of wine, two dainty little wine glasses, with gold rims, such as you can buy in seaside resorts or take away as a souvenir from glass factories.

They dismounted. Kruse had fastened his own reins round a stunted fir-tree and was walking the other two horses up and down while Crampas and Effi sat down in front of the table. Through a narrow gap in the dunes, they could see the beach and the pier. The November sun, already quite wintry, cast its pale glow on a sea still rough from the storm. There was a heavy swell. Now and again a great gust of wind carried the spray almost to where they were sitting. Wild oats were growing all round them and the acid yellow of the everlasting flowers stood out, despite their similarity of colour, against the yellow sand in which they were growing.

Effi acted as hostess. 'I'm sorry to have only cold meat to offer you, Major.'

'As long as it's not cold shoulder. . . .'

'However, Kruse is to blame. So there you are, Rollo. I'm afraid our provisions aren't really suitable for you. What shall we do about Rollo?'

'I think we'll give him everything; as far as I'm concerned, I'll do it out of sheer gratitude, because you see, my very dear Effi . . .'

Effi gave him a sharp look.

'. . . Because you see, Baroness, Rollo reminds me of something else that I wanted to tell you about, as a kind of continuation or supplement to Vitzliputzli, only much more piquant, because it's a love story. Have you ever heard of someone called Pedro the Cruel?'

'Vaguely.'

'A sort of Bluebeard.'

'Excellent. That's the sort of people one likes hearing about and I always remember what we used to say about my friend Hulda Niemeyer, that the only history she knew was Henry VIII's six wives, the English Bluebeard, if the expression fits in his case. And she really did know all six by heart. And you should have heard her when she recited the names, especially the name of Elizabeth's mother – she sounded so terribly unhappy, as if it was going to be *her* turn next. . . . Well, what about this story about Don Pedro?'

'Well then, at the court of Don Pedro there was a dark and handsome Spanish knight who wore on his chest the Cross of Calatrava – that's something like our two orders of the *Schwarzer Adler* and *Pour le Mérite* rolled into one. They had to wear this cross all the time, which was one of the special things about it, and this knight of Calatrava, whom the Queen, of course, was secretly in love with . . .'

'Why "of course"?'

'Because it's Spain.'

'Oh, I see.'

'And, as I was saying, this knight had a superb dog, a Newfoundland, although there weren't any such dogs at that time, because it was a hundred years before the discovery of America. Anyway, a wonderful dog, like Rollo let's say . . .'

As he heard his name, Rollo barked and wagged his tail.

'This went on for a long long time. But this secret love, which probably wasn't as secret as all that, became too much of a good thing for the King and as he wasn't very keen on the handsome knight of Calatrava in any case – because he wasn't only cruel but a dog in the manger or if the expression is inappropriate for a king or even more so for my charming listener, Baroness Effi, at least an envious man – so he decided to have the noble knight secretly executed for his secret love.'

'I don't blame him.'

'I'm not so certain, my dear Baroness. Let me continue. In some ways, it was right, but the King, I think, went slightly too far. He pretended that he wished to give a banquet in honour of all the military exploits of the heroic knight and so they had a long, long table and the King sat in the middle, with all the grandees sitting there too, and opposite him was the place for the man in whose honour the banquet was going to be given, the knight of Calatrava. But as he didn't come, in spite of the fact that they had waited quite a while for him, in the end the feast had to start without him and so there was a vacant place exactly opposite the King.'

'And so . . .?'

'And so, just imagine, Baroness, as the King, this Pedro, was just about to rise to his feet to express his regret that their "dear guest" had still not arrived, a dreadful outcry rose from the horrified servants outside on the stairs and before anyone knew what was happening, something rushed along the long banqueting table and sprang on to the chair and placed a decapitated head on the empty place; it was Rollo staring over this head at the person opposite, who was the King. Rollo had accompanied his master on his last journey and at the very moment the axe fell, the trusty beast had siezed hold of the head and now there was our friend Rollo sitting at the long banqueting table, accusing the royal murderer.'

Effi had become very silent. Finally, she said: 'Crampas, that's very splendid in its way, and because it's so splendid, I'll forgive you. But you would be doing me a better service and a kinder one if you told me some different kind of story, even something else from Heine. Heine surely didn't only write about Vitzliputzli and Don Pedro and your Rollo – because mine wouldn't have done a thing like that. Come on, Rollo, you poor dog, I can't look at you any more without thinking of the knight of Calatrava, who was loved in secret by the Queen. . . . Please call Kruse to come and pack all these things back into the hamper and while we're riding back you shall tell me another story, a story of a different sort.'

Kruse came up but as he was about to pick up the glasses, Crampas said: 'Kruse, leave that glass, the one there. I'll take that one myself.'

'Very good, sir.'

Effi, who had heard what had been said, shook her head. Then she gave a laugh. 'Crampas, what do you think you're doing? Kruse is stupid enough not to think anything more about it, and if he does, fortunately he won't realize what it's all about. But that doesn't justify your taking that glass . . . that tuppenny ha'penny glass from the Josephine factory. . . .'

'The ironic way you mention its price makes me value it all the more highly.'

'You never change. You're such a humorist but rather a strange sort of one. If I understand you correctly – it's laughable and I'm almost embarrassed to say it – you intend to become a König von Thule before your time.'

He gave a nod that was not without a touch of malice.

'All right then, as far as I'm concerned. On your own head be it; you know what you're doing. Only there's one thing that I should like to say to you: I don't find the role that you're forcing me to play in all this very flattering. I'm not keen on providing your König von Thule with an appropriate rhyme to finish the poem. Keep the glass but please don't draw any compromising conclusions from it as far as I'm concerned. I shall tell my husband about it.'

'You won't do that, Baroness.'

'And why not?'

'Innstetten is not the man to take this sort of thing as it needs to be taken.'

For a moment, she gave him a sharp look. But then she dropped her eyes, confused and almost embarrassed.

18

E F F I was dissatisfied with herself and glad that it had now been agreed not to continue these excursions for the remaining months of the winter. When she looked back over all that had been discussed, touched upon or hinted at during all those days and weeks, she could indeed find nothing directly to reproach herself with. Crampas was an intelligent man, experienced, humorous, free and easy, in the good sense as well, and it would have been petty and mean to have been too formal and observed the strict rules of propriety with him all the time. No, she couldn't blame herself for having fallen in with his manner of talking, yet she did have the vague feeling of having come through a danger and she congratulated herself that it was now all relegated to the past. It was, of course, most unlikely that there would be any social visits, since family visits were more or less impossible owing to the Crampas's domestic situation, while any meetings in the houses of the neighbouring gentry which were now, indeed, likely to be taking place during the winter, could only be extremely rare and fleeting. Effi realized all this with ever-increasing satisfaction and finally came to the conclusion that she would not feel any great loss at having to give up what she owed to Major Crampas's company.

In addition, Innstetten now informed her that he would not be undertaking his trips to Varzin this year: the Prince was going to Friedrichsruh, which he seemed to be increasingly fond of; in some ways, he was sorry about it, in others he was glad, for now he could devote himself to his home, and if she agreed, he suggested that they might go over their Italian trip again together, by looking over his Italian sketch-book. A review of this sort would be essential if they were to fix these things permanently in their minds and even things that they had only seen in passing and had barely been aware of could be really understood and remembered by this sort of supplementary study. He expatiated on this point and added that Gieshübler, who knew the whole 'boot of Italy' as far as Palermo, had asked whether he might be present too. Effi, who would have much, much, preferred an ordinary evening's gossip without any 'boot of Italy' at all (they were even going to hand round photographs), made rather a constrained reply. Innstetten, however, full of his project, noticed nothing, and continued: 'Of course, it's not only Gieshübler who must come, Roswitha and Annie must be there, too, and when I think that we'll be going up the Grand Canal and hearing the gondoliers singing in the distance while three yards away Roswitha will be bending over Annie, singing, 'Buhküken von Halberstadt' or some other children's song of that sort, I can see that our winter evenings will be very pleasant and you can be sitting there knitting me a big balaclava helmet. What do you think, Effi?'

Not only were these evenings planned; they actually started and in all probability would have gone on for several weeks if the innocent, harmless Gieshübler, in spite of his great reluctance to play a double role, had none the less found himself serving two masters.

One of them was Innstetten, the other Crampas, and although he had been delighted, if only for Effi's sake, to accept the invitation to the Italian evenings with very genuine pleasure, his pleasure at obeying Crampas was even greater. Crampas had planned that a performance of *Ein Schritt vom Wege** should be given before Christmas, and just before the third Italian evening Gieshübler seized the opportunity to mention the matter to Effi, who was supposed to be taking the part of Ella.

Effi was as if galvanized. What were Padua and Vicenza in comparison! Effi was not one for *réchauffé* dishes, she liked things fresh, she wanted variety. But as if a voice had warned her to be careful, she asked, in spite of her pleasurable excitement: 'Is it the major who planned this?'

'Yes, Baroness, you know that he was unanimously elected to the entertainment committee. At last, we can look forward to a lively winter in the club. He's made for the post.'

'And is he going to take part in the acting himself?'

'No, he refused. Unfortunately, I must say. Because he's very talented and he would make an excellent Arthur von Schmettwitz. He's merely going to be the producer.'

'So much the worse.'

'So much the worse?' echoed Gieshübler.

'Oh, don't take me too seriously. It's just a way of saying the opposite, really. On the other hand, it's true that the major is a dictatorial sort of man, he likes things done in his own way, so that we'll have to act as *he* wants and not as we want to ourselves.' She went on talking, contradicting herself and becoming more and more confused.

The *Schritt vom Wege* was, in fact, performed and for the very reason that there was only a fortnight left – since the week before Christmas was impossible – everyone made a great effort and it went off very well. The actors, and above all Effi, were warmly applauded. Crampas had been content with the role of producer and however vigorous his treatment of all the others during rehearsals, he had, equally, refrained from interfering with Effi's interpretation. Either Gieshübler had informed him of the conversation he had had with her or else he noticed for himself that Effi was taking pains to avoid him. And he was clever enough and had sufficient knowledge

* Literally, 'a step off the path': 'The Slip'.

of women not to interfere with the natural course of things, which, from his experience, he knew only too well.

The drama evening at the club went on till late and it was past midnight when Effi and Innstetten reached home. Joanna had stayed up in order to be of help, and Innstetten, who was not a little vain of his young wife, told her how charming Effi had looked and how well she had acted. It was a pity that he hadn't thought of it, because Christel and herself and even the old crone, Kruse's wife, would very easily have been able to watch from the music-gallery, for there had been a lot of people there. Joanna then left and Effi, who was tired, lay down on the bed. Innstetten however, who still wanted to continue chatting, pushed a chair up to her bed and sat down beside her, affectionately taking hold of her hand.

'Yes, that was a nice evening, Effi. I found that play pleasant and entertaining. And just imagine, the author is a high-court judge, it's really hardly believable. And from Königsberg at that. But what pleased me most of all was my delightful young wife, who turned everybody's head.'

'Oh Geert, don't say that! I'm vain enough as it is.'

'Vain enough, I expect that's quite true. . . . But not half as vain as the others. And that must be added to the seven beautiful things . . .'

'Everyone has seven beautiful things.'

'That was only a slip of the tongue; you may multiply that number by itself.'

'How complimentary you're being, Geert. If I didn't know you, I should be scared. Or are you really trying to cover something up?'

'Have you got a guilty conscience? Have you been hiding behind the door yourself?'

'Oh, Geert, now I really am scared.' She sat straight up in bed and looked at him with staring eyes. 'Shall I ring for Joanna to bring us some tea? You like that before going to sleep.'

He kissed her hand. 'No, thank you, Effi. After midnight even the Kaiser can't expect a cup of tea and you know I don't like putting people out more than necessary. No, all I want to do is to look at you and feel happy that I have you. There are often times when one realizes much more strongly what a treasure one has. After all, you might be like poor Frau Crampas; what a dreadful woman she is, not liking anyone, and she would have liked to wipe you off the face of the earth.'

'Oh, please, Geert, you're just imagining things again. Poor woman! I didn't notice anything.'

'Because you don't notice that sort of thing. But that's how it was, and poor Crampas was almost at a loss because of it and kept on avoiding you and hardly looked at you. Which was completely unnatural, first of all because he's a real ladies' man – and he has a particular weakness for your sort of lady. And I'll wager that no one knows that better than my little wife herself. When I think how – forgive the expression – how you both nattered away when he used to come and see you under the veranda in the morning or when we went riding or walked along the jetty. It's as I was saying, this evening he didn't dare because he was scared of his wife. And I can't blame him. The major's wife is rather like our Frau Kruse and if I had to choose between the two, I'd find it hard to make up my mind.'

'I shouldn't, after all there is a difference between the two. Crampas's wife is unhappy, Kruse's is uncanny.'

'And so you're more inclined to stand up for unhappiness?'

'Most definitely.'

'Well, that's a matter of taste. One can see that you've never been unhappy yourself yet. Incidentally, he has a gift for eluding the poor woman. He always manages to find a reason for leaving her at home.'

'But she was there this evening.'

'Yes, this evening she was. He couldn't avoid that. But I've arranged a party with him at Ring's, the head forester's house, with him, Gieshübler, and the pastor, on the third day of the Christmas holiday and you should have seen how cleverly he proved that she ought to stay at home.'

'So it's a party for men only?'

'Heaven forbid. In that case, I shouldn't have been going either. You'll be there and two or three other ladies, apart from those from the estate itself.'

'But in that case, it's horrible of him, I mean of Crampas, and he'll suffer for it.'

'Yes, sometimes people do. But I have the feeling that Crampas is one of those who doesn't lose very much sleep over anything he does.'

'Do you think he's a bad man?'

'No, not bad. Almost the opposite; in any case, he has a good side to his nature. But he's one of these half Poles, unreliable, and not to be trusted in anything, particularly with women. A gambler. He doesn't gamble at the table, but he continually takes risks in life and he needs watching closely.'

'I'm glad that you've told me that. I shall be careful with him.'

'Yes, do that. But not too much, because it doesn't help. Being natural is always best, and of course, the best thing of all is to have character and firmness and, if I may dare use a priggish word, purity of mind.'

She looked him full in the face. Then she said: 'Yes, no doubt. But now don't say anything else – and if you do, only say things that will make me really happy! Do you know, it seems to me that I can hear that dancing upstairs. Strange how it keeps coming back. I thought that you had only been joking about all that.'

'I wouldn't say that, Effi. But be that as it may, one must behave in such a way that one doesn't need to be frightened of anything.'

Effi nodded and suddenly found herself thinking once again of Crampas's words when he referred to her husband as an 'educator'.

Christmas Eve came and went in much the same way as in the previous year: presents and letters arrived from Hohen-Cremmen; Gieshübler again produced his greetings in verse and Cousin Briest sent a card of a snowy landscape with telegraph poles and little birds perched on them. Even Annie had a tree put up for her, a lighted tree which she stretched out to reach with her tiny hands. Innstetten, relaxed and cheerful, seemed to be enjoying his domestic happiness and spent a great deal of time with his daughter. Roswitha was astonished to see his lordship so affectionate and so good-humoured at the same time. Effi, too, talked and laughed a good deal; but it did not come really from the heart. She felt depressed, without knowing exactly whom she should blame for it, Innstetten or herself. No Christmas greetings had been received from Crampas, which pleased her on the whole, and yet, on the other hand, displeased her; even though his compliments had filled her with a vague feeling of dread, when he was indifferent it put her out of humour. She realized that things were not as they ought to be.

'You're so restless,' Innstetten remarked, after a time.

'Yes. Everybody is kind to me, you most of all; and that depresses me because I feel I don't deserve it.'

'People shouldn't worry about that sort of thing, Effi. At the end of the day, people deserve exactly what they get.'

Effi had been listening closely and her guilty conscience made her ask herself whether he had deliberately used such an ambiguous phrase. Later in the afternoon, Pastor Lindequist came to proffer his greetings and also to inquire about the party to the Uvagla forest, which was naturally going to be undertaken in sleighs. He explained that Crampas had offered him a seat in his sleigh but neither Crampas nor his orderly (who was going to drive as well as do everything else) knew the way, and so it would perhaps be appropriate for them to make the journey all together, with the governor's sledge leading the way and Crampas's following. Presumably, Gieshübler's as well, because Mirambo, to whom friend Alonzo, normally so cautious, seemed unaccountably prepared to entrust himself, seemed even less likely to know the way than the befreckled Uhlan of Treptow. Innstetten, amused by this small contretemps, fell in completely with Lindequist's suggestion, and arranged that he would drive through the market place at 2 p.m. precisely and take over the piloting of the cavalcade, without further ado.

The suggestion worked out as planned, and when, punctually at two o'clock, Innstetten passed through the market place, Crampas, having first greeted Effi from his sleigh, joined in behind Innstetten's. The pastor was sitting beside him. Gieshübler's sleigh followed, with Gieshübler himself and Dr Hannemann, the former in an elegant buffalo-skin coat, with marten fur trimmings, the latter in a bear skin which, as could easily be seen, had already done duty for at least thirty years. Hannemann had, in fact, been ship's doctor on board a Greenland boat. Mirambo sat in front, somewhat perturbed by his lack of knowledge of how to drive, just as Lindequist had suspected.

Within a couple of minutes, they had passed Utpatel's mill.

Between Kessin and Uvagla, where, according to legend, there had been a Wend temple, lay a stretch of wood not more than some thousand yards wide but a good mile and a half long, the right edge of which followed the line of the sea while on the left side it abutted on a large tract of extremely fertile and well-cultivated land which stretched far away to the horizon. It was along this side that the three sleighs were now speeding; some distance away, a few old carriages could be seen, containing, in all probability, the other guests who had been invited to the chief forester's house. One of these carriages, easily recognizable by its old-fashioned high wheels, came from Papenhagen. This was natural, for Güldenklee was considered the best speaker in the province – better than Borcke and even better than Grasenabb – and he would be unlikely to miss an occasion of this sort.

The journey did not take long – the gentry's coachmen were pressing the pace in order not to be overtaken – and by three o'clock they were drawing up in front of the head forester's house. Ring, an imposing man of military demeanour in his middle fifties, who had served in the first Schleswig campaign under Wrangel and Bonin and had distinguished himself in the assault on the Danish fortifications, was standing in the doorway to greet his guests who, after removing their coats and greeting the lady of the house, sat down at a long coffee table, already laid. The head forester's wife, a naturally timid or at least very awkward woman, showed herself to be equally so as hostess, a fact which plainly annoyed her exceedingly conceited husband, who was all for self-confidence and *élan*. Fortunately, his ill-humour did not lead up to any outbursts because what his wife lacked, his daughters amply made up for: a pair of young flappers of thirteen and fourteen, both as pretty as pictures and both evidently taking after their father. Cora especially, the elder of the two, immediately started flirting with Innstetten and Crampas, and they both played up to her. Effi was annoyed by this and then was sorry because she had been annoyed. She was sitting next to Sidonie von Grasenabb and said: 'Strange, I was like that, too, when I was fourteen.'

Effi was expecting Sidonie to disagree with her remark or at least to qualify it. Instead, Sidonie retorted: 'I can well imagine.'

'And how their father spoils them!' Effi went on, half embarrassed, for want of anything else to say.

Sidonie nodded. 'That's just the point. No discipline. That's typical of our times.'

Effi gave up.

Coffee was soon over and they all stood up to go for half an hour's stroll in the surrounding wood, first to a game enclosure. Cora opened the hurdle gate and hardly were they inside than the deer came up to her. It was really charming, as in a fairy-tale. But the vanity of the young miss, well aware what a pretty picture she was making, prevented her from creating a completely ingenuous impression, least of all upon Effi. 'No,' she said to herself, 'I wasn't like that. Perhaps I did lack discipline, too, as that horrible Sidonie was just hinting, and perhaps other things as well. They were too kind to me at home, they were too fond of me. But I must say all the same that I was never affected. It was always Hulda who was that. That's why I didn't like her when I saw her again this summer.' On the way back to the forester's, it began to snow. Crampas came up to Effi to say how sorry he was that he had not yet had the opportunity of wishing her good-day. At the same time, pointing to the large, heavy flakes of snow, he added: 'If it goes on like this, we'll be snowed up.'

'There are worse things than that. Being snowed up has always had pleasant associations for me, such as protection and help.'

'Such an idea never occurred to me, Baroness.'

'Yes,' Effi went on, trying to laugh, 'one's ideas are a funny thing. They don't only come from one's own personal experience but from what one has read somewhere or learnt quite by chance, as well. You've read a lot, Major, but I think I know one poem that you don't know – it's true it's not by Heine, a "Seegespenst" or "Vitzliputzli". It's called "God's Wall" and I learned it by heart from our pastor at Hohen-Cremmen many, many years ago, when I was still very small.'

' "God's Wall",' repeated Crampas. 'A charming title. What's it about?'

'Quite a short little story. There was a war somewhere or other, a winter campaign, and an old widow who was terrified of the enemy prayed to God to build a wall round her to protect her from her country's enemies. So God saw to it that the house became covered in snow and so the enemy went by it without stopping.'

Crampas was visibly confused and changed the subject.

By dusk they were all back at the head forester's.

19

THEY sat down to dinner at just after seven and everyone was pleased to see that the Christmas tree, a fir-tree decked out with numerous silver balls, was illuminated. Crampas, who was unfamiliar with the Ring's house, was visibly impressed. The damask cloth, the wine-coolers, the wealth of silver, all created an impression of magnificence far beyond what one would normally expect of a head forester, a situation explained by the fact that Ring's wife, however shy and awkward she might appear, came from a rich Danzig corn-merchant's family. This was also where most of the pictures came from that were hanging on the walls: the corn-merchant and his wife, the Remter* at Marienburg and a good copy of the well-known Memling altar-piece in the Marienkirche at Danzig. The Oliva convent was twice represented, once in oils and once cut out of cork. In addition, over the sideboard, there was a portrait of old Nettelbeck, extremely darkened by age, that had been part of the modest furnishings of Ring's predecessor, who had only died about eighteen months before. On that occasion, nobody had wanted to buy the picture of the old man at the traditional auction, until Innstetten had bid for it, angered by this lack of respect. Then Ring had patriotically realized what was happening and so the old defender of Kolberg against the French had remained in the forester's house.

The Nettelbeck portrait left a good deal to be desired, but otherwise, as already indicated, everything revealed an affluence almost bordering on magnificence and the meal served was also appropriately splendid. All the guests found something to enjoy in it, with the exception of Sidonie. The latter was sitting between Innstetten and Lindequist and as soon as she saw Cora, she said: 'There she is again, that unbearable little brat Cora. Just look how she's offering those small wine glasses, Innstetten, it's a real work of art, she could become a waitress on the spot. Quite revolting. And look at the way your friend Crampas is looking at her. That's a fine younger generation for you. I wonder what will become of it.'

* The dining-hall of the High Master of the Teutonic Order in East Prussia.

Innstetten really agreed with her, yet he found the tone in which she spoke so harsh and offensive that he ironically replied : 'Yes, my dear lady, what will become of it? I don't know either.' Whereupon Sidonie turned away from him towards her left-hand neighbour : 'Tell me, pastor, is this fourteen-year-old little flirt already being taught by you?'

'Yes, Fräulein Sidonie.'

'Then you must forgive me if I remark that you haven't been teaching her properly. I'm well aware that it's very difficult nowadays, but I know, too, that those who have charge of these young minds often lack proper conviction. The fact remains that parents and teachers bear the main responsibility.'

Adopting the same tone as Innstetten, Lindequist replied that that was all very well, but the spirit of the times was too powerful.

'The spirit of the times!' said Sidonie. 'Don't try that on me. I can't bear to hear that sort of thing, it's an expression of the sheerest weakness, an admission of bankruptcy. I know that kind of thing; never take the bull by the horns; always try to avoid anything unpleasant. Duty is unpleasant and so it's all too easily forgotten that what has been entrusted to us must sometimes be accounted for in return. One must intervene, my dear pastor, use discipline. The flesh is weak, I know, but . . .'

At this moment, some English roast beef was brought in and Sidonie gave herself a generous portion without noticing Lindequist's smile. And not having noticed it, it was not surprising that she went on completely unembarrassed : 'In any case, all that we're seeing here today could hardly be expected to be different; everything is twisted and misguided at its very source. Ring, Ring – if I'm not mistaken, over in Sweden or thereabouts, there was a legendary king of that name. Well, you can see, isn't he behaving as if he were descended from him, and yet his mother, when I knew her, took in ironing in Köslin!'

'I can't see any harm in that!'

'Harm? Neither can I. And in any case, there are far worse things. But as you're an ordained servant of the church, I must remind you of this much, that you should respect the social order. A head forester is not much more than a forester and a forester doesn't have wine-coolers like these and silver like this; it's all not right and that leads to girls growing up like this Fräulein Cora!'

Sidonie, always ready to make dreadful prophecies when she was pouring out the phials of her wrath, was now preparing to project her Cassandra-like gaze into the future as well, but the steaming punch-bowl, the usual conclusion to Ring's Christmas parties, was placed on the table at that moment – as well as fancy pastries, skilfully piled up in a way that far outshone the pyramid of cakes that had appeared a few hours earlier with the coffee. And now Ring himself, who had hitherto remained somewhat in the background, went into action, beaming yet solemn, as he began to fill the glasses standing in front of those present, large cut-glass rummers, into which, with artistic brio, he poured the punch in a flowing curve, which the ever-witty Frau von Padden, unfortunately not present on this occasion, had once described as *Ring's cascade*. The golden-red stream had to curve and fall without a drop being lost; and so it did today.

Finally, however, when everyone had received his drink – including even Cora of the auburn hair, who had meanwhile found a seat on 'Uncle Crampas's' knee – the old Baron von Güldenklee, from Papenhagen, rose to give the traditional toast of his excellent head forester.

'There are all sorts of rings,' such were, roughly, his opening words: 'Annual, curtain, wedding and as for engagement rings – because, lastly, mention should, no doubt, be made of those – and fortunately the guarantee has been given that one of them will very shortly make its appearance in this house and adorn the ring finger – in the double sense of the word – of a pretty little danny. . . .'

'Incredible,' Sidonie whispered to the pastor.

'Yes, my friends,' Güldenklee continued, raising his voice, 'there are many kinds of rings and there is even a story which we all know, called the "three rings",* something to do with Jews, which, like all the rest of the liberal twaddle, has brought and will continue to bring nothing but confusion and calamity. May God bring enlightenment. And now, in order not to strain your patience and consideration unreasonably, let me conclude. I am not for those three rings, my dear friends, I am much more in favour of one Ring, who is just the sort of Ring he should be, a Ring who can see gathered round his hospitable festive board all those of our old province of Pomerania who stand for what is good, all those who stand for God,

* From Lessing's *Nathan der Weise*.

King and Fatherland – and there are still some of us like that. (Loud applause.) That's the Ring that I support. I give you his health!'

Everyone joined in the toast and thronged round Ring, who was momentarily forced to relinquish his office as wine-pourer *en cascade* to Crampas, sitting opposite; however, the tutor hurried from his seat at the bottom end of the table and went to the piano to strike up the first chords of the Prussian national anthem, while everyone stood up and joined in: 'I am a Prussian . . . and Prussian will remain.'

'It really is splendid,' old Borcke said to Innstetten, as soon as the first verse had been sung, 'they don't have things like that in other countries.'

'No,' replied Innstetten, who was not very fond of this sort of patriotism. 'In other countries they have something else.'

They sang all the verses and then they were informed that the carriages were ready. Thereupon, the company rose, in order not to keep the horses waiting. This concern for 'the horses' took precedence over everything else even in the district of Kessin. In the hall there were two pretty maids (Ring attached importance to such things) to help the company on with their furs. Everyone was pleasantly stimulated, some more than others, and all seemed about to climb into their various vehicles without further ado when suddenly it became apparent that Gieshübler's sleigh was not there. Gieshübler was far too well mannered to show any disquiet or make any fuss at first but finally, since someone had to say something, Crampas asked what the matter was.

'Mirambo can't drive,' said the groom. 'The left horse kicked him on the shin while it was being harnessed. He's lying bawling in the stable.'

Dr Hannemann was naturally summoned and he went out, to return five minutes later and report with the sang-froid of the true surgeon: 'Yes, Mirambo mustn't go. There's nothing that can be done for the moment but lie still and apply cold compresses. In any case, there's no question of anything serious.' This was some consolation, but failed to remove the difficulty as to how Gieshübler's sleigh would manage to return home, until Innstetten announced that he would stand in for Mirambo and would personally pilot the twin stars of the doctor and chemist safely home. The suggestion was accepted with laughter and a certain amount of somewhat tipsy joking at the expense of this most obliging of governors who, in order to be of service, was even prepared to part from his young wife; then Innstetten, with Gieshübler and the doctor sitting at the back, once more led the way. Crampas and Lindequist followed at once. And then, as Kruse drove up immediately afterwards with the governor's sleigh, Sidonie came over to Effi and, with a smile, asked her, since she now had a seat free, whether she might travel with her. 'Our carriage is always so stuffy, my father likes it like that. And I'd so much like to chat with you, too. But only as far as Quappendorf. I'll get out where the path branches off to Morgnitz and then I'll have to get in our uncomfortable old crock. And papa smokes, too.'

Effi was not very pleased at the offer of such company and would sooner have travelled alone; but she had no choice, so Sidonie climbed in, and hardly had the two ladies taken their seats than Kruse gave the horses a flick of the whip and they moved down the raised drive of the forester's lodge over the somewhat steep dune on to the track beside the sea which ran in almost a straight line for a mile as far as the beach hotel, where it turned right and led into the town through the plantation. The snow had stopped falling some hours ago, the air was fresh and the crescent moon cast its even glow over the broad, darkening sea. Kruse drove close beside the sea, occasionally even through the spray from the breakers, and Effi, who was rather chilly, wrapped herself up more tightly in her cloak and continued, deliberately, to say not a word. She knew very well that the story about the 'stuffy carriage' was merely a pretext and that Sidonie had only come into her sleigh in order to say something unpleasant. And that would come soon enough. In addition, she was really tired, perhaps because of her walk through the woods, perhaps also because of the head forester's punch, to which, encouraged by her neighbour, Frau von Flemming, she had done ample justice. So, pretending to be asleep, she shut her eyes and let her head droop more and more over to the left.

'You oughtn't to lean so far over to the left, my dear Baroness. If the sleigh hits a rock, you'll be tipped out. Your sleigh hasn't got any safety straps, anyway, and not even any hooks for them that I can see!'

'I can't bear safety straps, they're so tedious. And then, if I were to tip out, I shouldn't mind, especially if I went straight into the

146

surf. Rather like a cold bath, of course, but what does it matter. . . .
By the way, can't you hear anything?'

'No.'

'Can't you hear something like music?'

'Organ music?'

'No, not organ music. In that case, I should think it would be the
sea. But it's something else, an extremely delicate sound, almost like
a human voice.'

'It's a hallucination,' said Sidonie, who thought that her moment
had come to attack. 'You must be suffering from nerves. You're
hearing voices. I hope to goodness that they're the right voices.'

'I can hear . . . well, of course, it's stupid, I know, but I almost
imagined that I could hear mermaids singing. . . . But, look, what's
that? There's lightning flashing right up to the sky. It must be the
northern lights.'

'Yes,' replied Sidonie. 'You almost seem to think it's a miracle.
It isn't, you know. And even if it were something of the sort, we
must be careful not to become nature worshippers. And incidentally,
how lucky we are that we're not in any danger of having to listen to
our friend the head forester, the vainest of mortals, on the subject of
those northern lights. I wager that he'd imagine that heaven was
doing it to please him and make his party all the grander. He's a fool.
Güldenklee had something better to do than propose his health.
And he pretends to be a church supporter, too. He's just recently
given an altar cloth. Perhaps Cora even helped stitch part of it. It's
frauds like that who are responsible for everything, because their
worldliness is always so obvious and then it's attributed to people
who really *are* concerned with saving their souls!'

'It's so difficult to see into anyone's heart!'

'Yes, that's so. But with many people it's quite easy.' As she
said this she looked at Effi with an insistence that was almost
offensive.

Effi said nothing and turned impatiently away.

'As I was saying, with many people it's quite easy,' repeated
Sidonie and having achieved her aim, she now went on with a
smile: 'And our head forester is one of these easy enigmas. Someone who brings up his children like that is to be pitied, but it has
one advantage – that it's obvious. And it's the same for his daughters as for him. Cora is going to America to become a millionairess

or a Methodist preacher, but whatever happens she's doomed. I've never seen a fourteen-year-old girl . . .'

At that moment the sleigh pulled up and as the two women looked around to discover what was the matter, they noticed that on their right, some thirty yards away, the other sleighs were also halted, the one driven by Innstetten on the far side and Crampas's somewhat nearer.

'What's the matter?' asked Effi.

Kruse half turned and said: 'It's the Slough, m'lady.'

'The Slough? What's that? I can't see anything.'

Kruse was wagging his head to and fro, as if trying to say that it was a question easier to ask than to answer. In which he was quite right, because it would take more than three words to describe what the Slough really was. But Kruse immediately received help in his embarrassment from Fräulein Sidonie, who knew all about everything in that part of the world and, naturally enough, all about the Slough, too.

'Yes, Baroness,' said Sidonie, 'it's a tricky thing. It doesn't matter much to me, I can get through comfortably, because when carriages are being used, they've got high wheels and also our horses are used to it. But with these sleighs, it's another matter, they get bogged down and so, for better or worse, you're going to have to find a way round.'

'Bogged down! I'm afraid I still don't quite see. Is this slough an abyss or something which always brings death and destruction to everybody? I can't imagine anything like that around here.'

'All the same, it is something rather like that, only in miniature, of course. This slough is really just a miserable little ditch, which flows down here on the right from Lake Gothen and seeps through the dunes. In summer, it occasionally dries out completely, and then you can easily drive over it without trouble and you don't even know you've done so.'

'And in winter?'

'Well, in winter, it's quite different, not always, but often. Then it turns into a sough.'

'Good God, what extraordinary words and names they have round here.'

'It turns into a sough and especially when there's a wind off the sea. Then the wind forces the sea up the ditch but not so that it can be seen. And that's the worst thing about it and the real danger. It all happens underground and the sand on the beach becomes soaked and filled with water to quite a depth. And then if you try to get over on top of a patch of sand like that, which isn't really sand at all any more, then you sink in as if it were a swamp or bog.'

'I've met that before,' retorted Effi quickly, 'it's like our Luch,' and amidst all her anxiety, she suddenly felt quite sad yet happy at the same time.

While this conversation was going on, Crampas had got out of his sleigh and walked across to Gieshübler's, which was some distance away, to discuss with Innstetten what ought to be done. He reported that, although Knut was ready to risk driving across, Knut was stupid and didn't realize what the position was; only those who knew these parts well ought to take the decision. Greatly to Crampas's surprise, Innstetten was also for risking it. Someone ought to make one more attempt; he knew that there was always this fuss; people were superstitious around here and afraid before they tried, while there was really nothing to it; but Knut didn't know the ropes and so he thought that Kruse should try a run at it and meanwhile Crampas could get in with the ladies (there was a small back-seat still free) so that he would be available if the sleigh overturned. That would really be the worst that could happen.

Crampas took Innstetten's message over to the two ladies and having fulfilled this mission with a laugh, he obeyed his instructions by taking the small back-seat, which was really nothing but a ledge covered by a piece of material; and then called to Kruse: 'Go on, then, Kruse!'

The latter had already reined the horses back some hundred yards in the hope that by taking a quick run, he might be able to get the sleigh across, but hardly had the horses even touched the Slough than they sank into the sand above their fetlocks so that it was only with difficulty that they could be backed out.

'It's no good,' said Crampas, and Kruse nodded his agreement.

While all this was taking place, the carriages had finally caught up, the Grasenabbs' in the lead, and when Sidonie had left Effi with a brief word of thanks and taken her seat in the back, opposite her father with his Turkish pipe, they set off towards the Slough without further ado. The horses sank in quite deeply but the wheels easily prevented any danger, and within half a minute the Grasenabbs were already trotting on their way home. The other carriages followed. Effi looked after them with a certain envy, but not for long, for meanwhile the sleigh drivers had also taken counsel by Innstetten's simple decision not to make any further attempt to force their way across but merely to adopt the more peaceful expedient of making a detour; in fact, by doing exactly what Sidonie had suggested from the very beginning. From the right, the governor's incisive voice could be heard directing them to remain on the side that they were for the moment and follow him through the dunes until they reached a plank bridge higher up.

When the two coachmen had understood, the major, who had got out at the same time as Sidonie in order to help her, came up to Effi again and said:

'I can't leave you all alone, Baroness.'

Effi hesitated for a moment and then quickly moved over to the other side and Crampas sat down beside her on her left.

All this might have been misinterpreted; but Crampas himself knew too much about women to explain it in a way flattering to his vanity. He could clearly see that Effi was merely doing the only possible thing in the circumstances. She could not possibly refuse his company. And so they flew along behind the two other sleighs, keeping close to the stream, on the far side of which rose dark banks of wood. Effi looked across and assumed that they would eventually be making their way along the inland edge of the wood, that is, on exactly the same path that they had followed earlier that afternoon. But Innstetten had meanwhile changed his plan and immediately his sleigh had crossed the plank bridge, instead of following the path along the edge of the wood, he swung into a narrower track that led right through the dense mass of wood. Effi was startled. Till now, there had been light and air around her but now the gloomy vault of the tree-tops cut them off. She was seized by a trembling and she locked her fingers hard together to take a grip on herself. Ideas and images swirled through her mind and one of these images was of the little old woman in the poem 'God's Wall', and like the little old woman, she prayed to God to build a wall around her. Two or three times her lips uttered the words, but all of a sudden she realized that they were dead, meaningless words. She was afraid yet, at the same time, as if under a spell from which she did not want to be released.

'Effi.' She heard the soft whisper in her ear, in a voice that trembled. Then he took her hand and untwined her fingers which she was still holding locked together and covered them with passionate kisses. She felt as if she would faint.

When she opened her eyes again, they were out of the wood and a short distance ahead they could hear the sound of the bells of the fast-moving sleighs in front. It became louder and louder and when, just short of Utpatel's mill, they left the dunes and turned off towards the town, the tiny houses with their snow-covered roofs could be seen beside them.

Effi looked around and a moment later the sleigh pulled up in front of the governor's house.

20

As Innstetten helped her out of the sleigh, he had looked closely at Effi but avoided any reference to the strange journey that she had made with her companion; and next morning, having risen early, he tried as far as possible to restrain himself, even though his ill-humour still persisted.

'Did you sleep well?' he asked when Effi came in to breakfast.

'Yes.'

'You're fortunate. I can't say the same for myself. I dreamt that you'd had an accident with the sledge in the Slough and Crampas was making every effort to save you and then sank down with you.'

'You sound so strange as you say that, Geert. There's a hidden reproach beneath it all and I can sense what it is.'

'How remarkable.'

'Don't you like it because Crampas came and offered us his help?'

'Us?'

'Yes, us. Sidonie and me. You must have completely forgotten that the major came with a message from you. And when he had to sit opposite me for a moment, unpleasantly enough on that wretched narrow ledge, am I supposed to have turned him out when the Grasenabbs came and everyone suddenly set off again? I should have made myself ridiculous, and that's something you're very sensitive about. Remember that with your agreement we've often been out riding together. And now you say I oughtn't to have gone driving with him. At home we used to say that it was very wrong to distrust a gentleman.'

'A gentleman,' repeated Innstetten with emphasis.

'Isn't he one? You said yourself that he was gallant, you even said he was the perfect gallant.'

'Yes,' Innstetten went on, in a friendlier tone of voice. 'Gallant, that he is, and the perfect gallant, he quite certainly is. But a gentleman! My dear Effi, a gentleman is something quite different. Have you ever noticed anything gentlemanly about him? I haven't.'

Effi looked straight in front of her and said nothing.

'It seems we're of the same opinion. Incidentally, as you have already pointed out, I'm to blame. I won't use the word *faux pas*, because it's hardly the appropriate word in these circumstances. But I myself am to blame and it won't happen again, if I can prevent it. But if I may give you some advice, be on your guard, too. He's an unscrupulous man and he has certain views on young women.'

'I'll accept what you say. Only one thing. I think you do him an injustice.'

'I'm not doing him an injustice.'

'Me then,' she said, steeling herself with an effort and attempting to look him in the eyes.

'Not you either, my dear Effi. You're a delightful young woman but firmness is not exactly your strong point.'

He got up to go. As he reached the door, Frederick came in to bring a letter from Gieshübler, addressed, naturally, to the baroness.

Effi took it. 'A clandestine correspondence with Gieshübler,' she said. 'More fuel for my worshipful master's jealousy. Or not?'

'No, not really, my dear Effi. I'm stupid enough to make a difference between Crampas and Gieshübler. They don't really have the same number of carats; the purity of gold is assessed by its carats and in certain circumstances, human beings too. Speaking personally, to avoid any misunderstanding, I like Gieshübler's frilly shirts considerably more than Crampas's sapper's whiskers. But I doubt if a woman would feel the same.'

'You think us weaker than we really are.'

'An extraordinarily small comfort! But let's not pursue it. Read your letter instead.'

Effi read: 'May I inquire as to your ladyship's health? I only know that you made a successful escape from the Slough, but there still remained perils enough going through the wood. Dr Hannemann has just come back from Uvagla with reassuring news about Mirambo. Yesterday, he thought the matter was more serious than he wished to tell us, today he no longer thinks so. It was a delightful trip. ... In three days' time we shall be celebrating New Year's Eve. While unable to have the sort of celebration that we had last year, we shall, of course, be having a dance and your presence there would delight all those with interest in such things, not least, Your respectfully devoted, Alonzo G.'

Effi laughed. 'Well, how about it?'

'Merely the same comment as always: I'd sooner see you with Gieshübler than Crampas.'

'Because you take Crampas too seriously and Gieshübler too lightly.'

Jokingly, Innstetten wagged a threatening finger at her.

Three days later, it was New Year's Eve. Effi wore a charming ball-gown, a Christmas present, but did not dance and took her seat amongst the older ladies, who had been provided with arm-chairs close by the music gallery.

None of the gentry whom Innstetten preferred to frequent were present, as the result of a small difference between them and the municipal club which had, as on previous occasions, been accused of 'subversive tendencies', notably by old Güldenklee. However, two or three other noble families, whose estates lay on the other side of the Kessine and who were not members of the club but were al-ways invited purely as guests, had come over the frozen river, some of them from a considerable distance, and were delighted to be taking part in the dance. Effi was sitting between the elderly wife of the councillor von Padden and the somewhat younger Frau von Titzewitz. The councillor's wife, an exquisite old lady, was a thorough-going eccentric and used to try to compensate for all the heathen and Slavonic disposition of her nature, especially notice-able in the formation of her cheek-bones, by the Christo-Germanic rigour of her beliefs. Her efforts in this direction had gone so far that even Sidonie von Grasenabb appeared a sort of *esprit fort* in comparison, whilst on the other hand she possessed that traditional humour of the Padden's with which that family had long been blessed and which delighted everyone who came into contact with her, even her political and ecclesiastical opponents.

'Now, my child,' said the councillor's wife, 'how are you then, in fact?'

'I'm well, Frau von Padden. I have a very fine man as my husband.'

'I know. But that doesn't always help. I used to have one, too! How are things with you? Any troubles?'

Effi was startled and, at the same time, rather touched. There was something uncommonly refreshing in the old lady's free and easy way of speaking and the fact that she was such a pious old lady made it all the more refreshing.

'Well . . .'

'Here it comes . . . . I can recognize it. It's always the same thing. Times don't change. And perhaps it's good that it is like that. Because the crux of the matter, my dear young woman, is the struggle. You must always wrestle with nature. And then, when you have got it down so that you would almost like to scream, the angels in heaven will rejoice!'

'Oh dear, Frau von Padden. It's often very hard.'

'Indeed it is. But the harder, the better. You must be glad that it's like that. The flesh is always with us and I see it every day. I've got grandsons and granddaughters. But to get the better of yourself in your faith, my dear, that's the crux of the matter, that is where the truth lies. Our old Martin Luther, that man of God, has made us recognize that. Do you know his table-talk?'

'No.'

'I'll send you it.'

At that moment, Major Crampas approached Effi to ask if he might take the liberty to inquire after her health. Effi blushed to the roots of her hair, but before she could reply, Crampas said: 'May I ask you, your ladyship, to be good enough to introduce me to the ladies?'

Effi said: 'Major Crampas!' He, for his part, was already completely *au fait*, and in his free and easy manner proceeded to enumerate all the Paddens and the Titzewitzes whom he had ever heard of. At the same time, he made his excuses for not yet having paid his calls on those living on the other side of the Kessine in order to present his wife; it was extraordinary the power that water had to keep people apart. 'It was just like the Channel, *la Manche. . . .*'

'What's that?' asked old Frau Titzewitz. Crampas thought it was inappropriate to give explanations that would, in any case, have led nowhere and so he went on: 'For twenty Germans who go to France, there's not one who goes to England. It's the result of the water, as I was saying, water has the power to separate people.'

Frau von Padden instinctively sensed something offensive, and was preparing to leap to the defence of water, but Crampas continued to speak with increasing eloquence, drawing the attention of the ladies to the lovely Fräulein von Stojentin, who, without doubt, was the queen of the ball, while saying which he none the less ran his eye admiringly over Effi. Then, quickly bowing to all three ladies, he took his leave.

'Handsome man,' said Frau von Padden. 'Do you see very much of him in your house?'

'Very little.'

'Really,' repeated the councillor's wife, 'a handsome man. Rather too sure of himself. And pride comes before a fall. . . . But just look, he's actually starting the dance with Grete Stojentin. He's really rather too old, at least in his mid-forties.'

'He's rising forty-four.'

'Well, well, you seem to know him quite well.'

At the very beginning of the New Year there were all sorts of distractions and this suited Effi very well. Since New Year's Eve, a sharp north-easterly wind had been blowing which increased almost to a gale in the following days, and on the afternoon of 3rd January news came that a ship had failed to make the entrance to the harbour and had been wrecked a hundred yards from the pier. It was said to be an English ship, from Sunderland, and as far as could be judged had seven men on board. In spite of all their efforts, the pilots could not pass round the jetty to get out of the harbour and it was quite unthinkable to try to launch a boat from the beach because of the breakers. This seemed sad enough. But Joanna, who brought the news, also provided some comfort: Consul Eschrich was on his way with his rescue-tackle and rocket-battery and he would certainly be successful; the distance was not as great as in '75 when it had succeeded, too, and they had even managed to rescue the poodle and it had been really touching to see how glad the dog had been and how it kept on licking the captain's wife and dear little girl, not much bigger than 'wee Annie', with its red tongue.

'Geert, I must come along with you, I can't miss that,' Effi said immediately, and the pair of them had set off in order not to be too late. They had chosen exactly the right moment, for as they came out of the plantation on to the beach, the first shot had just been fired and they could see quite plainly how the rocket, with the line attached, shot up below the storm clouds and fell beyond the ship. All hands on the ship set to at once and, with the help of the line, pulled in the thicker cable with the basket, and it was not long before the basket was coming back in a sort of curve and one of the sailors, a slim and extremely good-looking man wearing an oil-cloth, was safe on land and being eagerly interrogated, while the basket set off back once more, to fetch the second sailor, then the third and so on. They were all saved and as Effi went back home with her husband a half an hour later she felt like throwing herself down on the sands and crying her eyes out. A happy feeling had found its way into her heart again and great was her delight at such a feeling.

That was on the 3rd. Only two days later, on the 5th, there came a new excitement, although of quite a different kind. As he was coming out of the Guildhall, Gieshübler, who was of course a town councillor and magistrate, had met Innstetten and told him in conversation that the War Ministry had inquired how the town authorities would view the possibility of becoming a garrison-town. If they offered the necessary cooperation, that is, were willing to construct stables and barracks, they would be allotted two squadrons of Hussars. 'Well, Effi, what do you say to that?'

Effi's head swam. All the innocent happiness of her childhood suddenly came back to her, and for the moment it seemed to her as if the Red Hussars – because they would be Red Hussars, like those at home in Hohen-Cremmen – were really the guardians of paradise and innocence. But she was unable to say anything.

'You haven't replied, Effi.'

'Yes, it's wonderful, Geert. But it makes me so happy that I couldn't speak for joy. Will anything come of it? Will they be coming?'

'I think there's quite a way to go before that happens, in fact, Gieshübler was even saying that his colleagues, the city-fathers, didn't deserve it. Instead of just agreeing and being pleased about the honour or, if not the honour, at least the advantages of such a step, they were full of 'ifs' and 'buts' and very suspicious about the expense of the new buildings; the ginger-bread man Michelsen even said that it would ruin the town's morals and that everyone with a daughter would have to keep an eye open and put bars on all the windows.

'It's unbelievable. I've never seen better behaved men than our Hussars; really, Geert. Well, you know it yourself. And now this man Michelsen wants to put everybody behind bars. Has he got any daughters?'

'Yes indeed, three of them. But they're all *hors concours*!'

Effi laughed more heartily than she had laughed for a long time. But it did not last and when Innstetten had gone away and left her alone, she sat down beside her baby's cradle and her tears fell on the pillows. She felt like a prisoner, unable to escape.

This made her very unhappy and she would have liked to find some release. But although she was capable of strong feelings, she was not a strong character, she lacked endurance and all her good impulses came to naught. And so, she drifted on, one day because she felt unable to change anything, the next because she didn't want to. She was strongly affected by all that was mysterious and forbidden and so it came about that, though free and open by nature, she became involved more and more in a life of deception. Sometimes she was shocked to realize how easy she found it. In one respect only she remained true to herself: she saw everything clearly and made no excuses. On one occasion in her bedroom, late at night, she looked at herself in the mirror; the light and shadows were flickering and Rollo started barking outside, and at that same moment she felt that someone was looking over her shoulder. But she quickly pulled herself together: 'I know what it is, it wasn't *him*' – she pointed her finger towards the room upstairs – 'it was something else . . . my conscience . . . Effi, you're a lost woman.' But things took their course, the ball had been set rolling and the events of one day led inevitably on to the actions of the next.

Around the middle of the month, invitations arrived from families living in the surrounding districts. Four of the families which Innstetten particularly enjoyed visiting had agreed amongst themselves to issue invitations in succession. First the Borckes, then the

Flemmings and Grasenabbs and finally the Güldenklees. All with a week in between. As all four invitations arrived on the same day, they were obviously intended to create the impression of being methodical and carefully considered as well as showing particular friendliness and solidarity.

'I shan't be able to go, Geert. You must make my excuses straightaway on the grounds of the cure that I've been following all these weeks.'

Innstetten laughed. 'Cure. I've got to blame it on your cure. It's just a pretext; the truth is, you don't want to go!'

'No, I'm more honest than you're prepared to admit. You yourself insisted that I should consult the doctor. I did so and now I must follow his advice. The old chap thinks I'm anaemic, strangely enough, and you know that I drink some water with iron in it every day. If you imagine one of Borcke's dinners on top of that, with perhaps galantine and jellied eels, you must realize that it would be the death of me. And you wouldn't want to treat your Effi like that. It's true that sometimes I . . .'

'Please, Effi.'

'Incidentally, and that's the only pleasant thing about it, I do enjoy going some of the way with you every time you go off, certainly as far as the mill or the churchyard or up to the edge of the wood where the side-track from Morgnitz meets it. And then I'll get out and stroll back again. It's always nicest in the dunes.'

Innstetten agreed and when the carriage drove up three days later, Effi climbed in and accompanied her husband as far as the corner of the wood.

'Let me off here, Geert. Now you can go off to the left and I'll go on down to the beach and back through the plantation. Dr Hannemann keeps telling me every day that exercise is all-important. Exercise and fresh air. And I almost think he's right. Give my regards to everybody, but you don't need to say anything to Sidonie.'

The trips that Effi made in accompanying her husband as far as the corner of the wood took place once a week, but Effi saw to it that she followed the doctor's instructions in the intervening period as well. Not a day passed without her taking the prescribed walk, mainly in the afternoons, when Innstetten was starting to become engrossed in his newspapers. The weather was fine and mild,

with a hazy sky. As a rule, she would go alone and say to Roswitha:
'Roswitha, now I'm going down the main road as far as the square
where the merry-go-round is and I'll wait for you, so come and pick
me up there. And then we'll come back through the birch avenue
or the Reeperbahn. But don't come until Annie is asleep. If she won't
go to sleep, send Joanna. Or better still, don't worry; it's not
necessary; I'll be all right.'

The first day when they had made this arrangement, they did, in
fact, meet. Effi was sitting on a bench which ran alongside a long
wooden shed and was looking over towards a low frame-house,
yellow with black-painted beams, a modest inn where the locals
would come and drink a glass of beer or play a hand of whist. It
was barely beginning to be dusk but the windows were already lit
up and their light shone on to the heaped-up snow and a few trees
at one side. 'How lovely that looks, Roswitha.' This happened on
a few days. Generally, however, when Roswitha reached the merry-
go-round and the wooden shed, there was nobody there and when
she went back home and into the hall, Effi would come and meet
her and say: 'Where have you been, Roswitha, I got back a long
time ago?'

Some weeks passed in this way. The question of the Hussars
was as good as dropped, because of the difficulties raised by the
town-council; but since the negotiations had not quite come to an
end and had recently been conducted through a new authority, the
General Staff, Crampas had been called to Stettin to give his opinion
on the matter. The day after his arrival, he wrote to Innstetten:
'Forgive me for having taken French leave, Innstetten. Everything
happened so quickly. Incidentally, I'm going to try to spin out the
matter, because one's glad to have got away for a while. Please give
my regards to your charming wife and patroness!'

He read it to Effi. She remained still. Finally she said: 'It's a very
good thing.'

'How do you mean?'

'That he has gone away. He kept saying the same thing, really.
When he comes back at least he'll have something new to talk
about for a while.'

Innstetten looked her sharply up and down. But he could see
nothing and his suspicion subsided once more. 'I have to go away,
too,' he said after a pause, 'all the way to Berlin, in fact. Perhaps I

can bring something back too, like Crampas. My dear Effi always likes to hear something new; she's bored in our dear old Kessin. I'll be away about a week, perhaps one day longer. And don't be afraid ... he surely won't come back ... you know very well, that person up there ... And even if – after all, you've got Rollo and Roswitha.'

Effi smiled to herself and her smile was not without a certain melancholy. She was remembering the day when Crampas had first said to her that Innstetten was pretending about the ghost and about scaring her. The great educator! But wasn't he right? Was this little comedy really not appropriate?

And all kinds of conflicting thoughts, good and bad, went through her mind.

Three days later Innstetten left.

He said nothing concerning his intentions in Berlin.

21

INNSTETTEN had been away only three days when Crampas arrived back from Stettin with the information that the higher authorities had finally abandoned their intention of transferring two squadrons to Kessin; there were so many small towns competing for a cavalry garrison, and above all for Blücher's Hussars, that it was customary for such an offer to be greeted eagerly, not hesitatingly. When Crampas announced this, the town-council pulled a rather wry face; only Gieshübler was triumphant at seeing his colleagues' narrow-mindedness confounded.

When the news became known, some of the ordinary inhabitants of Kessin were somewhat upset and even some of the consuls (those with daughters) were momentarily displeased; in general, however, Kessin quickly got over the matter, perhaps because it – or at least its notables – were more interested in 'what Innstetten was up to in Berlin'. The latter were not keen on losing their universally popular governor and yet there were various rumours about it which, if not invented, were at least nurtured and widely disseminated by Gieshübler. Amongst other things, it was said that Innstetten was going to head a mission to Morocco, with gifts that not only included the traditional urn with Sans Souci and the New Palace but, above all, a big ice machine. In view of the Moroccan climate, this last seemed so probable that it induced people to accept the whole thing.

Effi heard the news, too. It was not so very long ago since she would have been delighted, but since the end of the year she felt little inclined to laugh freely and openly about such things. Her features now had quite a different expression and she had lost the half touching, half roguish, childlike quality which had been hers even after her marriage. While Crampas was in Stettin she had given up her walks to the beach and the plantation but now that he was back she started them again, undeterred by any unpleasant weather. As before, it was arranged that Roswitha should come to meet her at the end of the Reeperbahn or near the cemetery; but they used to miss each other even more frequently than before. 'I feel rather cross with you, Roswitha, because you can never find me. But it's not important; I'm not scared any more, even in the churchyard, and I've never yet met a soul in the wood.'

Effi said this the day before Innstetten's return from Berlin. Roswitha did not pay much attention, but instead busied herself with hanging garlands over the door; even the shark was given a fir-branch and looked more remarkable than ever. Effi said: 'That's right, Roswitha, he'll enjoy seeing all that greenery when he comes home tomorrow. Shall I go today, after all? Dr Hannemann is very insistent and keeps on saying that I'm not taking it seriously enough, otherwise I'd be looking better; but I don't really feel like it today, it's drizzling and the sky's so dull.'

'I'll bring your ladyship her raincoat.'

'Do that. But don't come for me today, I'm sure we wouldn't meet anyway!' She laughed. 'Really, Roswitha, you're not much good. And I don't like you catching a cold all for nothing.'

So Roswitha stayed at home, and as Annie was asleep she went to have a talk with Frau Kruse. 'Dear Frau Kruse,' she said. 'You were going to tell me some more about the Chinaman. Joanna stopped you from doing it yesterday, she's so stuck-up that she doesn't like that sort of thing. But I still reckon that there was something. I mean between the Chinaman and Thomsen's niece, unless it was his granddaughter.'

Frau Kruse nodded. 'Either,' Roswitha continued, 'it was an unhappy love affair' – Kruse's wife nodded again – 'or else it might have been a happy one and the Chinaman couldn't bear the thought that everything was going to come to an end all at once. Because the Chinese are human beings like us and I imagine everything is the same for them as it is for us.'

'Everything,' Frau Kruse assured her and was just about to prove it with her story when her husband came in and said: 'Mother, could you give me the bottle of leather polish? I must polish up the harness for when the master comes back tomorrow. He doesn't miss a thing and even if he doesn't say anything, you can see that he's noticed it.'

'I'll bring it out to you, Kruse,' said Roswitha. 'Your wife just wants to tell me something, but it won't take a minute and then I'll come and bring it.'

So a few minutes later Roswitha came out into the yard with the bottle of varnish in her hand and stood beside the harness which Kruse had just hung over the garden fence. 'It's not going to help much, dammit,' he said taking the bottle out of her hand, 'it's drizzling away and the polish won't last. But I suppose everything's got to be done proper-like.'

'So it must. And anyway it's real varnish, too, Kruse, I can see that straightaway, and real varnish doesn't stay sticky for long, it should dry off at once. And if it's foggy or damp next day, it doesn't matter any more. But I must say that that story about the Chinaman is very queer.'

Kruse laughed. 'It's a lot of nonsense, Roswitha. And my wife talks like that instead of looking after things, and when I want to put a clean shirt on there's a button missing. And that's how it's been ever since we've been here. Her head's full of nothing but stories and then there's the black hen as well. And the black hen doesn't even lay eggs. And why should it, after all, it never gets out and you can't get that sort of thing from just a cock-a-doodle-do. You can't expect that from no hen.'

'Now look you here, Kruse, I'll tell your wife about this. I always thought you were a decent sort of man and now you're talking about that business of a cock-a-doodle-do. Men are always worse than you think. And I really ought to take this here brush and paint you a black moustache.'

'Well now, from someone like you, I wouldn't mind.' Kruse, who was usually very much on his dignity, seemed to be just about to become even more playful when he suddenly caught sight of his

mistress, who today had come up from the other side of the plantation and was passing by the garden fence just at this moment.

'Good afternoon, Roswitha! You sound so cheerful! What's
Annie doing?'

'She's asleep, m'lady.'

But as she said this, Roswitha went red and quickly taking her
leave went towards the house to help her mistress change her
clothes. Because it was questionable whether Joanna was there. She
spent a lot of time over at the 'office' now that there was much less
to do in the house and she found Frederick and Christel too boring
and uninteresting.

Annie was still asleep. Effi leant over the cradle and then handed
Roswitha her hat and raincoat before sitting down on the small
sofa in her bedroom. She smoothed her damp hair slowly back off
her forehead, placed her feet on a low chair which Roswitha had
pushed up to her and, obviously enjoying the relaxation that comes
after a fairly long walk, said: 'Roswitha, I must remind you that
Kruse is a married man.'

'I know, m'lady.'

'Yes, one knows all sorts of things and still behaves as if one
didn't know. Nothing can come of it . . .'

'Nothing is meant to come of it, m'lady.'

'Because if you're thinking that she's ill, you're reckoning without your host. People who are ill live longest. And then she's got
that black hen. Beware of that because it knows everything and it
will blurt it all out. I don't know why, it makes me shiver. And I'm
sure all that business upstairs is connected with the black hen.'

'Oh, no, I don't think that. But it's awful. And Kruse, who's
always against his wife, can't make me change my mind.'

'What was he saying?'

'That it was only mice.'

'Well, mice are quite bad enough. I can't bear mice. But I could
see quite plainly how you were chatting with Kruse and being
familiar with him and I even think that you were talking about
painting him a moustache. That's going rather far. And then later
on, you'll be left all by yourself. You're still a pretty woman and
there's something about you. But all I can say is, be careful. What
was the first time like for you? Is it the sort of thing that you can
tell me . . .?'

'Oh, yes, I think so. But it was dreadful. And because it was so dreadful your ladyship can set her mind at rest where Kruse's concerned. When someone's been through what I've been through, they've had enough and they won't take any chances. I still dream about it sometimes, and I feel awful and horribly afraid. . . .'

Effi had sat up and was resting her head on her arm.

'Well, tell me. What was it like? I know from what I've heard at home that it's always the same with women like yourself.'

'Yes, I suppose the beginning is always the same and I don't imagine that there was anything special in my case, nothing at all. But when they asked me point blank and I had to say, "Yes, it is," all of a sudden, that was dreadful. With mother, it wasn't too bad; but father, who was the village blacksmith, he was strict, always in a rage, and when he heard it, he came at me with an iron bar that he'd just taken out of the fire and tried to kill me. And I screamed and ran up to the loft and lay there shivering and didn't come down until they called to me and told me I should come down. And then I had a still younger sister, who kept pointing at me and saying nasty things. And then when the child was on its way, I went into the barn next door because I didn't feel safe at home. Then some strangers found me half dead and carried me home to my bed, and two days later they took the child away. And when I asked later on where it was, they told me it was in good hands. Oh m'lady, may the Blessed Virgin protect you from misery like that.'

Effi started up and stared at Roswitha, wide-eyed. But she was more startled than indignant. 'What's that you're saying? I'm a married woman. You mustn't say things like that, it's not proper, it's indecent.'

'Oh, m'lady . . .'

'You'd better tell me instead what became of you! They'd taken the child away from you. . . . That's as far as you'd got.'

'And then a few days later someone came from Erfurt and drove up to the magistrate and asked if there wasn't a wet-nurse available. And the magistrate said yes, God bless him, and the strange gentleman took me away with him straightaway and since then times have been better for me. Even with the registrar's wife it was bearable, and finally I've come to you, m'lady. And that was the best thing of all.' As she said that, she went over to the sofa and kissed Effi's hand.

'Roswitha, you mustn't keep kissing my hand all the time, I

don't like it. And look out with Kruse! You're normally such a good, sensible girl. . . . With a married man . . . that's never a good thing.'

'Oh, m'lady, God's ways are strange and misfortune always has some good in it somewhere; and if it doesn't make us mend our ways, then there's no helping us. . . . I don't really mind men too much. . . .'

'You see, Roswitha, there you go . . . !'

'But if it ever happened again like that, with Kruse, I couldn't do anything about it – I'd just jump straight into the river. It was too dreadful. The whole thing. And what became of the poor little brat? I don't think it's still alive, they've let it die, but it's still my fault.' And she dropped on her knees beside Annie's cradle and rocked it to and fro and sang her 'Buhküken von Halberstadt' over and over again.

'Don't,' said Effi. 'Don't sing any more, I've got a headache. But bring me the papers. Or perhaps Gieshübler has sent the magazines over?'

'Yes, he has. And the fashion journal was on top. Joanna and I had a look through it before you came back. Joanna is always annoyed that she can't have something like that. Shall I bring the fashion journal?'

'Yes, and bring a lamp as well.'

Roswitha went off and when she was alone Effi said: 'The things one does to help oneself. A pretty woman with a muff and another with a half-veil, just fashionable dolls. But it's the best way to make me think of something else.'

In the course of the following morning, a telegram arrived from Innstetten in which he stated that he would now be catching the second train, so that he would not be arriving in Kessin until evening. The whole day passed restlessly. Fortunately, Gieshübler called in the afternoon and helped to pass an hour. Finally, at seven o'clock, the carriage drove up and the couple greeted one another. Innstetten was in a state of excitement unusual for him and thus failed to notice that Effi's cordial greeting was tinged with embarrassment. In the hall the lamps and lights were burning and their light was reflected in the tea-things which Frederick had already placed on one of the tables between the cupboards. 'That looks just as it did before when we arrived here. Do you remember, Effi?'

She nodded.

'Only the shark with his fir-branch is behaving rather more quietly and even Rollo is being reserved and not putting his paws on my shoulder. What's up with you, Rollo?'

Rollo rubbed against his master and wagged his tail.

'He's displeased either with me or with someone else. Well, I'll assume it's with me. Anyway, let's go in.'

So he went into his room and, taking his seat on the sofa, invited Effi to sit down beside him. 'It was so nice in Berlin, much nicer than I'd expected; but although I was so happy, I still kept longing to be back. And how well you look! A trifle pale and a trifle changed but it suits you.'

Effi blushed.

'And now you're blushing. But I'm telling you the truth. You used to look rather like a spoilt child and now all at once you look like a woman.'

'I like to hear you say that, Geert, but I think that you're saying it for the sake of it.'

'No, indeed not, you can take it to your credit, if you look on it as something creditable. . . .'

'I thought it was.'

'And now guess who sends his regards?'

'That's not difficult, Geert, and anyway, we women – and since your return, I suppose I may consider myself as one' – and she laughed as she stretched out her hand towards him – 'we women are good at guessing. We're not so dull as you are.'

'Well who?'

'Why, Cousin Briest, of course. He's the only person I know in Berlin, apart from the aunts, whom you won't have gone to visit and who are much too envious to send me their regards. Haven't you always found that old aunts are envious, too?'

'Yes, Effi, that's true. And now you've said that, I can recognize my old Effi again. Because you must know that the old Effi, the one who looked like a child, I was also rather fond of. Just as much as the present gracious lady.'

'Really? And suppose you had to choose between the two?'

'That's a leading question, I'm not going to be drawn by that. But here comes Frederick with the tea. How I've been longing for this moment. And I said as much, indeed, to your cousin, when we were sitting in Dressel's restaurant and drinking your health in champagne. ... Your ears must have been tingling. ... And do you know what your cousin replied?'

'Something silly, I'm sure. He's good at that.'

'That's the blackest piece of ingratitude that I've heard in all my living days. "Let's forget about my beautiful cousin Effi," he said. "Do you know, Innstetten, that the thing I'd like to do most would be to challenge you to a duel and shoot you dead, because Effi is an angel and it's through you that I lost her." And he looked so solemn and miserable as he said it that it was almost possible to believe him.'

'Oh yes, I've seen him in that sort of mood. How many glasses had you had?'

'I don't recall and even at the time I might not have been in a position to say. But I do believe that he was quite serious. And perhaps that would have been the best thing, too. Don't you think that you would have been able to live with him?'

'Live with him? That's not saying much, Geert. But I'm almost tempted to say that I wouldn't have been able to live with him.'

'Why not? He's really a nice pleasant young man and quite clever, too.'

'Yes, that's true ...'

'But ...'

'But he's a namby-pamby. And that's something that women can't bear even when they're still only half grown up, which you always reckoned me to be and perhaps still do, in spite of all the progress I've made. Namby-pambies aren't for us. Men should be men.'

'I'm glad to hear you say that. Now, by heaven, we must pull ourselves together! And fortunately, I can tell you that I've come more or less straight from something that looks rather like pulling oneself together, or at least that will require it in the future. ... Tell me, what do you say to a ministry?'

'A ministry? Well, that can mean two sorts of things. It may mean clever, distinguished men ruling a state, and it may just be a house, a palazzo, Palazzo Strozzi or Pitti or, if they're not suitable, any other one. You see that my Italian journey was not wasted.'

'And would you be willing to live in that sort of palazzo? I mean, that sort of ministry?'

'Heavens above, Geert – surely they've not made you a minister? Gieshübler said something about it. And Prince Bismarck can do anything. My goodness, he's managed it at last and I'm only eighteen.'

Innstetten laughed. 'No, Effi, not a minister, we're not quite as well in as that. But perhaps all sorts of talents will be sprouting in me and then it's not impossible.'

'So it's not yet, then, not a minister yet?'

'No. And to tell you the truth, we won't even be living in a ministry, but I'll be going to one every day, just as at present I go into the governor's office, and I'll be briefing the minister and travelling around with him when he goes to inspect the local authorities. And you'll be an under-secretary's wife and live in Berlin and within six months you'll hardly remember that you were once in Kessin and only had Gieshübler and the sand-dunes and the plantation.'

Effi said not a word but her eyes opened wider and wider; the corners of her mouth twitched nervously and her whole tender body trembled.

Suddenly she slid from her chair in front of Innstetten and grasping his knees, she said, almost as if she were praying: 'Thank God!'

Innstetten blenched. What did that mean? Something that had repeatedly, if fleetingly, passed through his mind for some weeks, now reappeared, and could be seen so plainly in his eyes that Effi was shocked to see it. She had allowed herself to be carried away by a feeling of relief that was not very different from a confession of guilt and in so doing she had said more than she ought. She had to put things right and find something, some pretext, at all costs.

'Get up, Effi. What's the matter?' Effi hastily stood up, though she did not sit down on the sofa again but moved towards a high-backed chair, apparently because she did not feel strong enough to remain upright without support.

'What's the matter?' repeated Innstetten. 'I thought that the time you'd spent here had been happy. And now you exclaim "Thank God" as if everything here had been one long torment.

Was it I who tormented you? Or was it something else? Do say.'

'How can you still ask me that, Geert?' she said, making a desperate effort to control her trembling voice. 'A happy time! Of course I've had a happy time, but other sorts as well. I've never been completely free from fear since I was here – never. Less than a fortnight ago, it looked over my shoulder again – the same face, the same sallow complexion. And these last few nights when you were away, it came back again, not the face but that rustling sound, and Rollo started barking again and Roswitha, who had heard it as well, came and sat on my bed and we didn't get to sleep again until the dawn was breaking. It's a haunted house and I've been made to believe that business of the ghost – because you're an educator. Yes, Geert, you are. But let's forget about that, all I know is that, for a whole year or more, I've been scared in this house and when I can go away, I think that I shall be rid of it and I'll be a free woman again.'

Innstetten had kept his eyes fixed on her and followed every word. What could be the meaning of the words: 'You're an educator'? And what she had said just before: 'And I've been made to believe that business of the ghost.' What was all this about? What had caused it? And he felt his vague suspicion stirring again and becoming stronger. But he had lived long enough to know that every sign is deceptive and that our jealousy, even with its hundred eyes, can still often mislead us even more than our blind trust. Things might be as she had said: and if that was so, why shouldn't she exclaim: 'Thank God!'

And so, quickly running over all these possibilities, he controlled his suspicions again and held his hand out to Effi over the table:

'Forgive me, Effi, but I was so surprised by everything. Of course it must be my mistake. I'm always too concerned for myself. We men are all egoists. But that's going to change now. Berlin certainly has one good thing about it: there aren't any haunted houses there. Where would they come from? And now let's go over so that I can see Annie. Otherwise Roswitha will be accusing me of being an unnatural father.'

As she heard these words, Effi had gradually become calmer and the feeling that she had had a lucky escape from a danger which she herself had created gave her back her resilience and poise.

22

NEXT morning they had a somewhat belated breakfast together. Innstetten had recovered from his ill-humour – and worse than ill-humour – while Effi was so completely absorbed in her sense of deliverance that not only had she regained her ability to feign a certain cheerfulness but she had almost become carefree again. True, she was still in Kessin, yet she already had the feeling that it was all a long way behind her.

'I've been thinking it over, Effi,' Innstetten said. 'You weren't really as wrong as all that about the things you said against this house. It was all right for Captain Thomsen but not for a spoilt young woman; everything so old-fashioned and not very much room. You'll be better off in Berlin with a drawing-room, too, but not like this one, and with tall, stained-glass windows in the hall and staircase, showing Kaiser Wilhelm with his sceptre and crown or something ecclesiastical, St Elizabeth or the Virgin Mary. Let's say the Virgin Mary, we owe that much to Roswitha.'

Effi laughed. 'Yes, let's do that. But who's looking for a place for us? I can't send Cousin Briest out searching for us. Nor the aunts either. They would think anything was good enough.'

'Ah yes, house-hunting. Nobody likes doing that. I think you'll have to go yourself.'

'And when do you think?'

'The middle of March.'

'Oh, that's much too late, Geert, everything will be gone by that time. The good houses are hardly going to wait for us.'

'That's true enough. But I only arrived back yesterday and I can't really say: "Leave tomorrow." It wouldn't be very nice for me and wouldn't suit me, either. I'm glad to have you with me again.'

'No,' she answered, collecting the cups and saucers together rather noisily in order to hide her growing embarrassment. 'No, we mustn't do that, not today or tomorrow, but in the next few days all the same. And if I find something I'll be back quickly. But one more thing: Roswitha and Annie must come with me. The nicest thing of all would be if you could come too. But I realize that it's not possible. And I think that our separation needn't last long. I already know where I can rent something. . . .'

'Where?'

'That's my secret. I want to have a secret, too, so that I can give you a surprise.'

At that moment, Frederick came in with the post. It was mainly official letters and newspapers.

'Ah, there's a letter for you,' said Innstetten, 'and if I'm not mistaken, it's your mother's handwriting.'

Effi took the letter. 'Yes, it's from mama. But that's not the Friesack post-mark. Look, it clearly says Berlin.'

'Really,' laughed Innstetten. 'You're behaving as if it were a miracle. No doubt your mother is in Berlin and has written to her darling from the hotel.'

'Yes,' said Effi, 'that's what it must be. But I'm almost scared and I can't console myself like Hulda Niemeyer who always says that when someone is scared, it's never as bad as one imagines. What do *you* think?'

'Not very high marks, for a parson's daughter. But now do read the letter. Here's a paper-knife.'

Effi slit open the envelope and read: 'My dear Effi, I arrived in Berlin a day ago, for consultations with Schweigger. As soon as he saw me, he astonished me by congratulating me and when I asked him why, he told me that the P.P.S. Wüllersdorf had just been to see him and told him that Innstetten had been given an appointment in the Ministry. I'm rather vexed to hear something like this from a third person. But I'm so proud and happy that you are both forgiven. Incidentally, I've always known (ever since Innstetten was with the Rathenowers) that he would become somebody. Now *you'll* be benefiting from it. Of course, you must have somewhere to live and a different establishment. If, my dear Effi, you think that you might need my advice with regard to this, then come to Berlin as quickly as your time-table allows. I'm staying here on a cure for a week, and if it doesn't work, perhaps rather longer; Schweigger won't commit himself exactly. I've taken rooms in Schadowstrasse and there are rooms free next door to mine. I'll tell you about the trouble with my eye when I see you; for the moment it's only the future of the two of you that concerns me. Your father will be tremendously pleased; he pretends to be indifferent to that sort of thing, but in fact it means more to him than to me. Give my best wishes to Innstetten and kisses to Annie, whom perhaps you'll be bringing with you.   Your ever affectionate Mother.'

Effi put down the letter and said nothing. She was convinced what she had to do, but she didn't wish to say it herself; Innstetten must propose it and then she would hesitantly agree.

Innstetten, in fact, fell into the trap. 'Well, Effi, you seem very quiet?'

'Oh, Geert, it's a difficult choice. On the one hand, I'd be glad to see my mother again, and possibly even in the next few days. But there is so much to be said against it.'

'And that is?'

'Mama is very determined, as you know, and only thinks what she wants to think. She always gets her own way with father. But I should like to live in a place which *I* like and furnished in *my* taste.'

Innstetten laughed. 'Is that all?'

'Well, it would be enough. But it's not all.'

And then taking her courage in both hands, she said: 'And then, Geert, I shouldn't like to leave you again so soon.'

'You rogue, you're only saying that because you know my weakness. But we're all of us so vain and so I'm prepared to believe it – prepared to believe it and at the same time play the part of heroic renunciation. So go as soon as you think necessary and when you feel you ought to.'

'You mustn't talk like that, Geert. What do you mean: "When you think you ought to"? By saying that you're trying to force me into the role of the affectionate wife, so that I have to say, coyly: "Ah well, Geert, in that case I can never go!" or something similar.'

Innstetten wagged a threatening finger at her. 'Effi, you're too sharp for me, I always thought you were a child and now I can see that you're as clever as any of them. But don't let's pursue that or, as your father always says, "that's too big a subject." But tell me, instead, when you're going.'

'It's Tuesday today. So let's say Friday noon by boat. Then I shall be in Berlin by the evening.'

'Agreed. And back when?'

'Well, let's say Monday evening. That makes three days.'

'Can't be done. That's too soon. You can't manage it in three days. And your mama won't let you go as quickly as that.'

'As I think fit, then.'

'Right.'

And Innstetten got up and went over to the governor's office.

The days before the departure passed in a flash. Roswitha was very happy. 'Oh, m'lady, Kessin is ... well, it's not Berlin. And the trams! And then the bell rings and you don't know whether to go left or right and sometimes I thought everything was going to run straight over me. No, it's not like that here. I think that lots of days we don't see half a dozen people. And nothing but sand-dunes and sea outside. And it booms and roars but that's all it does.'

'Yes, you're right, Roswitha. It keeps on roaring and roaring, but it's not a proper sort of life. And then you get all sorts of stupid ideas. You can't deny that that business with Kruse was not right.'

'Well, m'lady ...'

'All right, I don't want to go into that. Naturally, you won't admit it. And see that you don't take too few things with you. In fact, you can take all your things and Annie's, as well.'

'I thought we were coming back again.'

'Yes, I am. The master wants me to. But you can perhaps stay there with my mother. Only make sure that little Annie is not too spoilt; with me she was sometimes strict, but a grandchild ...'

'And wee Annie is such a little darling. She makes everyone feel fond of her.'

This was on Thursday, the day before their departure. Innstetten was out in the country, and was not expected back until evening. In the afternoon, Effi went into town as far as the market-place, and going into the chemist's asked for a bottle of sal volatile. 'One never knows whom one's going to be travelling with,' she said to the old assistant, with whom she was on chatting terms and who was as devoted to her as Gieshübler himself. 'Is the doctor in?' she asked when she had put the flask into her bag.

'Indeed, m'lady. He's in the next room reading the papers.'

'And I shan't be disturbing him?'

'You couldn't possibly.'

So Effi went in. It was a small, high-ceilinged little room, surrounded by shelves on which all sorts of alembics and retorts were standing, while on one wall there were boxes containing prescriptions arranged in alphabetical order and with iron rings attached.

Gieshübler was both pleased and embarrassed. 'What an honour! Here amongst all my retorts. May I ask you to sit down for a moment, Baroness?'

'Certainly, my dear Gieshübler. But literally only for a moment. I come to say good-bye.'

'But my dear Baroness, surely you'll be coming back. I heard that it's only for three or four days. . . .'

'Yes, I am expecting to return and it has been, in fact, agreed that I shall be back in Kessin within a week at the latest. But I might also not be back. I don't have to tell you all the thousand and one possibilities there are. I can see that you're trying to tell me I'm still too young, but even young people die. . . . And lots of other things can happen. And so I prefer to take my leave of you as if it were for ever.'

'But my dear Baroness . . .'

'As if it were for ever. And I want to thank you, dear Gieshübler, for being the nicest thing in Kessin, because, of course, you *were* the nicest man. And I'll never forget you even if I live to be a hundred. Sometimes I've felt lonely here and sometimes miserable, more miserable than you can imagine; I haven't always been able to work things out properly, but from the very first day, whenever I've been able to see you, I've felt happier, and better too.'

'Oh, my dear Baroness.'

'And I wanted to thank you for that. I've just bought myself a bottle of sal volatile; there are sometimes such strange people in the compartment and they won't ever let you open the window and then perhaps if – because it's really very strong, I mean the sal volatile – if it makes my eyes water, I'll think of you. Good-bye, dear, dear, Gieshübler and give my regards to your friend, Signorina Trippelli! In the last few weeks, I've often found myself thinking of her and Prince Kotschukoff. It seems a strange relationship, really. Yet I can see how it is. . . . And let us have news of yourself now and again. I'll write to you.'

On this, she left. Gieshübler accompanied her as far as the market-place. He was as if bewildered, so much so that he quite failed to grasp properly some of the enigmatic things that she had said.

Effi returned home. 'Bring the lamp, Joanna,' she said, 'but put it in my bedroom. And then I'll have a cup of tea! I feel so cold and I can't wait until the master returns.'

Both were brought. Effi was already sitting at her small writing-table with a sheet of paper in front of her. 'Put the tea on the table here, please Joanna.'

When Joanna had left the room, Effi locked the door, looked into the mirror for a moment and then sat down again and started writing:

'I'm leaving with the boat tomorrow and I'm writing to say good-bye. Innstetten is expecting me back in a few days but I shall not be returning. . . . *Why* I am not returning, you will surely know. . . . It would have been better for me never to have seen this place. I beg you not to take this as a reproach; it has all been my fault. If I think of your home-life your actions may be forgivable but not mine. I have a heavy burden of guilt but perhaps I can still save myself. Being called away from here seems to me a sign that I can still find forgiveness. Forget all that has happened and forget me! Your Effi!'

She rapidly read the letter through once again, struck by the strange formality of its tone; but that, too, was necessary; it was meant to show that there was no return. And so she thrust the letter into an envelope and went to a house that was set between the churchyard and the corner of the wood. A trail of smoke rose from the half tumbled-down chimney. There she handed in the letter.

When she got back, Innstetten was already there and she sat down beside him and told him about Gieshübler and the sal volatile.

Innstetten laughed: 'Where did you learn your Latin, Effi?'

The boat – a small sailing-boat, for the steamers only went during the summer – left at twelve. Effi and Innstetten were already on board a quarter of an hour beforehand, with Roswitha and Annie. There was more luggage than seemed necessary for a trip intended to be so short. Innstetten was talking with the captain. Effi, wearing a raincoat and light grey travelling hat, was standing in the stern,

175

near the rudder, letting her gaze run over the quayside and the row
of pretty houses that followed the line of the quay. Exactly opposite
the landing-stage was the three-storeyed building of Hoppensack's
Hotel; a yellow flag, with a cross and a crown on it, hung limply
down from the gabled roof in the still, hazy air. Effi looked for a
while at the flag and then she let her eyes fall until eventually they
settled on the people who were standing curiously on the
quayside.

At that moment, a bell rang. Effi felt a peculiar feeling; the ship
moved slowly away and as she looked once more towards the gangway, she saw that Crampas was standing in the very front row.
She was startled to see him and yet, at the same time, it pleased her.
For his part, Crampas's whole attitude seemed changed. He was
plainly moved and serious as he bowed to her from the quayside.
She returned his greeting with an equal seriousness, but at the same
time in a very friendly manner, although there was an entreaty in
her eyes. Then she went quickly to her cabin, where Roswitha was
already installed with Annie. Here, in the somewhat stuffy room, she
stayed until they had sailed out of the river into the wide Breitling
bay. Then Innstetten came to fetch her on deck. Over the surface
of the sea, grey clouds were hanging, occasionally pierced by a dull
ray of sun. Effi thought of the day when, exactly a year and a
quarter ago, she had driven along the bank in an open carriage. A
short span and an often quiet and lonely life. And yet how many
things had happened in between!

The boat continued upstream and by two o'clock they had reached the terminus, or very nearly. When, shortly afterwards, they
passed by the Prince Bismarck Hotel, Golchowski was once more
standing at his door and did not fail to accompany the governor
and her ladyship to the steps leading up the slope. The train was
not yet announced and Effi and Innstetten walked to and fro on the
platform. Their conversation was concerned with the question of
housing. They were agreed as to the quarter; they must live somewhere between the Tiergarten and the Zoological Gardens. 'I want
to hear the finches singing and the parrots as well,' said Innstetten,
and Effi agreed. And now the whistle was heard and the train
arrived; the station master was most obliging and Effi was given
a compartment to herself. A final hand-shake, a wave of the handkerchief and the train moved off.

23

ALTHOUGH the Friedrichstrasse station was thronged, as she looked out of the compartment Effi recognized her mother with Cousin Briest at her side. There was a joyful reunion and as they did not have to wait too long for their luggage, five minutes or so later the cab was rolling along beside the tram-lines into Dorotheenstrasse towards Schadowstrasse, where the guest-house stood on the first corner. Roswitha was delighted and enjoyed watching Annie reaching out with her little hands to try to catch hold of the lights.

And now they had arrived. Effi was given her two rooms, not, as she had expected, next door to Frau von Briest, but in the same corridor, and when all was arranged and Annie had been successfully installed in a drop-sided cot, Effi reappeared in her mother's room, a small drawing-room with a fireplace in which only a small fire was burning, because the weather was mild, almost warm. On the round table with its green lamp-shade three places had been laid and the tea itself was on a small side-table. 'What a delightful place you have, Mama,' Effi said, sitting down opposite the sofa, only to stand up again at once to see to the tea. 'May I take over my job as tea-pourer again?'

'Certainly you may, Effi dear. But only for Dagobert and yourself. I must do without, which I find rather hard.'

'I see, because of your eyes. But tell me now, what's wrong with them? In the cab – which was creaking too loudly anyway – we were talking much too much about Innstetten and our grand career and forgetting everything else, and we must stop it. Believe me, your eyes are more important for me and in one way, thank goodness, I can see that they haven't changed at all – they're still as kind as ever when you look at me.' And she dashed over and kissed her mother's hand.

'Effi, you're so violent. You haven't changed at all.'

'Oh yes, I have, Mama. I wish I hadn't. Marriage changes one.'

Cousin Briest gave a laugh: 'Well cousin, I don't notice much change. The only thing is, you're prettier. And I don't suppose that you've given up being violent yet, either.'

'Just like Cousin Dagobert,' said her mother, but Effi wouldn't hear of such a thing and said: 'Dagobert, you're good at everything except understanding people. It's strange. You officers don't understand people, certainly the young ones don't. You just keep looking at each other or at your recruits and the ones in the cavalry have got their horses as well. They really don't know anything.'

'But cousin, where did you learn all this great wisdom? You don't know any officers. I read that Kessin has decided against the Hussars that were intended to go there, a decision unique in world history, incidentally. And were you referring to the good old days? You were still almost a child when the Rathenowers used to come over.'

'I might reply that children are the best observers. But I won't, it's all a lot of tomfoolery and I want to hear about mama's eyes.'

Frau von Briest explained that the ophthalmic surgeon had given as his opinion that it was blood-pressure in the brain. This was causing the spots before her eyes. It would have to be brought under control by dieting: beer, coffee, and tea were all prohibited and with an occasional local blood-letting it would soon be better. 'He thought about a fortnight. But I know what doctors are like: a fortnight means six weeks and I shall still be here when Innstetten comes and you both move into your new accommodation. And I won't deny that that is the best thing about it and it consoles me in advance for the fact that the cure is likely to be a long one. Only you must find something really nice for yourselves. I thought of Land-grafenstrasse or Keithstrasse, elegant yet not too expensive. Because you're going to have to cut down on your expenses. Innstetten's job is very distinguished but it won't bring in all that much money. And now your father is complaining, too. Prices are dropping and every day he tells me that unless they provide pro-tective tariffs he'll have to leave Hohen-Cremmen and go begging. You know how fond he is of exaggerating. And now come along, Dagobert, and if possible tell us something nice. Illnesses are always boring and the most kindly disposed people only listen because they must. No doubt Effi will want to hear some story or other out of the *Fliegende Blätter* or the *Kladderadatsch*. But people say it's not as good as it was.'

'Oh yes, it's just as good as it was earlier on. They've still got Tweedledum and Tweedledee and that's good enough in itself.'

'My favourite is Charlie Miessnick and Wippchen von Bernau.'

'Yes, they're the best. But Wippchen – and by the way, Effi, forgive me for saying so but he's not in *Kladderadatsch* – Wippchen is no longer operating because there's no war at the moment. Unfortunately, people like us would like a chance to get rid of this horrible empty space,' and he ran his hand across his chest.

'Oh, that's just vanity. Go on with what you were saying. What's happening at the moment?'

'Well, cousin, it's a strange thing. . . . It's not to everybody's liking. At the moment, they have "Bible jokes".'

'Bible jokes? What on earth is that? Bible and jokes don't go together.'

'That's what I say and they're not to everyone's taste. But whether they're acceptable or not, their stock's high at the moment. It's the fashion, like lapwing's eggs.'

'Well, if it's not too extravagant, let's have an example! Is that possible?'

'Certainly it is. And I'm tempted to add: you've come just at the right time because the joke going round at the moment is something quite remarkably subtle: it's in the form of a double idea, and in addition to the quotation from the Bible there's a question of meaning. Incidentally all these jokes are in the form of a question – in this case it's extremely simple: Who was the first inefficient wine-waiter? Now guess.'

'Well, Ganymede, perhaps.'

'Very good. You really are brainy, Effi. I'd never thought of that. But all the same, you're a long way off the mark.'

'Well, who was it, then?'

'The first inefficient cupbearer was Satan, because in the Bible it says: "Satan setteth up a gin for the righteous; but the lot shall fall upon the wicked." You see, "gin" and "lot" in different senses.'

Effi repeated the sentence with a puzzled expression but in spite of all her efforts and Dagobert's comments, she was unable to see exactly what the point was; she was, indeed, one of those fortunate people who have no ear for that sort of pastime and so Cousin Briest was placed in the unenviable role of having to point out once more the similarity in sound and difference in meaning of the two words.

'Oh, I can see now. You must forgive me for having been so slow. But it really is too stupid.'

'Yes, it is stupid,' replied Dagobert, faintly.

'Stupid and inappropriate and enough to put one off Berlin. You leave Kessin in order to get back to civilization and the first thing you hear is a "Bible joke". Even mama isn't saying a word and that makes it plain enough. But I'll help you to retreat in good order. . . .'

'Please do, Effi. . . .'

'Retreat in good order and I shall take it, quite seriously, as a good sign that the first thing that my Cousin Dagobert said to me was that the wicked never prosper and the righteous do, strange as it may seem, and even though it's not a very good joke, I'm grateful to you for the sentiment.'

Dagobert, seeing that he was being let off, tried to poke fun at Effi for being so solemn, but realizing that he was annoying her he gave up.

Shortly after ten o'clock, he left, after promising to call next day to receive her orders.

As soon as he had gone, Effi went back to her own rooms.

Next day the weather was superb and mother and daughter set off early, first of all to the eye clinic, where Effi stayed in the waiting-room, looking through an album. Then they went on to the Tiergarten and nearly as far as the Zoo to look around there for accommodation. In fact, it so happened that in Keithstrasse they discovered something eminently suitable, except that it was newly built, damp and not yet ready. 'It won't do, Effi dear,' said Frau von Briest, 'if only simply on grounds of hygiene. And also, a privy councillor is not a drying agent.'

Although Effi liked the house quite well, she agreed the more readily with her mother's doubts as she was not at all interested in a quick solution, quite the contrary: 'Time is all-important', and so the best possible thing for her was to be able to postpone the decision on the whole matter. 'We'll keep this place in mind, Mama, because it's so nicely situated and it is basically what I wanted.' Then the two drove back into town, ate in a restaurant that had been recommended to them and then went to the opera in the evening, the doctor having given his permission on condition that Frau von Briest should listen rather than look.

The next few days passed in similar fashion; both were genuinely pleased to be together again after such a long interval and once more able to indulge in their lengthy conversations. Effi was outstanding, not only at listening and talking, but, when in good form, at scandal-mongering, and more than once showed signs of her old arrogance; her mother wrote home to say how happy she was to see her 'child' so cheerful and gay and that it was just like the lovely times they had all had nearly two years ago when they were buying the trousseau; even Cousin Briest was the same as before. Indeed, this was the case, with the one difference that he showed himself less frequently than before and when asked why, replied with apparent seriousness: 'You're too dangerous, Effi.' Each time this happened both mother and daughter laughed at him and Effi said: 'Dagobert, it's true that you're still very young, but you're no longer young enough to indulge in that form of flattery.'

So nearly a fortnight went by. Innstetten's letters became more and more pressing, and even almost sharp towards his mother-in-law, so that Effi realized that it was hardly possible to delay much longer and that she would have to rent something. But what then? There were still three weeks to go before the move to Berlin and Innstetten was insisting on a speedy return. There was only one thing to do; she must once more have recourse to subterfuge and fall ill.

While this was disagreeable for more than one reason, it had to be done, and as soon as this fact became plain to her, it also became plain, down to the smallest details, how she must play her part.

'Mama, as you can see Innstetten is becoming touchy over my delay in returning, so I think we must give in and rent something today. And I shall go tomorrow. Oh, it'll be so hard for me to leave you.'

Frau von Briest agreed: 'And which place will you rent?'

'The first one, of course, the one in Keithstrasse, which I liked so much from the beginning, and you did, too. I suppose it won't have dried out completely yet but it's the summer now, which is something of a consolation. And if the damp seems excessive and brings a bit of rheumatism, after all, I've always got Hohen-Cremmen.'

'My dear child, don't mention rheumatism, sometimes it's there without our realizing it.'

Her mother's words gave Effi inspiration. That very morning she rented the flat and sent a card to Innstetten saying that she was intending to leave on the following day, then she had the bags packed straightaway and all preparations made. But when the next morning came, Effi was still in bed. 'I can't travel. I've got all sorts of aches and pains and I can feel it all down my back. It almost looks to me like rheumatism. I wouldn't have believed that it could be so painful!'

'Well now, you see what I was saying. You must never talk of the devil. Yesterday you were talking about it without thinking and now today you've got it. When I see Schweigger, I'll ask him what you should do.'

'No, not Schweigger. He's a specialist. That's no use and he might even take offence at being consulted about something else. I think that the best thing for me to do is to wait and see. It may go away, after all. I'll live on tea and soda-water all day and if I can perspire, then perhaps I'll get over it.' Frau von Briest agreed, but insisted that she should eat well. The old-fashioned idea that you shouldn't enjoy anything was quite wrong and merely made you feel weak; in this respect, she belonged to the modern school: eat a lot.

Effi found not a little consolation in these comments, wrote a telegram to Innstetten, mentioning this unfortunate hitch and speaking of a tiresome but only temporary delay, and then said to Roswitha: 'Roswitha, you must go and get me some books; it won't be difficult, I want old ones, very old ones.'

'Of course, m'lady. The lending library is only just round the corner. What shall I bring you?'

'I'll write it down, an assortment to choose from because sometimes they haven't got just the one that you'd like.' Roswitha fetched pencil and paper and Effi wrote: Walter Scott, *Ivanhoe* or *Quentin Durward*; Cooper, *The Spy*; Dickens, *David Copperfield*; Willibald Alexis, *Die Hosen des Herrn von Bredow*.*

Roswitha read through the list and then, in the next room, cut off the last line; she was embarrassed, both for herself and for her mistress, at the thought of handing in the original list.

The day passed without incident. The following morning, Effi was no better, nor on the third.

* 'Herr von Bredow's Trousers'.

182

'Effi, we mustn't let it go on like this. When this sort of thing gets a hold, you can't get rid of it any more. The thing that doctors warn us about specially – and rightly – is any delay of that sort.'

Effi gave a sigh. 'All right, Mama, but whom can we have? Not a young doctor, though; I don't know why, but it would embarrass me.'

'A young doctor is always embarrassing and if he isn't, so much the worse. But you can reassure yourself, I'll bring quite an old one who's already treated me when I was still at school at Hecker's – that must be some twenty years ago. And he must have been getting on for fifty then and he had nice grey hair, all curly. He was a ladies' man but in the right kind of way. Doctors who forget that will never succeed, it's a foregone conclusion; we German women, at least those belonging to good society, are still basically sound.'

'Do you think so? I'm always glad to hear something like that, because occasionally you hear something quite different. And it must often be difficult. What's the name of this old privy councillor? I assume that he is a privy councillor?'

'Privy Councillor Rummschüttel.'*

Effi gave a hearty laugh. 'Rummschüttel! And he's a doctor for people who can't get up!'

'Effi, you're talking so strangely. You can't be in very great pain.'

'No, not at the moment. It's changing all the time.'

Next morning, Privy Councillor Rummschüttel appeared. Frau von Briest received him and when he saw Effi, his first words were: 'Just like her mother.'

The latter tried to reject the comparison and pointed out that twenty years and more were quite a long time, after all. Rummschüttel reaffirmed his view, stating at the same time that, although not every face left an impression on him, when it once had done so, it was indelible. 'And now, my dear Frau von Innstetten, what is the trouble, how can we be of help?'

'Oh, Dr Rummschüttel, I find it difficult to explain what it is. It keeps changing all the time. At the moment it seems to have gone. First of all, I thought of rheumatism but I could almost imagine that it might be neuralgia. Pains all down the back and then I can't stand upright. My father suffers from neuralgia, so that I've been in

* The name would suggest an association with (he)rumschütteln, to shake up.

a position to see what it's like. Perhaps I've inherited it from him?'

'Very probably,' said Rummschüttel, who had felt her pulse and given a quick but sharp look at his patient. 'Very probably, my dear lady.' But what he was saying under his breath to himself was: 'Malingering and putting on a remarkably good act. A real daughter of Eve.' However, he allowed nothing of this to show but with all appropriate seriousness said: 'Rest and warmth are the best things I can recommend. The rest can be done by medicine, not an unpleasant one, by the way.'

He stood up to write out the prescription: Aqua Amygdalarum ½ oz., Syripus florum Aurantii, 2 oz. 'Will you please take half a teaspoonful of this every two hours. It will quieten your nerves. And another thing I must insist on: no mental exertion, no visits, no reading.' He pointed to the book lying near her.

'It's Scott.'

'Oh, there's no objection to him. The best thing is books of travel. I'll call again tomorrow.'

Effi's attitude had been exemplary; she had played her part well. But once she was alone – her mother accompanied the doctor to the door – the blood none the less rose to her face; she had seen perfectly well that her pretence had been met by similar pretence from the doctor. He was evidently a thorough man of the world, who saw everything perfectly well but was prepared to turn a blind eye, perhaps because he knew that such things might now and again need to be humoured. Weren't there forms of pretence that deserved humouring and wasn't her own, at the moment, just such a one?

Soon afterwards, her mother came back and mother and daughter launched into praise of the civilized old gentleman who still had something so youthful about him, in spite of being nearly seventy. 'Just send Roswitha round to the chemist's straightaway. . . . You must only take it every three hours, he stressed this. He was just like that in the old days – he didn't often make prescriptions, or in large quantities, but always something energizing, and it used to work immediately.'

Rummschüttel came the next day and then every other day, because he could see that his visits embarrassed the young woman. This predisposed him towards her, and after the third visit, his judgement had been made: 'There's something happening here which is forcing this young woman to behave as she does.'

When Rummschüttel made his fourth visit, he found Effi up and sitting in a rocking-chair reading a book. Annie was beside her.

'Ah, my dear young lady! I'm delighted. I don't think that the medical faculty is responsible; it's the fine weather, these bright fresh March days that chase illness away. I congratulate you. And your lady mother?'

'She has gone out, doctor, to Keithstrasse where we've rented a flat. I'm expecting my husband to come in a few days' time and when we're properly settled in our home, I shall very much look forward to introducing him to you. I do hope, surely, that you'll be willing to look after me in the future.'

He bowed.

'Our new flat,' she continued, 'has just been built and it worries me, as a matter of fact. Do you think, doctor, that the damp walls ...?'

'Not in the least, dear lady. Make sure it's heated right through for three or four days with doors and windows open all the time and then I promise you that you can risk it. And that matter of your neuralgia was not as serious as all that. But I'm delighted that your cautiousness gave me the opportunity of renewing an old acquaintance and making a new one.'

He bowed once more, peered affectionately at Annie again, and took his leave, with his respects to Frau von Briest.

Hardly had he left than Effi sat down at her writing-table and wrote. 'Dear Geert, Rummschüttel has just been here and pronounced me cured. It would be possible for me to leave now, perhaps even tomorrow; but it's the 24th today and you intend to be here on the 28th. In any case, I'm still rather weak. I imagine that you will understand if I give up the idea of coming. Our things are already on their way in any case and if I were to come, we should have to put up as tourists in Hoppensack's Hotel. We ought also to consider the question of costs, because our expenses will be increasing anyway, apart from anything else. Rummschüttel will have to be paid, even if he is going to be our permanent doctor. Medically he's not said to be in the first rank – his rivals and critics say he's a "ladies' doctor". But that expression is praise as well, because not everyone knows how to handle us. It doesn't really matter if I don't take my leave of our friends and acquaintances in Kessin personally. I did see Gieshübler. The major's wife has never been anything but most ungracious towards me, ungracious to the point of rudeness. The only other people are the pastor and Dr Hannemann and Crampas. Give my regards to the latter. I'll send cards to our country friends; the Güldenklees are in Italy, so you tell me, and so that leaves only the other three. Make my excuses as best you can. You're good at formalities and you know the right sort of thing to say. As for Frau von Padden, whom I took such a liking to at the New Year's Eve ball, perhaps I'll send her a letter myself to say how sorry I am. Let me know by telegram if you're in agreement.   As ever, Your Effi.'

Effi took the letter to the post herself, as if that would bring a speedier reply, and the following morning the telegram that she had requested arrived from Innstetten: 'Entirely agree.'

Her heart rejoiced and she hurried downstairs to the nearest cab-rank. '1C, Keithstrasse,' and the cab sped away, first down Unter den Linden, and then down the Tiergartenstrasse and stopped in front of the new apartment.

Upstairs, their things which had arrived the day before were lying about higgledy-piggledy, but she paid no attention to them and when she went out on to the wide, walled balcony, she could see, beyond the canal bridge, the Tiergarten spread out with its trees already showing their fresh green, while overhead, there was a clear blue sky and a cheerful sun.

She shivered with excitement and took a deep breath. Then, leaving the balcony, she stepped back through the doorway and folding her hands, she raised her eyes: 'And now for a new life, with God's help! Things must be different.'

24

THREE days afterwards, rather late, at about nine o'clock, Innstetten arrived in Berlin. Everyone was at the station: Effi, her mother and her cousin; it was a hearty reception, most of all from Effi, and a whole host of things had already been discussed by the time the carriage which they had taken drew up in front of their new home in the Keithstrasse. 'Ah, you've made a good choice, Effi,' said Innstetten, as he walked into the hall. 'No sharks, no crocodiles, and we hope no ghosts, either.'

'No, Geert, all that sort of thing is finished with. A new era is beginning and I'm not scared any more and I mean to be better than I have been up till now and try to please you more.'

She whispered all this to him while they were going up the carpeted stairs to the second floor.

Cousin Briest accompanied her mother.

Upstairs, though there was still much to be done, care had been taken to give a homely impression and Innstetten expressed his pleasure: 'Effi, you're a little genius,' but she declined his praise and pointed to her mother as really deserving it. '*That's* where it must go,' had been her inexorable decision and she had always been right, thus saving a lot of time and preserving everyone's good temper. Finally, Roswitha appeared, too, in order to greet the master, and to say: 'Miss Annie sends her apologies for not coming,' a little joke with which she was very pleased and which completely achieved its purpose.

At this point they sat down at the table which had already been laid and when Innstetten poured himself out a glass of wine and everybody had drunk to 'Happy days' he took Effi's hand and said: 'Now, Effi, you must tell me what was the matter with you.'

'Oh, don't let's bother about that. It's not worth talking about; a trifle painful and a proper nuisance, because it cut across our plans. But it wasn't anything more and it's over now. Rummschüttel showed how good he is, a well-bred, charming man, as I think I already wrote to you. He's said not to be very brilliant intellectually, but mama says that's an advantage. And I expect she's right, as she always is. Our good old Doctor Hannemann was not brilliant either but he was always right. And now tell me, what is Gieshübler doing and all the others?'

'Well now, who are all the others? Crampas sends his regards.'

'Oh, very kind of him.'

'And the pastor wishes to be remembered to you, too. Only the country "gentry" were rather luke-warm and seemed inclined to blame me for your having left without saying good-bye. Our friend Sidonie was even rather cross and only dear Frau von Padden, whom

I drove over to see, myself, the day before yesterday, was genuinely pleased to receive your good wishes and your declaration of love for her! She said that you were a delightful girl but that I must take good care of you. And when I replied that you already thought that I was more of a tutor than a husband, she murmured, almost absent-mindedly: "a little lamb, white as the driven snow." And then she broke off.'

Cousin Briest laughed: 'A little lamb, white as the driven snow. Did you hear that, cousin?' And he was preparing to go on teasing her when he saw that she had gone pale.

The conversation, mainly concerned with past events, continued for some while and finally Effi gathered from the various items of Innstetten's news that out of their whole household in Kessin only Joanna had declared her readiness to migrate to Berlin. She had, of course, remained behind for the moment but would be arriving in two or three days' time with the rest of the things; Innstetten was pleased at her decision, because she had always been the most useful, as well as possessing a very definitely metropolitan elegance. Perhaps a little too much. Christel and Frederick had both declared that they were too old and it was plainly pointless to approach Kruse. 'What would we do with a coachman here?' concluded Innstetten. 'Horses and carriages are things of the past, in Berlin such luxury is over and done with. We shouldn't even have been able to find a place for the black hen to live. Or am I doing the flat an injustice?'

Effi shook her head and as a short pause now ensued, Effi's mother stood up: it was nearly eleven o'clock, she had a long way to go and as the cab-rank was only just round the corner, she wouldn't hear of anyone seeing her home – an idea which Cousin Briest naturally rejected. Shortly afterwards, they all broke up, after arranging to meet the following morning.

Effi rose fairly early and, since it was almost as warm as in summer, she had the breakfast table moved beside the open balcony door, and as Innstetten now appeared she went out with him on to the balcony and said: 'Well, what do you say about it? You wanted to hear the finches singing in the Tiergarten and the parrots in the Zoological Garden. I don't know if they'll both oblige you, but it's possible. Did you hear that? It came from over there, in that small park. It's not exactly the Tiergarten but almost.'

Innstetten was delighted and as grateful as if Effi had personally conjured it all up for him. Then they sat down and now Annie came in as well. Roswitha expected Innstetten to find a great change in the child, and this he eventually did. And then they went on talking, first about Kessin and then about the calls they would be making in Berlin and finally about their summer holiday. Halfway through the conversation they had to break off in order to be on time for their rendezvous.

As arranged they met at Helms's, opposite the Rotes Schloss, went to various shops, ate at Hiller's and were home again in good time. It had been a very successful occasion, with Innstetten heartily glad to be enjoying all the amenities of metropolitan life again. The following day, the first of April, he went to sign the book at the Chancellor's Palace – deliberately avoiding leaving a personal message – and then went on to report at the ministry. He was given an audience here in spite of the fact that it was, both socially and officially, an extremely busy day; indeed his chief went out of his way to receive him in a particularly obliging and friendly manner; he knew that they would get on well together.

In the flat at home, too, everything was working out well. Effi was genuinely sorry to see her mother go back to Hohen-Cremmen after having spent almost six weeks on her cure, as originally expected, and it was something of a consolation that Joanna installed herself in Berlin on the same day. That, at least, was something and though the pretty young blonde did not stand quite so high in Effi's affections as the completely unselfish and endlessly kind-hearted Roswitha, she was equally well thought of, both by Innstetten and by her young mistress, because she was very useful and good at her job and extremely reserved and self-possessed in her dealings with men. In Kessin, rumour had it that she owed her existence to an extremely high-ranking officer from the Pasewalk garrison, long since pensioned-off, which seemed to explain the refinement of her mind, her lovely blonde hair and her outstanding physical attractiveness. Joanna herself shared in the pleasure that her arrival aroused in everyone and was fully agreed to becoming Effi's general and personal maid, while Roswitha who, in the course of nearly a year, had more or less acquired Christel's skill at cooking, was put in charge of the kitchens. It became Effi's task to look after and care for Annie, a fact which caused Roswitha definite amusement. She knew what these young women were like.

Innstetten lived entirely for his work and his home. He was happier than he had been in Kessin because he did not fail to see that Effi appeared more relaxed and cheerful. And this was possible because she felt freer. True, the past still lingered on in her mind but it no longer frightened her, or, if it did, it was but fleetingly and far less often, and any nervousness that remained lent a peculiar charm to her whole manner. There was a kind of melancholy entreaty in everything she did and she would have liked to express it even more openly. But that was not to be thought of.

As they were making their round of visits in the first weeks of April, the social life of the big city, though not yet at an end, was drawing to its close, and so Effi was hardly able to play much part in it. In the second half of May, any social life died away completely and so, even more than before, they were glad to meet in the Tiergarten in the lunch-hour when Innstetten would be coming from his ministry or else to go for a stroll in the afternoon to the palace gardens of Charlottenburg. As she walked up and down the long façade between the Schloss and the trees of the Orangerie, Effi kept looking at the massive group of Roman Emperors standing there, finding a strange similarity between Nero and Titus, while she picked up pine-cones which had dropped from the weeping pines and then, arm in arm with her husband, went off in the direction of the Spree, towards the remote Belvedere.

'There's supposed to have been a ghost there once.'

'No, only spirits.'

'That's the same thing.'

'Yes, sometimes it is,' replied Innstetten. 'But there is a difference, really. Spirit manifestations are always produced, at least those in the Belvedere are said to have been, according to what Cousin Briest was telling me yesterday – but ghosts are never produced, they're natural.'

'So you do believe in them.'

'Certainly I believe in them. Such things exist. But I don't really believe in what we had in Kessin. Did Joanna ever show you her Chinaman?'

'Which one?'

'Why, ours. Before she left our old home, she unstuck him from

190

the back of the chair and put him in her purse. When I was getting change for a mark from her recently, I saw it. And she confirmed it, rather shamefacedly.'

'Oh, Geert, you shouldn't have told me that. Now there's something like that again in our house.'

'Tell her to burn it.'

'No, I don't want to do that and it won't help either. But I'll ask Roswitha ...'

'To do what? Ah, I understand, I can guess what you're going to do. She will have to buy a picture of a saint and put it in the purse. Is that it?'

Effi nodded.

'Well, do what you like. But don't tell anyone.'

In the end, Effi thought it would be better not to do anything about it and, still desultorily chatting, with their thoughts turning more and more to their plans for the summer holiday, they drove back as far as the Grosser Stern and then went along the Corso Avenue and the wide Friedrich-Wilhelm Strasse towards their flat.

They intended to go on holiday early, before the end of July, in order to visit the Bavarian mountains where the Oberammergau dramatic festival was being given again that year. It proved not possible to do so. The Privy Councillor von Wüllersdorf, whom Innstetten had known earlier and who was a particular colleague of his, fell suddenly ill and Innstetten had to stay and replace him. It was not until the middle of August that everything was finally arranged and they had the opportunity of leaving, but by now it was too late to go to Oberammergau and so they decided to stay in Rügen. 'First of all, to Stralsund, where there's Schill of course, whom you know about, and Scheele, whom you don't – he discovered oxygen but you don't need to know that. And then from Stralsund to Bergen, and the Rugard from where, according to Wüllersdorf, you can look out over the whole island and then, between the Big and Little Bodden of Jasmund, as far as Sassnitz. Because going to Rügen means going to Sassnitz. Binze would perhaps be all right but – to quote Wüllersdorf again – the beach is so full of pebbles and mussel-shells and we want to bathe after all.'

Effi fell in with all Innstetten's plans and especially with the arrangement that the whole household would close down for a month and Roswitha would go off with Annie to Hohen-Cremmen while Joanna would be going to a slightly younger half-brother who had a saw-mill in Pasewalk. So everyone would be properly accommodated. So, at the beginning of the following week the household dispersed and that same evening Effi and Innstetten were in Sassnitz. The hotel bore the name 'Hotel Fahrenheit'. 'I hope the prices are Centigrade,' added Innstetten after reading the name, and in high good humour the pair of them went for an evening walk over the cliffs beside the sea and looked out from a rocky promontory over the quiet bay shimmering in the moonlight. Effi was enchanted: 'Geert, it's just like Capri and Sorrento. We must stay here. But certainly not in the hotel; the waiters are so grand, you feel embarrassed to ask for a bottle of soda-water. . . .'

'Yes, nothing but *attachés*. But there's bound to be a private flat to be had.'

'I think so too. And we'll start looking round for one tomorrow morning.'

The following morning was as lovely as the evening and they took breakfast in the open. Innstetten received some letters which had to be dealt with promptly and so Effi decided to spend the free time by starting to look for accommodation straightaway. She went first of all past a paddock and then saw groups of houses and fields of oats and finally turned down a track that led steeply down to the sea. At the point where this precipitous track reached the sea, shaded by tall beech-trees there stood a modest restaurant, which, thanks to the early hour, was still quite empty. Effi sat down where she could see the view and she had hardly taken one sip of the sherry she had ordered when, partly out of curiosity and partly out of friendliness, the owner came out to engage her in conversation.

'My husband and I like it very much here,' she said. 'What a splendid view over the bay! The only thing that worries us is the question of accommodation.'

'Yes, madam, that will be difficult.'

'But it's already late in the season. . . .'

'All the same, here in Sassnitz there's certainly nothing to be found, I think I can guarantee that. But further along the beach, where the next village begins – you can see the roofs shining from here – there might be something.'

'And what's the name of the village?'

192

'Crampas.'

Effi thought that she had misheard the name. 'Crampas,' she repeated in a strained voice. 'I've never heard of that as the name of a place. Isn't there anywhere else in the district?'

'No, ma'am. Nothing round here. But further up towards the north, there are still some more villages and they'll be able to give you information in the restaurant just by Stubbenkammer. They'll always give you the addresses of people who would be prepared to let rooms.'

Effi was glad to have conducted this conversation all by herself and when she reported back shortly afterwards to her husband, though without mentioning the name of the village near Sassnitz, the latter said: 'Well, if there's nothing hereabouts, the best thing for us to do is to take a carriage (which always creates a good impression with a hotel, incidentally) and drive up the island towards Stubbenkammer without further delay. There's bound to be something quite idyllic up there, with an arbour covered in honeysuckle, and if we can't find anything, we can always make do with the hotel itself. They're all very much alike, after all.'

Effi agreed and towards noon they reached the hotel-restaurant near Stubbenkammer which Innstetten had already mentioned and where they ordered a snack.

'But only in half an hour's time. We intend to go for a walk first and take a look at Lake Hertha. I imagine you have a guide here?'

They had and a middle-aged man at once came up to the travellers. He looked as important and solemn as if he had been at the very least an assistant in the old rites of Hertha worship.

The lake, surrounded by tall trees, was quite near; it was fringed by rushes and countless water-lilies were floating on its still, dark surface.

'It really looks as if it's ready for the cult of Hertha,' said Effi.

'Yes, ma'am. Those stones are still there to remind us of it.'

'What stones?'

'The sacrificial stones.'

And pursuing their conversation, the three of them walked away from the lake and came to a vertical cliff of clay and gravel against which a number of smooth stones were leaning, each slightly hollowed out, with downward-sloping grooves.

'And what are they for?'

'So that it would flow away more easily, ma'am.'

'Let's go,' said Effi and taking her husband's arm, she went back with him to the restaurant where they were served with the lunch they had ordered beforehand. The bay lay in front of them, in the sun, and isolated sailing-boats were gliding over its surface and gulls were swooping on each other along the neighbouring cliffs. It was very lovely and Effi found it so, too; but looking beyond the sparkling surface of the water, she could once more see, to the south, the bright shining roofs of the scattered village whose name had so startled her early that morning.

Innstetten, although without any knowledge or suspicion of her thoughts, could clearly see that she was feeling neither pleasure nor enjoyment. 'I'm sorry that you're not very happy about being here, Effi. You can't forget Lake Hertha and especially those stones.'

She nodded. 'What you say is true. And I must confess to you that I've never seen anything in my life which made me feel so miserable. Let's stop looking for accommodation. I can't stay here.'

'And yesterday you thought it was like the bay of Naples and other beautiful places.'

'Yes, yesterday.'

'And today? No trace of Sorrento today?'

'Just a trace but no more than a trace. It's Sorrento in its death throes.'

'All right, Effi,' said Innstetten, giving her his hand. 'I won't trouble you with Rügen and so we'll give it up. Agreed? We don't have to stick to Stubbenkammer or to Sassnitz or further down the coast. But where shall we go?'

'I suggest that we stay one more day and wait for the steamer which will be coming from Stettin on its way to Copenhagen if I'm not mistaken. It's said to be very pleasant. Here I feel as if I should never be able to laugh again for the rest of my life and never had laughed either and you know how fond I am of laughing.'

Innstetten was very sympathetic towards her feelings, the more so as he recognized that, in many ways, she was justified. Everything really was melancholy, however beautiful it might be.

So they waited for the Stettin boat and two days later, very early in the morning, they landed in Copenhagen, where they found accommodation in Kongens Nytorv. Within a couple of hours they were in the Thorwaldsen Museum and Effi was saying: 'Yes, that is lovely, Geert and I'm glad that we've managed to find our way here.' A little while later, at luncheon, they made the acquaintance of a family from Jutland who were sitting opposite them at the *table d'hôte* and whose ravishingly beautiful daughter Thora von Penz at once attracted Innstetten's as well as Effi's attention and admiration. Effi's gaze returned again and again to her big blue eyes and flaxen hair, and when they rose from table an hour and a half later, the Penzes, who were unfortunately due to leave Copenhagen that very day, expressed the hope that they might shortly have the opportunity of seeing the young couple from Prussia in their castle at Aggerhus, half a mile from Limfjord, an invitation which the von Innstettens had little hesitation in accepting. In this way, they passed their time at the hotel; but this was not the final pleasure offered by this remarkable day, which, Effi insisted, ought to figure in the calendar as a red-letter day. To fill her cup of happiness to the brim, in the evening they went to a performance in the Tivoli theatre of an Italian pantomime with Harlequin and Columbine. Effi seemed almost intoxicated by their sly antics and when, late that night, they went back to their hotel, she said: 'Do you know, Geert, I really do feel that I'm slowly coming to myself again. I won't mention the lovely Thora; but when I think how we saw Thorwaldsen this morning and that Columbine this evening....'

'Whom you really preferred to Thorwaldsen.'

'Frankly, yes. I'm fond of that sort of thing. Our "good old" Kessin was a disaster for me. Everything about it got on my nerves. Rügen did, too, almost. I suggest we stay on for a few more days in Copenhagen, with a trip to Fredericksborg and Elsinore, of course, and then go over to Jutland. I'm genuinely looking forward to seeing the lovely Thora again, and if I were a man I'd fall in love with her.'

Innstetten gave a laugh: 'You don't yet know whether I won't.'

'That would be all right as far as I'm concerned. Then we'll be in competition and I shall show you that I've got hidden reserves, too.'

'You don't need to draw my attention to that.'

So their journey continued. When they reached Jutland, they drove up the Limfjord to the castle at Aggerhus, where they stayed three days with Penz and his family and then with many stops, and spending longer or shorter periods in Viborg, Flensburg and Kiel, they returned home via Hamburg (which they liked very much indeed), not going directly back to Keithstrasse but, of course, first to Hohen-Cremmen, where they wanted to take a well-earned rest. For Innstetten, this was only for a few days, because his leave was at an end. Effi stayed on for an extra week and said that she was not intending to come home until 3rd October, their wedding-day.

Annie had flourished in the country air and Roswitha's plan that her daughter should run and meet Effi in her little booties was entirely successful. Briest, while playing the fond grandpapa, was full of warnings about the dangers of too much affection and, even more, of being too strict. He was, in fact, completely unchanged. But his tenderness was really reserved only for Effi, who was always on his mind, especially when he was alone with his wife.

'How's Effi, do you think?'

'As kind and loving as ever. We can't be too thankful that God gave us such an affectionate daughter. And how grateful she is for everything and always so pleased to be living under our own roof again.'

'Yes,' said Briest, 'she's more pleased than I like. It's almost as if she still felt this was her home. After all, she's got a husband, and a child, and the husband's a model and the child's an angel and yet she behaves as if Hohen-Cremmen were still the centre of her life and her husband and child couldn't compete with us. She's a model daughter but to my mind she's too much of one. It worries me a little. And it's also unfair on Innstetten. What do you think the situation is there?'

'What do you mean?'

'Well, I mean what I say and you know what. Is she happy? Or is there something wrong? From the very beginning it seemed to me that she respected him rather than loved him. And to my eyes that's a bad thing. Love doesn't always last but respect certainly doesn't. Women get annoyed when they have to respect someone; first they get annoyed, then they get bored and finally they start laughing.'

'Is this a personal experience of yours?'

'I won't say that. I've never been sufficiently respected for that. But don't let's tease each other any more, Luise. Tell me how things are.'

'Oh, Briest, you always keep on coming back to that. We've

196

talked this over a dozen times and more and spoken our mind and you always want to know everything and you keep asking in such a terribly naïve way, as if I could see absolutely everything that goes on underneath. What do you think your daughter is like? Do you imagine that everything is all so straightforward? Or that I'm an oracle – I can't think of the name at the moment – or that the truth is clear as daylight when Effi has poured her heart out to me? Or at least what they call pouring out her heart. What does "pouring out" mean, in fact? She'll take good care not to let me know all her secrets. What's more, I don't know where she gets it from, she is . . . yes, she's a very clever young woman, and this cleverness is all the more dangerous, because she's so affectionate.'

'So you do admit that . . . affectionate. And good as well?'

'Good as well. . . . That is, she's very kindhearted. Where other things are concerned, I'm not quite sure; I think she has a tendency to look on God as a good, kind man and console herself with the hope that he won't be too strict with her.'

'Do you think so?'

'Yes, Briest, I do think so. Incidentally, I think that things are much better. Her character is the same, but since their move their living conditions are much pleasanter and they're getting more used to each other. She said something like that to me and, what's more important for me, I've seen evidence of it, with my own eyes.'

'What did she say?'

'She said: "Mama, things are better now. Innstetten was always a very fine man, there aren't many men like him, but I couldn't really get close to him, there was something remote about him and there was something remote even when he was affectionate. Yes, most of all then. There were times when I was frightened by it."'

'I know what she means.'

'What do you mean, Briest? Are you suggesting that I was frightened or are you saying that you were? I think both those ideas are ridiculous. . . .'

'You were telling me about Effi.'

'Well, she confessed to me that this feeling of strangeness had gone and it made her very happy. Kessin wasn't the right place for her, she said, with its spooky house and the people there, some of them priggish and the others too commonplace, but since her move to Berlin she felt that she had found the right place. He was one of the best of husbands, rather too old for her and too good for her, but now she was on top of things. She used that phrase which rather surprised me, actually.'

'Why so? It's not out of the top drawer, the expression, I mean. But . . .'

'There's something behind it. And she wanted to hint as much to me.'

'Do you think so?'

'Yes, Briest. You always think that she's a limpid stream. But there you're mistaken. She's fond of letting herself drift and if the current is going right, then so is she, too. She's not one for struggling or resisting.'

Roswitha now appeared with Annie and put an end to the conversation.

This conversation between Briest and his wife took place on the same day that Innstetten left Hohen-Cremmen for Berlin, leaving Effi behind for at least one more week. He knew that she found nothing pleasanter than gently dreaming away without a care, hearing nothing but kind words and being told all the time how nice she was. Yes, it was that which did her good more than anything else and, very thankfully, she indulged in it to the utmost, even though there were no distractions at all. There were few visits because, since her marriage, there was very little point of contact, at least with her younger friends, and even the vicarage and the school no longer meant to her what they had for so long. Especially in the school-house, everything was half empty. In the spring, the twins had married two teachers from near Genthin, a big double wedding with a report on the festivities in the *Havelland Observer* and Hulda was in Friesack looking after an old aunt from whom there were expectations and who, incidentally, as is not uncommon in such cases, was proving much longer-lived than Niemeyer had assumed. However, Hulda's letters always expressed satisfaction none the less, not because she really was satisfied, but because she did not wish there to be any suspicion that such an outstanding person as herself could fail to be prospering. Niemeyer, a weak father, showed off her letters with pride and pleasure, while Jahnke, who also lived entirely for his daughters, had worked out for himself that both the young women would be giving birth on the same day, on Christmas Eve. Effi laughed heartily at this and after first expressing the hope to the prospective grandfather that she might be invited to be godmother to the two grandchildren, she turned from family affairs to talk about 'Kjöbenhavn' and Elsinore, Limfjord and Schloss Aggerhus and, above all, about Thora von Penz, whom she could only describe as 'typically Scandinavian', with blue eyes, flaxen hair and always in a red plush, waisted dress. Whereupon Jahnke's face lit up as he said over and over again: 'Yes, they're like that. Pure Aryans, much more German than the Germans.'

Effi intended to be back in Berlin on 3rd October, her wedding-day. It was now the evening before and on the pretext that she must get packed and have everything ready for her return, Effi had gone up to her room relatively early. In fact, all she wanted to do was to be alone, because, however much she enjoyed talking, there were also times when she longed for peace and quiet.

Her rooms were at the top of the house and looked out over the garden; Roswitha was sleeping with Annie in the smaller of them, with the door ajar; in the larger one, which she occupied herself, Effi was walking to and fro; the lower casement windows were open and the small white curtains blew out with the wind and then slowly settled on to the back of the chair until a fresh gust would lift them again. As it did so, the light became so bright that you could clearly read the inscriptions on the pictures in narrow, gold-edged frames hanging over the sofa: 'The assault on Düppel, redoubt No. V' and beside it: 'King William and Count Bismarck on the heights of Lipa'. Effi shook her head and smiled: 'Next time I'm here, I must ask for some other pictures, I can't bear those ones all about war.' And then she closed one of the windows and sat down beside the other one, which she left open. How lovely everything was! Beside the church-tower, the moon was shining on the lawn with its sundial and beds of heliotropes. Everything was bathed in a silvery shimmer and white strips of light lay next to the bands of shadows, like white linen put out to bleach. Further on were the tall rhubarb plants, their leaves already tinged with autumn yellow, and she was reminded of the day, now little less than two years ago, when she had been playing down there with Hulda and the Jahnke girls. And when the visitor had come, she had gone up the few steps beside the bench and an hour later she was engaged to be married.

She stood up and went to listen at the door. Roswitha was already asleep and Annie as well.

And all of a sudden, as she was looking at her child, all sorts of memories of her life in Kessin came crowding, unbidden, into her mind: she saw the governor's house with its gable and its view over the plantation and she was sitting in the rocking chair and rocking to and fro; and now Crampas approached to wish her good-day and then Roswitha arrived with the baby and she took it and lifted it high in the air and kissed it.

'That was the first day. That was the beginning.' And still reflecting on this, she left the room where the two of them were asleep and sat down again at the open window and looked out into the silence of the night.

'I can't get away from it,' she said. 'And the worst thing, the thing that completely puzzles me about myself, is that . . .'

At that moment the clock in the tower started striking and Effi counted the strokes.

'Ten. And this time tomorrow I'll be in Berlin and we'll be talking about how it's our wedding-day and he will say nice, kind things to me and perhaps affectionate things. And I'll be sitting there listening with this guilt on my mind and conscience.'

She propped her head on her hand and stared straight ahead in the silence.

'And this guilt on my conscience,' she repeated. 'Yes, it's there – but is it a weight on my conscience? No, it's not and that's what makes me frightened about myself. The thing that weighs on me is something quite different – fear, a dreadful fear, the constant apprehension that one day it will all be discovered. And then, apart from the fear, there's the shame. I'm ashamed. But in the same way as I'm not properly repentant, so I'm not properly ashamed either. I'm ashamed only because of the constant lying and deception; it was always my boast that I couldn't lie and didn't need to, either; lying is so vile. And now I've had to lie all the time and in front of everybody, in small things as well as large ones, and Rummschüttel realized it and shrugged his shoulders and who knows what he thinks of me – at any rate, not very highly. Yes, I'm really afraid and ashamed of all my lying. But I don't feel ashamed of being guilty, not really, or at any rate, not ashamed enough, and that is what's destroying me, because I'm not ashamed. If all women are like that, then it's horrible and if they aren't like that, which I hope is the case, then it's a bad thing for me, there's something wrong with my soul, I don't have the proper feelings. And old Niemeyer, when he was still in his prime, once said that to me when I was still not much more than a child: the important thing was to feel properly and if you could do that, the worst could never happen to anyone and if someone couldn't do that, then they'd always be in constant danger, and what people call the devil would always have you in his power. O merciful God, is that what has happened with me?'

And sinking her head in her arms, she broke into bitter tears.

When she lifted her head again, she was calmer and looked out once more into the garden. Everything was very still and from the plane-trees she could hear a gentle rustle, as if it were raining.

Time passed. A voice rang out from across the village street: it was the old night-watchman Kulicke calling out the time, and when he stopped, she could hear, half a mile away, the clatter of the train passing through Hohen-Cremmen. Then the noise grew fainter and died away completely and only the rustle of the plane-trees remained, like the sound of gentle rain.

But it was only the night breeze passing.

25

NEXT evening, Effi was back again in Berlin and Innstetten met her at the station with Rollo, who trotted beside them as they drove chatting through the Tiergarten.

'I was half thinking you might not keep your word.'

'But really, Geert, I do keep my word, that's the least one can do.'

'Don't say that. It's a big thing, always to keep your word. And occasionally one can't do it. Just think back. I was expecting you in Kessin that time, when you were renting the flat and who was it who didn't come? Effi.'

'Well, that was different.'

She did not want to say: 'I was ill,' and Innstetten failed to notice. In any case, his head was full of other things, connected with his post and his social position. 'Really, our life in Berlin is only just beginning. In April, when we moved in, the season was coming to an end, so that we hardly had time to pay our calls and Wüllersdorf was the only person we knew at all well and unfortunately he's a bachelor. From June onwards, everything goes to sleep and all the shutters that are down give you plenty of warning: 'Everybody's gone', even if it's true or not makes no difference .... So what was left? The odd chat with Cousin Briest, the odd meal at Hiller's – that's not what's meant by Berlin life. But now everything's going to change. I've noted the names of all the senior officials active enough to entertain. And we're going to entertain, too, and when winter comes, the whole ministry will be saying: "Well, the most charming of all the wives is Frau von Innstetten."'

'Oh Geert, you're unrecognizable, you sound as if you're making up to me!'

'It's our wedding-day, so you must make allowances for me.'

Innstetten was determined to change the quiet life that he had led as governor for one socially more active, both for his own and Effi's sake; but initially this was only possible to a limited extent, because the time was not yet ripe and the pleasantest side of their new life was, exactly as it had been during the last six months, their home life. Wüllersdorf used to call often, as well as Cousin Briest, and when these two were there, word was sent up to the Gizickis, a young married couple who lived above them. Gizicki himself was a district-court councillor and his clever, lively wife was *née* von Schmettau. Occasionally there was music and for a short while they tried whist but they gave it up again because they found that it was pleasanter to chat. The Gizickis had, until a short while ago, been living in a small town in Upper Silesia, and Wüllersdorf, albeit some years ago now, had served in the dreariest little towns of the province of Posen and, in consequence, he used to quote, with equal enjoyment and mock solemnity:

> Schrimm
> Ist schlimm,
> Rogasen
> Zum Rasen,
> Aber weh dir nach Samter
> Verdammter.*

* Schrimm is bad, Rogasen makes you mad, but woe betide if you are condemned to reside in Samter.

No one was more amused than Effi and this generally led to re-counting a whole host of stories about life in petty provincial towns. Kessin, with Gieshübler and la Trippelli and the head forester Ring and Sidonie Grasenabb, obviously had its turn as well and when Innstetten was in good form, he would really let himself go: 'Ah yes,' he would say on such occasions, 'our dear old Kessin! I must confess that it really was full of characters, led by Crampas, Major Crampas, the perfect beau and something of a bluebeard, who had taken a great fancy to my wife, I don't know whether I ought to say understandably or unaccountably ...' 'Let's say understandably,' interjected Wüllersdorf, 'because I assume that he was the president of the club and liked acting, either the part of the lover or the man of the world. And perhaps he was even some-thing better still, he may even have been a tenor.'

Innstetten confirmed both these suppositions and Effi tried to join in the fun, but it was a strain and when the guests had left and Innstetten had gone to his room to try to finish off a pile of papers, she always fell prey once again to all her former preoccupations and she had the feeling that there was a shadow hanging over her.

Anxieties of this sort still pursued her. But they were becoming less frequent and less intense, which was not surprising in view of the way in which her life was now developing. The affection which was shown, not only by Innstetten but by people far less close to her, not least the almost tender friendship shown her by the minister's wife, a youngish woman herself – all this at least reduced the fears and cares of her past life, and when another year had passed and, for the ceremony of a new foundation, the Empress picked the 'wife of the privy councillor' and made her one of the ladies-in-waiting, while old Kaiser Wilhelm at the Court Ball had addressed a few gracious words of compliment to the beautiful young woman 'of whom he had already heard', her cares gradually fell away. It *had* happened, but a long, long time ago, as if on another planet, and everything was becoming hazy and dreamlike.

The parents from Hohen-Cremmen came to visit them occa-sionally and were glad to see how happy their children were; Annie was growing up – 'as pretty as her grandmother' old Briest said – and if there was any cloud at all, it was the fact that it now had to be more or less accepted that little Annie would not be having a brother or sister; the house of Innstetten, since there were not even any cousins on the male side, was thus, presumably, going to die out. Briest, who could not take the question of the perpetuation of other families seriously, since he really believed only in his own, used occasionally to joke about it and say: 'Well, Innstetten, if things go on like this, then no doubt Annie will marry a banker in due course – I hope a Christian, if there are any left by that time – and out of respect for the old baronial house of Innstetten, His Majesty will allow her banking progeny to continue in Gotha's Almanach, or what's less important, in Prussian history, under the name of 'von *der** Innstetten' – observations which were always received by Innstetten himself with embarrassment, while Frau von Briest shrugged her shoulders, and Effi, on the other hand, merely laughed. She was proud of being of noble birth, but only as far as it concerned herself and she would certainly have had no objection whatsoever to an elegant, experienced, worldly and, above all, very, very rich son-in-law.

Yes, Effi took the question of inheritance lightly, as charming young women do; but after a very long time – they had already been in the new post more than six years – old Rummschüttel, who had something of a reputation as a gynaecologist, was consulted by Frau von Briest. He prescribed a visit to Schwalbach. But since Effi had been suffering from catarrh ever since last winter and had even had her lungs sounded two or three times, finally he said: 'Well then, my dear Frau von Briest, let's say three weeks in Schwalbach to begin with and then the same amount of time at Ems. But during the cure at Ems, Innstetten may join his wife. So all in all, it means being separated for three weeks. I can't do better than that for you, my dear Innstetten.'

So the matter was settled, and it was further decided that Effi should be accompanied by the wife of a privy councillor called Zwicker, 'for the latter's protection', as Briest said, in which he was not entirely mistaken, because Frau Zwicker, in spite of being well on the wrong side of forty, was in considerably more urgent need of protection than Effi. Innstetten, once again heavily involved in representing the minister, complained that, quite apart from Schwalbach, he would probably have to give up the idea of spending any time with Effi in Ems. Meanwhile 24th June, Midsummer's Day, was fixed as the date of the departure and Roswitha helped her mistress

* i.e. on the mother's side.

204

in her packing and marking the linen. Effi had kept all her old affection for her, and indeed Roswitha was the only person with whom she could speak freely about the past, about Kessin and Crampas, the Chinaman and Captain Thomsen's niece.

'Tell me, Roswitha, you're a Catholic, aren't you. Don't you ever go to confession?'

'No.'

'Why not?'

'I used to go. But I still didn't confess properly.'

'But that's very wrong. In that case, it can't help.'

'Oh, m'lady, in our village everybody did that. And some of them just giggled.'

'Didn't you ever feel, then, that it was a good thing, if you've got something on your mind, to be able to get it off your conscience?'

'No, m'lady. I was afraid that time my father came after me with the red-hot iron; yes, I was very afraid then but it wasn't anything else.'

'Not afraid of God?'

'Not really, m'lady. If you're as afraid of your father as I was, then you're not so afraid of God. I just kept thinking that God was good and would help a poor miserable creature like me.'

Effi smiled and did not pursue the matter further; it seemed natural to her that Roswitha should talk as she did. But she added: 'You know, Roswitha, when I come back, we must talk about all this seriously some time. It really was very sinful.'

'About the child and because it went hungry? Yes, m'lady, it was. But it wasn't me, it was the other people. And then it was all such a long time ago, too.'

26

EFFI had now been away more than four weeks and was writing cheerful, almost aggressively cheerful letters, especially since her arrival in Ems, where, as she said, she was in the company of people, that is of men, of a sort that had rarely appeared in Schwalbach. Her companion, Frau Zwicker, had, indeed – she continued – raised certain doubts as to the suitability of these additions to their company, in the interests of the cure, and even voiced strong objections to them, naturally with an expression on her face that more or less suggested the opposite. The Zwicker woman was delightful, rather free and easy and probably even a woman with a past, but extremely amusing and one could learn a great deal from her; she herself had never felt so much a child, in spite of being twenty-five years old, as she had since she had got to know her. She was so well read, too, even in foreign literature, and when for example she, Effi, had recently been talking of *Nana* and asked if it were really so dreadful, Frau Zwicker had replied: 'But my dear Baroness, what do you mean by dreadful? There are all sorts of things that are quite, quite different.' 'She seemed to want to tell me about all these "different things",' Effi's letter concluded, 'but I declined because I know that you blame the moral decline of our times on that sort of thing, I expect rightly. But I didn't find it easy to do. Another thing is that Ems is like an oven and we're suffering terribly from the heat.'

Innstetten had read this last missive with mixed feelings, half amused and yet somewhat out of humour. Frau Zwicker was really not the sort of woman for Effi who, at the moment, had a tendency to drift towards the left; but he abandoned any idea of writing to her on this subject, for one reason because he didn't wish to put her out and also for the even better reason that he told himself that it wouldn't have any effect anyway. At the same time, he was longing for his wife's return and felt it unfair that, when every senior officer in the ministry was either away or about to go on leave, he found himself doing not merely the same but unfortunately double the amount of work.

Yes, Innstetten was longing for a break in his work and in his loneliness, and similar feelings were shared in the kitchen, where Annie liked to spend her time after school, as was quite natural in as much as Roswitha and Joanna not only both loved her equally well but were also both on the same good terms with each other as they had always been. This friendship between the two maids was a favourite topic of conversation between the various friends of the house and Gizicki said to Wüllersdorf: 'I see it as fresh proof of the old saw: "I would have men about me that are fat." Caesar knew all about human nature and realized that being agreeable and sociable is really a question of *embonpoint*.' Indeed, this foreign expression, difficult to avoid in this case, while applicable to both girls, was complimentary to Roswitha, whereas when applied to Joanna, it was nothing but the simple truth. The latter could, in fact, hardly be called corpulent but merely a sturdy, strapping girl of normal proportions who looked everyone straight in the face with her blue eyes, and her own peculiar conquering air that was yet entirely in keeping. Full of high principles and with a strong sense of decorum, she based her life on her convictions as servant in a good family and her feeling of superiority over Roswitha, who had never completely outgrown her peasant origins, was so strong that when, as occasionally happened, Roswitha enjoyed temporary preference, she would merely smile. To be sure, if such things had to be, such a preference was just a minor, likeable eccentricity of her mistress, which poor old Roswitha, with her everlasting tale of how her father chased her with the red-hot iron bar, could certainly be permitted. 'If people don't behave in that way, that sort of thing doesn't happen.' Such were her thoughts, which, however, she kept to herself.

In fact, they lived together in friendly harmony. The most important factor in their peace and good understanding was the fact that, by unwritten agreement, they had divided Annie's care and even, almost, her education between the two of them. Roswitha had the poetry department, the fairy-tale and story-telling, whereas Joanna was in charge of good manners, a division of labour which was so deeply rooted on both sides that questions of jurisdiction hardly ever arose; a state of affairs certainly helped by Annie's own character, for she had a marked tendency to be the 'little miss', in which she could have had no better teacher than Joanna.

To repeat, therefore: both stood equally high in Annie's eyes. At present, however, in view of the preparations for Effi's return, Roswitha was slightly ahead of her rival because, in accordance with the protocol, it was she who had been put in charge of arrangements for welcoming Effi on her return. This welcome fell into two parts: a flower garland and in conclusion a poetry recitation. Once the lengthy hesitation as to whether it should be 'W' or 'E. v. I.' had been settled, the garland had not offered any special difficulty; the choice had fallen on a 'W' woven in forget-me-nots, but the question of the poem seemed likely to provoke much more embarrassment and would perhaps have been insoluble, had Roswitha not had the courage to stop the judge on his way up to the second floor as he was returning from a court sitting and courageously ask him for his views as to a piece of poetry. Gizicki was a very friendly man and later that same afternoon the cook received the following piece of verse, as requested:

> Mama, we've been waiting for you
> Days and weeks and hours too.
> We welcome you with bated breath
> And make for you a lovely wreath.
> Our kind papa has lost his pain,
> His wife, our mother's back again.
> Roswitha laughs, Joanna too,
> Annie jumps up from her shoe
> And cries 'Welcome to you!'

Of course, the words had to be learnt by heart that very evening, while at the same time their suitability or lack of it had also to be subjected to critical scrutiny. The emphasis on wife and mother, in Joanna's opinion, although it seemed at first very appropriate, yet somehow contained a suggestion that might give offence, and personally, as a 'wife and mother', she would feel offended by it. Rather worried by this remark, Annie promised to show the poem to her teacher next day and returned with the comment: Miss was completely in agreement with 'wife and mother', but on the other hand against 'Roswitha and Joanna', whereupon Roswitha declared that 'Miss' was a silly goose, and that was what came from too much learning.

This conversation between the maids and Annie to settle the question of the disputed lines had taken place on a Wednesday. Next morning, Innstetten went off to the ministry; a letter from Effi fixing the probable date of her arrival had not yet arrived, although it was expected to be at the end of the following week. It was twelve o'clock, school was over and just as Annie was coming into Keithstrasse from the direction of the canal, with her satchel on her back, she met Roswitha in front of the flat.

'Let's see who can get to the top of the stairs first,' said Annie. Roswitha refused to have anything to do with such a race but Annie dashed ahead and when she reached the top she stumbled and fell so awkwardly that her forehead struck against the scraper standing beside the stairs and blood started pouring from it. Laboriously puffing and blowing, Roswitha came up and quickly rang the bell, and when Joanna had carried the child, now somewhat scared, indoors, they tried to decide what was to be done: 'We must send for the doctor ... we must send for the master ... the porter's little girl Lene must be out of school by now, too.' But then they decided against doing anything like that because it would take too long; something had to be done at once and so they bundled the child on to the sofa and began to apply cold water compresses.

Everything went well and they began to feel calmer. 'And now we must bandage her up,' said Roswitha finally. 'There must still be that long bandage which the mistress cut up last winter when she twisted her foot on the ice. ...' 'Of course, of course,' said Joanna, 'only where can the bandage be? Yes, that's right, I remember, it's in her sewing-table. It's bound to be locked but the lock is child's play; just go and fetch the chisel, Roswitha. We'll break the lid open.' And so they began to rummage around in the drawers, high and low, but the roll of bandage could not be found. 'But I know I've seen it,' said Roswitha and as she testily went on searching, everything she came upon was hurriedly piled on the broad windowsill: all sorts of sewing things, pin-cushions, reels of thread, skeins of silk, dried posies of violets, cards, notes and finally, on the third and bottom layer, a small bundle of letters rolled up and tied together with red silk thread. But there was still no bandage.

At this moment, Innstetten came in.

'Oh my God,' said Roswitha and stood, horrified, beside the child. 'It's nothing, master. Annie fell on the iron scraper ... oh my goodness, what will the mistress say! Yet it's a good thing that she wasn't here when it happened.'

Meanwhile Innstetten had taken the temporary compresses off and saw that it was a deep cut but not a dangerous one. 'It's not too bad,' he said. 'All the same, Roswitha, we must let Rummschüttel see it. Lene can go, she'll have time now. But what on earth has happened to the work-table?' And Roswitha explained how they had been looking for the roll of bandage; but now she would rather cut a fresh piece of linen.

Innstetten agreed and he sat down beside the child as soon as the two maids had left the room. 'You're so wild, Annie, you get that from your mother. You dash about like a whirlwind. But it doesn't get you anywhere or at best, somewhere like this.' And he pointed to the wound and gave her a kiss. 'But you didn't cry, you're a good girl and so I'll forgive you for being so wild. . . . I think the doctor will be here in an hour's time; just do as he says and when he s bandaged you up don't pull it about or touch it or press on it and then it will get well quickly, and when your mother comes everything will be all right again, or almost. But it's a good thing that it's not until next week, the end of next week, so she says. I've just had a letter from her; she sends her love and is looking forward to seeing you.'

'Couldn't you read me the letter, please, Papa?'

'Yes, of course I will.'

But before he could do so, Joanna came to announce that the meal was served. In spite of her wound, Annie stood up and sat at the table with her father.

27

FOR a while Innstetten and Annie sat opposite each other without saying a word; finally, as their silence was becoming embarrassing for him, he asked her a few questions about her headmistress and which teacher she really liked best. Annie replied unenthusiastically, for she felt that Innstetten was not really interested. Things only improved when, after the second course, Joanna whispered to her 'little Annie' that there was something else to come. And in fact Roswitha, feeling herself partly responsible towards her darling for the unfortunate event of the day, had made an extra effort and produced an omelette with apple slices.

At this, Annie became somewhat more talkative; Innstetten's mood also improved, and then, very soon afterwards, the bell rang and Rummschüttel came in. He was merely making a social call without any inkling that he had been sent for. He expressed satisfaction at the compresses. 'Fetch a little more antiseptic and let Annie stay at home tomorrow. Above all, rest.' Then he asked after Effi and what news there was from Ems. He would come in again tomorrow for a further examination.

When they had risen from table and gone into the next room – the one where they had been so urgently and fruitlessly looking for the bandage, Annie was made to lie down on the sofa again. Joanna came and sat down beside the child while Innstetten began to put back into the sewing-table the motley collection of things that were still lying scattered over the window-sill. Once or twice he was uncertain where the things belonged and had to ask:

'Where did the letters come from, Joanna?'

'Right at the bottom,' she replied, 'in this compartment here.'

During this question and answer, Innstetten looked rather more closely than before at the little packet, tied round with red thread, which looked like a packet of notes rather than letters. He slid his thumb and index finger down the side of the bundle, as if it were a pack of cards, and caught a glimpse of a few odd lines, or rather, isolated words. While it could not be said that he clearly recognized anything, none the less it seemed to him that he had seen the writing before somewhere.

Should he look more closely?

'Joanna, you may bring us the coffee. Annie will have half a cup, too. The doctor didn't forbid it and anything that is not forbidden is permitted.'

As he said that, he unwound the red thread, and as Joanna left the room he ran his fingers over all the letters in the packet. Only two or three of the letters bore an address: Frau Landrat von Innstetten. Now he recognized the writing; it was the major's. Innstetten was unaware of any correspondence between Crampas and Effi; his head began to spin. He pocketed the packet and went back into his room. A few minutes later Joanna tapped gently on the door as a sign that the coffee was ready. Innstetten replied but nothing further happened: silence reigned. It was not until a quarter of an hour had passed that he could be heard once more walking up and down on the carpet. 'What's wrong with daddy?' Joanna said to Annie. 'The doctor told him that it was nothing.'

The footsteps in the next room went on and on. Finally, Innstetten came out again and said: 'Joanna, look after Annie and see that she stays quietly on the sofa. I'm going out for an hour or possibly two.'

Then he looked closely at the child and went off.

'Did you see how daddy looked, Joanna?'

'Yes, Annie. Something must have made him very angry. He was quite pale. I've never seen him looking like that before.'

Hours passed. The sun had already set and only a red glow was reflected on the roofs opposite when Innstetten returned. He took Annie's hand, asked her how she was and then instructed Joanna to bring the lamp into his room.

The lamp was brought. In its green shade were set some oval-shaped, semi-transparent photographs, all different portraits of his wife which had been taken in Kessin at the time of the production of Wickert's *Schritt vom Wege*, to be given to all the various actors and actresses. Innstetten slowly turned the shade from left to right as he examined each photograph. When he stopped doing this, he opened the balcony door, since he found it rather sultry, and then picked up the packet of letters again. It seemed that while looking through them the first time he had picked out some of them straightaway and put them on the top. In a low voice, he now read them over again to himself.

'Be in the dunes again, behind the mill, this afternoon. We can talk undisturbed in old Frau Adermann's place – the house is quite isolated. You must not be so scared about everything. We have *our* rights, too. And when you can convince yourself of that, I think that you'll stop being afraid. Life wouldn't be worth living if things always had to be just as they happen to be. The best of life goes beyond any consideration of that sort. Learn how to enjoy it!'

' . . . get away, you wrote to me. Impossible. I can't abandon my wife, even more so because it would be leaving her in need. It's not possible and we must not take things too seriously, otherwise we shall be helpless and miserable. Our best card is *not* to be serious. Fate is responsible. Everything had to be as it is. And would you have wanted it otherwise, so that we had never met?'

Then came the third letter:

'Be at the same place again today. How can I possibly live here without you? In this poky old town! I'm beside myself and there's only one thing in which I agree with you – it will be our salvation and in spite of everything we must bless the hand that has decreed that we have to separate.'

Hardly had Innstetten put the letters down when the outdoor bell rang. A moment later, Joanna announced: 'Privy Councillor Wüllersdorf!'

Wüllersdorf came in and saw at first glance that something was amiss.

Innstetten's first words were: 'Forgive me, Wüllersdorf, for asking you to call on me immediately. I don't like disturbing people in the evening and least of all an overworked under-secretary. But I couldn't do anything else. Please make yourself comfortable. Have a cigar.'

Wüllersdorf took a seat. Innstetten started walking up and down again. Consumed by agitation, he would have liked to have kept moving but realizing that it could not be done, he took a cigar himself, sat down opposite Wüllersdorf and tried to compose himself.

'I've asked you to come and see me on two matters,' he began. 'First, to issue a challenge on my behalf, and secondly to be my second in the duel itself; the first is not very agreeable and the second even less so. What's your answer?'

'You know that I'm at your disposal, Innstetten. But before you tell me any more about it, forgive me if I ask you the naïve preliminary question: is it necessary? Hasn't the time passed for you to be handling a pistol and for me to be watching you do it? But don't misunderstand me, this doesn't mean I'm saying no. How could I refuse such a request from you! But now tell me what's it all about.'

'It's about my wife's lover, who was at the same time a friend of mine, or almost.'

Wüllersdorf stared at Innstetten. 'Innstetten, that's not possible.'

'It's more than possible, it's certain. Read these!'

Wüllersdorf skimmed through them. 'Are these addressed to your wife?'

'Yes, I found them today in her sewing-table.'

'And who wrote them?'

'Major Crampas.'

'So these refer to things that took place when you were still in Kessin?'

Innstetten nodded.

'So it's six or six and a half years ago?'

'Yes.'

Wüllersdorf said nothing. After a pause, Innstetten spoke: 'It almost seemed as if those six or seven years set you wondering. There's the question of time limit, of course, but I don't really know whether this is a case where such a limit could properly apply.'

'I don't know, either,' said Wüllersdorf, 'and I frankly confess that everything seems to turn on that question.'

Innstetten looked him full in the face.

'Do you mean that quite seriously?'

'Quite seriously. It's not a matter for joking or being clever about. . . .'

'I'm curious to know what you mean by that. Tell me frankly what your attitude is.'

'Innstetten, you're in a frightful situation and your happiness has been destroyed for ever. But if you kill the lover, then your wife's happiness is, as it were, doubly destroyed and the grief or sorrow that you have caused will be added to the grief or sorrow that you have *been* caused. It all turns on this question, do you really have to do it? Do you feel so injured, so insulted, so enraged that one of you must disappear, he or you? Is that how it is?'

'I don't know.'

'You must know.'

Innstetten had sprung to his feet and gone to the window where he was nervously tapping on the panes. Then he spun round again, went up to Wüllersdorf and said: 'No, that's not how it is.'

'How is it then?'

'It's just that I'm infinitely unhappy, I'm humiliated, I've been shamefully deceived and yet in spite of that I have no feeling of hatred at all, or even a thirst for vengeance. And if I ask myself why not, then the first reason that comes to me is merely – the lapse of time. People always talk about an unforgivable sin and in God's eyes this is wrong, but not in man's eyes. I should never have believed that time, purely as time, could have such an effect. And then the second thing is that I love my wife, yes, strange to say, I still love her, and however frightful all these things appear to me, yet I'm so much under her spell, she's so lovable and so gay, she has such a special charm all of her own, that, in spite of myself, I feel tempted, in my heart of hearts, to forgive her.'

Wüllersdorf nodded. 'I can understand very well what you're saying, Innstetten, I'd perhaps feel the same myself. But if you feel like that on the subject and are saying to me: "I love this woman so much that I can forgive everything" and if we also add the other thing, that this all happened long, long ago, like something on another planet – well, if things are like that, Innstetten, then I must ask you this question: why all this fuss?'

'Because it's got to be done, nevertheless. I've turned this thing over and over again in my mind. We're not isolated persons, we belong to a whole society and we have constantly to consider that society, we're completely dependent on it. If it were possible to live in isolation, then I could let it pass. I should then be bearing a burden that I had myself accepted, my true happiness would have disappeared, but so many people live without "true happiness" that I should have had to do so, too – and would have. No one *needs* to be happy, and least of all no one has any claim to be, and we don't necessarily have to rid the world of someone who has robbed us of our happiness. If we're turning our backs on the world, we can let him go on living too. But with people living all together, something has evolved that now exists and we've become accustomed to judge everything, ourselves and others, according to its rules. And it's no good transgressing them, society will despise us and finally we will despise ourselves and not be able to bear it and blow our brains out. Forgive me for giving you this lecture which, after all, is only saying what everyone has said to himself hundreds of times. But how can anyone really say anything new? So once again, there's no hatred or anything of that sort and I don't want to have blood on my hands merely for the sake of the happiness I've been deprived of, but that *something* which forms society – call it a tyrant if you like – is not concerned with charm or love, or even with how long ago a thing took place. I've no choice, I must do it.'

'I'm still not sure, Innstetten . . . .'

Innstetten smiled. 'You shall decide for yourself, Wüllersdorf. It's now ten o'clock. Six hours ago, I'll grant you this in advance, the cards were still in my hand and I could have done one thing or another, there was still a way out. But not any longer, I'm in an impasse. I've only myself to blame; if you like, I should have been more guarded and shown more self-control, have kept everything to myself and fought it all out in my own mind. But it came so suddenly and so violently that I can hardly blame myself for not having been able to control my reactions more successfully. I went to your place and wrote you a note and by doing that the game passed out of my hands. From that moment onwards, there was someone else who knew something of my misfortune and, what is

215

more important, of the stain on my honour; and as soon as we had exchanged our first words, there was someone else who knew all about it. And, because there is such a person, I can't go back.'

'I'm still not sure,' repeated Wüllersdorf. 'I don't like using a stale cliché but there's no better way of putting it: "I'll be as silent as the grave," Innstetten.'

'Yes, Wüllersdorf, that's what people always say. But there is no keeping a secret. And if you do as you say and are discretion itself towards others, even so *you* know about it and it doesn't help me where you're concerned if you've just expressed approval and even said: "I can understand all that you're saying." The fact of the matter is, that from this moment onwards I'm dependent on your sympathy and every word that you hear me exchange with my wife will be checked by you, whether you want to or not, and if my wife talks about being faithful or, as women do, sits in judgement on another woman, then I shan't know where to look. Or suppose it happens that, in some quite ordinary question of an affront having been given, I suggest that allowances might be made because no harm has been done, or some such thing, then a smile will cross your face or at least start to cross it and in your mind you'll be saying to yourself: "Good old Innstetten, where insults are concerned he really has a passion for analysing the exact amount of offensive material they contain and he never finds a sufficient quantity of poison gas. He's never been able to discover anything that smells too strongly for him . . ." Am I right, Wüllersdorf, or not?'

Wüllersdorf had risen to his feet. 'It's terrifying to think that you're right, but you *are* right. I won't worry you any longer with my question as to whether it's necessary. The world is how it is and things don't go the way that we want but the way that others want. All that high-falutin' talk about "God's judgement" is nonsense, of course, and we don't want any of that, yet our own cult of honour on the other hand is idolatry. But we must submit to it, as long as the idol stands.'

Innstetten nodded.

They stayed talking for another quarter of an hour and it was arranged that Wüllersdorf should set off that very evening. There was a night train at twelve.

Then they parted with a brief: 'See you in Kessin!'

28

THE following evening, as arranged, Innstetten set off himself. He travelled in the same train which Wüllersdorf had taken the day before and shortly after five a.m. he arrived at the station where he had to change for Kessin. As always in the season, the steamer which has so frequently been mentioned was leaving immediately after the arrival of the train and by the time he reached the bottom of the steps leading down the railway embankment Innstetten could already hear its bell ringing. It was less than three minutes' walk to where the boat was moored and Innstetten made his way thither, wishing 'good day' to the captain, who seemed somewhat embarrassed and must presumably have heard about the whole affair in the course of the previous day. Innstetten installed himself beside the helmsman.

The ship at once cast off from the jetty. The weather was superb, with a bright morning sun, and there were few passengers on board. Innstetten remembered the day when, returning with Effi from their honeymoon, they had driven in an open carriage along the bank of the Kessine – a grey November day, he recalled, but there was joy in his heart; and now the position was reversed: outside, all was light and November was in his heart. He had gone this way many, many times since then, and the peacefulness which lay over the fields, the cattle in their pastures which looked up as he drove past, the people as they worked, the fertile soil, had all brought contentment to his mind; and now, in harsh contrast, he was glad when clouds appeared and began to obscure the laughing blue sky. So they continued down the river and soon, once they had crossed the magnificent expanse of Breitling Broad, the tower of Kessin church came in sight and shortly afterwards the quayside and the long line of houses with the ships and boats in front. Now they had arrived. Innstetten took leave of the captain and walked over to the gangway which had been wheeled up to make it easier to disembark. Wüllersdorf was already there. They greeted each other without a word being spoken and then walked diagonally across the quayside to Hoppensack's Hotel, where they sat down under an awning.

'I took a room here yesterday morning,' said Wüllersdorf, who was not anxious to go into details straightaway. 'When one thinks what a miserable hole Kessin is, it's amazing to find such a good hotel here. I've no doubt that my good friend the head waiter speaks three languages: in fact, to judge by his hair-parting and his low-cut waistcoat, he might well go up to four. . . . Jean, will you please bring us coffee and brandy.'

Innstetten understood perfectly well Wüllersdorf's motive in striking this note and approved of it, but he was still not quite able to control his agitation and, without thinking, pulled out his watch.

'We've got time,' said Wüllersdorf. 'Still about an hour and a half or almost. I've ordered the carriage for 8.15. We shan't have to drive more than ten minutes.'

'Where to?'

'First of all, Crampas suggested a corner of the wood just behind the cemetery. But then he interrupted himself and said: "No, not there," so then we agreed on a spot somewhere among the dunes. Close to the beach; the front line of sand-dunes has a gap and you look on to the sea.'

Innstetten smiled. 'Crampas seems to have selected a beauty spot for himself. That always was his style. How did he take it?'

'Wonderfully well.'

'Arrogant? Facetious?'

'Neither the one nor the other. I frankly confess, Innstetten, that I was shaken. When I mentioned your name, he went as pale as death and struggled to control himself and I saw the corners of his mouth twitching. But that was over in a flash and then he'd regained his self-control and from then onwards he showed only a sort of resigned melancholy. I'm quite convinced that he has the feeling that he won't come out of this safe and sound and that he doesn't want to. If I assess him correctly, he's fond of life and at the same time indifferent towards it. . . . He takes everything that comes while still realizing that it's not worth much.'

'Who's going to be his second? Or rather, who's he bringing with him?'

'As soon as he'd taken a grip on himself, that was his chief concern. He mentioned the names of two or three local gentry but then he didn't pursue it because they were too old and too pious, and he said he would telegraph to his old friend Buddenbrook in Treptow. He's arrived, a capital fellow, dashing and yet childish at the same time. He couldn't keep calm and he kept on walking up and down in the greatest excitement. But when I had told him the whole story, he said, just as we did: "You're quite right, it's got to be done." '

The coffee came. They each took a cigar and once again Wüllersdorf set about guiding the conversation on to more casual matters.

'I'm surprised that none of the inhabitants has come to welcome you. I know that people were very fond of you. And even your friend Gieshübler . . .'

Innstetten smiled: 'You don't know the people who live along the coast here. Half of them are narrow-minded and half of them are crafty, not very much to my liking. But one virtue they do have, they're all very polite. And even my old friend Gieshübler. Naturally, they all know what's happening but for that reason they'll be careful not to be inquisitive.'

At this moment, a chaise-coach with the hood down made its appearance on their left. It was early and so it was not hurrying.

'Is that ours?' asked Innstetten.

'Presumably.'

Immediately afterwards the carriage stopped in front of the hotel and Innstetten and Wüllersdorf stood up.

Wüllersdorf went up to the driver and said: 'To the pier. . . .'

The pier lay on the opposite side of the beach, right instead of left, and the false instruction had been given merely to obviate any possible incidents which might still occur. Moreover, whether you intended to keep left or right eventually, you had in any case to go through the plantation, and so their way led them inevitably past Innstetten's old home. The house was more silent than ever; even the ground-floor rooms looked relatively neglected, so the state of the upstairs rooms could well be imagined. And the feeling of weirdness which Innstetten himself had so often attacked or gently made fun of in Effi now impressed him too and he was glad when they had passed it.

'That's where I used to live,' he said to Wüllersdorf.

'It looks strange, rather empty and deserted.'

'It may well be. People in the town thought it was haunted, and looking at it today I don't blame them.'

'What was wrong with it then?'

'Oh, a lot of rubbish: an old ship's captain with a granddaughter or a niece who disappeared one fine day and then a Chinaman who was perhaps her lover and in the entrance hall a shark and a crocodile hanging from the ceiling and always swaying. An extraordinary story, but not for now. We've other things on our minds, after all.'

'Don't forget that it may all go off smoothly.'

'It need not. And earlier on, Wüllersdorf, when you were talking about Crampas, you were speaking differently yourself.'

Soon afterwards, when they had passed the plantation, the driver was about to turn right. 'No, let's keep left. We can go to the pier later.' So the coachman turned left into a wide drive which led straight towards the wood behind the men's bathing beach. When they were three hundred yards from the wood, Wüllersdorf stopped the carriage and, still in the loose sand, the two walked on down a fairly wide track cutting at right angles through the dunes which formed three ridges at this point. Thick clumps of wild oats were dotted about on all sides and around them were growing everlasting flowers and a few blood-red carnations. Innstetten bent down and put a carnation in his buttonhole. 'We'll keep the everlasting flowers for later.'

They walked thus for five minutes. When they arrived at the fairly deep hollow which separated the first two ridges, they could see the opposing party already standing on the left: Crampas and Buddenbrook and, with them, good old Dr Hannemann, who was holding his hat in his hand, so that his white hair was fluttering in the wind.

Innstetten and Wüllersdorf climbed up the slope while Buddenbrook came to meet them. They shook hands and then the two seconds went briefly to one side to arrange the final details. It was agreed that the two should advance simultaneously and fire at a distance of ten paces. Then Buddenbrook went back to his place. No time was lost; the shots rang out. Crampas fell to the ground.

Walking back a few yards, Innstetten turned away from the scene. Wüllersdorf had gone over to Buddenbrook and they both waited for the doctor to speak. He shrugged his shoulders. At the same moment, Crampas made a gesture: he was trying to say something. Wüllersdorf bent down over the dying man, nodded in agreement to his barely audible words and then went over to Innstetten.

'Crampas wants to speak to you, Innstetten. You must humour him. In less than three minutes he'll be dead.'

Innstetten went up to Crampas.

'Will you . . .' These were his last words.

A look of pain that seemed somehow touched with friendliness flickered across his face, and then it was all over.

29

INNSTETTEN returned to Berlin that same evening. Without going into Kessin again, he had taken the carriage that he had left waiting at the crossing in the sand-dunes and driven straight to the railway station, leaving the two seconds to inform the authorities. During the journey – he was alone in the compartment – he went over everything that had happened, turning it all over in his mind once again. His thoughts were no different from those of two days ago, except that now they followed the reverse order and, starting with the certainty of what was his right and duty, they finished with less conviction. 'If guilt has any meaning at all, it's not tied to any time or place and can't cease to be guilt overnight. Guilt demands expiation: that makes sense. But a time limit is neither one thing nor the other, it's feeble or at least prosaic.'

And so he clung to his idea and repeated to himself that everything had happened as it was bound to happen. But as soon as he had reached that conclusion, he had another volte-face. 'There must be a time limit, because a time limit is the only sensible thing and it doesn't matter whether it's prosaic as well; what's sensible usually is prosaic. I'm forty-five now. If I'd found the letters twenty-five years later, I'd be seventy. Then Wüllersdorf would have said: "Innstetten, don't be a fool!" And if Wüllersdorf hadn't said it, then Buddenbrook would have and even if Buddenbrook hadn't, then I should have said it myself. That's quite plain to me. If you push something to extremes, then you exaggerate and become absurd. No doubt about that. But where does it begin? Where is the limit? A ten-year interval makes a duel still necessary and then it's called honour and after eleven years, or perhaps even after ten and a half, it's called nonsense. The limit, the limit! Was that what it was? Had it already been passed? When I think of his last look, resigned and yet smiling in his misery, it seemed to be saying: "Innstetten, always standing on principle ... You might have spared me that and yourself as well." And perhaps he was right. I can hear myself saying something similar. True, if I'd felt deep hatred, if I'd had an irresistible urge for vengeance. . . . Revenge is not a pretty thing but it's human and has a natural human justi-fication. So it was all done merely to support a fantasy, an abstrac-tion, it was just a made-up story, a bit of play-acting. And now I must continue to play-act and send Effi away and ruin her life and mine as well. . . . I should have burnt the letters and the world should never have heard of them. And when she came to me, all unsuspecting, I should have said to her: "There's where you belong" and cut myself off from her. Inwardly, not in the eyes of the world. There are so many lives that aren't real lives and so many marriages that aren't real marriages, either. . . . And my happi-ness would have come to an end, but I shouldn't have the memory of that gentle questioning look of silent reproach.'

Innstetten arrived in front of his flat shortly before ten o'clock. He went upstairs and pulled the bell. Joanna came to open the door.

'How's Annie?'

'She's well, sir. She's not asleep yet. . . . If you would like . . .'

'No, no, that'll only excite her. I'd sooner see her tomorrow. Bring me a cup of tea, Joanna. Who called?'

'Only the doctor.'

And Innstetten now found himself alone again. He walked up and down, as he liked doing. 'They already know everything. Roswitha is stupid, but Joanna is an intelligent girl. And if they don't know it for certain, they'll have worked it all out so that they discover it. It's remarkable how everything can be interpreted and stories are blabbed about as if everyone had been present when it happened.'

Joanna brought the tea. Innstetten drank. He was dog-tired after all his exertions and went to sleep.

Next morning, he rose early. He saw Annie, had a few words with her, praised her for being such a good patient and then went off to the ministry to report to his chief all that had taken place.

The minister was very gracious: 'Well, Innstetten, good luck to those who are able to come safe and sound through all the trials life faces them with. You've managed it.' He gave his approval to everything that had happened and left the rest to Innstetten.

It was not until late that afternoon that Innstetten returned home, where he found a few words from Wüllersdorf. 'Arrived back early today. All sorts of experiences, painful, touching, with Gieshübler in the forefront. The nicest hunchback I've ever met. He didn't say much about you but kept exclaiming all the time about your wife. He found it impossible to keep calm and in the end he broke into tears. What strange things happen. A pity there aren't more people like Gieshübler. But there are more of other sorts. And then the scene in the major's house. . . . Frightful. I can't talk about it. One's learnt one's lesson again: be careful. See you tomorrow. Yours, W.'

As he read the letter, Innstetten was deeply shaken. He sat down and wrote a few letters. When he had finished, he rang: 'Joanna, post these letters.'

Joanna took the letters and was preparing to go.

'And one more thing, Joanna: the mistress won't be coming back. Others will be telling you why not. Annie is not to know anything, at any rate not at the moment. Poor child! You must slowly try to convey to her that she no longer has a mother. I can't do it. But use your intelligence. If only Roswitha doesn't upset everything!'

Joanna stood there for a moment as if completely dazed. Then she went up to Innstetten and kissed his hand.

When she had gone back to her kitchen, she was filled with an immense feeling of pride and superiority, almost of happiness. Not only had the master told her everything, but, at the end, he had even added: 'If only Roswitha doesn't upset everything!' That was the main thing, and although she had a good heart and even felt sympathy towards her mistress, her chief concern, above all else, was the feeling of triumph at being on a certain footing of intimacy with her master.

In normal circumstances it would have been easy for her to flaunt and exploit this triumph, but today she was less fortunate, because, although her rival was not yet in anyone's confidence, she yet turned out to be better initiated. At about the same time as all

223

this had been taking place, the porter downstairs had, in fact, called Roswitha into his little lodge and as soon as she had come in, had thrust a paper under her eyes: 'There's something for you, Roswitha. You can let me have it back later on. It's only the *Fremdenblatt* but Lene has already gone to fetch the *Kleines Journal*. I expect there'll be more in that, they always know everything. Well now, Roswitha, who would have thought a thing like that!'

Although she was not normally inquisitive, when she heard these words Roswitha went up the back-stairs with all possible speed and had just finished reading when Joanna came in.

The latter put the letters that Innstetten had given her down on the table, looked at the addresses, or pretended to (because she had long since been aware whom they were addressed to) and with well-simulated calm, said: 'One's for Hohen-Cremmen.'

'I can well imagine,' said Roswitha.

Joanna was somewhat surprised by her remark. 'The master never writes to Hohen-Cremmen normally.'

'Yes, normally! But now ... Just imagine, the porter downstairs has just given me this.'

Joanna took the paper and, under her voice, read a paragraph that had been heavily marked in ink:

'Shortly before going to press we have learnt from a well-informed source that yesterday morning at the seaside resort of Kessin in Upper Pomerania a duel took place between Under-Secretary von I. (Keithstrasse) and Major von Crampas. The latter was fatally wounded. It is said that a relationship had existed between him and the beautiful and extremely young wife of the under-secretary.'

'The things these papers write,' said Joanna, upset because her news was already out of date.

'Yes,' said Roswitha, 'and now people will read it and say unkind things about my poor dear mistress! And the poor major. Now he's dead.'

'Well, Roswitha, what are you thinking about! Oughtn't he to be dead? Or ought our master be dead instead?'

'No, Joanna, our master ought to be still alive, everybody ought to be alive. I'm not for shooting people and I can't even bear to hear a shot fired. But just think, Joanna, that's ages and ages ago and those letters, which looked strange to me the moment I saw them, bound round two or three times with that red thread, and then tied into knots, without a bow – they'd already gone all yellow, because it's so long ago. We've already been here six years and for an old story like that, how anyone can . . .'

'Well, Roswitha, you're saying how *you* see it. But if you examine it closely, you're to blame. It all comes from those letters. Why did you fetch the chisel and break open the work-table, which one never ought to do; you ought never to break open a lock that someone else has fastened.'

'But that's really too bad of you, Joanna, to put the blame for something like that on me, because you know quite well that you're to blame and that you rushed into the kitchen like an idiot and told me the work-table had to be opened because the bandage was inside it and then I fetched the chisel along and now it's supposed to be my fault. It's not, I say. . . .'

'Well, I won't say it then, Roswitha. But don't you come along and say: "the poor major". What about the "poor major"? The poor major was no good at all. Anyone who has a ginger moustache like that and is always twirling it can't be any good and can only do harm. And when you've always been in service with distinguished families – which you haven't, Roswitha, that's just your trouble – then you know what is fit and proper and all about honour and you know, too, that when something happens like that, then there's nothing else to do about it and so you have what they call a challenge and one of them gets shot dead.'

'Oh, I know that as well. I'm not so stupid as you always try to make out. But when it was so long ago . . .'

'Oh, you and your "so long ago". That shows that you don't understand what it's all about. You always keep telling that old story about how your father came after you with a red-hot iron bar and every time I have a red-hot ironing heater in the fire, I find myself thinking of your father and can see him trying to kill you because of the child, who's dead now itself. And you talk about it all the time and the only thing that you haven't done is to tell Annie, and when she's confirmed she'll certainly learn about it, perhaps even the very same day; and it annoys me that all those things happened to you and your father was only a village blacksmith and shod horses or put rims on wheels and now along you come and expect our master to keep quiet and say nothing, just because it's "so long ago". And what does "not long ago" mean? Six years isn't long ago. And our mistress – who won't be coming back here, anyway, the master has just told me so – our mistress is only rising twenty-six, her birthday's in August and you bring up your "long ago". And even if she was thirty-six, let me tell you that it's at thirty-six that you really have to be careful and if the master hadn't done anything, then all the "right people" would have cut him. But you don't even know that word, Roswitha, you don't know anything about it.'

'No, I don't know anything about that and I don't want to. But one thing I do know, Joanna, and that is that you're in love with the master.'

Joanna gave a nervous laugh.

'Yes, laugh away! I've seen it for a long time. There's something about you. And it's a good thing that our master doesn't see such things. . . . The poor lady, the poor lady . . .'

Joanna was anxious to make peace. 'Let's forget it, Roswitha! You're getting in a rage again, but I know everyone from the country gets into rages.'

'Perhaps they do.'

'Now I'll go and take the letters and see downstairs if the porter has got the other paper yet. I was right in thinking that he'd sent Lene to get it, wasn't I? There must be some more about it there; there's really nothing at all in this one!'

30

EFFI and Frau Zwicker had been staying in Ems for almost three weeks, occupying the ground-floor of a charming villa. In their shared drawing-room, which lay between their two living-rooms and had a view over the garden, there was a rosewood grand-piano on which Effi would now and again play a sonata and Frau Zwicker now and again a waltz; she was completely unmusical and mainly confined herself to praising Niemann's* Tannhäuser.

It was a splendid morning. In the tiny garden the birds were twittering, and from the neighbouring house, which contained a 'saloon', you could already hear the click of the billiard-balls, in

* Niemann was a well-known tenor.

spite of the early hour. The two ladies had taken their breakfast not in the sitting-room itself but on a slightly raised, walled-in, gravel terrace, with three steps leading down into the garden. The awning overhead had been drawn back so that the fresh air might be enjoyed to the full, and both Effi and her companion were sewing with some concentration. Only occasionally were a few words exchanged.

'I can't understand,' said Effi, 'why I haven't had a letter for four days. He usually writes every day. Is Annie ill? Or is he?'

Frau Zwicker smiled: 'My dear friend, your news will be that he's in excellent health.'

Effi was not favourably impressed by the tone in which this had been said and seemed on the point of retorting when at that moment the maid came out of the sitting-room on to the terrace to clear away the breakfast things. She came from the region of Bonn and ever since spending her youth there, she had been accustomed to judge the most manifold aspects of life by standards based on the behaviour of the undergraduates and Hussars of that town. ... She was called Afra.

'Afra,' said Effi. 'It must be nine o'clock already. Has the post come yet?'

'No, not yet, ma'am.'

'Why is that?'

'Naturally, because of the postman. He comes from the district of Siegen and he's got no "go"! I've already told him he's just a clod. And by the way he does his hair, I shouldn't think he knows the meaning of the word "parting".'

'Afra, you're being too harsh again. Just think of being a postman day in, day out, in all this heat.'

'You're right, m'lady. But there are others who can manage it; if you've got it in you, you can do it.' And as she spoke, skilfully balancing the tray on the five fingers of one hand, she went down the steps to take a short-cut to the kitchens through the garden.

'A pretty little thing,' said Frau Zwicker, 'and so neat and nimble, I'd be tempted to say, naturally graceful. Do you know, my dear Baroness, that that Afra ... incidentally, what a wonderful name. I think they say there was even a Saint Afra, but I don't think ours is descended from her ...'

'And now, my dear Frau Zwicker, you're allowing yourself to

be sidetracked into the theme of Afra and thereby forgetting what it was you really wanted to say.'

'Not at all, *chère amie*, or at any rate, I've found my way back to it. I was intending to say that our Afra put me quite uncommonly in mind of that superb young woman whom I saw in your house . . .'

'Yes, you're right. There is a similarity. Only our maid in Berlin is considerably prettier and in particular her hair is much lovelier and thicker. I've never seen such lovely flaxen hair as our Joanna's anywhere. You see something like it, but never so thick and long.'

Frau Zwicker smiled. 'It's really quite unusual to hear anyone speak with such enthusiasm about her maid's flaxen hair, and thick and long at that! D'y know, I find that quite touching? After all, choosing a maid is a continual embarrassment. They have to be pretty because it puts any visitor off, particularly the men, to see a bean-stalk of a woman with a muddy complexion and black round the edges appear in the doorway and it's a good thing that corridors are usually so dark. But if you pay too much attention to the effect that she's going to produce and the so-called "first impression" and if you keep on giving a pretty girl like that one dainty little white apron after another, then you'll find you don't get a moment's peace of mind and you ask yourself whether you're not too vain and over-confident in yourself, whether you ought not to find a *remedy*. Remedy was one of Zwicker's favourite words, and he often bored me with it; but of course, all privy councillors have favourite words of that sort.'

Effi was listening with mixed feelings. If Frau Zwicker had only been rather a different sort of woman, all this might have been charming, but because she was the sort of woman she was, it was with a certain reticence that Effi received these remarks which, in other circumstances, would have amused her.

'That's very true what you say about privy councillors, my dear Frau Zwicker. Innstetten has also got into that sort of habit but always laughs when I remark on it and then excuses himself on the grounds of officialese. Your husband was in the service longer, of course, and was no doubt older. . . .'

'Just slightly,' said Frau Zwicker, sharply, in a challenging tone.

'And all in all, I really find it hard to explain to myself the anxiety that you just mentioned. Surely what goes by the name of morality still has some force. . . .'

'Do you think so?'

'And especially I cannot think, dear Frau Zwicker, that it should have been your lot to experience worries and anxiety of that kind. Forgive me for touching so frankly on the point, but you definitely have what men call "charm". You're gay, fascinating and stimulating and if it's not indiscreet, in view of all these advantages, might I ask whether what you were referring to is based on any painful personal experience?'

'Painful!' retorted Frau Zwicker. 'Ah, my dear, dear Baroness, painful is too grand a word, even if one has perhaps really experienced a great deal in one's life. Painful is too strong, much too strong. And then, of course, one has after all one's remedies and means of counter-attacking. You mustn't take things too tragically.'

'I can't quite imagine what you're trying to suggest. It's not that I don't know about guilty behaviour, indeed I do; but all the same, there is a difference between having all kinds of guilty thoughts and letting such things take a complete or even a considerable hold over you. And then in one's own home ...'

'I'm not talking about that, I didn't mean to say quite that, although, speaking frankly, I'm also full of misgivings there, too, or, as I now have to say, I *was* full of misgivings, since that all belongs to the past. But there are other more out-of-the-way places. Have you ever heard of country excursions?'

'Of course. And I wish Innstetten were more fond of them.'

'Do think what you're saying, *chère amie*. Zwicker was for ever lurking in cornfields. I assure you that just *hearing* the word still gives me quite a turn. All those resorts on the outskirts of our dear old Berlin anyway! Because I do love Berlin in spite of everything. But even just the names of those places conjures up a whole world of care and anxiety. You're smiling and yet tell me, my dear, what can you expect the moral state of a big town to be like when almost at its very gates – because there's no longer any real difference between Berlin and Charlottenburg – confined within a distance of not much more than half a mile, you find a Pichelsberg, a Pichelsdorf and a Pichelswerder. Three Pichels is really too much. You can go to the four corners of the earth and not find anything like that.'

Effi nodded.

'And all that,' continued Frau Zwicker, 'takes place in the green belt on the Havel side. It's all in the west, where there's culture and civilization. But now go the other way, up the Spree. I won't mention Treptow and Stralau. They're quite formless, mere bagatelles, but if you take a look at the large-scale map, in addition to names which are strange, to say the least, such as Kiekbusch and Wuhlheide – you should have heard the way my husband used to pronounce that one – you'll find also names that are really so brutal that I won't offend your ears by mentioning them. But of course, those are the places that everybody prefers. I loathe these country excursions which the public looks on as a typically patriotic Prussian pastime but in reality they contain all the seeds of social revolution. When I say "social", I mean of course, "moral" revolution; the other sort has already taken place and Zwicker was saying to me at the end of his life: "Believe me, Sophie, Saturn devours his own children." And whatever faults and whatever weaknesses Zwicker may have had, he was a thinker and had a real sense of historical evolution. ... But I can see that my dear Frau von Innstetten, who's usually so polite, is only listening with half an ear; why, of course, the postman has just made his appearance and so one's heart gives a leap and is busy imagining all the loving words that are in the letter. Well, what have you got for us, Böselager?'

The postman had meanwhile come up to the table and was unloading his bag: a number of papers, two advertisements for hairdressers and last of all, a large registered letter addressed to: 'The Baroness von Innstetten, *née* von Briest.'

The recipient signed for the letter and the postman left. Frau Zwicker flicked through the hairdressing advertisements and laughed at the reduction in the charge for a shampoo.

Effi was not listening; she was turning her letter over between her fingers and feeling an inexplicable reluctance to open it. Registered, with two large seals and a thick envelope. What could it mean? The postmark was Hohen-Cremmen and the address was written in her mother's handwriting. And not a line from Innstetten for five days.

She took a pair of sewing scissors with mother-of-pearl handles and slowly cut along the envelope. And now a new surprise awaited her. The letter itself was, indeed, closely written in her mother's hand, but there was a bundle of bank notes fastened round with a wide paper band, on which was written, in red, the amount it contained, and this was in her father's hand. She pushed the bundle on one side and leaning back in her rocking-chair, she began to read. But before she had gone far, the letter fell from her hand and the blood drained from her face. Then she bent down and picked the letter up again.

'What's the matter, my dear? Bad news?'

Effi nodded but said nothing except to ask her to hand her a glass of water. She took a drink and said: 'It won't last, my dear Frau Zwicker, but I should like to leave you for a moment. . . . If you could please send Afra to me.' And she stood up and went into the drawing-room, where she was clearly glad to find something to hold on to as she felt her way along the rosewood grand-piano. With this support, she arrived at her room, on the right-hand side. Groping to open the door, she made for her bed on the opposite side of the room and collapsed in a faint.

31

MINUTES passed. When Effi had recovered, she sat down on a chair beside the window and looked out on to the quiet street. If only there could have been noise and conflict down there! But there was merely the sun shining on the roadway and the shadows cast by the railings and the trees. The feeling of being alone in the world came over her in all its gravity. Only an hour ago, she was a happy woman, the darling of everyone whom she knew, and now an outcast! She had read only the beginning of the letter but enough to have a clear view of her situation. Where should she go? She could find no reply to that question, yet she felt a deep longing to escape from her surroundings, away from the Zwicker woman who looked on everything merely as 'interesting' and whose sympathy, if she were capable of such a thing, was surely not as lively as her consuming curiosity. Where could she go?

The letter was lying on the table in front of her but she hadn't the heart to read on. Finally, she said: 'What am I afraid of now? What can anyone tell me that I haven't already told myself? The cause of it all is dead; it's impossible for me to return home, the divorce will be pronounced in a few weeks' time and the custody of the child will be given to the father. Of course, I'm the guilty party and a guilty woman can't bring up her child. And how could she find the means to do it anyway? I expect I'll be able to fend for myself all right. I must see what mama writes on the subject, what she thinks I ought to do.'

As she said this, she picked up the letter again to read the end as well:

'... And now as to your future, my dear Effi. You'll have to fend for yourself and as far as material resources are concerned, you may depend on our support. Berlin will be the best place for you to live (this sort of thing can be best concealed in a big town) and there you'll be one of the many who have been forced to do without fresh air and sunlight. You'll be living a lonely life and, if you don't want to do that, you'll probably have to move out of your social class. You'll be excluded from the society in which you've been moving up till now. And the saddest thing for us and for you (even for you if we understand you rightly) is that you will be excluded from our house, too. We can't offer you any asylum in Hohen-Cremmen, there can be no refuge for you in our house, because that would mean cutting ourselves off from everyone we know and this we are emphatically not inclined to do. Not because we are particularly worldly and would look upon it as completely unbearable to have to say good-bye to so-called "society". No, that's not the reason, but simply because we want to make our position plain and show the whole world that we condemn – I'm afraid I must use this word – your actions – the actions of our only daughter, the daughter whom we loved so dearly. ...'

Effi could not read on. Her eyes filled with tears and after vainly struggling against them, she finally burst into a violent fit of sobbing and weeping which brought relief to her feelings.

Half an hour later there was a knock on the door and when Effi said 'Come in,' Frau Zwicker appeared in the doorway.

'May I come in?'

'Of course, my dear Frau Zwicker,' said Effi who, with her hands clasped together, was lying on the sofa, with a light covering over her. 'I'm tired out and I've settled myself here as well as I could. Won't you please sit down.'

Frau Zwicker sat down so that the table, on which there was a bowl of flowers, was between her and Effi. Effi showed no signs of embarrassment and remained in the same attitude, not even unclasping her hands. All at once, it was completely indifferent to her what this woman thought; all she wanted to do was to get away.

'You've had some sad news, my dear Baroness. . . .'

'Worse than sad,' said Effi. 'At any rate, sad enough for us to have to part company. I must leave today'.

'I don't want to appear indiscreet but is something wrong with Annie?'

'No, it's nothing to do with Annie. The news wasn't from Berlin at all, it was my mother who was writing to me. She's worried about me and so I must try to dispel her worries or, if I can't, at least be on the spot with her.'

'Of course, I understand perfectly, even though I shall regret having to spend these last few days in Ems without you. Can I help you in any way?'

Before Effi could reply, Afra came in and announced that lunch was about to be served. All the guests, she said, were greatly excited; the Kaiser was probably coming to stay for three weeks and there were to be important manoeuvres at the end of his visit and the Bonn Hussars were coming, too.

Frau Zwicker immediately wondered to herself whether it would be worth while to stay on till then, answered with an emphatic 'Yes' and then went off to make Effi's excuses for missing lunch.

As Afra was on the point of following her, Effi said: 'And then, Afra, if you're free, will you come and help me for a quarter of an hour to pack my things, I want to leave by the seven o'clock train today.'

'Today? Oh, m'lady, that is a pity. It's just beginning to be nice here.'

Effi smiled.

Frau Zwicker still hoped to hear more and was only persuaded with difficulty not to see the baroness off. 'People are always thinking of something else at the railway-station,' Effi had assured her, 'and only concerned with getting a seat and seeing to their luggage; and it was just those people whom one was fond of whom one said good-bye to beforehand. . . .' Frau Zwicker confirmed this, although she recognized perfectly well what lay behind these pretexts; she had not been born yesterday and could distinguish unerringly the false from the genuine.

Afra went with Effi to the station and made the baroness give her the firm promise to be back next summer; once you'd been to Ems, you always wanted to return. Ems was the nicest place, apart from Bonn.

Frau Zwicker had meanwhile sat down to write some letters, not at the somewhat rickety rococo secretaire in the drawing-room, but outside on the veranda, at the very table where she had been breakfasting with Effi barely ten hours earlier.

She was enjoying writing her letter, which was destined for a woman-friend from Berlin who was at the moment staying in Reichenhall. Their two minds had long since come together and culminated in a sturdy scepticism embracing the whole male world: they considered men thoroughly inadequate in what might reasonably be expected from them, and most inadequate of all were the so-called 'mashers'. 'The shy ones that hardly know which way to look are, after a short preliminary study, always the most reliable, but the real Don Juans turn out disappointing every time. Why should that be, after all?' Such were the pearls of wisdom exchanged by the two friends.

Frau Zwicker was already on her second page and, pursuing her subject, which was, of course, Effi – a subject more than welcome – she wrote: 'All things considered, she was very bearable, affable, apparently sincere, without any trace of aristocratic "side" (or else extremely clever at hiding it) and always ready to listen to something interesting, a gift which, I hardly need to tell you, I exploited to the full. As I said, a charming young woman, of twenty-five or thereabouts. And yet I never felt certain about this relaxed air of hers and even now I don't feel certain about it, either. That business with the letter – there must be something or other behind that. I'm as good as sure of it. The fact that she used to be fond of talking about the fashionable Berlin preachers and was anxious to determine the exact amount of godliness of every single person, added to the occasional innocent Gretchen-like sort of look that seemed to indicate that butter wouldn't melt in her mouth – all those things didn't shake my belief that ... But here comes our Afra, whom I think I mentioned to you – a pretty girl – and she has put a newspaper down on the table which, she says, our landlady has given her for me to read the paragraph marked in blue pencil. Excuse me while I read it. . . . P.S. The newspaper was rather interesting and providential. I've cut out the piece marked with blue and am enclosing it. You can see from it that I was *not* mistaken. Who can Crampas be? It's incredible – first of all writing notes and letters herself and then keeping those from the other man! What are stoves and fireplaces for? Anyway, as long as this idiotic custom of duelling continues, such thoughtlessness is not permissible; future generations may perhaps be able to indulge this passion for corresponding, because it will have lost its dangers. But we're still a long way from that. Incidentally, I feel full of sympathy for the young baroness and, vain as one is, my only consolation is that I myself wasn't taken in concerning her. And it wasn't such a straightforward case as all that. A less efficient diagnostician might well have been taken in! As always, Yrs, Sophie.'

32

THREE years had gone by and Effi had been living for almost the whole of that time in a small flat in Königgrätzstrasse, between Askanischer Platz and the Halle Gate: two rooms, one behind the other, and beyond the second one a kitchen with maid's room; the whole lay-out was as ordinary and commonplace as possible. Yet the flat had distinction and charm and it impressed everyone who called, most of all, perhaps, the old Privy Councillor Rummschüttel on his occasional visits. He had long since forgiven the poor young woman, not only for her pretended rheumatism and neuralgia, which already belonged to the past, but for all those other events that had happened since, if, indeed, he needed to forgive them at all, because Rummschüttel had seen all sorts of things in his time. He was now in his late seventies but whenever Effi, who had often been ailing in recent times, wrote to ask him to call, the next morning he would appear, refusing to listen to her excuses that she lived so high up. 'Please, no excuses, my dear young lady, because first of all, it's my profession, and secondly, I'm happy and almost proud to climb those three floors so well. If I weren't afraid of disturbing you – because after all, I'm calling on you as your doctor and not as a lover of nature or connoisseur of scenery –

I should like to come more often, merely to see you and sit down here at your back window for a few minutes. I don't think you're sufficiently appreciative of the view.'

'I am, really,' said Effi, but Rummschüttel went on unperturbed: 'Please, dear lady, come over here, just for a moment, or allow me to lead you to the window. It's magnificent again today. Look at all those different railway embankments, three, no, four of them and all the traffic going to and fro all the time ... and now there's that train disappearing behind a clump of trees. Look how the sun shines through the smoke. If it weren't for the St Matthew's cemetery in the background, it would be ideal.'

'I like cemeteries.'

'Yes, it's all right for you to say that. But we doctors, we always inevitably ask ourselves the question whether there couldn't be fewer people buried there. By the way, my dear young lady, I'm pleased with you and I only regret that you refuse to consider going to Ems. For your catarrh, Ems would do wonders. ...'

Effi said nothing.

'Ems would do wonders. But since you don't want to and I accept that, then you must drink the waters here. In three minutes, you can be in Prince Albert's garden and even if the music and the dresses and all the distractions of a proper spa are lacking, the waters are, after all, the main thing. ...'

Effi agreed and Rummschüttel picked up his hat and stick. But then he went over once more to the window. 'I hear talk of terracing the Kreuzberg, God bless the town council, and if only that bare spot at the back there could be made greener ... A charming flat, I almost envy you. ... And there's something I've been wanting to say for a long time, my dear lady, you write such a kind letter every time and who wouldn't enjoy receiving that? But it must be a trouble every time. ... Why not simply send Roswitha along?'

Effi thanked him and they parted.

'Why not simply send Roswitha along,' Rummschüttel had said. Was Roswitha with Effi, then? Was she in Königgrätzstrasse instead of Keithstrasse? Indeed she was and had been for a very long time, as long as Effi herself had been living in Königgrätzstrasse. Indeed, three days before Effi had moved in, Roswitha had come to see her beloved mistress and it had been a great day for both of

236

them, so much so that we must go back and report how it had happened.

When she had received her parents' letter of renunciation from Hohen-Cremmen and had caught the evening train to Berlin from Ems, she had not, in the first instance, taken her own flat but had moved into a room in a boarding-house. It had been a fairly successful experiment. The two ladies who ran the *pension* were educated women and full of consideration; they had long since ceased to be inquisitive. So many factors were always involved that it would have been far too complicated to try to penetrate into everyone else's secrets. Such things were bad for business. Effi, still remembering Frau Zwicker's inquisitorial glances, had been very pleasantly impressed by the discretion of the landladies. But after a fortnight, she realized plainly that the whole physical and moral atmosphere there was not really bearable for her. At meal-times there were usually five people, in addition to Effi and one of the landladies – the other was seeing to the service behind the scenes: two English girls studying at the University, a titled lady from Saxony, a very pretty Galician Jewess, whose business no one exactly knew, and a schoolmaster's daughter from Polzin in Pomerania who wanted to be a painter. The various forms of snobbishness in which, strangely enough, the English girls were not completely superior but had to compete with the highly artistically-minded young woman from Polzin, were not very edifying, yet Effi, prepared to be neutral, would have been able to overlook this depressing moral environment but for the other, purely external, physical atmosphere of the boarding-house. It was perhaps beyond the powers of investigation to discover its real composition, but it was only too certain that it took the over-sensitive Effi's breath away, and so, for this external reason, she very soon found herself looking out and around for a new place to live, and she succeeded in finding one relatively close by. This was the flat that has previously been described in the Königgrätzstrasse. She was going to enter into occupation at the beginning of the Michaelmas quarter, had made the necessary arrangements, and during the last few days of September had been counting the hours until her release from boarding-house life.

On one of these last few days, she had left the dining-room a quarter of an hour earlier and was just thinking of taking a rest on her lumpy sofa, wool-upholstered in a large floral pattern, when there was a gentle knock at the door.

'Come in.'

The one maid of the establishment came in, a sickly-looking woman in her mid-thirties who, as she never left the corridor of the boarding-house, carried the local miasma about with her in every fold of her clothes. 'If madam would please excuse me. Someone wishes to speak to madam.'

'Who?'

'A woman'

'And did she give her name?'

'Yes, Roswitha.'

Barely had Effi heard the name than she shook off her lethargy, jumped up, ran out along the corridor, seized hold of Roswitha and dragged her into her room.

'Roswitha. It's you. How lovely. But what's brought you here? Something nice, of course. A kind old face like yours can only bring something nice. Oh, how happy I am, I could kiss you. My dear old Roswitha, how are you? Do you remember those times with the Chinaman's ghost? Happy days. And I used to think then that they were unhappy because I didn't know how hard life can be. I've learnt since. Oh dear, ghosts aren't the worst thing, by far. Come here, dear Roswitha, come and sit down beside me and tell me. . . . Oh, I'm so longing to know. What's Annie doing?'

Roswitha could hardly speak and she looked round the strange room at its grey, dusty-looking walls with their narrow gold border. Finally, however, she came to herself and said that the master was now back from Glatz, the old Emperor had said that 'in such cases, six weeks would be just right' and she had only waited until the master had returned because of Annie, who had to have someone to look after her. Because although Joanna was of course a respectable person, she was all the same rather too pretty and too much preoccupied with herself and perhaps was getting all sorts of ideas in her head. But now that the master was there to take charge and see that everything was all right, she thought that she would make the effort to come and see how her mistress was. . . .

'That's right, Roswitha.'

'. . . and see whether m'lady needed anything or needed her

perhaps, because if so, she would stay on here right away and help and do everything and see that everything was all right for her mistress again.'

Effi had leant back in the corner of the sofa and closed her eyes. But all of a sudden, she sat up and said: 'Yes, Roswitha, that's a thought, there's something in what you've just said. I ought to tell you that I'm not going to stay in this guest-house. I've rented a flat near by and found some furniture and I'm moving in in three days' time. And if I went along there with you and could tell you: "No, not there, Roswitha, the cupboard's got to go there and the mirror over there," yes, that would be something, I'd like that, I'm sure. And when we were tired by all the fuss and bother, then I'd say: "Now, Roswitha, you go over and fetch a jug of Spatenbräu beer, because when someone's been working they need a drink and if you can, bring something nice back from the Habsburger Hof restaurant, you can take the crockery back afterwards" – well, Roswitha, it really does make me feel much more cheerful when I think of that. But I must ask you if you have thought it all over? I won't mention Annie, although you're fond of her, she's almost like your own child – but Annie will be looked after anyway, and Joanna is fond of her too. So we won't talk about that. But you must remember how everything has changed if you want to come back to me. I'm not like I was in the old days. I've taken just a small flat and I don't suppose the porter will worry much about you or me. And we shall only be able to live very modestly, every day it'll be what we used to call our Thursday dinner, because that was the day we finished up the left-overs. Do you remember? And do you recall how good old Gieshübler once came, and had to eat with us and how he said he'd never eaten anything so delicious? You must still remember that, he had such terribly good manners, but in fact he was the only man in town who knew anything about food. The others thought everything was good.'

Roswitha was enjoying every word that Effi was saying and thinking everything was all right, and then her mistress repeated: 'Have you thought it all over? Because, although it was my own household, I have to say this, that over all these years you've become spoilt and we never had to bother about having to economize; but now I have to economize, because I'm poor and I've only got what people give me, you know, from Hohen-Cremmen. My parents

239

are very good to me, as far as they can be, but they're not wealthy. And now tell me, what do you say?'

'I say that I'll move in next Saturday with my trunk, not in the evening but in the morning so that I'm on the spot when you're settling in. Because I can manage much better than m'lady ...'

'Don't say that, Roswitha. I can manage too. One can do everything if one has to.'

'And you don't need to be afraid for me, m'lady, as if I could ever think: "It's not good enough for Roswitha." Everything that I have to share with you, m'lady, is good enough and most of all if it's sad. I'm already really looking forward to that. And you'll see that I can understand. And if I didn't understand, then I should learn. Because I've never forgotten, m'lady, how I was sitting there in the churchyard, all alone, and thinking to myself that the best thing would really be to be lying there with the others. And who was it who came along and saved my life? Oh, I've been through such a lot. When my father came after me that time with the red-hot crowbar ...'

'I've heard about that, Roswitha.'

'Yes, that was bad enough. But when I was sitting there in the cemetery so deserted and poor, that was even worse. And then your ladyship came along. And may I never go to heaven if I ever forget that.'

She stood up and went over to the window. 'Look, m'lady, you must have a look at *him* again.'

Effi also went over to the window. ...

There, on the other side of the street, Rollo was sitting, looking up at the guest-house windows.

A few days later, with Roswitha's help, Effi moved into her flat in the Königgrätzstrasse and she liked it from the very beginning. Of course, she lacked company, but during her stay at the guest-house she had had such little pleasure from her contacts with her fellow-men that she did not find it difficult to be alone, at least not at first. There was, indeed, no possibility of artistic conversation with Roswitha, not even of talking about the news, but when it was a question of simple human feelings and Effi began her sentence with the words: 'Oh Roswitha, I'm scared again ....' then the

240

good soul always knew the right answer and on every occasion could offer consolation and, generally, advice.

Until Christmas things went very well, but Christmas Eve passed very sadly and when the New Year came, Effi began to feel very melancholy. It wasn't cold, merely grey and raining, and if the days were short, the evenings were all the longer. What was there to do? She read, she sewed, she played patience, she played Chopin but his nocturnes were not calculated to bring much light into her life and when Roswitha came in with the supper tray and, in addition to the tea, put two small plates with an egg and a Wiener Schnitzel cut into small slices on to the table, Effi shut her piano and said: 'Come and keep me company, Roswitha.'

So Roswitha came: 'I know what it is, your ladyship has been playing too much again, you always look like that then, with red spots on your face. The doctor forbade it.'

'Ah, Roswitha, it's easy for the doctor to forbid it and for you to repeat what he says. But what am I to do? I can't sit all day at the window looking at the Christuskirche. I always look at it during the Sunday evening service when the windows are all lit up, but it doesn't do any good, it makes me sadder than ever.'

'Well, m'lady, then you should go there sometimes. You did go once.'

'Oh, more often than that. But it didn't help me much. He preaches quite well and I'd be happy to know the hundredth part of all that he knows. But it's all rather like reading a book; and when he talks so loudly and waves his arms about and shakes his long black hair, then he makes me forget my devotions.'

'Forget?'

Effi laughed: 'You mean that I didn't have any. Perhaps you're right. But whose fault is it? Not mine. He always talks such a lot about the Old Testament. And even if it is a good thing, I don't find it edifying. Anyway, all this listening is not the right thing for me. You see, I ought to have so much to do that I don't know which way to turn. That's what I need. There are all sorts of girls' clubs for domestic science or dress-making or training kindergarten teachers. Haven't you ever heard of them?'

'Yes, I have heard of them. Little Annie was going to go to a kindergarten once.'

'Well you see, you know more about it than I do. I'd like to join a club like that, where you can make yourself useful. But it's no good thinking about it. The ladies on the committee won't accept it and they can't either. And that's the most horrible thing about it, the fact that the world is so closed to one and that one's even forbidden to help in some good work. I can't even give extra lessons to poor children. . . .'

'That wouldn't be suitable for you either, m'lady. The children always have such grubby boots and when the weather's wet, there's such a steam and fug that your ladyship wouldn't be able to bear it.'

Effi smiled. 'I expect you're right, Roswitha, but it's a pity that you are right and I can see that I've still got too much of the old Adam in me and I'm still too well off.'

Roswitha refused to hear of this. 'Anyone as kind as your ladyship can't be too well off. Only you mustn't keep on playing such mournful music and now and then I think things will turn out all right and that something will turn up.'

And something did turn up. In spite of her horrible memories of the schoolmaster's daughter from Polzin with her artistic arrogance, Effi decided to take up painting, and although she laughed about it herself, because she realized that she would never rise beyond the lowest amateur level, she worked at it passionately, because she now had an occupation which, being quiet and noiseless, was entirely to her liking. She went to an elderly teacher of painting who was both a keen student of the Brandenburg aristocracy and extremely pious, so that from the start Effi was close to his heart. Here, no doubt, he thought, was a soul to be saved and so he showed her particular affection and treated her like a daughter. Effi was very pleased at this and their first painting lesson was a happy turning point in her life. Her poor life was now less poor and Roswitha was triumphant at having been proved right and that something had turned up after all.

This went on for a time, indeed quite a long time. But the fact of having re-established contact with people, although it made her happy, filled her with the desire to renew and increase her contacts. Sometimes she was seized with an immense longing for Hohen-Cremmen and even more passionately did she long to see Annie. She was her child, after all, and as she yearned for her and at the same time remembered Trippelli once saying that the world was so small that even in Central Africa you could be certain of suddenly meeting an old acquaintance, she was rightly amazed that she had never met Annie. But that, too, was going to change. One day, she was coming from her painting lesson, close by the Zoological Garden, and not far from the stop she got on one of the horse-trams going along the long Kurfürstenstrasse. It was very hot and the curtains flapping to and fro in the strong wind refreshed her. She was leaning back in the corner facing the front platform and was looking at some sofas painted on to the panes of glass – blue with bobs and tassels – when, as the tram was moving slowly along, she saw three schoolgirls jump on, with their satchels on their backs and tiny pointed hats, two of them fair-haired and gay, the third dark and serious. It was Annie. Effi started and the thought of meeting her child, something for which she had been hoping for so long, now filled her with a dreadful fear. What should she do? With quick decision she opened the door to the front platform where only the driver was standing and asked him to let her off at the front at the next stop. 'Forbidden, missy,' the driver said; but she gave him a gold piece and looked at him so pleadingly that the man obligingly changed his mind and muttered: 'Shouldn't really, but I suppose it's all right once in a way.' And when the tram stopped, he removed the safety-grill and Effi jumped down.

Effi arrived home still in a state of great emotion. 'Just imagine, Roswitha, I've seen Annie.' And she told her of the meeting in the tram. Roswitha was disappointed that mother and daughter had not celebrated a reunion on the spot and was with difficulty persuaded that such a thing would have been hardly appropriate in the presence of so many people. Then Effi was made to relate how Annie had looked and when, with a mother's pride, she had done so, Roswitha said: 'Yes, she's half one and half the other. Her looks and her strangeness, if you'll pardon me saying so, come from her mother, but she's serious like her father. And thinking it over, she's probably more like the master.'

'Thank goodness,' said Effi.

'Well, m'lady, that's a question. And I think there's many a one who's more on her mother's side.'

'Do you think so, Roswitha? I don't.'

'Well, well, I know my own mind and I think your ladyship knows very well, too, where the truth of the matter lies and what men are really like.'

243

'You mustn't talk like that, Roswitha.'

Here the conversation came to an end and the subject was not referred to again. But even although Effi deliberately avoided talking to Roswitha about Annie, she still could not expunge the meeting from her heart and she was sad at the thought of having run away from her own child. Her worry became shame and her longing to meet Annie became morbid. It was impossible to write to ask Innstetten. She was well aware of her guilt, indeed she cultivated the feeling with almost passionate eagerness; but in the midst of this awareness of her guilt she was filled on the other hand with a kind of revolt against Innstetten. She would say to herself: he was right, again and again, and yet in the end, he was wrong. All that had happened was now so remote, a new life had begun – he could have let it die a natural death, but instead it was poor Crampas who had died an unnatural death.

No, she couldn't write to Innstetten, but she did want to see Annie and speak to her and hold her in her arms and after thinking it over for a whole day, she decided how she could best do it.

The very next morning she dressed carefully in a subdued dress and went to Unter den Linden, where she asked to see the minister's wife. She sent in her card, on which was printed only: Effi von Innstetten, *née* von Briest. Everything else had been left off, even the title of baroness. 'Please come this way'; and Effi followed the servant into an ante-room, where she sat down and in spite of her excitement, looked round at the pictures decorating the walls. First of all there was Guido Reni's *Aurora*, but on the opposite wall there were some English prints, after Benjamin West, in the well-known chiaroscuro style of aquatints. One of the prints was of King Lear in the storm on the heath.

Effi had hardly time to look around before the door of the adjoining room opened and a tall, slim lady, whose appearance was immediately reassuring, came over to the petitioner and held out her hand. 'My dear Frau von Innstetten,' she said, 'what a pleasure to see you again. . . .'

And as she spoke, she went over to the sofa, drawing Effi with her, and made her sit down beside her.

Effi was touched by this impression of frank kindheartedness. Not a trace of superiority or reproach, nothing but true human

244

sympathy. 'What can I do to help you?' were the Minister's wife's next words.

Effi's mouth twitched. Finally she said: 'The reason that brings me here is a request which your Excellency can perhaps help me realize. I have a ten-year-old daughter whom I haven't seen for three years and should very much like to see again.'

The Minister's wife took Effi's hand and gave her a friendly look. 'When I say that I haven't seen her for three years, that's not quite exact. I saw her three days ago.' And she gave a vivid description of her meeting with Annie. 'I ran away from my own child. I know, of course, that as one makes one's bed so one must lie in it and I don't wish to change anything in my life. It's right that things should be as they are; I have made them what they are. But it's too hard about the child, and so I feel that I should like to be allowed to see her now and again, not secretly and furtively, but with the full knowledge and agreement of all concerned.'

'With the full knowledge and agreement of all concerned,' the Minister's wife repeated. 'That means with your husband's agreement. I can see that he is bringing the child up to keep her away from her mother, a course which I won't claim the right to judge. Perhaps he's right; forgive me for saying that, Frau von Innstetten.'

Effi nodded her head.

'You yourself accept your husband's attitude and are merely asking to satisfy your natural feeling, indeed one of our noblest feelings – at least, we women like to look on it as such. Am I right?'

'Entirely.'

'And so I'm to try to obtain permission for occasional meetings in your house, where you can try to win back a place in your daughter's heart.'

Effi once more expressed her agreement and the other continued: 'Well, dear Frau von Innstetten, I'll do what I can. But it won't be an easy task for us. Your husband – forgive me if I refer to him as I used to – is not a man who acts according to moods and whims but according to principles, and he'll find it hard to give them up or even to relax them temporarily. If such were not the case, his disciplinary methods would have changed long ago. Anything that is hard on you he considers right and proper.'

'So your Excellency thinks it would be better for me to withdraw my request?'

245

'Not at all. I merely wanted to explain your husband's actions, not to justify them, and I wanted at the same time to point out the difficulties which we shall in all probability be meeting. But I think we'll succeed all the same. Because we women, if we set about it cleverly and don't press too hard, can manage all sorts of things. Especially as your husband is one of my particular admirers and he'll not easily refuse any request that I make him. Tomorrow there's a meeting of a little society when I shall see him, and the day after I'll let you have a note in the morning to tell you whether I've been clever, that means successful, or not. I think we'll win and you'll see your daughter again and be pleased with her. She's said to be a very pretty child. No wonder.'

33

Two days later, as promised, the note came and Effi read: 'I am delighted to be able to give you good news. Everything went as hoped. Your husband is too much a man of the world to refuse a lady's request; at the same time, I mustn't disguise the fact that I could see quite plainly that his agreement was not in accordance with what he himself considered wise or right. But don't let's niggle when we ought to be rejoicing. It's been agreed that your Annie should come and see you at the lunch hour. May good luck attend your meeting!'

Effi received this letter by the second post and so there were presumably barely two hours before Annie would appear. A short time but still too long and Effi walked restlessly up and down through the two rooms and then into the kitchen, where she talked with Roswitha about everything under the sun: about how next year the ivy on the Christuskirche would probably completely overgrow the windows or about how the porter had failed once again to close the gas stopcock properly, they'd all be blown up soon, or how she'd rather get the paraffin from the big lamp-shop in Unter den Linden again than from the Anhaltstrasse. Indeed, she talked about everything under the sun, except Annie, because she did not want to face up to the fear which she felt in spite of or perhaps even because of the note from the Minister's wife.

Noon had come, and gone. Finally, the door-bell rang, discreetly,

246

and Roswitha went to look through the peep-hole. Yes, it was Annie. Roswitha gave the child a kiss but without saying a word and very quietly, as if there were someone ill in the house. She led the child from the corridor first of all into the back room and then up to the door of the front room.

'Go in there, Annie!' And so saying, because she didn't want to disturb them, she left the child and went back to her kitchen.

When the child went in, Effi was standing at the other end of the room, with her back to the cheval-mirror. 'Annie!' But Annie remained standing by the half-opened door, partly through embarrassment but partly on purpose, too, so that Effi hurried across to her, lifted her up and kissed her.

'Annie, darling, how glad I am. Come and talk to me!' and she took Annie's hand and went to sit down on the sofa. Annie remained standing and, still looking shyly at her mother, reached out with her left hand to catch hold of the edge of the table-cloth. 'Do you know that I saw you once, Annie?'

'Yes, I thought so too.'

'And now tell me all sorts of things. How you've grown! And there's the scar, Roswitha told me about that. You were always so wild and reckless when you were playing. You've got that from your mama. She was like that. And how about school? I expect you're always top, you look like that to me, like a model schoolgirl who always brings home very good reports. I've heard that Fräulein von Wedelstädt thinks highly of you, too. That's as it should be. I was ambitious, too, but I wasn't so good at school. My best subject was always mythology. What's your best subject?'

'I don't know.'

'Oh, you must know. Everyone knows that. What did you get your best marks in?'

'In religious instruction.'

'So you see, I was right. Well, that's very nice. I wasn't so good at that but it may have been something to do with the teaching. We only had an ordinand.'

'We had an ordinand too.'

'And he's left?'

Annie nodded.

'Why did he leave?'

'I don't know. We've got the vicar again now.'

247

'Whom you all like very much.'

'Yes; two girls in the first class want to change their religion.'

'Oh I see. That's very nice. And what's Joanna doing?'

'Joanna came with me as far as here.'

'And why didn't you bring her up with you?'

'She said she'd sooner wait downstairs, over by the church opposite.'

'And I suppose she'll fetch you?'

'Yes.'

'Well. I hope she won't become impatient. There's a little garden in front and the windows are already half overgrown with ivy, as if it were an old church.'

'I shouldn't like her to have to wait too long for me.'

'Ah, I can see that you're very considerate and I'm pleased to see that, of course. Only you have to make sure you're considerate towards everybody.... And now tell me something else, how's Rollo?'

'Rollo's very well. But papa says he's getting so lazy, he's always lying in the sun.'

'I can believe that. He was like that when you were still quite young.... And now tell me, Annie, because we've only just seen each other today for a little while – will you come and see me more often?'

'Oh yes, if I may.'

'Then we can go for a walk in Prince Albert's Garden.'

'Oh yes, if I may.'

'Or we'll go to Schilling's and eat ice-cream, pineapple or vanilla, those were the sorts that I used to like best.'

'Oh yes, if I may.'

This third 'if I may' was the last straw for Effi. She jumped up and looked at the child with a glance that contained something like disgust.

'I think it's time to go, Annie, Joanna will be getting impatient.' She rang. Roswitha, who was already in the next room, came in.

'Roswitha, go with Annie as far as the church. Joanna's waiting there. I hope she hasn't caught cold. I'd be sorry. My regards to Joanna.'

And they both left.

But hardly had Roswitha closed the outside door than Effi tore open her clothes, because she felt that she was suffocating, and burst into hysterical laughter. 'So that's what it's like to meet someone again,' and so saying she flung herself forward, opened the casement-windows and looked around for some support. And in her desperate need, she found something. Beside the window stood a bookshelf with a few volumes of Schiller and Körner on it, and on the books of poetry, all of the same height, there lay a Bible and hymnal. She picked them up, because she had to have something to kneel and pray to, and placing the Bible and hymnal on the edge of the table, exactly where Annie had been standing, and flinging herself violently on her knees in front of it, she murmured to herself: 'Oh heavenly Father, forgive me for what I did; I was a child ... No, no, I wasn't a child, I was old enough to know what I was doing. I did know, too, and I won't try to diminish my guilt ... but that was too much. Because what has happened with the child is not God punishing me but just *him*. I thought he had a noble heart and I've always felt small beside him but now I know it's he who is small. And because he's small, he's cruel. Everything small is cruel. *He* taught the child that; he always was a schoolmaster, Crampas called him one (he was joking then but he was right). "Oh yes, if I may!" You don't need to say that, because I don't want either of you any more, I hate you both, even my own daughter. Too much is too much. He was always thinking of his career and nothing more. Honour, honour, honour ... and then he shot that poor man, whom I didn't even love, and whom I'd forgotten because I didn't love him. It was all just stupidity and then blood and murder. And it's my fault. And now he's sent me my daughter because he can't refuse a minister's wife anything and before he sent her, he trained her like a parrot and taught her the phrase: "If I may." What I've done disgusts me but what disgusts me even more is how virtuous they both are. Go away, the pair of you! I have to go on living but I suppose it can't go on for ever.'

When Roswitha came back Effi was lying, face downward, apparently lifeless.

34

WHEN Rummschüttel was sent for, he found Effi's health in some danger. The feverishness, which he had observed for some considerable time, seemed more marked and, what was worse, there were the first signs of nervous disturbance. His quiet, friendly manner, however, to which he succeeded in adding a touch of humour, did Effi good, and as long as Rummschüttel was there she remained calm. When he eventually left, Roswitha accompanied the old gentleman down to the hall and said: 'Oh Doctor, I'm so frightened; if it happens again and it easily can, oh God, then I won't have a moment's peace. What happened with the child was too much. Poor mistress! And still so young, at an age when many people are just beginning to live.'

'Don't worry, Roswitha. Everything will still be all right. But she must go away. We'll see. A different atmosphere, different people.'

Two days later a letter arrived in Hohen-Cremmen: 'My dear Frau von Briest, My long and friendly relationship with the Briest and Belling families and not least the deep affection that I feel for your daughter are my justification for writing. Things cannot go on like this. If nothing happens to relieve the loneliness and suffering which your daughter has been undergoing for some years now, then she will pine away. There already existed a predisposition to consumption, which was why I prescribed Ems, and to this old weakness has now been added a fresh one: her nerves are going to pieces. To counteract this trend, she must have a change of air. But where can she go? It would not be difficult to pick one of the Silesian spas; Salzbrunn would be good and Reinerz even better, because of the nervous complication. But Hohen-Cremmen is the only place. You see, my dear lady, it's not only a change of air that can help your daughter to recover. She is pining away because she only has Roswitha. Faithful servants are an excellent thing but parental love is better. Forgive an old man for interfering in matters outside the range of his profession as doctor. And yet that is not really the case, because it's as a doctor that I'm writing to you and making this *demand* on you from my sense of duty, if you will pardon that word. . . . I have seen so much of life . . . but I won't pursue that. . . . Please give my regards to your husband, Yours very truly, Doctor Rummschüttel.'

Frau von Briest read the letter out to her husband; they were both sitting on the paved path in the shade, with their backs to the conservatory, facing the circular bed with the sundial. The creeper climbing round the windows rustled in a passing breeze and dragonflies hovered over the water.

Briest said nothing but tapped his finger on the tea-tray.

'Please don't tap. Say something.'

'What am I to say, Luise? The fact that I'm tapping says enough. You know what I've thought about this for a long time. At the time when Innstetten's letter came like a thunderbolt out of a clear sky, I was of your opinion. But that's half an eternity ago. Do I have to go on being the Grand Inquisitor till the end of my days? I assure you that I've tired of it long ago.'

'Don't go blaming me, Briest. I love her as much as you do, perhaps more; everyone has their own way. But we've not been sent into the world just to be weak and forbearing and show respect for all that's against the laws of God and man and that society condemns and, for the moment at any rate, rightly condemns.'

'Oh, really, Luise. One thing's more important.'

'Of course, one thing's more important, but what is it?'

'Parents' love for their children. And when one's only got one child . . .'

'Then the catechism and morality and the claims of society are to be brushed aside?'

'Oh, Luise, you can quote the catechism as much as you like but don't quote society!'

'It's difficult to get along without society.'

'And difficult without one's child, too. And believe me, Luise, if society wants to, it can turn a blind eye. My view is this: if the Rathenowers come, so much the better, and if they don't come, so much the better, too. I'll just send a wire saying: "Come, Effi." Do you agree?'

She stood up and kissed his forehead. 'Of course I do. Only don't blame me. It's not an easy step to take. Our life will be changed from now on.'

'I can bear it. The rape-seed crop is a good one and in the autumn I can course a hare. And I still enjoy drinking red wine. And I'll enjoy drinking it even more when I've got my daughter at home again. . . . And now I'll send that telegram.'

Effi had been in Hohen-Cremmen for more than half a year now. She was occupying the two rooms on the first floor which she had occupied when she had been staying before; the larger of them was arranged for her personally, while Roswitha slept in the adjoining room. All that Rummschüttel had hoped for from the stay and all the other benefits had been realized, as far as could be expected. She coughed less and the harshness which had robbed her really kindly face of a good deal of its charm vanished too, and there were days when she was able to laugh again. Little was said of Kessin and the past, with the exception only of Frau von Padden and, of course, Gieshübler, for whom old Briest had a lively affection. 'This Alonzo, this precious Spaniard who kept a Mirambo in his house and brought up a Trippelli – he must have been a genius, you can't persuade me that he wasn't.' And then Effi had to agree to put on the whole act of Gieshübler, hat in hand, making his endless polite little bows, something which, with her special gift of mimicry, she did very well, albeit unwillingly because she always felt it unfair towards that good, kind man. Innstetten and Annie were never mentioned, although it was understood that Annie would inherit Hohen-Cremmen.

So Effi was reviving and her mother who, like all women, was not entirely averse from looking on the whole business as an interesting case, however painful it might be, vied with her husband in manifesting her love and attention.

'We've not had such a good winter for a long time,' said Briest. And then Effi would get up and brush the thinning hair back from his forehead. But although everything was going so well, appearances were deceptive as far as Effi's health was concerned for, in fact, her illness was pursuing its course and silently consuming her life. Effi was once again wearing the loose-belted blue and white striped smock that she had worn on the day she became engaged and when she crossed the room, with her brisk, elastic step, to bid her parents good morning, they would look at her with pleasure and admiration but also with sadness, because they could not fail to see that it was not the brightness of youth but a transfiguration that was giving her slender build and shining eyes this special expression. Everyone who looked closely could see this, except Effi herself, who went on living completely absorbed in the happiness at being once again in this peaceful, affectionate atmosphere, reconciled with all those whom she had always loved and by whom she had always been loved, even in her miserable years of exile.

She did a lot of the housekeeping, introducing all sorts of small improvements and looking after the decorations. Her sense of beauty was always infallible. Reading and, above all, any artistic activity, she had, however, completely abandoned. 'I've done such a lot of it that I'm glad to be able to fold my arms and do nothing!' No doubt it also reminded her too much of her sad days in the past. Instead, she developed the art of looking at nature with silent delight and when the leaves dropped from the plane-trees, the rays of the sun glinted on the ice of the pond or the first crocus bloomed in the still rather wintry flower-bed, all these things comforted her and she could look at them for hours and forget all that life had denied her or, rather, that she had lost for herself.

There were callers, too, for not everyone turned against her; but mainly she frequented the schoolmaster's and the pastor's houses.

It was no great harm that the daughters had left the schoolhouse, because things would not have been the same as before, but her relationship with Jahnke himself was better than ever, for this old friend viewed not only the whole of Swedish Pomerania but the district of Kessin also as a promontory of Sweden and continually asked her questions about it. 'Yes, Jahnke, we had a steamer and as I think I once wrote to you or perhaps told you, I even almost went over to Wisby one day. Just imagine, almost to Wisby. It's funny, but I can say "almost" for lots of things in my life, really.'

'What a pity, what a pity,' said Jahnke.

'Yes, indeed, it is! But I really did go round Rügen. And you'd have enjoyed that, Jahnke. Just imagine, Arkona, with a big Wendish storage pile, which is supposed to be still visible, because I didn't go that far; but not too far away is Lake Hertha with its white and yellow water-lilies, I thought a lot about your Herta when I was there. . . .'

'Ah yes, Herta. . . . But you were saying something about Lake Hertha.'

'Yes, I was. . . . And just imagine, Jahnke, right by the lake there were two big sacrificial stones, all smooth, and still with the grooves to let the blood run away. Ever since then I've always had a dislike for the Wends.'

'Now please, Frau Effi, forgive me, but those weren't Wends. That business with sacrifices and Lake Hertha was much, much earlier, long before B.C.; they were pure Aryans, whom we're all descended from. . . .'

'Of course,' laughed Effi, 'whom we're all descended from, certainly the Jahnkes and perhaps even the Briests.'

And then she left the subject of Rügen and Lake Hertha and asked after his grandchildren and which he liked best, Bertha's or Herta's.

So Effi's relations with Jahnke were excellent indeed, but in spite of his familiarity with Lake Hertha, Scandinavia and Wisby, he was still nothing but a simple man and so it was inevitable that the lonely young woman enjoyed her talks with Niemeyer much more. In the autumn, while it was still possible to walk in the park, she was able to indulge in such talks to her heart's content; but with the onset of winter, they were interrupted for many months, because she did not like going to the pastor's house by herself. Niemeyer's wife had always been an unpleasant person and now took a very high-handed attitude, in spite of the fact that, in the view of the community, she was not irreproachable herself.

The whole winter went by in this way, much to Effi's regret, but when at the beginning of April the bushes showed their outline of green and the paths in the park rapidly dried out, the walks were resumed.

One day they were walking in this way and in the distance they could hear the cuckoo. Effi counted the number of times it called. She was holding Niemeyer's arm and said: 'Yes, there's the cuckoo. I don't dare ask him. Tell me, pastor, what do *you* think of life?'

'Ah, Effi dear, you mustn't ask me leading questions like that. For that you must address yourself to a philosopher or apply to a faculty. What do I think of life? A lot and not much. Occasionally, it's a good deal and occasionally very little.'

'That's right, my friend, I like that, I don't need to know any more.' As she said that, they had reached the swing. She jumped on it as nimbly as she had done when still a young girl and before the old man who was watching her could recover from the shock, she was crouching down between the ropes and was setting the seat swinging by skilfully swaying her body up and down. In a few seconds she was flying through the air and, hanging on with only one hand, she tore a small silk scarf from her neck and chest and waved it with a sort of gay abandon. Then she let the swing slow down and, jumping off, she caught hold of Niemeyer's arm again.

'Effi, you haven't changed at all!'

'No. I wish it were true. But that all belongs to the past and I just wanted to try it once more. Oh, how lovely it was and how refreshing the breeze was. I felt as if I was flying up to heaven. Shall I ever go there? Tell me, pastor. You must know. Please, please. . . .'

Niemeyer took her head between his two old hands, gave her a kiss on her forehead and said: 'Yes, Effi, you will.'

35

EFFI used to spend all day in the park because she needed the fresh air. Old Doctor Wiesike from Friesack gave his consent but left her too much discretion to do what she wanted in this respect, and during the chilly days in May she caught a violent cold: she had a temperature, coughed a great deal and the doctor who normally came over every other day now came daily and was puzzled as to what best to do since, because of her fever, he could not give Effi the sleeping drugs and pectoral that she required.

'Doctor,' old Briest asked him, 'what is going to happen? You've known her ever since she was a baby, you fetched her into the world. I don't like all this. She's visibly losing weight and then there are those red patches and her shining eyes when she looks at me so strangely all of a sudden. What do you think? What's happening? Is she going to die?'

Wiesike wagged his head slowly to and fro. 'I wouldn't say that, Herr von Briest. I'm not pleased at this temperature. But we'll get it down again and then she must go off to Switzerland or Menton. Pure air and pleasant surroundings to help her forget the past. . . .'

'Ah, Lethe, the river of forgetfulness.'

'Yes, Lethe,' smiled Wiesike. 'What a pity that those old Swedes, the Greeks, only bequeathed the word and not the source itself. . . .'

'Or at least the recipe for it, because you can imitate all sorts of waters these days. My goodness, Wiesike, that would be a good piece of business if we could set up a sanatorium like that here: Friesack as a source of forgetfulness. Well, for the moment we'll try the Riviera. Menton is on the Riviera, isn't it? It's true that the price of grain at the moment is not very good again but what must be, must be. I'll talk to my wife about it.'

This he did and received immediate support from his wife who, no doubt as the result of her quiet way of life, had recently conceived a strong desire to visit the south herself, and this favoured his proposition. But Effi would not hear of it. 'How good you are to me! And I'm selfish enough to accept your sacrifice if I expected some benefit from it. But I'm convinced that it'll only do me harm.'

'You're just imagining that, Effi.'

'No. I've become so irritable that everything annoys me. But not when I'm here with you both. You spoil me and prevent anything from standing in my way. But on a journey that's not possible, you can't push everything unpleasant to one side; at the start you've got the porter, and at the finish you've got the waiter. Just to think of all their smug faces makes me hot all over. No, let me stay here. I don't want to leave Hohen-Cremmen, my place is here. I like the heliotrope in the flower-bed round the sundial better than Menton.'

Following this conversation, the plan was dropped and although he had expected great things from Italy, Wiesike said: 'We must respect that, because it's not just a whim. When people are ill like that they have a very delicate flair and they know with remarkable accuracy what is going to benefit them and what not. And what Frau Effi was saying about porters and waiters is really quite right and there's no air wholesome enough to make up for the vexations of hotel life, if one really is vexed by it. So let her stay here; if it's not the best thing, at least it's not the worst.'

Wiesike proved right. Effi got better, put on a little weight – old Briest was a fanatical believer in weighing – and lost a good deal of her irritability. At the same time, however, her need for fresh air continued to grow and especially when there was a west wind and grey clouds sped across the sky, she would spend hours in the open air. On such days as these she would go out into the fields and as far as the Luch, often half a mile wide, and when she was tired, she would sit down on a hurdle fence and, lost in dreams, look at the buttercups and red sorrel swaying in the wind.

'You always go alone,' Frau von Briest said. 'You're safe with the people from round here but there are all sorts of horrible strangers lurking about.'

This made an impression on Effi, who had never thought of danger, and when she was alone with Roswitha, she said: 'I can hardly take you with me, Roswitha, you're too fat and not very steady on your feet any more.'

'Now, m'lady, it's not so bad as that yet. I might still get married.'

'Of course,' laughed Effi. 'One always can. But you know, Roswitha, if only I had a dog to go with me. Papa's shooting dog is not very fond of me. Shooting dogs are so stupid and he never moves until the sportsman or the gardener takes the gun down from the rack. It often makes me think of Rollo.'

'Yes,' said Roswitha, 'they haven't got anything like Rollo round here. But I don't mean to say anything against "here" when I say that. Hohen-Cremmen is very good.'

It was three or four days after this conversation that Innstetten went into his study an hour earlier than usual. The early morning sun which was very bright had awakened him and because he thought that he would not go to sleep again, he had got up to do some work that had been waiting to be finished for some considerable time now.

It was now a quarter past eight and he rang. Joanna brought in the breakfast tray on which, beside the *Kreuzzeitung* and the *Norddeutsche Allgemeine*, two letters were lying. He briefly scanned the addresses and from the handwriting recognized that one of them was from the minister. But what about the other one? The post-mark was not clearly legible and the 'Baron von Innstetten, Esquire' bore witness to a happy unfamiliarity with the customary modes of address. Similarly, the handwriting was of a very primitive character. On the other hand, the address was remarkably accurate: W. Keithstrasse 1c, 2nd floor.

Innstetten was sufficiently a Civil Servant to open the letter from 'His Excellency' first. 'My dear Innstetten, I am glad to inform you that His Majesty has been pleased to sign your nomination and I send you my sincere congratulations.' Innstetten was delighted to receive the minister's friendly note, almost more than at the honour itself. As far as climbing higher up the ladder was concerned, since that morning in Kessin when Crampas had taken leave of him with a look that was ever before his mind's eye, Innstetten had become somewhat critical in such matters. Since then, his standards of judgement had changed and he saw things in a different light. What was distinction, after all? More than once, as the days went forlornly by, he had had to recall a half-forgotten anecdote told in the ministry, and dating from the time of the older Ladenberg, who when, after much waiting, he received the Order of the Red Eagle, hurled it furiously to one side with the exclamation: 'You can stay there until you're black.'* Probably it did become a Black Eagle later on, but many a long day too late and certainly with little satisfaction for the recipient. Anything that is to please us depends on time and circumstance and something that will make us happy today will be worthless tomorrow. Innstetten was strongly conscious of this and, however true it may have been that honours and favours from the highest quarters meant a great deal to him, or, at least, had meant a great deal in the past, he now realized the equal truth that there was little to be gained from this splendid outward display and that what people call 'happiness', if it exists at all, is something different from such display. 'If I'm right, happiness consists of two things: first, in being where you belong – but what government official can ever say that of himself? And secondly, and best of all, that one's ordinary, everyday life should follow a smooth and easy course, that is, that you've slept soundly and your new boots don't pinch you. If the seven hundred and twenty minutes of your twelve hour day have gone by without particular annoyance, then you can talk of a "happy day".' Today, Innstetten was feeling once again tempted to give rein to such painful considerations. He took up the second letter. When he had read it he ran his hand over his forehead, realizing to his grief that happiness did exist, that it had once been his but that he had it no longer, nor would he ever have it again.

Joanna came in to announce: 'Privy Councillor Wüllersdorf.'

He was already standing in the doorway. 'Congratulations, Innstetten.'

'I can believe you when you say it. The others will be annoyed. What's more ...'

'What's more ... Surely you don't want to start complaining at this juncture?'

'No. His Majesty's kindness is overwhelming and the good-will of the minister, to whom I owe everything, even more so.'

'But ...'

'But I've forgotten how to enjoy anything. If I were to say such

* The order of the Black Eagle being a higher grade.

a thing to anyone but yourself, that remark would seem merely a figure of speech. But you will appreciate it. Just look around you and see how empty and bare everything is. Whenever Joanna comes in, that so-called jewel, then I'm really scared. This attitudinizing' – – Innstetten mimicked Joanna's attitude – 'this half-comic offering of a well-shaped bust, which seems to demand special attention, either from humanity or myself, I'm not quite sure which – I find all this so gloomy and depressing that if it weren't so ridiculous it would be suicidal.'

'My dear Innstetten, in the mood you're in, do you want to become head of a department?'

'Bah, how can I avoid it? Read this; it's a note I've just received.'

Wüllersdorf took the second letter with the illegible postmark, noticed the 'Esquire' with amusement and then took it over to the window in order to read it more easily.

'Dear master, You will no doubt be surprised that I am writing to you but it is about Rollo. Wee Annie told us last year that Rollo had got very lazy but that does not matter here, he can be as lazy as he likes, the lazier the better. And the mistress would like him so much. She always says when she goes to the Luch or into the country: "I'm really scared, Roswitha, because I'm all alone but who is there to come with me? Rollo would be all right, I don't dislike him. That's the advantage of animals, they don't worry about things so much." Those were the mistress's very words and I won't say any more and just ask you to give my love to little Annie. And to Joanna as well. Your faithful servant, Roswitha Gellenhagen.'

'Yes,' said Wüllersdorf, folding up the letter, 'she's worth more than we are.'

'I think so, too.'

'And that's why you feel so doubtful about everything else.'

'You're quite correct. I've been thinking about it for a long time now and those simple words with their deliberate or perhaps unintentional accusation have quite upset me. It's been tormenting me for years and now I'd like to get out of the whole business. I've lost all pleasure in everything. The more distinctions I earn, the more I feel that it's been valueless. I've made a mess of my life and so I've been thinking to myself I ought to have absolutely nothing to do with ambition and vanity and everything connected with them and try to employ my gifts as a schoolmaster, which is my real forte, as a sort of superior moral leader. There have been such people. So if it were possible, I ought to try to become someone terribly famous, like for example that Doctor Wichern in the *Rauhes Haus** in Hamburg, that wonderful man who could quell any criminal with his piety and a look.'

'Hm, that sounds quite all right, that would do.'

'No, it won't do. Not even that. The fact is that there's nothing open to me. How can I grip the soul of a brutal murderer? To do that you have to be still guiltless yourself. And if you're no longer guiltless and have blood on your own hands, then you must at least pretend to be a fanatical penitent and put on a colossal act of contrition for the edification of the fellow humans you want to convert.'

Wüllersdorf nodded.

'You see, now you're nodding. But I just can't do that any more. I just can't bring myself to put on sack-cloth and ashes now and even less to be a dervish or fakir dancing myself to death in a welter of self-accusation. And as that's all quite impossible, I've worked out in my mind what else I could best do and that is to leave everything and go where everybody's coal-black and doesn't know anything about culture and honour. Happy people! Because it's just that, all this fiddle-faddle, that's responsible for everything. One doesn't do that sort of thing for passionate reasons, which might be acceptable, but merely because of certain conceptions ... conceptions. . . . And then someone collapses and then you collapse yourself. Except that it's worse.'

'For goodness sake, Innstetten, those are just fancies, just ideas. Into deepest Africa indeed, what on earth's the good of that? That's only for lieutenants who're in debt. But someone like yourself! Do you want to preside over a palaver in a red fez or become blood-brother to King Mtesa's son-in-law? Or do you want to grope your way along the Congo in a pith helmet with seven holes on top until you come out in the Cameroons or thereabouts? Impossible!'

'Why is it impossible? And if it is, what else is there to do?'

'Simply stay on here and practise resignation. Who doesn't feel depressed? Who doesn't say every day: "It's all a very doubtful business"? As you know, I've got my own little burden to bear, not exactly the same as yours but not much lighter. All this crawling about in the jungle or spending the night on a white ant heap is

* An institution for deprived children set up in 1833.

260

nonsense; it's all right for those who like it but it's not for such as us. The best thing is to hold the fort until you drop. But first of all, to get as much as you can out of the small things, the very small things of life, and to have an eye for violets in bloom or the Luise Monument decked out with flowers or little girls skipping in long lace-up boots. Or to drive out to Potsdam and go into the Friedens-kirche where Kaiser Friedrich is buried and where they're just starting to build him a vault. And while you're standing there, just think what *his* life was like, and if that doesn't reassure you, then you're beyond all help.'

'All right, all right. But a year is a long time and there's every single day . . . and then there's the evening.'

'That's the easiest thing to deal with. We've got *Sardanapalus* or *Coppelia* with dell'Era,* and when that's over, we've got Siechen. Not to be despised. Three tankards are infallible. There are lots of people, lots and lots of them, who think the same as we do about the whole business, and one man who'd also had a lot of trouble once said to me: "Believe me, Wüllersdorf, you can't do without make-shift constructions." The man who said that was an architect and he knew what he was talking about. And he used the right expression. Not a day passes without my being reminded of those "makeshift constructions".'

Having thus unbosomed himself, Wüllersdorf took his hat and stick, while Innstetten, who, as he listened to his friend's words, must have been reminded of his own previous meditations on the subject of 'miniature happiness', nodded in partial agreement and smiled to himself.

'And where are you going now, Wüllersdorf? It's still too early for the Ministry.'

'I'm making myself a present of today. First of all an hour's stroll along the canal as far as the Charlottenburg lock and back again. And then a call on Huth, in the Potsdamer Strasse, being careful going up the little wooden stairs. There's a florist's under-neath.'

'And you'll enjoy that? That'll satisfy you?'

'I wouldn't say that exactly. But it helps a bit. I'll find a number of regular customers there, always in for an early drink, whose names I shall cunningly refrain from mentioning. One of them will talk

* A prima ballerina.

about the Duke of Ratibor, another about the Prince Bishop Kopp and the third one, no doubt, about Bismarck. There's always a certain amount of rubbish. Three quarters of it is wrong but if it's funny you don't complain too much, and you go on listening gratefully.'

So saying he left.

36

MAY was fine, June still finer and once Effi had successfully overcome the feeling of sorrow that was aroused when Rollo first arrived she was delighted to have the faithful beast with her again. Roswitha received praise and old Briest expressed to his wife his approval of Innstetten, who was a perfect gentleman, not petty, whose heart was always in the right place. A pity about that stupid business between them. They really were a model couple!

The only person who remained calm in the course of this reunion was Rollo himself, either because he had no instrument for measuring time or because he saw the separation as an aberration which was now ended. The fact that he was now old no doubt contributed to his calm. He remained sparing with his affection, just as he had been sparing with his manifestations of pleasure on seeing his mistress again, but he was, if anything, even more faithful than before. He never left his mistress's side. He treated the shooting dog benevolently but as a creature on a lower plane. He spent the nights lying on a rush mat in front of Effi's door, the mornings, when breakfast was taken in the open, beside the sundial, always quiet, always sleepy, and not until Effi got up from the breakfast table and walked towards the hall to pick up, first, her straw hat and then her parasol did he recover his youth and then, without caring whether his strength was to be put to a stern or a gentle test, he dashed up the village street and down again and would not calm down until they were among the first fields.

Effi, for whom the open air was even more important than the beauty of the scenery, avoided the small patches of woodland and kept largely to the main road leading to the station, a road planted, first of all, with ancient elms and then, when they reached the highway, with poplars, a good hour's walk. She took delight in everything, breathing in the sweet scent wafted from the fields of rape and clover or following the soaring of the larks and counting the drinking fountains and troughs where the cattle went for water. She could hear the tinkling of their bells. And then she felt that she should close her eyes and lose herself in sweet oblivion. Close to the station, right beside the highway, there was a roller. This was where she rested every day and from here she could follow all the activity on the railway embankment; trains would come and go and occasionally she saw two plumes of smoke which merged with each other for a moment and then went off separately again to left and right until they disappeared behind the village and the tiny wood. Rollo would sit beside her, sharing her morning snack, and when he had caught the last mouthful, he rushed like a madman along a furrow, no doubt to express his gratitude, only stopping when a startled brace of resting partridges shot up from a neighbouring furrow.

'What a lovely summer it is! A year ago, I should never have thought that I could be so happy, dear Mama.' Each day Effi would say this as she walked with her mother round the pond or plucked an early apple from the branch and bravely took a bite from it. She had splendid teeth. Frau von Briest stroked her hand and said: 'Just get well, Effi, quite well. Then you'll find happiness, not past happiness but a new one. There are many types of happiness, thank God. And you'll see that we'll find something for you.'

'You're both so kind. And yet I've changed your life for you and turned you into old people before your time.'

'Oh, don't talk about that, Effi dear. When it happened, I thought the same. But now I know that quiet is better than the noise and bustle of the old days. And if you continue to make progress, we can still travel. When Wiesike suggested Menton, you were ill and irritable and because you were ill, you were quite right in what you said about porters and waiters, but when your nerves are stronger it will be all right, because you won't be annoyed, you'll just laugh at the grand airs and the frizzy hair. And then there's the blue sea and the white sails and the cliffs all covered in red cactus – I've never seen it but that's how I imagine it. And I should like to get to know it.'

So the summer went by and the nights of shooting stars were over.

Effi had spent these nights sitting at her window until after midnight and never tired of watching them. 'I never was a very good Christian but suppose we perhaps do come from up there and when everything is all over on earth we go back to a heavenly home, to the stars up there or even beyond! I don't know and I don't want to know, but how I long for it!'

Poor Effi, you spent too long looking up at the marvels of the heavens and thinking about them and in the end the night air and the mists rising from the pond stretched her once more on a bed of sickness, and when Wiesike was summoned and saw her, he took Briest to one side and said: 'There's no hope, you must prepare yourself for a sudden end.'

He had spoken only too truly, and a few days later, quite early, for it was not yet quite ten o'clock, Roswitha came downstairs and said to Frau von Briest: 'Ma'am, the mistress is in a bad way. She keeps talking quietly to herself and sometimes she seems to be praying, but she won't admit it, and I don't know but it seems to me as if it might be all over at any time.'

'Does she want to speak to me?'

'She didn't say so. But I think she would like to. You know how she is, she doesn't want to disturb you and make you frightened. But I think perhaps you ought.'

'Very well, Roswitha,' said Frau von Briest, 'I'll come.'

And before the clock struck, Frau von Briest went upstairs into Effi's room. The window was open and she was lying on a day bed next to the window.

Frau von Briest drew up a little black chair with three little gold rods in the ebony back, took Effi's hand and said:

'How are you, Effi? Roswitha says you're very feverish.'

'Oh, Roswitha is always so scared of everything. I just looked at her and she thinks I'm dying. Well, I don't know. But she thinks that everyone should be as scared about it as herself.'

'Are you not afraid about dying, Effi dear?'

'Not at all afraid.'

'Aren't you mistaken about that? Everybody is fond of living, young people most of all. And you're still so young, Effi.'

Effi kept silent for a while and then said: 'You know, I've never read much and Innstetten was often surprised at that and didn't like it.'

It was the first time that she had mentioned Innstetten's name. This made a strong impression on her mother and made her realize plainly that the end was near.

Frau von Briest spoke: 'You were going to tell me something, I think.'

'Yes, I did want to, because you said something about my still being so young. But that doesn't matter. It was at the time when I was still happy and Innstetten used to read to me out loud in the evenings; he had very good books and in one of them there was this story about someone being called away from a dinner party and the following day the man who had been called away asked how it had been after he'd left and he received the reply: "Oh, there were all sorts of things, but you didn't really miss anything." You see, Mama, those words stuck in my mind – it doesn't mean a great deal if you're called away from table rather early.'

Frau von Briest remained silent. Effi sat up a little and said: 'And since I've mentioned old times and Innstetten too, I must tell you something else, Mama dear.'

'You're exciting yourself, Effi.'

'No, not really. When you're speaking from deep down in your conscience, it doesn't excite you, it calms you. So I wanted to tell you that I'm dying reconciled with God and man and even reconciled with him.'

'Did you feel such bitterness in your heart towards him? In a way, forgive me, Effi dear, if I say this to you at such a moment, you really brought your sorrow, yours and his, on yourself.'

Effi nodded: 'Yes, Mama. And it's sad that I did. But when all those dreadful things took place and last of all what happened with Annie, you remember, then, if I may use the ridiculous expression, I turned the tables on him and quite seriously made myself think that he was to blame because he was dull and calculating and even, in the end, cruel. And it was then that I cursed him.'

'And now that weighs on your conscience?'

'Yes. And I'm anxious for him to know that during the time I've been ill, which is almost the loveliest time of my life, I've come to see plainly that he was right in all he did. In what he did to poor Crampas – well, what else could he do, after all? And then the thing that hurt me most deeply, the way he had brought up my own child to be on her guard against me, however hard it is for me and however much it grieves me, he was right about that too. Let him know that I died believing that. It will console him and lift him up and perhaps reconcile him. Because he had a great deal of good in his nature and was as fine a man as any one can be who doesn't really love.'

Frau von Briest saw that Effi was exhausted and seemed to be sleeping, or wanting to sleep. She quietly stood up and went. Meanwhile, hardly had she left than Effi got up, too, and sat down by the open window to breathe in once again the cool night air. The stars were twinkling and, in the park, not a leaf stirred. But the longer she listened, the more clearly she could hear once more the gentle rustling of the plane trees. A feeling of release came over her. 'Peace, peace.'

It was a month later and September was on the wane. The weather was fine but in the park the foliage was already showing a good deal of red and yellow and since the equinox, which had brought three days of storm, the leaves were lying scattered all around. On the round flowerbed, a small change had been made, the sundial had gone and in its place, there could be seen, since yesterday, a white marble stone on which was written merely: 'Effi Briest,' with a cross underneath. This had been Effi's last request. 'On my stone, I'd like you to give me back my old name; I didn't bring any honour to my other one.' And the promise had been made.

And so the marble stone had come yesterday and been laid and now, facing it, Briest and his wife were seated looking at it and at the heliotropes which had been spared and now framed the stone. Rollo was lying at the side, his head in his paws.

Wilke, whose gaiters were getting wider and wider, brought the breakfast and the post and old Briest said: 'Wilke, order the small carriage. My wife and I want to go for a drive in the country.'

Meanwhile Frau von Briest had poured out the coffee and was looking over to the round bed and its flowers. 'Look, Rollo is lying by the stone again. It really has affected him more deeply than us. He's stopped eating altogether.'

'Ah yes, Luise, the beasts of the field. That's what I'm always saying. We're always talking about instinct. All in all, it's really the best thing.'

'Don't talk like that. When you start philosophizing . . . don't take offence, Briest, but that sort of thing's beyond you. You've got common sense but with questions like that you can't. . .'

'I suppose not.'

'And if we must ask questions at all, Briest, they're quite different ones and I can tell you that not a day goes by, since that poor child was buried there, without such questions occurring to me. . . .'

'What questions?'

'Whether we're not perhaps to blame?'

'Nonsense, Luise. How do you mean?'

'Whether we ought not to have brought her up differently. We ourselves. Because Niemeyer is a nonentity, since he leaves everything in doubt. And then Briest, sorry as I am to have to say so . . . your constant prevarication . . . and finally, what I accuse myself of, because I don't wish to remain blameless in this matter, whether she wasn't perhaps too young?'

While she was saying this, Rollo woke up and slowly wagged his head to and fro, while Briest said calmly: 'Ah, Luise, don't go on. . . . That is *too* big a subject.'

MORE ABOUT PENGUINS

If you have enjoyed reading this book you may wish to know that *Penguin Book News* appears every month. It is an attractively illustrated magazine containing a complete list of books published by Penguins and still in print, together with details of the month's new books. A specimen copy will be sent on free request.

Penguin Book News is obtainable from most bookshops; but you may prefer to become a regular subscriber at 3s. for twelve issues. Just write to Dept EP, Penguin Books Ltd, Harmondsworth, Middlesex, enclosing a cheque or postal order, and you will be put on the mailing list.

Some other Penguin Classics are listed on the following pages.

Note: *Penguin Book News* is not
available in the U.S.A., Canada or Australia.

TURGENEV

SKETCHES FROM A HUNTER'S ALBUM

TRANSLATED BY RICHARD FREEBORN

For most of its present-day readers Turgenev's early masterpiece is quite simply one of the most beautiful books in any
language: a lyrical, almost magical account of wanderings in
the Russian countryside, to read which is an unforgettable
experience. Yet when it was published in 1852 it was regarded
by Tsarist officialdom as a subversive work which appeared
to denounce the whole Russian social system. Perhaps the
secret behind this apparent contradiction lies in that combination of urbanity, compassion, and intellect which is
Turgenev's special genius. Condemning nothing, he reveals
the peasants of his beloved country as individual human
beings, suffering and oppressed in what might have been a
paradise.